Past Prai

"This story will permeate your imagination long after you've finished the last page."

D. J. Williams, author of *King of the Night*

"Readers will be eager to take this twisty, suspense-filled ride."

Publishers Weekly on *Specters in the Glass House*

"Wright is in a class by herself, writing her own twists into the classic gothic mystery trope."

Publishers Weekly on *Night Falls on Predicament Avenue*

"Wright is an expert in her element. She elevates the classic haunted-house tale with this exceptional story of fear, unexamined grief, and hope through faith."

Booklist on *Night Falls on Predicament Avenue*

"*The Lost Boys of Barlowe Theater* is a story that stays with you long after you close the book."

Lynette Eason, award-winning author of the EXTREME MEASURES series

"In *The Vanishing at Castle Moreau*, Wright pens an imaginative and mysterious tale that is both haunting and heartwarming."

Rachel Hauck, *New York Times* bestselling author

TEMPEST
at
ANNABEL'S
LIGHTHOUSE

Books by Jaime Jo Wright

The House on Foster Hill
The Reckoning at Gossamer Pond
The Curse of Misty Wayfair
Echoes among the Stones
The Haunting at Bonaventure Circus
On the Cliffs of Foxglove Manor
The Souls of Lost Lake
The Premonition at Withers Farm
The Vanishing at Castle Moreau
The Lost Boys of Barlowe Theater
Night Falls on Predicament Avenue
Specters in the Glass House
Tempest at Annabel's Lighthouse

TEMPEST  ANNABEL'S LIGHTHOUSE

JAIME JO WRIGHT

BETHANYHOUSE
a division of Baker Publishing Group
Minneapolis, Minnesota

© 2025 by Jaime Sundsmo

Published by Bethany House Publishers
Minneapolis, Minnesota
BethanyHouse.com

Bethany House Publishers is a division of
Baker Publishing Group, Grand Rapids, Michigan

Printed in the United States of America

Library of Congress Cataloging-in-Publication Data
Names: Wright, Jaime Jo, author.
Title: Tempest at Annabel's Lighthouse / Jaime Jo Wright.
Description: Minneapolis, Minnesota : Bethany House, a division of Baker
    Publishing Group, 2025.
Identifiers: LCCN 2024039019 | ISBN 9780764243790 (paperback) | ISBN
    9780764244612 (casebound) | ISBN 9781493449019 (ebook)
Subjects: LCGFT: Christian fiction. | Novels.
Classification: LCC PS3623.R5388 T46 2025 | DDC 813/.6—dc23/eng/20240826
LC record available at https://lccn.loc.gov/2024039019

Scripture quotations are from the King James Version of the Bible.

Cover design by Jennifer Parker

Published in association with Books & Such Literary Management,
www.booksandsuch.com.

Baker Publishing Group publications use paper produced from sustainable forestry
practices and postconsumer waste whenever possible.

25 26 27 28 29 30 31   7 6 5 4 3 2 1

To Elizabeth Olmedo

This is proof that sometimes stories not only cross an ocean but they light the way to an entirely new adventure of friendship and togetherness. Thank you for your endless enthusiasm, last-minute patience, and the copious amounts of pleas for a lighthouse story. This one is for you.

ANNABEL

THIS GREAT WATER will be my sepulcher. I will not be the first to find eternal slumber in its depths. I will not be the last. It is a peaceful monster that, when awakened, becomes a ravenous beast, with icicles as its teeth and fathoms of deep blue that freeze one's soul. A spirit that divides you from the inside and takes you on a journey—a quest.

At least this is what my father taught me. His interpretation of what was taught to him by those who inhabited this place long before the White man's arrival. Waters surrounded by the mountains of the Porcupine. A world of wilderness, of copper and iron. A great sea that claims and devours, and in its moments of serenity, slumbers. It becomes a mirror clearer than the scarred one whose blackness peers through as it reflects my face in the mornings. This mirror made of water shines back the light from the sun and pretends to be gentle and kind.

This is the *Anishinaabewi-gichigami*.

This is where I will die.

1

Rebecca

It was many and many a year ago, in a kingdom by the sea . . .
Annabel Lee

SILVERTOWN
UPPER PENINSULA OF MICHIGAN
SPRING, 1874

THE VIOLENT WATER RAGED with waves that swallowed everything in its path. A vicious foe, it drove any living creature on the shore inward to the insignificant shelter of the woods. The trees took the brutal abuse of the wind that blew its frigid gales and turned otherwise peaceful blue-green water into a chilling, gray killer.

She clawed her way through the forest, rain pelting her face, assaulting the bare skin of her shoulders and neck. The blood that ran down the side of her face mingled with the rain and tasted like iron as it dripped from her lips. Her head raged with pain. She had been struck, and her coming back to consciousness had not been part of their plan. Darkness cloaked her slight form and seemed to laugh with wicked undertones. A tree branch raked her face. She wrestled with it, her breath tearing at her lungs. The pain of needing air not sodden, air not claimed by gasps of desperation, left her whimpering in the night.

Beneath her feet, the pine needles and ferns warred between spearing and cushioning her. She stumbled, her knee colliding with a rotting log lying on the forest floor. The agony was no worse than that which already flayed her body as she tried to gulp deep breaths but came up short of anything that would bring calm or comfort. She heard nothing over the sounds of the wind and the waves, but she knew. They were coming.

A glance over her shoulder revealed only darkness, outlined by shadows of trees, boulders and crevices, the lake beyond. The storm had come tonight. Then *they* had come. A formidable offense that captured her, incapacitated her, and now chased her once more. They were hunters—*her* hunters—those who answered the call of the demons, rising to claim their victims.

And they were coming for her. Again. Relentless, like the waves of *gichigami*.

A songbird awakened her. That and the warmth she felt as the morning sun filtered through the treetops waving overhead. The earth beneath her was saturated, and mud caked between her toes and her fingers. A gentle breeze lifted her hair, once soft like corn silk but now matted with dried blood and clumps of mud. She ran her tongue across her lips. They were dry, but she still tasted blood. Her vision blurred as she opened her eyes, and her head seemed to split with the mighty blow of a nonexistent ax.

Confusion cluttered her mind. She pushed herself from the ground, her hip sinking into the half-drowned earth. Her left hand braced her, mud oozing between her fingers. Blinking furiously, she tried to clear her thoughts. Looking around her, she tried to assess where she was.

Clothed in soiled, torn undergarments, she attempted to sit straighter, hugging her torso as if to hide herself from the trees that glowered at her. The sun seemed to flicker and twinkle, not unlike a very large star might, and for a moment she thought perhaps it was the only friendly thing here.

She stretched her leg and startled as her toes scraped across something cold and hard. The realization of it horrified her, and in spite of the pain in her joints and the obvious bruises on her legs, she shoved herself backward with a cry.

The base of the gravestone lay flat on the earth, the four-sided monument like a marker pointing directions.

Bewildered, she twisted onto her knees, her breath catching as a sharp pain told her that her injuries spanned more than just her legs and torso. Her shuddering breath was echoed by the warble of another bird—a bird she couldn't identify. She should know what it was. She *knew* that she should know, but she didn't.

Leaning toward the gravestone, she reached out a hand, her fingernails broken with flecks of blood and dirt beneath them. Her fingers traced the engraved name on the stone, *Annabel*, and a date, *1852*.

So many years ago. It was, wasn't it? Many years ago? She fell back onto her heels, sitting before the marker as if kneeling in prayer. Today was . . . well, it was—

Her breaths came quicker now. She couldn't recall the year. Not the month. Not even yesterday. Nor why she was here now, bruised and bloodied, alone, and barely clothed.

A quick assessment of her body and she knew something terrible had happened to her. Something she would never put into words and never tell a soul. Part of her took a deep solace that she couldn't remember, but another found it all the more frightful that she didn't even know her own name.

The feel of something trailing the skin of her neck awakened her dulled senses. She cried out, batting at its feathery touch. Even a spider or a beetle was ominous to her now. But her hand connected with a chain. A delicate chain. One that was miraculously still clasped around her neck. A locket was attached to the chain, lying demurely between her breasts.

She pulled it away from her chest. The locket was open, empty inside, but covered with dried mud as though it had been pressed into the earth. Looking down, an oval-shaped bruise on the upper skin of her left breast confirmed her assumption. Yes. It had been viciously squashed between her and the ground at some point in her not-so-distant past. It would require careful cleaning.

Turning it over, her breath caught.

Sitting there at the base of Annabel's grave, she read her own name as if for the first time.

Rebecca.

That was all.

Rebecca.

2

SHEA RADCLYFFE

*That a maiden lived there whom you may
know by the name of Annabel Lee . . .*
Annabel Lee

**SILVERTOWN
UPPER PENINSULA OF MICHIGAN
PRESENT DAY**

A NUT-BROWN CURL BOUNCED in front of her right eye. Shea Radclyffe blew it away with an irritated puff. Lightning streaked across the sky, illuminating the ocean between her and Canada. Only it wasn't the ocean; it was Lake Superior. Or "Gitche Gumee," as Longfellow had dubbed it in his poem. Her wipers swept back and forth across her windshield as rain pelted the glass. She squinted, hardly able to see through the darkness of the night and the sheets of rain. The rain was like the tears she had shed on much of her drive here. Tears that mimicked the storm in her heart, in her marriage, in her life.

More lightning revealed the stretch of highway ahead, bordered to the left by endless miles of forest, and to the right by the lake whose waves were—well, she certainly couldn't measure them, but she'd read online that they were capable of reaching thirty feet.

"Oh, thank the good Lord." Her acclamation was less a prayer and more an outburst of relief.

Thunder rolled and thrummed in the air, the lightning acting as a beacon, for the silhouetted lighthouse had been dark since the late 1930s. Decommissioned. Retired. No longer needed. The same words were on repeat in Shea's mind, but about herself. And she was only thirty. Just thirty and already feeling washed up and forgotten.

She swiped at a rogue tear. Another mile and Shea saw the gravel drive. She didn't bother with her indicator but turned onto the path, stuffing down the trepidation she felt as she approached the abandoned site. Her car pointed toward the lake, toward the roiling whitecap waves that were terrifying in their rage. Dark waters beneath tsunami-like emotion, the parallels between the darkened lighthouse and herself were frightening. She had come here on impulse, but now Shea doubted her common sense. She'd been doubting it since leaving Wisconsin in her rearview mirror. Since she'd left Pete.

Pulling the car to a halt, she shifted into park. A lone light shone in the window on the arched door of the lighthouse. This one wasn't like those she'd toured in Oregon on the West Coast— tall, stately, majestic lighthouses with beacons that stretched for miles. No. This lighthouse was different. It was Midwestern. Before coming, she'd seen pictures of the historic building that stood outside of Silvertown, U.P. of Michigan.

The lighthouse sat on an expansive lawn that topped a vast cliff above the lake. For the most part, it looked more like a brown brick, two-story farmhouse with a single gable roof and a small attic window at its peak. The lighthouse was abutted to the house, rising taller than the roof, reminding Shea of a grain silo rather than the picturesque lighthouse often shown on calendars. It was squatter while still boasting the iron catwalk that encircled the lamp room. The entire lighthouse was made of brick, its beacon designed to wage war against angry thirty-foot waves, rising on a shoreline of basalt cliffs and a wilderness of pines that hid darkness in its depths.

She could hardly see anything now. Shea grimaced as she pulled a water-resistant parka from the passenger seat behind her and flung it over her head.

Wrestling her body from the car, her feet vanished into puddles. She kicked the car door shut behind her and ran through the rain, stepping onto a white, wooden stair. Shea grabbed the old doorknob, which in the light of day was probably its own bit of historical curiosity, and then burst into the entryway. The smells of woodsmoke and age met her nose, along with that of cinnamon and citrus. The warmth of the interior space permeated her soaking-wet feet.

Two hands reached out and swung her parka off her head. The accumulated water slid down the side and onto the floor, avoiding giving her another shower, all while Shea yelped in surprise at the human form waiting inside the lighthouse.

A male voice greeted her. "Welcome to Annabel's Lighthouse!"

Shea ran her hands over her unruly, now sopping-wet curls, sweeping them back so she could see clearly.

The man hung her parka on an antique hall tree. Light filtered into the entry from the room beyond, which looked to be an old kitchen. Small, cozy, a woodstove filling the room with dry, comforting heat.

He turned to her, a sideways grin mixed with a wince. "Not the greatest weather, but that's life here in the U.P."

"Guess I'll get used to it!" Shea managed a laugh, her stomach curling beneath the kindness of the man of obvious Viking descent. He had blond wavy hair, brilliant blue eyes, and a jawline that could slice bread.

He stuck out his hand. "Holt. Holt Nelson."

The lighthouse's private owner. Yes. She had exchanged multiple emails with him when she'd booked the place as a rental for the next month.

She accepted Holt's handshake. "Shea Radclyffe."

"I know." His eyes twinkled as he held out his other arm to show her into the warm kitchen. "The bestselling author extraordinaire."

"Hardly." Shea really wasn't that famous. Her nonfiction book that featured the history and legends of obscure places had only just hit a bestseller list, and while her agent had sent her a dozen roses from her office in New York, Shea tended to be more pragmatic.

"Either way, glad to have you!" Holt's shoes echoed on the scarred hardwood floor. A pot of tea perched on a hot pad on a small, round wooden table with chipped white paint. A yellow ceramic teacup beckoned her. Holt gave it a casual nod. "I figured you'd like something to warm you up. I'd recommend staying inside tonight and getting your bags out of the car in the morning. This storm isn't going to let up anytime soon."

Shea shot a nervous look over her shoulder toward the doorway she'd just entered. "Is there any reason to be concerned? Will the water rise and be more of a threat?"

Holt's chuckle was reassuring. "Nah. The lake can't get at you here. The waves won't get any higher than they already are, plus it's why the lighthouse was built in this spot—just out of reach of the monsters of Lake Superior."

"That makes sense." Shea felt silly for having asked. It stood to reason no one would build a lighthouse where the waves could destroy it.

Holt's smile warmed her as much as the nearby woodstove.

He wasn't mocking her or even acting as if she was the outsider that she was.

"I'll head out now and leave you to it," he said. "Some of the light switches are dimmers, so just be aware you may need to turn the knob. A bit old-fashioned, I know."

"Charming," Shea said.

"I left some basics in the icebox for you since I knew the storm was moving in. Milk, eggs, bread, that sort of thing. As you can see, the stove is a woodstove. We don't have natural gas this far out, and besides, it's more authentic if you ask me. There's the woodbox"—he pointed—"and if you need more firewood, just give me a call. I'll stop by and refill it for you." Holt pointed to a yellow rotary phone that hung on the wall. "You probably won't get a cell signal, at least not much of one. It's sketchy out here."

"But there's Wi-Fi, yes?" Shea needed it to research and write, and she was sure it had been listed as an amenity.

"Yeah, but it's moody too, though. It's not like we have fiber optic out here." He waited, and Shea thought she was supposed to laugh or something. So she did.

Holt nodded, apparently happy with her reaction. "It's satellite Wi-Fi, but for the most part it works fine. Best we can do in the Porkies."

The Porcupine Mountains. Yes. She was going to need to explore those too.

Holt bid her farewell, but Shea dogged his heels as he retreated into the little alcove and shrugged into his rain jacket.

"Are you . . . going to be okay out in this storm?" Not that she wanted to spend the night with a complete *male* stranger.

Holt winked. "Born and raised here, Radclyffe. This is nothin'."

His cavalier way of launching his form into the storm gave her all sorts of Aquaman vibes, even though he more closely resembled Thor.

Shea shut the door and flicked the lock—not that she'd need

it. She turned and leaned against it, staring into the kitchen, which led to the darkened rooms beyond.

She was here.

At Annabel's Lighthouse.

The infamous haunted lighthouse of Silvertown.

The ghostly lighthouse, shrouded in mystery and lore, was much preferred to a husband whose most exciting contribution to their marriage of late was to change the oil on her car before she left. Thirty years old and she wasn't sure who she was anymore. She wasn't sure who Pete was either. Their past had included an intoxicating teenage romance, with a reunion when she returned home from college. Pete, the homeboy, the blue-collar mechanic, and Shea the travel-hungry, literature-chasing adventurer. Opposites might attract, but after time they also repelled. If there weren't enough commonalities between them, how long could it last really?

Shea lifted her eyes to the kitchen ceiling. The markings of old coal fires and days gone by scarred it.

Maybe Annabel had once drank tea here.

Maybe Annabel had once mourned the loss of a man who was supposed to love her.

The twisted part was that Annabel was dead. And Shea? She didn't feel much different inside. Still, a spirit lingered here that begged to be awakened. She just didn't know if either her spirit or Annabel's was going to be friendly or something darker than what she'd bargained for.

3

LAKE SUPERIOR WAS AN ENIGMA to Shea. It had been ever since she was a young girl of nine running barefoot on its shores, skipping over driftwood and water-smoothed rocks, dodging blistering cold waves that threatened to bite her toes with frost.

Sunshine shed the torrents from the night before. Shea stepped onto the front stoop of the lighthouse. With a mug of coffee in hand, her flannel pajama pants pressed against her legs as the morning breeze soothed her skin. Such a stark difference from the tempestuous violence of the night before. The lake was mostly calm now, and a soft *whoosh-whoosh* could be heard as little waves caressed the shoreline. An innocence had returned this morning, one that belied the lake's underlying unpredictable temperament.

Shea had wrangled her dark spiral curls back with a headband and only taken time to slip on a fleece sweater over her nightshirt. In the early light, Annabel's Lighthouse didn't scream terror or poltergeists. It didn't have the haunted allure written about in travel magazines and old Upper Peninsula history books. Instead, it too was much like the lake. Gentle and charming in its quiet way, and not even much of a lighthouse if one wanted to argue.

"Oregon lighthouses have more aesthetic interest."

That had been the legitimate argument of her publisher when she'd raised the idea of writing her next compilation of true-life historical hauntings centered around a lighthouse. He wanted her to pursue one on the West Coast.

"They're taller. Prettier. More . . . lighthousey."

Pat Franz, her acquisitions editor, had a strange ability to create his own words, which seemed odd considering he was an editor. In the end, Shea was able to convince Pat that Annabel's Lighthouse would stand up to the Pacific Northwest ones because of its history. Annabel. The strange occurrences surrounding it. The fact that it had sat abandoned for a decade before finally being entered into the National Register of Historic Places and sold in the 1980s to a private owner.

"Morning."

The sound of Holt's voice as he rounded the corner of the lighthouse startled Shea. She yelped, splashing coffee from her mug onto the step.

Her host and the current owner of the lighthouse looked to be around her age, rugged yet clean-shaven with red tints in his blond hair, a square jawline, broad shoulders, a Roman god of a man . . .

Shea cleared her throat—and her thoughts.

She was staring.

"Morning," she answered back with a shameful belatedness that was more than evident.

"You survived last night's storm." It was an observation, and Holt draped his arms over the iron railing that edged the walk from the lighthouse to the lawn. There was an easygoing air about him, gentle, his smile warm and inviting.

"I did." Shea gathered her wits about her and shoved away the inappropriate attraction. Taking a sip of her coffee helped to settle her nerves, and she felt her middle-school-girl self slip away and be replaced by her authorly self who was accustomed to interactions with strangers, all in the name of research. "It was a doozy, though."

Holt laughed. "That it was. Not the worst, though there were a few branches down across the road this morning, and they lost electricity in town for a bit." He turned to look out over the lake that stretched to the horizon. "So you write books, huh?"

Shea nodded even though he wasn't looking at her. "I write about the historical tales and legends that surround different sites across the country."

Holt swiveled and squinted in thought. "Did you write that book on the ghost stories connected with that old house in Wisconsin?"

"Foster Hill?" Shea couldn't help but smile in the realization he was familiar with it. "I did. That was a fascinating story to write. A bit lighter on the ghosts, but so much family ancestry and tragedy. When I met with the current owner, Kaine Prescott, talking to her and touring the old place was like stepping into a time machine."

Holt nodded, seemingly satisfied that he'd pegged her and her books. "Edna Carraway is a lifetime native here. You'll want to meet up with her. She has lots of tales about the goings-on around the Porcupine Mountains. She knows the stories handed down by the Ojibwe people too. Some of her family married into the tribe over a century ago. She's a walking history book for Silvertown and the Porkies."

Shea couldn't help the spark of intrigue that lit her soul. This is what she loved about writing books and gathering old tales— true ones or otherwise. These were the stories that would die someday if they weren't passed along.

"The indigenous people are fantastic at preserving their ancestral legacies," Shea observed.

Holt nodded in agreement. "You seem familiar with the area."

Shea smiled as she readjusted her hold on her coffee mug and leaned back against the side of the house. "I used to come to the

U.P. with my family when I was a kid. When I got . . ." She bit off her words and rephrased them. "Lately it's been tough getting to this area. Travel has been . . . tricky."

A frown creased the region between Holt's eyes. "But aren't you a writer who writes about places all over the country?"

Shea managed a nervous laugh. "Funny, huh?" It was all she was going to offer him for a response. Holt's question made sense. It was the same issue Shea struggled with. Her husband Pete's resistant expression flashed across her mind. He liked staying put and preferred she do the same. He hated to travel by air. Trains and buses weren't any better—too many people. Shea knew he'd be happy as a hermit and thought he wanted her to share his opinion. Some of her friends argued that he was a bit controlling and she needed to just do her thing. Shea wasn't sure. Pete's personality wasn't domineering, he just didn't like her being away. Or so he said.

So it was always tense when Shea left him to travel for her books. No one understood her situation, it seemed—even herself at times. She pictured the glower on his face every time she pulled out of the driveway for a trip away, recalled the silence from his phone while she was gone, his aloof greeting when she returned home. So Shea had made it a habit not to travel unless it was necessary for her work. That was another reason she'd chosen Annabel's Lighthouse. She'd played on the shores of Lake Superior as a child. Dreamed here, imagined here, and fell in love with the lore and legend of the place, the untapped wildness. But she hadn't been back since she'd graduated from college and married Pete, her sweetheart who, at the time, seemed to be her answer to life's dreams.

Shortsighted twenty-two-year-old that she was.

Shea squashed her thoughts. No. She'd come here to reflect on who she was without Pete. Not that she would ever leave him for good . . . Well, that *had* crossed her mind, if she was being honest. Pete was like having a roommate who split expenses.

Romance had dissipated eons ago. Thank God they'd never had kids—she'd never wanted them—but Pete? Who knew. He was barely able to deviate from his daily menu routine of Raisin Bran in the morning, a ham sandwich for lunch, and a hamburger for supper. If she never ate another hamburger, it'd be too soon.

"What brings you to the lighthouse this morning?" Shea shoved aside her thoughts and focused on the steady cadence of waves washing up onshore. A steady cadence of blessed predictability—until a storm blew in.

Holt slid his arms from over the railing and turned toward the lake. "Just wanted to make sure everything was in one piece after the storm." He glanced at Shea as he thumbed over his shoulder toward the wilderness road and expanse behind them. "I live about a half mile that way. I have a cabin in the woods. I don't mean to butt in, but some of my property is part of an old silver mine from back in the day."

Shea frowned, clutching her coffee that was fast cooling in the morning air. "I thought this area was known for copper."

Holt dipped his head. "True. But there was a brief boom of silver in the late nineteenth century. Silvertown was pretty much a ghost town after the silver dried up."

"Makes sense." Shea took a sip of her lukewarm coffee. "Silvertown doesn't seem much more than a highway between a strip of small businesses."

"The town?" Holt's chuckle was deep. "If you can call Silvertown a *town*. We've got one little dive bar, a small grocery store, and a gas pump."

Shea nodded. "Mining towns go from boom to bust rather quickly in the course of history."

"That they do." Holt's expression shadowed for a moment, and Shea wondered why something from so long ago would bother him.

"So you own the old mining property?" she ventured.

Holt motioned for her to join him on the lawn. Shea glanced

at her feet and decided the moccasin slippers with rubber soles would suffice for now. The yard was less squishy than she'd imagined after the amount of rain from the night before. As she joined Holt at the end of the short walkway, she made a mental note to research the geology of the area. A lighthouse would be built on firm ground.

He led her across the lawn, past a grove of evergreens. His voice was a soothing rumble, and it matched the cadence of the waves as they approached the embankment.

"As you know," Holt explained, "the lake stretches north to Canada." He extended his arm toward the horizon, where blue water met blue sky.

Shea noted with a little surprise that the so-called cliff the lighthouse stood on was actually not that high but more of an outcropping. A well-worn trail led down to the shore, which was littered with driftwood, weeds, and debris that had washed up during the storm.

"This whole region is the Porcupine Mountains, but go about twelve miles that way"—Holt pointed eastward—"and you'll enter the state park." He did an about-face, and Shea followed suit, both now taking in the lighthouse with its arched windows set into the brickwork. "That way leads to the forest where the mining took place." Holt tipped his head in the opposite direction. "To the west is Silvertown, a few rentals and the like in the form of cabins or small houses. You can still find remnants of the mining era hidden in the woods and scattered among private properties. Back in its heyday, there were plans to make Silvertown into a port for the shipping of ore." Holt shifted his attention back to Annabel's Lighthouse. "That's what made her so important in the late nineteenth century. Lots of hopes and dreams died here. This place—as beautiful as it is—is also a wasteland."

Holt's tourism spiel ended, and Shea took an absent sip of her now cold coffee. She assessed the area, filing it all away in her mind along with Holt's information. Some of it she already knew, but she'd not been aware of the intent to make Silvertown a port. That would've potentially changed the area's future tremendously.

"Do you know why the port never materialized? I mean, was it because the silver wasn't sustainable?"

Holt rolled his lips together in thought before giving a nonchalant shrug. "What's been told and what actually happened is still up for debate."

Her curiosity was piqued by Holt's vague answer. "What's been told?"

Holt shot her a sideways glance. "Like you just pointed out, there wasn't enough silver. The place went bust."

"But there was copper. Why didn't they just adapt? This entire region is known for that, so it obviously would have been an option, right?"

"Sure, but Ontonagon is just west of here. That village was already established in the copper industry, and it has its own harbor."

"Suppose the silver mining *had* prospered, why wouldn't they have used Ontonagon to ship out the silver too?" Shea was growing confused. "Based on your argument that Ontonagon was an established port, why would they need a separate one here in Silvertown just for silver?"

Holt laughed. "Well, there's the rub. Like I said, there's what's been told and what actually happened. Intrigue, betrayal, greed, murder—Silvertown has it all." He gave a sweep of his hand up the length of the lighthouse. "And Annabel's Lighthouse has seen it all, long before the silver boom of the 1870s. The one thing you'll learn really fast, Shea Radclyffe, is that this land is harsh, and it holds its secrets with ferocity." He winked, then grew more somber. "Don't get too close. It may bite you."

4

REBECCA

And this maiden she lived with had no other
thought than to love and be loved by me . . .

Annabel Lee

SILVERTOWN
UPPER PENINSULA OF MICHIGAN
SPRING, 1874

A COLD HAND CARESSED HER FACE, brushing her damp hair away from her bruised skin. It was feathery and so light in its touch, Rebecca wondered if she might be dreaming. Her eyes fluttered open, searching for the ministering hand of care. No one was there. It was only the trees, the hard ground beneath her, the rustling wind that permeated her chemise and chilled her body. But she had felt a presence. A feminine presence. The kind that nurtured and under whose influence a person's soul was warmed and began to rest. "Missy."

The gruff growl broke through the haze of her mind.

"Missy, you best wake now, ya hear?"

Rough fingertips—so unlike the cool, comforting ones—grazed her neck, poked the side of it, then slapped her cheek.

Rebecca moaned, drawing her knees to her chest, only to have them collide against the side of the grave marker where she'd lost consciousness.

Annabel's grave.

The world between reality and dreams stilled for Rebecca, and she kept her eyes sealed against reality. Annabel. It had been Annabel's soothing touch a moment ago. Reaching from the grave, from the beyond. Calling to her from death's cavern and—

"Missy!" This time the voice was sharper, as was the slap on her face.

Rebecca managed to open her eyes, squinting against the midday sunlight that sparkled through the treetops.

"You're not dead."

The voice belonged to a grizzled face, lined and weathered as though the lake itself had beaten channels into his skin. A white beard, scruffy white sideburns, and a fisherman's cap squashed onto a nest of equally white hair, framing dark eyes that squinted back at her. He smelled of woodsmoke and fish.

"Well?" He straightened from his crouched position over her. "Are you hurt?" The toe of his boot nudged her bare leg.

Rebecca whimpered.

Hurt? Yes.

She opted to nod and not say anything. The old man scared her. His beady eyes were fogged by so many layers of stories and time that she wasn't sure she could trust him.

"You *are* hurt." He groaned as he bent and shoved his left hand between the ground and her shoulder. Not gently, the man pulled on her arm, coaxing her up from her position by the gravestone.

"No." Rebecca tugged against him, shrinking away. His hand released her, and Rebecca edged backward, bracing her palms on Annabel's grave. She stared up at the old man, who studied her through narrowed eyes. His faded blue shirt was covered with a worn-out wool vest that had long since lost its buttons.

"I can't help ya if you're going to lie down an' die."

Rebecca eyed him.

He grunted. "Fine place you picked. Won't have to dig deep to bury ya, I s'pose. Reckon I'll come back tonight and take care of your remains, seein' as the wolves'll be by to do it themselves if'n I don't."

Rebecca whimpered again, this time the sound of her own voice inspiring a clearer thought. She reached out. "Help. I-I . . ."

She was lost. So very lost. She searched the fisherman's face, trying to recollect whether or not she knew him. There was a brief moment when his voice sounded familiar and touched something inside her, but then it dissipated just as quickly.

He gave no indication that he knew her.

"I've been tryin' to help you." The old man widened his stance for better balance, then reached down with a thick hand. "Grab it. I'll yank ya up."

Injured or not, it was all the gentility she would receive.

Rebecca cautiously placed her hand in his and scrambled to her feet. Her chemise gave her little comfort of modesty, and he seemed to note that, giving a harrumph as he looked around the forest floor as though a blanket or a coat would miraculously appear.

"Ain't got nothin'," he simply said.

Rebecca wrapped her arms around herself, a shiver passing through her.

There was a moment of awkward silence. It felt as if he expected something from her, but when she didn't give it— whatever it was—he accepted its absence.

"Edgar's my name," the man said, nodding.

Rebecca stared at him.

Edgar harrumphed again. "Tell me yours."

"R-Rebecca." Her voice sounded unfamiliar to her ears.

"Rebecca what?"

She shook her head.

Edgar palmed his beard, petting it as if it were a cat, then dropped his hand to his side. "Now what do I do with ya?" He stared at her, giving Rebecca the feeling that she was an inconvenience and yet he still liked her at the same time.

And she didn't know why. Rebecca stared back at him.

"Let Annabel lie in peace, for pity's sake. She's already a tempest that can't be silenced." Edgar's cryptic words sank into Rebecca, and she cast her gaze back to the stone of the woman who had died so many years before. A woman Rebecca knew nothing about and yet somehow felt as though she had just met her—been nursed and cared for by her.

Edgar motioned her away from the gravestone with knobby fingers. "Follow me." He turned and started forward, not bothering to look over his shoulder to see if she would follow.

Rebecca hesitated. An old man seemed harmless enough, but she'd learned last night that brutality came in various forms. It was enough to make her doubt even the tiniest bit of kindness Edgar had shown her.

He maneuvered ahead through the trees and undergrowth. "You comin'?" he asked, his voice trailing behind him.

Rebecca started forward after him. She had little choice but to follow.

The forest opened into a clearing. Rebecca squinted at the sun's boldness. She shielded her eyes, cupping her hand over them, grateful the old fisherman wasn't fast on his feet.

To her right, the lake sparkled in its expanse, smooth with small waves pretending to be kind. Ahead of her stood a two-story brick house, and from its west side rose a tower—the lighthouse. They were one unit with two separate purposes. Shelter from the house, rescue from the light.

"You're the lightkeeper?" Rebecca blurted out between chapped lips, trying to ignore the throbbing in her head and the way the world around her spun. She struggled to keep upright.

Edgar was oblivious to her malady as he pointed at the lake. "The lake, she's a saucy woman. Someone needs to warn the ships of her devilry."

Rebecca scanned the horizon, then returned her gaze to the lighthouse. She should remember this place if she had been here before. It was remote and unpopulated. Yet the only thing that looked familiar to her were the twin arched windows on the second story. Had she looked out from those windows before today, out toward the lake or . . . ?

She squeezed her eyes shut against the brightness of the lake reflecting the sun. So many homes heralded arched windows. That was hardly a memory specific to this place. If she hailed from this region or somewhere else, Rebecca didn't know. Her mind was an empty black slate, all words and letters erased, leaving behind not even a trace of chalk.

"Come into the house," the lightkeeper said.

Rebecca followed Edgar up the path that led to the back door. It stood open, its wooden panels hanging solid on its hinges. There was a distinct and lingering smell of woodsmoke mixed with the pungent sweet of tobacco.

Rebecca paused. The aroma was eerily familiar. It should prompt a recollection, but it didn't.

Edgar glanced at her as he shuffled through the small entryway into the kitchen beyond. He puttered about at the stove, the kettle scraping as he pulled it toward him. A few moments later, he returned, a tin cup of coffee in hand and an expectant look on his face.

Rebecca stood frozen in the doorway. If she was supposed to make herself at home, she hadn't. Something inside—something innate—told her to remain where she was until invited in.

"Sit." Edgar set the cup on the table, and coffee sloshed over the side.

Still aware of her lack of modesty due to her ripped chemise, Rebecca entered the kitchen with unease. She eyed the corners, the darkened room beyond. They were alone. She slipped onto a hard wooden chair, and the smell of the coffee awakened her senses. Her stomach rumbled, and her body, though aching from the battering from the night before, craved the warmth of the brew. "Thank you."

Edgar gave a short nod. He waited until Rebecca lifted the coffee to her lips and took a sip. It was bitter and strong. Some coffee grounds made their way through her teeth into her mouth, but Rebecca swallowed them.

"Hungry?" Edgar huffed.

Rebecca gave a quick nod.

Soon Edgar had a plate of hard biscuits in front of her. "Don't got any butter. Nothing fancy here."

"That's all right," she replied. She felt unnerved, disconnected from who she was, where she'd come from, what had happened . . .

"So who are ya?" Edgar wanted to know as well.

"Rebecca" was all she could manage as a reply.

His brow furrowed. "Knew that. What's your full name? Where're you from?"

Rebecca labored to remember, to access the dark corners of her mind. There weren't even images. No shadows. Just darkness. And fear. So much fear that another whimper escaped her without her permission.

Edgar held up a hand. "S'okay. We'll deal with that later. Let me go get you somethin' warm to wear."

He shuffled his way from the kitchen into the innards of the keeper's house. In his absence, Rebecca's shoulders lowered and released a small bit of the immense tension that had coiled her neck and shoulder muscles into knots.

Edgar returned with a long piece of cloth draped over his arm. Rebecca eyed it as his large fingers rubbed the cotton between them. He dropped it in a pile in front of Rebecca.

"Try that," he said and then continued on his way to the door they had entered through.

After he left, the silence in the house enveloped Rebecca. She set aside her coffee cup and reached for the garment. She held it up and saw it was a woman's dress. It was small like Rebecca and looked compatible with her slight form. A serviceable gray, worn beneath the arms, without any frills or embroidery. The material appeared to be homespun, its style so simplistic it was impossible to put a date to it.

Rebecca stood and made the effort to slip into the dress. She was pleasantly surprised to find she was able to button the gown over her bosom. It was comforting to have something covering her body besides just her undergarments.

Moving to the doorway that led into the house, Rebecca peered into the darkened room. It was a cramped, seemingly unused dining area with brick walls and no decor on them. Sunlight streamed through the windows, exposing the table in the room's center. A lace cloth draped across the middle of the table, where a tapered candle in an iron base stood unlit and boasted a new wick. The unused candle indicated that Edgar the old lightkeeper didn't often entertain visitors in his home.

Just off the dining room was a small pantry. It too had brick walls, and aside from the shelves stacked with various items, there was a washbasin with a hand crank to squeeze water from clothes after cleaning them. Rebecca was hard-pressed to imagine Edgar at work standing over the washbasin.

The only other room on the first level was a square sitting room with a fireplace, stuffed chairs with a small table between them, and kerosene lamps mounted on the walls in cast-iron holders. At the far end of the room was a set of stairs that led to the second floor. Rebecca made her way up the stairs, careful not to trip on the narrow treads. Once at the top, she entered another small living space that housed a desk, a bookshelf with volumes covered in cobwebs, and what appeared to be a lightkeeper's log.

She ran her hand over the inked words dried on the page. The handwriting was clear with pen strokes that emphasized the writer's confidence. The entry for yesterday was already penned: *Routine work. Standing by—rain and strong winds.* For whatever reason, Rebecca caressed the words. They seemed to come alive beneath her fingertips, to beat like a heart, strong and purposeful. The words exuded strength and didn't match the perception Rebecca had drawn from the stooped-shouldered Edgar.

Her eyes blurred as her head pounded. Rebecca pushed her hair behind her ear, leaning against the desk while she composed herself. Once she had gathered her wits again, she took note of the solitary room beyond.

A narrow bed had been shoved into a corner between two windows, one at its head and one by its feet. That it was the keeper's sleeping quarters was obvious by the shirt hanging off the scarred iron post of the footboard, the suspenders in a pile on the floor, and a few toiletry items littered about the top of a compact dresser.

Beyond that stood one more door that led into a little alcove. Rebecca moved closer but with hesitation, then peered into the alcove. It was clear where it went. She saw a landing and then metal stairs that spiraled upward to the lighthouse above.

Rebecca took a few steps upward, gripping the metal rail that curved along the stairs. She came to another landing, where a doorway on one side led to what she assumed was the attic, while the stairs continued their upward spiral to the lantern room.

She peered through the doorway into a short hallway. This was a space that wasn't meant to be a living area and yet had been converted into one. It was dark with no windows. It smelled musty, yet there was the scent of spice and even the faint scent of lavender. There were two doors across from each other.

After a quick inspection, she noted one of the doors opened to a tiny bedroom with barely enough space for a single bed. It was plain and dull with a sloping ceiling that would make it necessary for anyone taller than Rebecca to duck. The bed had a navy-blue patchwork quilt and a sagging mattress, with a rag rug on the wooden floor. Rebecca turned from the room and saw that the other door—the only other entry into the constrictive space—was closed. She tried the knob, but the door remained solidly secured.

"It's locked."

Rebecca cried out in shock, spinning around and hitting her shoulder against the wall. She stared at the form who blocked the entrance back to the lighthouse stairwell. He was tall and bent over so as not to hit his head on the top of the doorframe. He had dark straight hair that hung over his forehead. His eyes were piercing, and yet he addressed her as a man might when coaxing a trapped, frightened animal.

"I won't hurt you," he assured, his voice rumbling in the hallway between them.

Desperation filled her at the sight of him. She blinked against the thrum of pain in her head, straining to recall if he was the man from the previous night who'd partaken in chasing her and beating her, and if she should claw her way to escape, or if he was in fact safe.

"I'm Abel." Frosty eyes searched hers. When she didn't respond, he took a careful step toward her, his hands up as if to indicate he meant her no harm.

Rebecca eyed him warily.

"I'm the assistant here. I work alongside Edgar. I'm training to eventually keep the light on my own." He eyed her for a second, and Rebecca couldn't find her tongue to utter a reply. Abel pointed to the sparse room and the sagging bed. "That's where I sleep."

Rebecca glanced at the open room, her hand still resting on the locked door she'd just tried to open.

Abel cleared his throat. "Edgar sent me to fetch you."

Rebecca stared at him, searching her memory for something—anything—that would bring clarity to this moment. He was a stranger. Or was he? His eyes were so vivid, so sharp, she wondered if he could see into her soul and knew more about her than she did about herself.

"Do you know who I am?" she asked.

Surprise swept across his angular features. "Me? *No.* I mean, no."

"You've never seen me before?" she pressed, her voice echoing in the small passageway.

Abel's eyes narrowed as though trying to comprehend. "Don't *you* know who you are?"

His question, though innocent and perfectly sensible, sparked something inside Rebecca. She had been here before. She'd walked the shores of this lake many times. She'd breathed in scent of the fir trees and the poplar. She'd been caressed by the same breeze that turned into a gale when one least expected it.

But no. She did not know who she was. And with nothing more to give the man in front of her, Rebecca simply shook her head and responded, "No. I am . . . no one."

5

SHEA

I was a child, and she was a child, in
this kingdom by the sea . . .
Annabel Lee

ANNABEL'S LIGHTHOUSE
PRESENT DAY

*D*ON'T GET TOO CLOSE. *It may bite you."*
    Shea mouthed the lightkeeper's words to herself as she explored the place that would be her home for the next month. Annabel's Lighthouse. A two-story building with cramped rooms, a metal spiral staircase that led from the keeper's bedroom up to the little attic bedrooms and then on to the lighthouse itself.

    Curiosity demanded that she ignore the inner rooms and head to the beacon or lamp room. The square iron gallery accommodated a platform and rail, while the decagonal beacon room held an old Fresnel lens and light. Though it was no longer working, no longer warning ships of the rocky shoreline, the light remained intact, like a time capsule that held memories only it could recall. She eyed heavy curtains hanging over several of the panes of glass, wondering at their existence when the purpose of the lighthouse was to shine the light outward, not hold it inside.

Pulling her phone from her pocket, she typed a note into an app to remind herself to research the curious curtains. The room was a tad chilly, the wind clanging against its metal framework.

Annabel's Lighthouse.

Shea was here for Annabel as much as she was for the inner workings of a lighthouse built in the 1860s. She scanned the horizon. It was said a person could see twelve miles out on a clear day. Twelve miles of blue-green waters, icy cold even on a hot July day. Waters that never gave up their dead but preserved them for years because of the freezing temperatures. Corpses didn't have the normal "bloat and float," as Shea liked to call it. They sank along with their ships, which became permanent caskets in a watery grave.

But then there was Annabel.

Not much was known of the woman who had taken over the name of Silvertown Lighthouse and claimed the place as her own. It was said that some nights she could be seen walking the shoreline, barefoot and wearing a white gown. Annabel's story comprised a marriage and an outside lover, thwarted love, a raging tempest, and a man who had never given up hope of finding her—the young woman lost to the lake's frigid depths.

The lighthouse had been kept for years, the beacon said to have searched for the lost woman even on calm nights. Its light shone over the waters, a silent cry for Annabel to come home, to rise from the lake and take her place beside the man who'd loved her for decades until his death.

Today, Annabel was a mere ghost story. Her spirit was said to haunt the lighthouse. She was a restless spirit, visiting people when least expected, acting as though she pled for rescue, sometimes heralded as a nurturing specter, other times so haunting she was almost like a siren one wished to follow. Some said her husband killed her. Most believed the man who'd truly loved her—her lover—joined Annabel after he died. An old man curled on his cot in the lightkeeper's room, alone and decrepit.

Shea didn't believe in ghosts, but she did believe in lore and in telling the stories of the ones whose lives had been captured in ways that made them ghostly.

Annabel had a story.

Shea planned to unravel it, and then she would write it. And when Shea was done, Annabel would no longer be a ghost, but a human who had lived and died, plagued by the same tempestuous waters of love that Shea herself was attempting to navigate.

As she did on any research trip, Shea took the first day to explore the area and gather information. Following a fifteen-minute drive from the lighthouse, she entered the Porcupine Mountains State Park and its miles of wilderness. Once she'd found a place to park, she set off, hiking along the Escarpment Trail that led to a scenic overlook, where she could look down at the vastness of the region and the famed Lake of the Clouds, which sparkled at the foot of the dramatic cliffs. The old-growth forest below burst into full spring foliage, a deep emerald green and invitingly lush.

While she'd been enticed to hike the trail, she wasn't prepared for a several-mile-long walk, nor was it the purpose of her day. Turning away from the Lake of the Clouds, she traveled back toward the lighthouse and then beyond it toward Ontonagon. Lunch in a small diner brought her face-to-face with locals, and she spent some time exploring the town, poking her head into a small museum, and afterward walking the pier. She'd gathered a few names of people to reach out to for more information about lore, history, and the like.

The name Edna Carraway had come up a few times, just as Holt had mentioned earlier that morning, and so had the names August Fronell and Captain Gene. Apparently all three were locals, born and raised, with Captain Gene being the one who interested her the most. Maybe it was the *Captain* ahead of his name, or maybe it was merely because he'd been described as "cranky and crotchety." And while she might get the most stories out of him concerning Annabel and the lighthouse, she'd be lucky to find the man.

It seemed the captain was as elusive as "Pressie," the lake's mysterious serpent that was not unlike the Loch Ness Monster. In fact, they said it was Captain Gene who had been the last known person to spot Pressie in the lake, although that had been back in the 1970s. Regardless, Captain Gene was someone Shea wanted to interview.

With leads noted in her phone app, Shea made her way back to the lighthouse, stopping briefly at the diner once again where the Wi-Fi was reliable. She scanned her inbox, wrote and sent an email to her editor, and thumbed through text messages.

Pete had texted her once: *Make it there?*

She eyed it for a long moment, debating whether she felt like giving Pete the satisfaction of knowing she'd arrived safely. He could have at least taken the time to call her. Finally, she ignored the sting of her stagnant marriage and sent him a quick response: *Yep.*

There. If Pete could write in short sentences, so could she.

Back at the lighthouse, Shea heated soup in the kitchen, enjoying the cast-iron pot and the old-fashioned stove that still worked. She'd followed the instructions Holt had left on a laminated card—wood in the firebox to get it started and to keep it warm. Back in the day, they would have followed up the wood with coal for longer and more consistent burning. But tonight, she just needed enough to heat the iron range, which took far longer than Shea anticipated.

That was the allure of Annabel's Lighthouse, and she knew when she'd reserved the place that she'd be stepping back in time. A microwave oven was available as another option for heating up the soup, but the call of the prior century had wrapped itself around Shea as darkness set in. She could hear the ebb and flow of the waves on the shoreline. The strength in the waves filled the lighthouse with a consistent, rhythmic song.

The lights in the kitchen were kept purposefully dim. Shea could see why Holt had attempted to recreate an early twentieth century appeal. The simplicity of life was emphasized by the solitude of the lighthouse, a cozy environment that belied the dangers of the lake and wilderness just outside the door.

With a bowl of hot soup in hand, Shea moved to the sitting room, settling on a green couch long out of style. It sagged in the middle but was remarkably comfortable when Shea sank onto it. She propped her feet on a faded blue-velvet ottoman and, with a sigh of relief for the familiar, retrieved the remote control for the small TV mounted on the wall above a table that held coasters, a few locally written books on the area, and a guest book for visitors to sign.

She wasn't sure what she'd find for channels, and it was obvious to her the moment she turned on the TV that her choices were limited. But there was a true-crime documentary on, and now that it was dark outside and the 60-watt lightbulb in the lone lamp created shadows around the room, it only seemed appropriate to watch something creepy.

Maybe Annabel would pay a visit too . . .

Shea smiled to herself, pleased with the solitude, the silence, and the overwhelming feeling that she was alone. Truly alone. A wild country, a temperamental lake, a legendary ghost, and just herself. It was almost delightful, if she could set aside the realities of life.

The documentary proved to be one she'd seen before, but Shea found a few DVDs on the table next to the books. She set her soup bowl aside and looked through them, her attention perking up when she noted one of them was about the Silvertown Lighthouse.

Within a few minutes, Shea had popped the DVD into the player and located its remote. She hit play, retrieved her soup, and settled in for what she hoped would be helpful research.

"In 1968, the keeper of the lighthouse in Silvertown, Michigan, finally allowed the lamp to go out for the last time . . ."

Shea leaned forward, her spoonful of soup hoisted partway to her mouth. Her eyes were glued to the documentary. The camera lens panned the lighthouse, undoubtedly filmed with the use of a drone, and then swept over the roof of Annabel's Lighthouse, along the shoreline, then back to glide past the gallery.

Shea let the spoon fall into the soup bowl.

". . . but this wasn't the last that would be heard of the Silvertown Lighthouse." An edge of suspense tinged the male narrator's voice. "Ghost stories aside, the lighthouse would once again make the news in 2010 when the body of Jonathan Marks was found in the living area of the lighthouse."

Enthralled, Shea set down the bowl.

"At the time, the lighthouse was owned by Marks. The coroner confirmed he'd been dead for at least seventy-two hours before his body was found. An investigation into the death of Mr. Marks was launched, and living up to the lighthouse's mysterious and secretive reputation, Mr. Marks's death, while being ruled a suicide, has long since been debated."

The couch she sat on changed from cozy to downright creepy.

The narrator droned on. "Reports claim that Mr. Marks's body on discovery had the telltale signs of a gunshot wound to his right temple. People who knew Mr. Marks claimed this simply didn't add up. Jonathan Marks was not only left-handed, but he was known in the U.P. for his unpopular stance against firearms as a whole. A conservationist, Marks was an outspoken critic of the hunting of wildlife and a proponent for nationwide gun-control laws."

Shea sank into the couch cushions, unable to peel her eyes away from the TV. A suspicious death? Here at the lighthouse? This she had *not* heard of prior to coming, nor in her first day of research in the nearby town. And how could that be? She'd think a more current lighthouse death would even trump the old ghost story of Annabel for telling rights.

"With a lack of resources to fund an investigation that had already been determined to be a suicide, the case of Jonathan Marks and what may have been his potential murder was closed. To this day, many locals believe that fifteen years is far too long for this murder to go unsolved. But if Marks was indeed murdered, his body found on the floor beneath a painting of the elusive Annabel from a century prior, was it really a man who took his life, or was it, as some have claimed, Annabel who exacted revenge for the tragic circumstances surrounding her death back in 1852?"

Shea sprang up from the couch, sweeping her eyes around the cramped room and alighting on a painting that hung on the wall to her left. She'd noticed it before, but only as a beautiful landscape of the Lake Superior shoreline. Now, on closer inspection, Shea noted that just off to the right of the shore, what appeared to be filmy white foam from the waves was actually the obscure form of a woman. Annabel.

Shea's gaze dropped to the wood floor beneath it. Jonathan Marks had died right there. Right where her bare feet were planted. She scrambled backward.

No one had mentioned to her the murder of Jonathan Marks fifteen years ago. Or was it really a death by suicide? Everyone spoke of Annabel. Annabel's Lighthouse. The dead woman of

1852, back when Silvertown didn't even have a name yet, when the wilderness was truly wild and the indigenous people still traded and interacted with the trappers and miners moving into the area.

In 1852, the lighthouse hadn't been built yet, and Annabel's spirit hadn't begun to haunt the place.

But possible murder?

Shea grabbed her soup bowl and retreated into the kitchen, where somehow she felt more in control. Heat still emanated from the stove. She set the bowl on the table.

This changed things. The lighthouse's cozy sense of peace had morphed into an eeriness reminiscent of Edgar Allan Poe. Actually, this brought the lighthouse well into the twenty-first century. It brought death directly into its inner sanctum.

The lightbulb in the fixture suspended over the kitchen table flickered. Shea froze, eyeing it. It buzzed, flickered again, and then, like an exclamation point marking the moment, it popped, swallowing both the kitchen and Shea in complete, terrifying darkness.

6

REBECCA

But we loved with a love that was more than love . . .
Annabel Lee

ANNABEL'S LIGHTHOUSE
SPRING, 1874

FOG WAS SETTLING IN, and the waters were churning as the sun went down. Rebecca hugged her knees to her chest as she cowered in the corner of the oil room in the lighthouse, listening to the wailing of the wind as it rattled the windows. Another storm, another tumultuous night reminiscent of the one prior. She had spent the entire day here in the oil room, the small room with the washbasin just off the dining area. Its floor-to-ceiling shelves were stocked with colza oil, stored in tanks, there to keep the flame of the lantern burning.

She'd sequestered herself in this room for the last several hours. While the sitting room with the rocking chair might have been more comfortable, something inside of Rebecca had landed her here, on the floor, curled into a ball and hopeful that she'd be left alone. The oil room seemed a lonelier place and, by being so, felt safer.

She'd heard the low timbre of the men's voices—probably discussing her. What to do with her, why she was here, who she was. There was a deep fear rooted within her, a nauseating fear that kept her stomach churning and her soul indecisive. The man, Abel, had told her he didn't know who she was. Edgar had been impassive. But there were tiny familiarities here in this lighthouse, and even more outside. Like distant dreams or another life. She had lived here once, and there had been peace. At least that was what one side of Rebecca felt convinced of. The other side was certain this lighthouse and the men within it were strangers, were dangerous, were somehow tied to the men from last night.

Even now, Rebecca closed her eyes tightly and then opened them, yet the memories of last night remained.

She ran through the woods, tree branches scraping wildly at her face. Rain pelted her with the stinging prickles of cold drops forming into miniature frozen spears. The men had come at her from both the east and west. They had encircled her like a pack of wolves.

They shoved Rebecca to the ground. The leering smile of the otherwise faceless assailant loomed over her, fading in and out of her memory. She felt his hands on her torso. Felt them in places no man had touched her before, and he was unkind in his force. Another man's growling voice was no omen of rescue, and though he had shoved her assailant from his straddled position atop her, he had only taken his place. But it was his hands that had lifted her head and then brought it to the earth. She had choked on the rain. She had suffocated on the air stolen from her with the action and the subsequent pain.

A moment of scuffle between her attackers. Rebecca had broken free. She had run through woods at a breakneck pace and—

"Rebecca?"

She screamed, flailing her arms and legs.

The lightkeeper's assistant—Abel, was it?—knelt beside her. She could hear him trying to calm her. His hand was on her arm. She screamed again, slapping at him. She couldn't allow him to hurt her. She needed to get away. But the lighthouse was safe. It was a haven in the thunderstorm. It was—

"Rebecca!"

The sharp tone of Abel's command snapped something aware inside of her. Rebecca froze, her chest heaving in terrified breaths, her eyes wide as she stared at Abel with fear.

His frigid look seemed to match the growing storm outside the lighthouse.

"You're safe, Rebecca." Abel reached for her, but she shrank back from his hand.

A shadow flickered across his face. Irritation? Anger? She couldn't tell, but it wasn't sadness—it wasn't pity either.

She wanted to reach out to him, but his dark silence intimidated her. She wanted to flee from him, but the gentleness of his touch confused her.

"A storm is coming," he informed her. "Please stay in the oil room. You'll be safe here."

Rebecca pulled herself into a sitting position, scooting away from him on her bottom until her back hit the wall.

Abel's expression was troubled. "Rebecca . . ." he began.

He knew her. He at least knew something of her. Rebecca could see it in his eyes. But he withheld it from her. He let her believe they had only just met.

"Will you stay here?" he asked for reassurance.

She nodded. Lying. The moment he left her alone would be the moment she would run from the lighthouse. Back into the storm. Back into the proximity of her attackers from last night. Back into the unknown . . . Rebecca sucked in an unwelcome sob.

Where did she run when she didn't know from whom she ran or why?

Abel eyed her, then strode to the corner of the room where he gripped a large metal, boxlike contraption. It had what appeared to be a trumpet configured to one side, like the earpiece of an elderly soul hard of hearing. He appeared to sense her curiosity, so Abel provided a brief explanation.

"The fog is getting dense, and the lake is turning wild. I need to sound the warning horn."

Rebecca frowned, unsure of what he meant.

Abel tipped his head with instruction. "Stay here."

Rebecca nodded, but while she answered him, a strange, overwhelming desire took over her, as though the lake were calling to her despite its anger. Perhaps its spirit was furious at the wrongs committed against her, and now it rose in her defense. Perhaps the lake was not a violent murderer, but a vigilante exactor of justice, devouring ships and sailors who dared to brutalize the innocent.

It made sense in Rebecca's mind, yet it wouldn't if she were to voice it. So she remained mum as Abel departed the oil room and headed toward the gale.

Fierce winds plastered Rebecca's dress against her legs, whipping her hair and slapping it across her face. She had reacted to her strongest instinct. Flee. She saw Abel forging ahead, his rain slicker shedding water, unaware that Rebecca was mere paces behind him. The rain was cold, the wind blowing off the lake akin to a monster's icy breath. She could hear nothing but the roaring and crashing of the waves, which had been unleashed from their morning calm into white-crested walls, rising to heights that would swallow men standing on one another's shoulders.

The storm stunned Rebecca as she pled with her senses to

align with reason. Run—to the woods. Run—to the lighthouse. Run. Her need swirled inside her with a similar violence to the storm building off the lake.

She stood, the rain pelting her, as Abel pushed into the storm. He neared the edge of the embankment. Perched above the rocky shoreline, he began to pump a small handle up and down on the metal box until, through the volume of the waves, Rebecca could hear the warning wail of the foghorn.

The lighthouse behind them cast its beam onto the lake, attempting to bust through the thick fog and the curtain of rain.

Rebecca regretted the lack of clarity in her thoughts. She regretted that nothing triggered recollections but only reinforced the utter fear that rose from her gut into her throat. Nausea claiming her, strangling her, and the already dark of night devouring her whole.

She dropped to her knees, leaning forward on her hands and gagging onto the sodden earth. Abel continued to sound the horn.

"A ship!" His shout interrupted Rebecca's momentary fade as she felt the world closing in around her. "A ship!"

Another shout behind Rebecca told her that Edgar was fighting his way toward them.

"What are you doing out here?" A sharp reprimand laced his voice.

Edgar's meaty hand clamped around Rebecca's arm and hauled her to her feet. His bearded face pressed close to hers, and his snappy black eyes speared her with concern. "Get inside! Go!"

His shove sent Rebecca stumbling back toward the lighthouse. She struggled across the lawn, the warmth of the light beckoning her. Edgar had made her decision for her, and something in her responded to his direction.

Go back. Go back to the lighthouse.

A yell behind her made her twist in her position.

The foghorn had stopped.

The wind tore at her with wicked derision, but Rebecca fixated on Abel and Edgar as they scrambled down the embankment.

"—sinking!"

She raised her eyes to the lake and saw the outline of a ship. A steamer. The lake bludgeoned it, wrecking it into pieces.

The next moments might have been mere minutes or perhaps hours, but Rebecca lost sight of her own horror and instead surged after the two lightkeepers. There was naught they could do but watch as the lake ate the ship, debris already lifting on the high waves and pummeling onto the shore.

"Look for survivors!" Abel's shout was cut off by the raging storm.

Far ahead along the shoreline, the flicker of lanterns awakened her to the realization that while remote, the lighthouse was not solitary in its existence. Other men were fighting their way through the storm toward the lighthouse, drawn by the shipwreck that occurred just offshore.

Rebecca clawed her way up the sandy bank, skinning her knees on driftwood and rock as she did so. She took refuge in a grove of trees, watching as a group of men arrived, all dressed in oiled coats and floppy hats that drained water from their faces.

Their yelling was unintelligible above the lake's own voice. Ropes were uncoiled. A rowing skiff was hauled from its mooring on the shore toward the water.

Edgar waved his arms over his head, his wobbling run toward the men indicative of disagreement.

A shouting match ensued.

One man pointed toward the ship that was now in pieces, then at the skiff.

"You'll sink!" Edgar's hoarse cry reached Rebecca's ears.

She wrapped her arms around a tree trunk, stabilizing her. Mesmerized by the chaos, she squinted into the rain. She could see people in the water now. One was lifted high with a wave that then crashed and appeared to roll over them. The depth of the darkness swallowed the victim, along with the violence of the lake.

She released the tree and hurried along the embankment, holding her hand over her eyes, a futile shield against the rain. A head bobbed in the lake and disappeared.

People were drowning before her very eyes, and she was help-less. The men were helpless. She searched the shoreline until her gaze landed on Abel. He stood like a solemn sentinel, bathed in the swath of light from the gallery, staring at the abyss as he watched the ship's passengers drown. Helpless.

She hid in the oil room once again, uncertain as to why Edgar had directed her back there. He had spotted her on the em-bankment, the lighthouse most likely silhouetting her drenched form, and he'd waved her back. When she didn't move, the old man had clamored up the ridge and shoved his face near hers.

"Get in the oil room an' stay there!" His command was so brusque and sharp it had snapped Rebecca from her sodden stupor.

How long had she stood there, unmoving, spellbound and horrified not only by the storm but by the shipwreck and the destruction left in the wake of it all? It matched her very soul, she felt, and as the minutes ticked by, she had been less terrified and more entranced by the lake. By its majesty and its power. By the way it imitated every part of her. A tumult warring within her whose forecast refused to predict a calm anytime soon.

Now clanging and banging came from the kitchen as someone filled the range with coal. Rain still pelted against the window just across from the wall of shelves.

Rebecca shivered, soaking in her dress, unable to get warmth back into her bones. She peered out the window into the night.

Men rushed to and from the lake in what appeared to be a for-naught rescue mission. No bodies were being carried to the lighthouse, but as the storm had begun to wane and dawn seeped into the sky, the waves continued to wash pieces of the doomed steamboat ashore.

"Goodness, you're sopping wet, Rebecca."

Rebecca was startled at the matronly voice and banged into the windowsill. She stared at the woman. Lucky if she was over five feet tall. A dry muslin dress swathed her frame, and a ser-viceable shawl draped her shoulders, the ends tucked in a band that stretched around the woman's plump waist.

"What was Edgar an' Abel thinking?" She tsked as she hurried from the oil room and then soon returned with a wool blanket in her hands. "Get out of your things. Even your skivvies. You need to get warm before you die of hypothermia or shock." The woman glanced over her shoulder, as if the two lightkeepers were standing behind her, and scowled regardless of their ab-sence. "Men. Half a brain and no mind to nurture." She shook the blanket and held it up like a curtain. "There now. Out of your things. Hurry now. There may be more I need to help with besides you."

"I'm not from the shipwreck." Rebecca felt it necessary to inform the woman if for no other reason than that she felt guilty stealing attention from others in more dire need.

"Don't I know that?" The woman's gruffness was laced with kindness. Rebecca stilled and eyed her, whose blue eyes met hers. Confusion flooded the woman's face. "Rebecca? Come now . . ." She shook the blanket again. "What are you doing?"

Rebecca stared at her. This woman knew her. Rebecca could see that she did. She took a step toward her. "Who—who are you?"

Drawing back, the woman eyed Rebecca, and an awareness crept over her that brought with it both an air of worry and a strong sense of caution.

"I'm Abel's mum," she explained, seeming to watch for Rebecca's recognition. "You can call me Niina."

The name was unfamiliar. It sounded different—accented, pronounced like the number nine with an *ah* at the end. Rebecca surprised herself when she asked, "Are you Finnish?"

The woman stared at her for a long second and then gave a quick nod. "*Joo.* Yes," she answered and then shook the blanket to emphasize. "Hurry, child."

Rebecca did as she was told, pausing at her soaked chemise until she noted that Niina had turned her face toward the window to give Rebecca privacy. She stripped and reached for the blanket, which Niina released when she felt Rebecca's tug. Wrapping it around herself, Niina turned back to Rebecca. Her eyes did quick work of skimming the bare skin that was still exposed regardless of the blanket.

"I'd like to flay the person who gave you those bruises." Niina beckoned with her hand. "Come. We'll head up to—we'll get you dressed."

Rebecca didn't miss Niina's falter and switch mid-sentence. She was going to refer to a place that should be familiar to Rebecca, but instead she'd bitten her tongue.

Rebecca followed without a word. The wind and rain still rattled the windows and echoed loudly in the spiral iron staircase. They climbed to the attic level, and Niina led Rebecca straight to the room with the locked door.

"No one goes in there," Rebecca parroted Abel from earlier.

Niina huffed as she took a skeleton key from her apron pocket. "Says Abel." She unlocked the door and pushed against its whitewashed wood. It opened, hinges protesting the movement. A musty smell laced with lavender greeted Rebecca. She sucked in a breath, the scent releasing a nostalgic emotion in Rebecca she could not identify. A lone bed with a thin mattress covered with a patchwork quilt was tucked against the far wall just under the slanting roof. There was no other furniture except for a trunk that sat at the end of the bed. Niina opened the chest and rummaged through its innards.

"Here we are." She pulled out another dress, this one a dusty blue. "It's not fancy, but it'll do." A chemise and underthings followed. Rebecca shed the blanket and quickly dressed, relishing the warmth. Niina gave her a hand-knitted sweater with leather buttons. "This will keep you warm."

"Whose clothes are these?" Rebecca had to ask. First the gray dress Edgar had given her earlier, and now these things? She had a feeling she had seen them before, yet she also was certain she'd never worn them.

"Well, they're not yours, if that's what you're thinking," Niina answered, refolding a garment that had come undone and tucking it carefully into the trunk.

"These were Kjersti's." Niina's voice broke. She glanced at Rebecca, seemed to wait for something, and when it didn't happen, continued. "Kjersti was my daughter." Niina closed the lid of the trunk. "She stayed here at the lighthouse with Abel and Edgar when I was on my deathbed. No one expected me to live. I surprised them all. My fever broke the day Kjersti came down with it. She was gone within three days. Before they could bring her home to me, and before I could nurse her as an *äiti* should. Abel locked up the room, and no one can enter now. No one but me, mind you. I've the right."

Of course she did. She was Kjersti's mother.

"Abel locked the room." For some reason, Rebecca had assumed the locked room was Edgar's doing. A broken heart perhaps. Harbored memories. She'd not expected it to be at the hand of Abel, and for his sister.

Niina's eyes shone with tears, and she blinked rapidly. "Kjersti and Abel were always close. She was the eldest and looked after him. He was lost without her—" Niina's words hitched, and she shook her head. Waving her hand, she motioned for Rebecca to exit the tiny room. "He'll have to manage with you being here in Kjersti's room. There's nothing to be done about it now. We'd best go down and see if there are any survivors. I'll need your help if there are."

As Niina led the way, Rebecca snuck a glance into the room opposite Kjersti's. The room that must be Abel's. Surely as an unmarried woman she'd not be expected to board across the hall from an unmarried man, with only a male lightkeeper a level down in the keeper's bedroom?

"Might I . . . ?" Rebecca hesitated, then plunged ahead with her question. "Might I stay with you instead?"

Niina's stopped abruptly. She turned from her perch two steps below Rebecca as they curved downward. "No." Niina's hand rose and hovered over Rebecca's cheek, her eyes softening. "It's not safe." She didn't offer an explanation, and Rebecca knew instinctively that to inquire further would be useless. Her suspicions had to be true. Abel and Niina and even Edgar—yes, they knew who she was, but they did not want to tell her. They harbored her here in the lighthouse, along with secrets, and along with the truth of whoever she really was.

7

THERE WERE NO SURVIVORS.

The lake had claimed the steamship, with few bodies having washed up onshore. Hours later, the men who had joined Edgar and Abel had left the vicinity.

"This is the harsh side of life here in Silvertown." That was the only sorrow expressed by Niina. She had set to work baking bread, and the kitchen was filled with an inviting aroma. Niina asked Rebecca to assist, and then she eyed Rebecca as she stood there hesitantly, unsure of what to do.

"You've never baked bread before." Niina's observation was terse but softened with a smile. "Well, watch and learn."

Rebecca did so, sipping tea from a tin cup and worrying about how she could possibly stay at the lighthouse with two men. But she couldn't even recall her surname, let alone where she was from. Still, the men—the ones who'd come from down the way with lanterns, ready to battle the storm with Edgar and Abel— they had to come from Silvertown.

"Perhaps I should go with you," Rebecca tried again. "To Silvertown."

Niina shook her head, keeping her back to Rebecca as she kneaded more dough. "No. You'll stay here. Where it is safe."

"Surely someone there can help me."

A small laugh escaped the older woman. "Of course. A throng of copper and silver miners, the one-legged captain who owns the merchant shop, and more miners? Homes are scattered about. It's less a town and more a wilderness dotted with ramshackle shacks, mining camps, and a main street. Have you *no* recollection of where you are, child?" Niina turned, her hands covered in flour, a questioning expression on her round face.

Rebecca gave her head a sheepish shake. "None."

"And no recollection of what happened to you?"

Another shake of her head.

A deep frown creased the skin between Niina's eyes. "Your family? Do you remember them?"

"Do I have a family?" Rebecca challenged. Niina knew Rebecca could not bake bread. Niina was surprised that Rebecca had asked for her name. Niina also knew there was danger associated with her. It felt as though the truth was being dangled in front of her like a steak in front of a dog but kept just out of reach because they believed the steak to be laced with poison. "You say it isn't safe," Rebecca said, running her hand up her arm, not needing to remind herself of the bruises hidden beneath her dress sleeve. "Do you know why?" She was hopeful, and she breathed a prayer that Niina would take pity on her and tell her what she knew.

Niina continued to knead her dough. "Few of us have family in Silvertown." She had sidestepped Rebecca's question. "Down the way in Ontonagon, you'll find civilization. Women, children, a church, a post office, and the like. But Silvertown and this lighthouse, well, it's a dream, that's what it is. A rich man's dream to get richer. There is no *family* in Silvertown."

"Maybe I'm from Ontonagon. Perhaps I should go there." The door opened, cutting Rebecca's musing short.

Edgar and Abel entered the living space, making the small kitchen even more cramped. Edgar pushed through the room and disappeared into the house beyond. Abel paused, and Rebecca didn't miss the quick survey he gave her person. That he recognized his sister's clothes was evident by the shadow that crossed his face.

Instead of commenting, he moved to the short counter and lifted a slice of warm bread. "Mmm, it is delicious, *Äiti.*"

Niina batted his chest, snatching the slice of bread from his hand. "Go. You get dry and warm before you catch your death, and then come back and I will slice more for you."

Abel dropped a kiss on his mother's cheek, bending over a significantly long way to do so. The difference in their heights was stark. Rebecca shrank into her chair as Abel passed by. His clothes were damp, his dark hair was ruffled and stuck out in multiple directions. He paused by Rebecca and looked down at her.

"You are dry now. Good. I should not have left you to yourself in the lighthouse." Gentle reprimand tinged his voice.

"*Joo!*" Niina spun from where she had pounded the dough into a firm ball. "What were you thinking?"

Abel shrugged. "That Rebecca would stay put, just as she promised." He turned to Rebecca, and they locked gazes. His look was expectant, the cool ice blue of his eyes such a stark contrast to his dark hair that they appeared almost ethereal.

Rebecca felt warmth leave her face, then it swept back up in a rush to her cheeks. Something inside of her craved him. But he was dangerous too. She could sense it.

He looked away from her and back to his mother. "I'm going to get dry."

Minutes later, both men had returned to the kitchen, and their presence made Rebecca wish to hide. Between Edgar's glowering and undisguised surveyance of her and Abel's attempts to not look at her, she felt a bit like a porcelain doll in the midst of rough little boys who didn't know what to do with it.

She was never more grateful for Niina's presence, and she dreaded the moment Abel's mother took her departure. Why the woman wouldn't take Rebecca along struck a nerve with her, and she wished to demand a reason for this. But she didn't. Because she was afraid. There was no other reason. Rebecca didn't know who to trust, but something in Niina's refusal to take Rebecca home with her to Silvertown was emphasized by caution and intent. It made Rebecca believe that Niina was being sincere in her offer of security here at the lighthouse.

Niina set plates with fresh bread in front of both men. "Do we know anything about last night's wreck?"

"It wasn't a passenger ship. The ship was due in Ontonagon and was carrying mining supplies." Abel's response was muffled around a bite of bread. "The men lost were the ship's crew."

"Such sad loss of life." Niina clucked her tongue.

Edgar huffed. "I pity the dead, but the wreck . . . it sticks it to Hilliard and his cronies."

"Edgar." Niina's voice held warning.

He jerked his head up to spear her with a look. "What? Truth is what truth is." He glanced at Rebecca, then back at Niina. "Hilliard has no respect for the land round here. No respect for those what been here long before he ever came. I remember when this place was just an outpost and we traded with the Ojibwe. Respectable men—*good* men—and then people like Hilliard come in. They ignore all local knowledge and think they can get rich."

"Hilliard was already rich," Abel groused around another bite of bread.

"And not everyone was respectable even before Hilliard," Niina inserted with reprimand.

Edgar snorted. "Every group has their bad apples, sure, but Hilliard?"

"Who is Hilliard?" Rebecca dared to ask, and the sound of her voice must have startled the other three, who all stilled. She squirmed under their frank gazes, surprise on their faces as if Rebecca had asked who the president of the United States was—which she hadn't, even though she realized now she wasn't entirely sure.

"Hilliard owns half the copper mines around Ontonagon," Niina explained. "A year ago, silver was found here, not far from the Iron River. Silvertown is a bit like California just before their gold rush. Find a little, look a bit more, and then silver fever breaks out."

"Only Hilliard is monopolizing the entire construct. And he won't listen." Edgar took a draw from his cup of water before setting it back on the table with a thud. "He's garnerin' investors from as far off as Pennsylvania. Thinks Silvertown will be the next big vein of money."

Rebecca glanced between the three people she shared the small kitchen with. "You don't want that to happen?" She bit her tongue. An ominous feeling descended on her. She was a part of this somehow. A part of it that skirted the perimeter of her memory, taunting and frightening her simultaneously.

Edgar worked his bearded jaw back and forth, then settled his stare on Rebecca. "Years ago, before the war, this place was known for furs. It was quiet here. Good relations between the traders and the Chippewa. But about thirty years ago, the chiefs met with the government and gave all their lands in this area to the United States. That meant the White man now owned a heap of the land to the west and much of the land east of the American Fur Company's trading post. 'Course, that meant permits were issued for mining, and the rest is a short history of the last thirty years."

"The fact that there's a stamp mill now in Silvertown to process the ore says a lot." Abel's musing brought Rebecca's eyes to his face. He caught her gaze. "Not that mining is bad. It boosts the economy in the area. It's just—"

"Progress will happen," said Niina, "and mining has supported us since you were a boy, Abel. Your own father worked the mines."

Abel nodded.

Edgar gave his customary snort. "And then there's men like Hilliard." He eyed Rebecca for a long moment, until it made her shift in her chair, as if she were somehow to blame. "Shortsighted and feverish with greed. He's the kind that makes progress worse than better."

"Where are the Chippewa now?" Rebecca asked Niina.

Niina's face softened into a smile. "They were granted land, and most have moved there. But there are still some in the area."

Edgar harrumphed. "Hilliard won't hire them even though one of them found a big copper load years ago. I've no respect for men like Hilliard. Don't care what color a man is, greed is greed. And then there's dominatin' folks—that's what Hilliard does. Throws his money around like he's everyone's boss. He don't even like the foreigners."

"Foreigners?" Rebecca asked.

Abel gave her a sheepish smile. "Folks like my *isä*. My father came from Finland, but he didn't speak English. Some don't like the immigrants."

Rebecca didn't respond. Instead, she calculated the stories in her mind, desperate to find something to trigger a memory, a familiarity, anything. But there was nothing. A dark void in her recollection meant the brief history lesson surrounding her newest home meant little to her outside of the fact that the world of the Porcupine Mountains was no friendlier than other places. There were pockets of separation. The rich and the poor. The born-and-raised and the immigrant. The White man and the Indian.

And then there was her. Rebecca. Only Rebecca, and three

people who had already left her on her own side of the table. Tentative in their care, suspicious in their gazes, with a welcome that held her at arm's length while simultaneously trying to offer her safety.

She was an outsider.

At least Rebecca had learned that much about herself.

8

SHEA

I and my Annabel Lee . . .
Annabel Lee

ANNABEL'S LIGHTHOUSE
PRESENT DAY

T HAT SHOULD DO IT." Holt finished screwing in a new bulb, and light flooded the room, relieving Shea of that little detail.

She rubbed her hand against her thigh, apprehension swirling in her gut. "You didn't mention there was a murder here fifteen years ago."

Holt zipped shut the duffel bag of tools and supplies he'd brought with him after Shea's call that the light fixture had blown out. He smiled, dimples creasing his cheeks. "You mean suicide?"

"That's not what the documentary I just watched implied."

Shea didn't mean to sound accusatory, but she was still unnerved.

"Oh, *that* documentary?" Holt leaned his hip against the table and crossed his arms over his broad chest. "A small crew came up here about three years ago and filmed that. Until that point, no one thought much of Jonathan Marks's death being more than what was concluded in the end."

"The documentary brought up good points," Shea countered.

"Yeah? So did that streaming-service documentary about that killer from your neck of the woods in Wisconsin. Anyone from these parts knows it turned a murderer into a hero."

"Did it?" Shea tried to squelch her nerves, which brought out the challenger side of her personality.

"I don't know." Holt dismissed her with a laugh. "I've never paid much attention to true crime—or supposed crime. I live in this area to avoid that sort of thing."

Shea matched his smile, drew a deep breath, and released it. "Sorry. I don't know why I'm so edgy."

"Sure you do." Holt reached for his duffel bag and swung the strap over his shoulder. "You just saw a show that told you a guy died in the living room you're staying in. That's weird. And then Annabel goes and blows a lightbulb on you."

"Annabel?" Shea offered a dubious grin.

Holt winked. "She's blamed for just about everything odd that goes on here at the lighthouse. Just wait. One of these nights you'll look out onto the shore and see a wispy, white form of a woman and you'll know it's true. All the tales of Annabel haunting the area are true."

"You believe that?" Shea's curiosity was doing away with the final remnants of her anxiety.

Holt shrugged. "When you're born and raised around legend, you tend to take it seriously. Stories must come from somewhere, even if they're not all true."

Shea motioned for Holt to put down his duffel bag and make

himself comfortable. The world outside was dark. The sound of the lake was rhythmic in its pattern. She was alone in a lighthouse, and with her curiosity and anxiety both piqued, she wouldn't be sleeping anytime soon. She didn't mind the company.

A sideways glance at Holt as he made his way home reminded her that there was also probably a bit of selfish motive in her invitation. He was intoxicating. The way he listened to her. Bantered with her. Interacted with her. Heck, he even completed a full coherent sentence versus one-word grunts. Maybe she should feel guilty for her attraction, and part of her did. The part of her that remembered the Sunday school teachers pounding the Ten Commandments into her as a kid. But it was obvious to even a mosquito on the wall that her and Pete's marriage had an expiration date. Didn't it?

"So then. What do *you* believe about Annabel?" Shea reached for a mug. "Tea?" She followed up her first question with a second.

"Sure." Holt nodded. "What do *you* know about Annabel?" He countered Shea's original question with his own. As he did so, he sank onto a chair at the table and hoisted his boot-clad feet onto the seat of another.

Shea set a kettle under the farmhouse sink's faucet and turned the water on to fill it. "Well, I know she was one of the first group of European women who moved to and settled in this area."

"Back in the late 1840s, yes," Holt responded.

"And I know she died in 1852, but no one knows where she's buried."

"Fact." Holt's words reassured Shea she was going in the right direction.

She placed the kettle on the stove and reached for the knob to increase the heat on the burner, then laughed when she remembered it was literally an old-fashioned cookstove.

"Add some wood to the firebox," Holt suggested with a side-ways smile.

Shea laughed softly. "Yes, sir." As she reached for kindling in the woodbox next to the stove, she continued, "Lore states that Annabel's cause of death is up for debate. She drowned in Lake Superior, we know that, but why and how is what's questioned."

"Yep." Holt reached for a paper napkin from the middle of the table and began to fold it into a triangle. "Some say she rowed the skiff out as far as she could and waited for the lake to claim her. Others say she was fleeing something or someone and drowned."

Shea paused and turned with a frown. "Well now, this brings up a question in my mind. I wonder . . ."

"Wonder what?" Holt matched her furrowed brow.

"Well, Jonathan Marks died here. Annabel died here."

"Mmm, not exactly." Holt shook his head. "The lighthouse wasn't built when Annabel died."

Shea frowned, trying to understand. "That's even weirder. How is it she haunts the lighthouse then? Why is it called 'Annabel's Lighthouse'?"

Holt's chuckle warmed her insides. "Because even ghosts need a place to live." His grin blindsided her with its charm. "I mean, it's hardly fair she has to wander the shore forever. As for her death and then Jonathan Marks's death, well, that's just an interesting coincidence."

Shea held her index finger in the air. "Gibbs's rule number thirty-nine: There's no such thing as coincidence."

Holt shifted in his chair. "Quoting fictional television characters won't win you an argument." He chuckled.

Shea tipped her head. "Sure, but it's still true."

"So your plan now is to tie Annabel's and Jonathan Marks's deaths to the lighthouse and solve both of their deaths?" Holt's mouth was set in a teasing line, and Shea couldn't help but laugh at herself.

"No. I'm just here to learn about Annabel and who she was. I want to feature the lighthouse and its lore. I just wasn't expecting more current 'lore' to impact the story. It just makes me think, that's all, nothing more, I guess. That being said, Annabel is an icon for this lighthouse, but I need more info than what I've got. I need to know her full name, where she was born, what brought her to the U.P., who she was attached to here, and so on. I still want to know more about why she's associated with a lighthouse that wasn't built until the 1860s, after her death."

"That last part is easy." Holt slid his feet off the chair and leaned forward, resting his arms on the table.

Shea waited, even as the teakettle began to whistle.

"This is where Annabel wanders. The shore out front of the lighthouse. It was right off this point that she's said to have drowned. When the lighthouse was built, it wasn't just the keeper who moved in and took over the quarters. Annabel did too."

Shea curled up in the bed, its pillow-top mattress most assuredly not original to the lighthouse. With three bedrooms to choose from, Shea had opted for the keeper's room, where she had a good view of the lake. And she wasn't far from the bathroom, which had been added on in later years. Nor did she have to climb the metal stairs up to the attic with its claustrophobic rooms.

It was past midnight. Holt had stayed for tea, and their conversation soon deviated from Annabel and the lighthouse and the death of Jonathan Marks to more personal history. She'd learned Holt had grown up in the U.P. and later moved to Ontonagon, where he'd been able to put in a bid for the Silvertown Lighthouse—its official name. He'd spent the last two years fixing it up, making sure it met all the necessary requirements for a historical site, and prepping it for rentals. She also learned he'd been married to his high-school sweetheart but was now divorced. He was an only child who didn't give details about his parents. He was just a good ol' northern boy with dimples who could swallow her whole.

Shea gave her pillow a punch and tossed onto her side in a restless fit of energy. Her research instincts were in high gear. After the recent revelation about Jonathan Marks, she really wanted to investigate more—and she wanted to not think about the fact that a man had bled all over the floor just below the bedroom she was trying to sleep in.

If she could just sleep, then tomorrow morning she'd plan a trip into Ontonagon and look up Captain Gene, Edna Carraway, and—wasn't there another person? Her mind was getting foggy, yet her muscles felt taut with energy.

Sleep was elusive.

The floor creaked.

Her eyes popped wide open.

The window rattled.

It was just the wind.

Right?

It had to be just the wind.

The floor creaked again, like the weight of footsteps.

Shea propped herself up on an elbow, narrowing her eyes to see through the darkness.

Silence.

Thirty seconds later, she lowered herself back onto her pillow.

The floor creaked.

"Go to sleep, Annabel," Shea commanded out loud.

But it didn't make her feel any better. Especially when she swore she'd heard a whispered "no" echo back from outside the keeper's bedroom door.

9

THE ENGINE PROTESTED. Grinding and moaning as though she were asking it to drive to Alaska, not just to Ontonagon.

"You've got to be kidding me." Shea caught a glimpse of her frustrated face in the rearview mirror. Shadows under her eyes marred her features. She blamed Annabel for that.

A glance at her phone and she eyed the signal. All was calm in nature today, so apparently it had decided to allow her to gather one bar of signal that was coming from some random, unseen cell tower.

She snatched it up and, out of habit, dialed Pete. The long pause before the phone even connected was long enough for her to rethink her instinctive impulse to call her husband. Shea yanked the phone from her ear and was just about to end the call when she heard Pete.

"Yeah?"

She gritted her teeth and sucked in a breath, pleading for patience. She lifted the phone back to ear. "My car won't start."

No hellos. No pleasantries.

She could picture Pete, six hours away in Wisconsin, his flannel shirt hanging loose over his beat-up T-shirt. Grease under his fingernails and permanently embedded in his calluses. His nose, crooked at the end, and it wasn't because of some cool sports injury—he'd just been born that way. His brown eyes, the whiskery face, the shaggy hair. The man was as Midwestern-rural as they came. She'd been attracted to him once. Years ago. Now?

"What's it doing?"

Pete's question startled her back into the present.

"It's groaning."

"Groaning?"

"I don't know. Like it's trying to start but can't." She hated trying to describe mechanical issues to Pete.

"Is the battery dead?"

"I don't know. I don't know how to check it."

"It's not making a clicking sound?"

Shea tried not to be irritated. In the end, this wasn't Pete's fault. "No. It's—groaning."

"Like a slow engine crank?"

"Sure?"

"I can't help you if I can't identify the issue." Pete's frankness was never meant to sound harsh, but she always took it that way. Why couldn't he couch his statements in something nice, like *I know you're trying, and I appreciate it, but it's difficult for me to identify the issue. Perhaps you could try starting the car and I could listen on this end*? But no. There was none of that. Just "I can't help you if . . ."

"It acts like it wants to start, but then it runs out of energy and dies." She made another attempt and then waited.

A pause.

"It's probably the battery."

She waited longer and then realized Pete wasn't going to offer if she didn't ask. "What do I do then?"

"You'll need to have someone jump-start it. You should have cables in the trunk. I made sure they were there before you left."

Shea winced. She was hard on him, but then in times like these, he always seemed to come through.

"I also checked the fluids in the car. I hooked it up to the reader and didn't get any error codes, so it shouldn't be giving you trouble."

"I don't need this right now." Shea sagged in the seat and eyed the dashboard. It was ritzier than what Pete had wanted her to get. He preferred older vehicles that didn't have so many electronics and things that could go wrong that weren't fixable with a spark plug or an easy-to-get part.

"Want me to drive up and help?" His offer wasn't unusual. That was Pete's way. If she couldn't fix it on her own, he'd just come and do it himself. She could never tell if he was *okay* with coming and helping or if he did it because he was her husband and had to.

"I can find someone to jump-start the car."

"K. If you can't, call me back. I could make it there by tonight."

Anyone else might find Pete a tad heroic, but Shea knew better. It wasn't her he was coming for; it was the car. Vehicles were his best friends. Mechanics. Tools. Grease. He lived for it. If Pete loved her as much as he adored his cars, she'd be as valued as his 1969 Javelin.

She'd give Holt a ring.

Shea ended the call with her husband and checked the phone's signal. Still one bar. Barely enough. She rang Holt, and within seconds he answered.

"Sure. Man, that stinks. I'll be right over."

He hadn't said anything much different from Pete, yet something in Shea had jump-started, even if her car hadn't. She appreciated how Holt empathized with her frustration. It touched her soul. It was nice to have someone who cared about her.

Finally, the battery jump-started successfully, and Shea made it to Ontonagon without further incident. She was just in time for midmorning coffee at the diner, so she slipped inside and ordered a basic cup that was fast-served to her in the cream-colored coffee mug most diners had. The waitress smiled down at her.

"Can I get you anything else?"

"I was wondering." Shea took the invitation, although she was sure it wasn't what the waitress expected. "Do you have any idea how I would go about finding Captain Gene?"

"The captain?" The waitress's crow's feet beside her eyes deepened as a knowing grin stretched across her face and touched the graying hair at her temples. "You and everyone's mother's brother want to find Captain Gene. He comes out of hiding when he feels the mind to, not before."

"Someone must know where he lives," Shea said.

The waitress propped her hand on her hip. "You'd think, but no one does. Man doesn't even have an address. Not even a P.O. box. He's like a hibernating bear that pokes his nose out when he wakes up in the spring."

"So he comes out in spring? Like about this time of year?" Shea straightened in her booth.

The waitress, whose name tag read *Marnie*, gave an offhanded shrug. "I was speaking metaphorically. I don't know when he'll pop up. He just does. Gets a can of Folgers from the market, matches, toilet paper, and peanut butter. The man is predictable when it comes to his shopping list. But that's about as predictable as he gets. Why do you want to talk to him? Are you a reporter or something?"

Shea took a sip of the black coffee, which was burnt and desperately needed help. She shook her head. "No. I'm a writer. I'm researching for a book surrounding the lighthouse."

Marnie threw her head back in understanding. "Oh, gotcha! Annabel's Lighthouse? That makes sense. You should talk to my mother, Edna Carraway. She could at least get you started."

"Edna is your mother?" Shea perked up.

"You bet she is. I live with her. We're just about three blocks over. The little yellow ranch house with the rusty metal bike out front. Can't miss it. Head on over and give the door a knock. Tell her Marnie sent you, and my mother will prattle your ear off with so much info you'll probably want to run away."

"Oh, you're a gem!" Shea took another sip of the coffee to be polite, then pushed it away. "I'll head over there now if you think your mom won't mind?"

"Not at all!" Marnie waved her hand as if to brush away any inconvenience. "Small town, and we love company."

Shea handed Marnie a five-dollar bill for the coffee and tip and then exited the diner. Meeting Edna Carraway's daughter— who had to be in her mid-fifties—meant she had an instant in with Edna. Always a plus when it came to building rapport.

Within a few minutes and after a short drive, Shea stood in front of the Carraway house. Sure enough, the rusted bike was in the front, a basket hanging from its handlebars and a few small sprigs of marigolds freshly planted. She walked up the slanted and cracked sidewalk to the front porch, which was also cement and certainly not fancy. She rang the doorbell and waited until the door opened and the most adorable elderly lady peered out at her from behind wire-rimmed glasses. Her lenses were so thick they made her eyes twice their actual size. Her hair was white and permed into a short, curled cap on her head. Her skin was wrinkled and soft, her hands dotted with age, and her height came to the bottom of Shea's chin.

"Yes?" Edna's voice quivered with age.

Shea took a moment to introduce herself, quick to add that Marnie had sent her, and she was hoping Edna had some time to spare.

Edna's door widened, and her eyes brightened. "Come in! Come in!"

Shea stepped inside and gave the front room a quick once-over. Rose wallpaper consistent with the nineties adorned the walls. The furniture was nothing special: a La-Z-Boy recliner, a brown couch, a purple crocheted afghan folded and hanging over the arm of a rocking chair, and a tube TV that still boasted dials for changing channels. A large painting of a dog hung over the couch—a spaniel with long ears and brown eyes that looked happy.

"That's Ralph." Edna pointed. "Marnie painted him about ten years ago right before he passed. Such a good dog, and once Ralph crossed the rainbow bridge, I just didn't have the heart for another one." Edna wobbled across the living room in such a tenuous fashion that Shea found herself reaching out in case the woman fell.

"Let's head to the dining room and sit down," Edna directed. Soon Shea found herself at a wooden table, sitting in a wooden chair, with a plate of store-bought cookies in front of her and a glass of milk. "I don't drink anything with caffeine," Edna explained as she eased herself onto a chair opposite Shea. "Doctor says it's bad for my heart."

"I understand." Shea smiled.

"Tell me more about your book!" Edna folded her hands in front of her, and her buggy, faded blue eyes stared intently at Shea. "And speak up 'cause my hearing isn't the best, and those silly ear things that are supposed to help me hear just fall out, so I don't wear them."

Hearing aids. Shea was absolutely in love with Edna already. The woman was pure joy in a petite bundle, and her forthright conversation eased Shea's frayed nerves. She took a few minutes to describe her career to Edna, ending with how she was staying in Annabel's Lighthouse and researching lore from the locals.

Edna's eyes sparkled. "I can never talk about this area too much. So much history here, and so many tales. The lake is alive with them, you know. It breathes the ghosts of the dead."

Shea pulled out her phone. "Do you mind if I record this?"

Edna glanced at the phone and lifted her hand in welcome. "Go right ahead. No reason for me to take everything I know to the grave with me. I highly doubt the worms and beetles will be interested."

Shea bit back a smile as she opened the recording app on her phone. "Well, first and foremost, I'm really interested in learning about Annabel. Who was she beyond just the lore?"

Edna's expression softened. "Oh, Annabel. Sweet thing. I imagine she was a tortured soul, and that's the truth of it." She picked at a piece of lint from the cuff of her sweater. "The way it's been told since I was girl was that Annabel came here with her father. She was motherless, and seeing as most of the people in the area were either fur trappers or Chippewa . . . well, she was a special little thing. Mining was just getting started. It was a time of change for this area, a move into the modern age. Well, modern for them, I suppose."

Shea considered Edna's words. "What was Annabel's last name?"

"Oh, honey." Edna's already large eyes grew wider. "Nobody knows *that*. It happened too long ago, and her grave was lost to time. She's just known as Annabel. Of course, the lighthouse was built not long after she drowned. Just a wooden structure at first, until they rebuilt it as you see it mostly today. I think they rebuilt it in the 1860s, and then the new keeper took it over."

"And what was that keeper's name?" Shea knew names would be helpful as she pieced the story together.

"Edgar. Edgar Wolf. He was of German roots, so his surname sounded more like *Voolf*. Anyway, he ran the lighthouse until the early 1880s, I believe, and then a younger man took over—Abel Koski, I think his name was."

"And when were the sightings of Annabel first recorded?" Shea found excitement growing inside of her. The lightkeepers' names were golden.

Edna's lips pressed together in a thin, knowing smile. "Well, from the moment she drowned really. Her lover—and some say Annabel was also married, so that in itself was scandalous—

claimed to have seen her the very next night. 'An aimless wandering' were the words used. After that, various sailors would spot her on the shoreline, or a miner would notice her slip behind trees and vanish into the forest. Once the lighthouse was built, she seemed to take up residence there."

"Why do you think that was?" Shea wasn't sure if Edna was a firm believer in the existence of Annabel's ghost or merely an intrepid storyteller.

Edna chuckled. "That's all been conjecture for decades. Some say she moved into the lighthouse to haunt the keeper and anyone else who lived there. That she made it her mission to keep them from sleep so that none died or drowned on their watch. Others claim Annabel moved into the lighthouse because she had an attachment to someone who once lived there. Probably one of the keepers."

"Was one of the keepers perhaps her lover?" Shea speculated.

Edna nodded. "That's been the theory. You see"—she leaned forward—"the same way Annabel's identity was lost to time, so too was her lover's. No one really knows the truth of it outside of the tragedy of her drowning."

What Edna shared matched what Shea had already researched and what she'd learned from Holt. But she couldn't help but feel somewhat disappointed. She had imagined Edna would know more specifics and not just embellishments to the legend.

"And what can you tell me about Jonathan—"

Shea's inquiry was cut off by the high-pitched sound of shattering glass.

Edna cried out. "Sweet dandelion stems! What was that?" Her hands clutched at her throat.

Shea shot up from her chair, sweeping the living space with investigative observation. None of the house windows were shattered, but the front ones were open, allowing the warmer spring breeze to freshen up the house.

She patted the air between her and Edna. "Stay here. I'll go look."

"Oh, be careful!" Edna was struggling to rise from her chair, ignoring Shea's instructions. "I've never heard the likes of that before!"

Shea hurried through the front room and cautiously pushed open the door. Her eyes caught sight of her car parked on the road just yards from the house.

"You've got to be kidding!" She sprinted down the walk to approach her car from the front. The windshield was completely shattered. Glass decorated the inside of the car, the windshield boasting a large hole dead center.

"What happened?" Edna had emerged from the house, and she held tightly to the fence post at the end of the walk. "Oh no. Is that your car?"

"Yes." Shea's answer was curt, but not because she blamed Edna. She knew before she looked inside the vehicle that someone had launched something hard through her windshield. She yanked open the door and surveyed the inside. There was nothing. No stone, no item that would explain the gaping hole in the windshield. Shea struggled to pull her emotions into control so she didn't cry or scream, or worse, swear like a sailor. *That* would probably make Edna's eyes pop right out of her head. Shea had a strong feeling that Edna Carraway never swore. Ever.

She reached for her phone in her jeans pocket. She'd call the police. This was absurd.

Edna teetered up beside Shea and laid a hand on Shea's wrist. Edna's head began to shake from side to side. "You've ruffled feathers, Miss Radclyffe."

"Ruffled feathers?" Shea dialed the police. "Who on earth would want to vandalize my car? And where did they go?" She looked around as if the culprit would be standing there to take ownership of the act.

Edna lifted enormous eyes and pushed her wire frames higher

up her nose. "Annabel has a reputation, you know." Edna clucked her tongue as though Shea should have foreseen this happening. "A nice ghost, for all sakes and purposes, but if anyone asks too many questions, well now, Annabel doesn't like that."

"What are you talking about?" Shea was losing patience. The story was cryptic enough without adding another level of ludicrousness to it.

Edna's features turned stern, her mouth set in a grim line. "Annabel's history is sacred to her spirit. She's a private ghost, Miss Radclyffe, and she wants to have a voice in things."

Shea eyed the elderly woman. "You're saying *Annabel* traveled from the lighthouse all the way to Ontonagon in order to break my windshield to keep me from asking questions about her life?"

Edna offered a wobbly shrug. "No one ever said spirits can't travel."

10

REBECCA

With a love that even the winged seraphs
of heaven coveted of her and me . . .
Annabel Lee

ANNABEL'S LIGHTHOUSE
SPRING, 1874

S HE HAD CLEANED UP, her hair freshly washed—
thanks to Abel for filling the bathtub in the oil room with
hot water. Nothing had felt better than slipping into the
bath and allowing the warmth to saturate her body, to take the
cloth Niina had provided her with and wipe away the grime and
dirt. The bar of soap Niina had given her was made of goat's
milk, a soft, moisturizing experience Rebecca believed she'd
never had before. The scent of lavender permeated the room
and overwhelmed the lingering smell of oil for the lamp.

Now clean, Rebecca slipped back into the dress Niina had

provided, then braided her hair into one long plait down her back. She opened the door to the main area of the house and glanced around.

"The men are outside. Things to do after the shipwreck." Niina's voice startled Rebecca as it came from the corner of the sitting area.

"Are they hopeful they may still find survivors?" Rebecca padded across the faded carpet, her bare feet relishing its softness.

Niina's knitting needles clicked away as she rocked. "No. They'll clean up the beach of any wreckage that washes ashore. If any of the goods from the ship happen to make it to shore intact, they'll have to notify the port in Ontonagon." She glanced up at Rebecca and then back to her craft. "You need to rest now. Up all night and then having to listen to the men grouse about Hilliard and the mines. You must be exhausted."

Rebecca eased onto a worn, blue velvet sofa, its cushions threadbare in spots. "I'll be fine."

The needles clicked more, and the silence felt as calming as the bath had. Rebecca was grateful Niina had not left the lighthouse. In fact, she seemed very at home here.

"Do you come here often?" Rebecca ventured.

Niina smiled, though she didn't raise her head. "Frequently, yes. The men would starve or end up eating dry oats with water poured over them to get by. I'm not concerned about Edgar, but my boy, Abel—he's all I have left."

Rebecca recalled how Abel had mentioned his father earlier, but it had been in the past tense. This made Rebecca's own situation even more stark to her. If she had family, wouldn't they be looking for her? She felt like there were voices just on the edges of her recollections. She caught glimpses of them in split seconds and then they dissipated into oblivion.

She toyed with the locket around her neck. The locket engraved with her name—or what she assumed was her name—on the back of it. Someone had given this to her. Someone had cared enough to bestow a piece of custom jewelry. The locket was made of silver, and if she were correct, it had taken some coins to purchase it for her. Yet it was empty—stark and bare. That made the locket and its giver even more of a mystery. For why give a locket if it was to remain empty?

Niina's voice broke through Rebecca's pondering. "You'll be able to sift through your confusion better if you let your body rest."

"I know." Rebecca's acknowledgment didn't mean that she intended to obey. While bed sounded like a refuge, she was also afraid to be alone with her thoughts. "What if I remember?"

"Hmm?" Niina lifted her chin to look at Rebecca.

Rebecca's cheeks warmed. She hadn't intended on asking it aloud. "What do I do if I remember, and things fall into place?"

"Then you must share it with us." Niina's eyes darkened with sincerity. She set her needles in her lap, though she didn't let go of them. "So that we may assist you."

There it was. Rebecca could see the glimmer of half-truth on Niina's face.

"You know me, don't you?" She posed the question less as an accusation and more as a plea.

Niina returned to her knitting. "We know you were attacked, and that alone puts you in danger." A stern look from the woman made it clear she wished for no more probing from Rebecca. It was hardly fair. Rebecca wanted to protest, but Niina continued quickly as if to fill the stillness, so Rebecca didn't have a chance to inquire further. "You are best off here in the lighthouse. I realize you don't see it as ideal or even proper. But if you were to come to my cabin—well, Edgar and Abel will keep you safe here. I, as a woman, cannot do that. Neither man will bring you harm, and who knows who is out there looking for you!"

Rebecca strained to examine the recesses of her memory. She hadn't slept since her attack and since Edgar had found her in the woods. Her mind was cloudy, exhaustion warring with a louder voice than any memories she could conjure.

A wave of dizziness came over her, and for a moment she tried to camouflage it by digging her fingernails into the palms of her hands. But it was no use. Niina set aside her knitting and rose.

"See? You need to rest. You're as pale as the whitecaps on the lake."

"I'll be fine." Rebecca struggled to sound convincing.

Niina shook her head. "You need to eat something."

"I just had bread."

"You need meat. You need sustenance." Niina hustled past Rebecca, who took the liberty to lie against the arm of the sofa. The idea of food made her stomach roil both in hunger and disgust. It was a strange feeling, and Rebecca swallowed against the bile that rose in her throat.

Niina hurried back into the room, a piece of jerky wrapped in a cloth napkin. "Chew on this while I heat up some stew."

"No." Rebecca pushed Niina's hand away, then realized how rude she'd sounded. "Please. I-I don't think I can eat right now."

"You won't think you can eat for a long time, but you must."

Rebecca furrowed her brow. Sleep. Yes. Sleep would be good, and then when she woke, hunger could be satiated and her recollections explored. She ignored the jerky that Niina held and managed to sit up. "I believe I will go lie down."

Niina set the jerky on an end table and reached to assist Rebecca as she pushed off the sofa. "I will help you."

Rebecca hated to be such a bother. "I'll be fine. Is it all right if I used Kjersti's room?"

"Of course it is." Niina ignored Rebecca's protestations and gripped her elbow gently. "I will tuck you in."

Rebecca experienced a familiar and yet strange pang of longing. Something stung her heart with Niina's actions. Her mother would have done as Niina did. Had she a mother? The ache in her chest told her she either had one whom she was desperately homesick for and did not remember, or she had no mother, and the ache came from the empty chasm created when there was no one left to fill it.

She stumbled as another wave of dizziness washed over her.

"You are not fine, *raksu*, my dear. Come."

This time, Rebecca leaned more heavily on Niina, and it wasn't until she felt the soft mattress beneath her exhausted body that she noticed the room slow its spinning.

Niina pulled the sheet and quilt up, tucking it gently around Rebecca. "You sleep for as long as you need to. If you awaken and it's dark and I'm no longer here, you go right back to sleep. I will leave instructions for Abel to feed you in the morning. I will leave plenty of food. You need nourishment as soon as you're able to hold it down."

"I'll be fine," Rebecca mumbled again as she turned her face into the pillow, wondering why she had fought against giving in to resting when Niina had suggested it earlier.

Niina's next words washed over her as sleep claimed Rebecca. Enough to jolt her eyes wide open before sheer exhaustion forced them closed again, trouble to be faced only when she awakened.

"Sleep now, *raksu*. For you and for the babe within you."

Her hair was brushed away from her face, tenderly, with the cool touch of a feminine hand. Rebecca breathed deeply, embracing the overwhelming peace of being watched over. Being nurtured and cared for.

"Be still." The words passed over her skin on breath that brushed like a feather. "Shhh . . ."

Rebecca drank in the solace, and then she allowed her eyes to open, slowly at first, to take in the room. She was in the attic. The ceiling was directly over her, within arm's reach as it angled over her head. She was curled beneath a quilt, her head resting on a pillow, the scent of lavender mingling in the sheets and on the air.

At the end of the bed, Rebecca saw her. The woman. She sat with her back to Rebecca, and her hair, long and white-blond, hung down her back unbound. Her form was thin, her shoulders clothed in a simple white blouse.

Rebecca could see the woman's profile, but nothing more. Just a small, straight nose, long eyelashes against the of ivory skin of a high cheekbone. The woman spoke, her words breathy and almost difficult for Rebecca to hear.

"It is all a mystery," she said, and echoed the words in Rebecca's soul. "Who are you, you ask? Who and why and where does the heartbeat merge with the mind and make sense? What are memories if they are only to be lost, and what is the lost unless it has potential to once again be found?"

Rebecca frowned, curling her fingers into the bedcovers and pulling them tighter around her. An uneasy feeling needled at her. At the same time, she wanted to sit up and address the woman.

The woman sat as if frozen there, as if waiting for Rebecca to respond. Rebecca swallowed, wishing in a way that she hadn't opened her eyes. So she closed them. She hoped that she would feel the comforting hand once again, its cool touch against her skin. The tender ministrations of someone who cared only that Rebecca find peace.

Then it returned as the hand adjusted the bedcovers, tucking them in gently around Rebecca's neck.

"Shhh," she said.

Rebecca opened her eyes, forming a grateful smile. This time, dark hair framed the woman's face. A young face, not much older than Rebecca's twenty years. A curl teased at her temple. Blue eyes, so blue they were almost white, smiled back at her. Rosy lips curved upward in a relieved and playful smile.

"You're all right. You're safe."

Startled by the change in appearance, Rebecca shot a glance at the end of the bed. The woman with the corn-silk hair had disappeared. There was no one there. Only this friendly face, someone she knew, someone so close to her that Rebecca could almost taste her name on her lips.

The young woman smiled and reached out, but she didn't touch Rebecca. Only the blanket, adjusting it once more as if she hadn't already done so. "He'll keep you safe," she whispered, her smile warm.

Rebecca could hear it—the dark-haired woman's name. She could see it reflected in the lake-water eyes. She could hear it echoing in the hall of the lighthouse and up the spiral metal staircase.

"Kjersti." She said the name as she blinked.

Her eyes opened.

The vision was gone.

Rebecca shot up in her bed, sweat trickling down her face, her gown sticking to her back. The thud of her heart against her chest almost hurt, and the apprehension closed her throat in a stranglehold.

Rebecca swung her legs over the side of the bed to stand. As her nightgown slipped over her hips, damp from the turmoil of nightmarish sleep, it brushed over her abdomen, a small mound she'd not taken note of prior to this.

Kjersti.

But no. There had been another.

It was as though they had both been in the room and one had merged into another and—

Rebecca was momentarily distracted as a wave of dizziness overcame her. She leaned against the metal frame of the bed.

Niina's words came back to her like the rush of unwelcome waters.

A baby?

Her hand swept up to rest over her womb. She strained to remember—anything. How had she—where had this pregnancy come from?

Rebecca knees weakened at the unexpected observation from Niina. And how did Niina know? Did she only assume because Rebecca was nauseated and exhausted, that it meant she was with child? She stumbled to the door and opened it. The short hall was stuffy with unmoving air. There were no windows, just the ceiling that melded with the roof. Just the room next door where Abel would sleep.

"You're a chilling reminder . . ."

The words came back to Rebecca as she stood in the doorway. Darkness permeated the room and the hall. She was alone—or so she thought. But now a memory was returning. Stronger and more present than Kjersti had been, or the woman at the end of her bed had been.

Rebecca's breaths came in short, frightened gasps. She was seeing things now. Or the dead were visiting her. She had *known* Kjersti. She didn't know how, but she *knew* the dead Kjersti who had just visited her. Which meant the other woman was likely dead too. This lighthouse was filled with spirits that—

"You're a chilling reminder . . ."

Rebecca spun back to the bedroom, facing the bed. It was a man's voice. Gruff and frightening.

"Go away." Her voice trembled as she attempted to ward off the wandering dead that were roaming the lighthouse. The sudden picture of the gravestone she had fallen on while running, the place where Edgar had found her—Annabel's grave—fluttered through Rebecca's memory.

Who was Annabel? Was she the woman at the end of the bed? Rebecca was shaking now, her body quivering with the unknown and the dead, who at this moment seemed very much alive.

"You're a chilling reminder . . ."

That voice was so familiar, and in a way that Rebecca knew her mind didn't want to remember.

The image of a piece of shoreline swept over her. A large rock outcropping, black basalt, with water crashing on it and splashing her legs.

". . . chilling reminder . . ."

It was enough of a memory to engage Rebecca's urgency. She slid her feet into leather slippers Niina had pulled from Kjersti's trunk. They were tight on her toes, but she ignored that and instead reached for a green wool lap blanket hanging from a peg on the wall. Rebecca wrapped it around her shoulders and then opened her door, slipping from Kjersti's bedroom into the hallway. It was dark. Abel's door was mostly closed. Curious, Rebecca peered through the crack.

Abel lay sprawled on his stomach, shirtless, his back to the ceiling and illuminated by the moonlight that washed over his body from the window. He wore his trousers, suspenders hanging down over his hips. It was as if he'd been awake long enough to begin to undress and then ceased caring and simply collapsed onto the bed. He must be exhausted after last night's shipwreck. Which meant perhaps Edgar was awake still? Surely both lightkeepers didn't sleep at night. Or maybe they took shifts?

Rebecca stared at the sleeping man, and a momentary impulse to race in and curl up beside him came over her. Strength. He exuded a strength while he slept that mystified her. Was it Abel's voice she'd heard?

No. No, and she dared not wake him. He would be certain

the injuries she'd sustained had addled her mind—and maybe
they had.

A large rock outcropping.

Black basalt.

Water crashing on it and splashing her legs.

"...*chilling reminder*..."

Rebecca eased away from Abel's room and tiptoed to the door
at the end of the short hall. She pulled it open, revealing the
spiral metal staircase. Stepping out onto it, Rebecca winced as
the tread squeaked beneath her weight. Light from the lamp up
in the galley spilled onto the steps. She craned her neck to look
upward. If old man Edgar was up there, she mustn't alert him to
her presence. She knew that he would never allow her to leave
the lighthouse at night again, especially not alone—and yet it
was as though she was being beckoned there.

"*You're a chilling reminder*..."

Not spotting Edgar, Rebecca worked her way around and
down until she came to the door of most concern. The door
into the living area was directly off the lightkeeper's room. If
Edgar was asleep, she would need to sneak past his bed to get
to the living area on the second floor and finally make her way
downstairs to the entrance.

Rebecca pushed the door open, catching her breath as the
hinges protested. She peered into the tiny closet-like room
just off the lightkeeper's domain. There was no obvious form
of Edgar on the bed, which did nothing to relieve Rebecca of
worry. If he wasn't in the gallery and he wasn't asleep, then at
any moment Rebecca could come face-to-face with the gruff old
man. She wasn't afraid he would harm her, but his stern and
beady gaze was intimidation enough.

She slipped through the rooms as quietly as she could and
made her way to the first level and the kitchen. Having not run
into Edgar, Rebecca made fast work of slipping from the house
and into the night.

Immediately her body was assaulted by the cool spring wind that danced its way off the lake. The blast of cold awakened Rebecca's senses, sharpening her mind and shocking her from the stupor that had captivated her. The lighthouse behind her swathed the water with a shaft of light. The waves appeared relatively calm, considering the lake's aptitude to be temperamental.

"You're a chilling reminder . . ."

It was a memory now.

But it *was* a memory!

She crossed the yard on her way to the embankment. Unlike the night before, no ship was sinking, no waves were threatening the lives of would-be rescuers, no men from Silvertown were racing up the shoreline.

All was still aside from the waves' repetitive caress of the shore.

Rebecca scampered down the rocky path along the embankment, her feet slipping into the sand as she reached the shore. But it was no gentle shoreline. Instead, it was littered with driftwood and rocks, making a stroll along the sand out of the question. The obstacles were enough to make Rebecca wish to turn around to find refuge in the lighthouse once more, but the image of the basalt outcropping and the words replaying in her mind—her only clear recollection—urged her forward.

She maneuvered her way along the shore until she reached a stretch where the sand dominated the rocks and invited her to ease her breath and her body. Rebecca walked to the water's edge, the waves lapping at the sand hungrily. The sound of their rushing and rolling didn't cease or pause, not even for the weary of heart and mind. She stared out into the darkness, the giant expanse of water like a deep grave.

"You're a chilling reminder . . ." Each time she recalled the words from her dream, they became shorter, until now only the word *chilling* remained. It adequately captured the lake. It

enveloped Rebecca with a deep ache and a void that left her questioning why. Why did she remember those words? Who had spoken them? She knew—oh, this she recalled!—that *she* was the chilling reminder. The words had been spoken to her, about her. Who had said them? What man had looked upon her and seethed the words of disdain? It was that person Rebecca could not remember. But she could recall the feeling of revelation as she was told that *she* was someone's curse. Someone's chilling reminder of . . .

Rebecca turned toward the east, squinting into the night to see if she could make out the familiar landmark, even the shadow of it. She froze as a form emerged from the woods some two hundred yards down the shoreline. It was vaporous in nature, with long and loose hair so white it almost glowed in the moonlight, blowing around the figure's face. A white gown not unlike the one Rebecca wore made it evident that this was a woman.

Rebecca fixated on the wispy figure as it crossed the beach, seeming to float across the sand. Rebecca caught a glimpse of a bare leg and foot as the woman, without hesitation, walked into the water. Concern quickly overwhelmed Rebecca. The woman was walking to her death! The water was still frigid from winter's ice melt. No one could survive long in the lake.

The woman was up to her knees now, and it was then Rebecca found her voice and her ability to move. She ran across the sand, dodging rocks and scampering over driftwood. "Stop!" she shouted, but the wind and the roar of the waves carried away her voice.

The figure turned toward her, faceless in the moonlight, her white-blond hair covering her face like a veil. She stared at Rebecca, and then, just as Rebecca drew close enough to believe her shout of caution might be heard, the woman crouched into the water, letting it cover her shoulders, her neck, and finally her head.

Rebecca sprinted as much as she was able, her feet twisting and sinking into sand that acted like a trap. She fell forward, her knees scraping against the damp shore.

A voice, whether in her mind or in the wind, drifted over the waters where the woman had vanished and made its way into Rebecca's soul.

"You're a chilling reminder to me."

11

EDGAR PUSHED THE DOOR OPEN in frustration as Rebecca approached the entrance to the house. She was bathed in the light shed from the lamp above, and Edgar's face was illuminated as well. His bushy eyebrows were drawn together in a V, his hair askew, his clothes rumpled. She didn't know where he had come from, but she had been exposed in her secret dalliance with the lake and the lake's ghostly memories.

"You're like to get yourself killed." Edgar's grumble was more of a growl as he stepped aside to allow Rebecca entrance.

She caught him poking his head back into the night, looking to the left and the right as if he himself had been the one sneaking out and hoping no one had seen. He shut the door firmly, then waddled into the kitchen behind Rebecca. His legs were arthritic and bowed, his hips twisted, lending toward imbalance, but the elderly man was still intimidating as he locked eyes with her sheepish expression.

"You know we've black bears in these parts, and wolves, and even a cougar now and then. You want to be eaten in the night, your innards gnawed on like a dead deer's?"

Rebecca's intuition told her wild animals weren't truly the root of Edgar's warning. Still, she shook her head. "No. I'm sorry." She felt like a child standing before her reprimanding father.

Edgar's jaw was set, his agitation evident. "You didn't bruise yourself, you know. Someone was out to get you, an' you can't expect they're just going to throw their hands up and go 'oh shucks' if they catch wind of your being alive."

Rebecca reached for the back of a chair to steady herself. She had not forgotten. She had not forgotten *anything* since Edgar had found her broken atop Annabel's grave.

Edgar nodded as he saw the realization on her face. "See? You don't know who's out there hunting you. Any one of them have teeth they'd love to sink in and finish you off with. Wolf or man, they'll tear you to shreds. He nodded toward her abdomen. "And it's no secret you're caring for two. Best act like a mother and be responsible with the life God gave you."

The lake-grizzled man was finished now, and he turned his back to her to move to the stove and pick up the kettle. He poured black coffee into a mug and plunked it down before her, motioning Rebecca to sit down.

"Warm your insides," he directed, this time his tone gentler.

Having weathered what Rebecca hoped to be the worst of Edgar's anger, she did as he asked and slipped onto a chair. Her stomach was churning with anticipation that was now stifled by truth. Echoes of shouting and criticism vibrated through her with unbidden resurgence, and she knew then that fierce anger was a part of her past. She shrank against retribution, and yet her soul fought containment. Even now she stifled irritation that Niina had so obviously spoken to Edgar of Rebecca's supposed condition. She preferred to keep this quiet for now, at least until Rebecca herself was certain of Niina's claim regarding the babe.

"Told ya to drink up." Edgar sank onto a chair opposite her and gestured at her coffee.

Rebecca lifted the cup and took a sip, wincing at the brew's bitterness.

"Tell me the truth. What were you doing out there?" Edgar cheeks were reddened from the wind. There was a desperation in the way he drummed his fingers on the table. Rebecca could sense he was testing her, though for what, she wasn't sure. He gave no allowance for Rebecca to evade his question as he leaned forward across the table.

"I . . ." She paused. Dare she share her flimsy recollection and the haunting words that still replayed in her mind even now? Her vision of Kjersti, so strong in her memory and yet so clouded. It had been real! So very real. And yet it had not. *Could* not have been. Kjersti was dead. Which could only lead Rebecca to conclude that the woman at the end of her bed, the one who had spoken such odd and cryptic words to her, was also dead. A ghost. This ghost had followed Rebecca to the lake and disappeared into its depths. A person simply did not announce that she was visited by the dead, that she was nurtured by the dead, or that her only clear memory was that she was someone's worst reminder.

Edgar's eyes narrowed, an awareness touching his features. His voice was more hushed when he spoke this time, and more knowing. "You saw her, didn't you?"

"Her?" Rebecca stilled. The old man could read minds?

"Annabel." The way he spoke the name was almost reverent, but it was also tinged with fear.

Rebecca couldn't tear her eyes from Edgar's.

He nodded and sipped his coffee, still locking gazes with her. "She comes at night. Did you hear her? Did she call to you?"

Rebecca remained wordless. The woman at the end of her bed was Annabel? The grave on which Rebecca had collapsed? That woman had been dead for over two decades. Why would she haunt Rebecca? Or had a bond been formed between Rebecca and Annabel as she'd lain prostrate over the earthen tomb? Had

Annabel's spirit determined that Rebecca was hers to guard, to watch over?

Edgar accepted Rebecca's silence by releasing her from his stare. "She's in your mind, Rebecca." Edgar's words wove through Rebecca with a warning attached to them. "Once she's there, she won't leave ya. She'll fill your mind and then your soul." He breathed heavily, his fingers thrumming the tabletop. "She's as insistent as the lake, she is. Annabel pounds away at your heart like the waves pound the shore." Edgar clamped his mouth shut, staring at his fingers that he stopped from their insistent drumming on the table. "She'll not leave ya." He lifted his aged eyes, staring deeply into hers.

Edgar's stare sucked Rebecca in with the power of his belief. Just when she'd begun to feel as though the lighthouse was safe, it seemed to become dangerous again. Yet something inside her was tied to the lighthouse, and she didn't know if it was simply because it was all she knew now, or if something in her past had led her here in the first place.

Yet no one wished to be visited by ghosts they didn't know, didn't understand, and didn't know the intentions of. Least of all her who had awakened tonight in the world of the dead, about which she knew nothing. Nothing at all.

Edgar cleared his throat and shook his head slowly. "She comes out at night from time to time, Annabel does. She's a phantom, and has been since she died twenty years ago."

"Did you know her in life?" Rebecca dared to ask, fingering the handle on her tin mug.

"Annabel doesn't claim any living person. She's a manifestation that claims you and then never sets you free." He leveled a stare at Rebecca again. "The lake took her life, they say, but did it? Or was it something more?"

"You mean—did someone aid in her death?" Rebecca asked, all the while feeling a strange kinship with Annabel. Despite her inability to remember the events, she knew how it felt to be hunted, to feel as though someone saw you as a *chilling reminder*. But a reminder of what? Of what they couldn't have? Of what they wanted her to be?

"Heartbreak," Edgar said. "That's what aided in Annabel's death." He took a long, noisy sip of his coffee and looked out the lone window behind Rebecca. His gaze reflected the light from the lighthouse that shone across the lake. "She's a mystery to this place, Rebecca. No one understands her. She'll appear one day, and no one will know where she came from. Then she vanishes into the lake, leaving behind a vague feelin' that you should understand somethin'—but ya don't."

The parallel was eerie. Rebecca wrapped her arms around herself and considered her words carefully before posing the question. "Does anyone know how she died?"

A sad smile touched Edgar's mouth and made his beard and mustache twitch. "Does anyone know the truth about anyone's story? Life is just a busted-up vessel, its pieces floating to shore. Years later, folks try to patch them together, but the life's story is never what it really was. The only one who can retell it truthfully is the one who lived it. When you die, Rebecca, the truth dies with you. All that's left is speculation." He shook his head and sipped his coffee. "And there's not much comfort in that, now, is there?"

ANNABEL

KNOW ME AFTER I AM GONE.
Chase after me in the wind—the memory of me.
Catch my spirit between your fingers and I will caress your skin as I pass through.

Be wistful about what could have been.

Remember the melancholy of grief.

Recall the chilling and the killing, the taking of life, and the last first look into the eyes of the dying.

Because I know you, after I am gone.

I will chase after you in the wind and catch your spirit while you sleep.

I will be wistful for what I have no longer, and I will not sever my soul from yours.

Where you will be, I will be too.

In the wind.

In the water.

In the light.

I will come, once I am dead. And you will know I am there. Watching. Waiting. Remembering.

12

SHEA

And this was the reason that, long ago,
in this kingdom by the sea . . .
Annabel Lee

ANNABEL'S LIGHTHOUSE
PRESENT DAY

SHE HAD A SPLITTING HEADACHE. The kind that made a woman want to shower, bathe, curl up in bed, drink wine, and engage in a thousand other self-care attempts to make oneself feel better. Instead, Shea waved to Marnie, Edna's daughter, who had given her a ride back to the lighthouse after having her car towed to a nearby repair shop.

Entering the lighthouse, Shea dropped her bag onto the table so she could dig through it to find aspirin. Popping two, she opted to avoid the wine since that wouldn't be much help in collecting her thoughts.

Who in their right mind would throw a brick through someone's windshield? And as much as she liked Edna Carraway, the elderly woman believed that a spirit could break a windshield, that Annabel had somehow risen from the dead and vandalized Shea's car. Shea snorted, feeling a tad guilty as she did so.

The logic simply wasn't there. Poor Edna. The elderly woman was so shaken by the incident that the police had called Marnie at the diner and asked her to come home. After finally getting Edna settled with a cup of tea and an old black-and-white western, Marnie had joined Shea back outside as Shea filed her report with the cops and helped her arrange to have the windshield repaired.

She had little to no hope the culprit would be found. Streets in Ontonagon weren't lined with cameras.

"Am I in personal danger?" she had inquired of the police, who shrugged and explained that without a clear motive, it was hard to know what, if anything, was meant by the act of vandalism. It could be just bored kids with nothing to do. Or kids who didn't like having tourists in town.

"It's not the first time it's happened here," Marnie had chimed in, seconding the officer's conclusion.

They'd do their best to figure it, but Shea could tell they had already dismissed it as unsolvable. That was the police response, and Shea really couldn't fault them. It wasn't as if they had a lot to go on, and motive was sketchy at best.

In the end, finding Edna relaxed and content with John Wayne, Marnie had offered to bring Shea to the lighthouse, and Shea had accepted.

Now she traipsed through the century-old house to the lightkeeper's room. She slipped into a pair of joggers and a hoodie sweatshirt, hoping Holt didn't decide to drop by tonight and see her in her slothful clothes that did nothing to aid her already curvy figure.

She needed to relax. Gather her thoughts. Maybe write an

opening chapter in her book. She didn't have much information on Annabel yet, aside from what she already knew. But then there *was* the Jonathan Marks angle she could capitalize on. She could also safely investigate the basics of that in the security of the lighthouse with the help of the internet.

Returning to the first floor, Shea glanced out the window. Dusk was settling in, and soon it would be dark. With the lighthouse dormant, there were no streetlamps to illuminate the yard, and the lake would become a black, moving shadow, beckoning lost souls with its rhythmic call.

She checked the lock on the window, then did a quick sweep of the place to make sure all the ground-floor windows were battened down against intruders. That she was unnerved from today wasn't something Shea would even try to deny herself. Padding to the sitting area, she curled up on the couch with her laptop and prayed the satellite Wi-Fi would be reliable enough.

Jonathan Marks.

Murder or suicide? Shea hesitated as she glanced at the spot on the floor the documentary had indicated to be the place Jonathan's body had been discovered. An involuntary shiver passed through her. The lighthouse looked friendly in the day-time, but after today—and now that night was setting in—Shea had to admit she was starting to become afraid of two ghosts— Annabel's *and* Jonathan Marks's.

First things first. She needed to make a spreadsheet of facts she knew about Annabel—which weren't many up to this point. Then she would do the same with Jonathan Marks. Her editor would love the parallel angle of dead woman near the light-house from 1852 and dead man in the lighthouse from 2010. Two deaths would make for a creative approach to the historical setting of the place. The Porcupine Mountains area provided the perfect level of seclusion, and with Lake Superior's incessant power and mystique, her approach to this tale would be like a book version of a chilling documentary exposé. Only, if she was going to go with that angle, she needed the material that would expose something other than what was already known by those who cared to research it themselves. She needed to uncover the local secrets, the lore that was never spoken of. She needed to know what secrets Jonathan Marks hid before he died, for everyone had them. And she needed to—

Someone pounded on the door.

Shea shrieked and almost flipped her laptop onto the floor as she jumped.

"Good grief!" She didn't even bother to temper the volume of her voice, and she hoped whoever was outside banging would hear her. Shea set her laptop on the coffee table and smoothed back the wayward spiral curls that had escaped her scrunchie. She hurried to the tiny entryway. "I'm coming. For the love of Pete!"

"Yeah?"

"Huh?" Shea frowned, then grimaced at the familiar voice on the other side of the door.

No.

He hadn't.

She jerked open the door, every emotion from the day releasing with the sigh she expelled and the tears that burned her eyes. Tears of frustration, need, hope, and preparation for the inevitable disappointment.

Pete stood there in his customary grease-stained jeans, his ratty old T-shirt, and an unbuttoned green flannel shirt. He hadn't shaved—at least it didn't look like he had—since Shea had left their place three days ago.

"What are you doing here?" She stared at Pete, unsure what her response should be. This was exactly why she'd left to come to the lighthouse. Six hours away wasn't enough to deter him? He didn't like to travel. But now here he was. His motivation was *her*? Or the car. It had to be something to do with the car. Sometimes Shea wondered if it would be easier to dislike an interloping female rather than the soulless vehicles that competed with her for Pete's faithful attention.

"I got a text from the insurance company saying they're processing your claim." Pete rubbed his chin. "Broken windshield, huh?"

"It's okay," Shea mumbled. She didn't like that while she wanted to be away from him, there was also a sense of relief at the familiarity of his presence. Pete. Average Pete. But for a second, Shea caught a whiff of his deodorant—spices she could identify—and while he had nothing on Holt in the alpha-male hottie looks department, he was . . . *familiar.* There was comfort in the familiar, but there was danger too. It meant settling for mediocrity. This was what Shea had come here to get away from. "You didn't have to come," she finished.

"I was already on the way. I got to thinking about the battery, and it probably needs replacing. I should have done that before you left, but I figured it was still fine for a bit longer."

"The car is running okay. I don't need a new battery. I need a new windshield, and you can't help with that." Shea should feel guilty she hadn't asked him to come in, but she didn't. Asking Pete to come in would be dangerous to her emotional well-being.

"Right. I debated." Pete shifted his weight onto his other steel-toed boot. "But then when the text came through, I called the insurance company to follow up and found out someone had vandalized the car."

She grimaced. She should have thought to call Pete, so he wouldn't do what he'd just done. Touch one of his cars and the man would take whatever anxiety meds were necessary to have the guts to fly to Siberia or wherever to rescue the thing.

He was waiting for her to respond. Shea sucked in an irritated breath. "Yes. Someone threw a brick through the windshield. The cops found it under the passenger-side seat. But according to one lady, I've upset a ghost."

Pete's expression didn't change. It was, for all sakes and

purposes, expressionless. "A ghost. Okay. Anyway, I figure I'd stay the night at least. That way I can go to the shop tomorrow and see what the plan is for replacing the windshield."

Shea should have bit her tongue, but she didn't. "You can go home, Pete. They don't need you hovering over them at the repair shop, plus where are you planning to stay?"

"Here." With that, Pete lifted his backpack he'd been holding by the canvas loop at its top. "I know there's more than one room here. I'm not looking to snuggle up for the night."

"You never are," Shea muttered, then stepped aside to let him inside, knowing it was fruitless to suggest Pete get a room in Ontonagon or at his own lakeshore cabin. He'd just inform her that it would be "poor stewardship" of their finances.

Pete entered the lighthouse and looked around, poking his head into the rooms, a logical scowl on his face. "You're paying to stay here?"

"Yes." Shea crossed her arms as she stood in the doorway between the kitchen and the living area.

He glanced at her. "It's small. And that's a wood cookstove." Pete pointed at it and then shot her a doubtful smile. "You know how to work a wood cookstove?"

"I never said it was the Ritz."

"No, but for the price, you could've rented something nicer, more up to date. Something that has an electric stove."

The man didn't miss much when it came to functionality. For him, it was the practical that was important. Ambience was wasteful, even annoying to him.

"I'm here for the atmosphere and the history," Shea mumbled. She wasn't even going to try to explain it further. If Pete ever comprehended the importance of mood and sentiment and beauty, then she'd dye her hair green. It was a safe bet to make with herself. So safe that she didn't bother to imagine what it'd be like if Pete appreciated the ambiance.

Another knock on the door. Shea groaned. She knew who it

was before she opened it. Holt. It had to be. This place was turning into Grand Central Station for the collection of men who did things to her nerves. One who she'd slept with, and another who, well . . . Reining in her thoughts, Shea eyed her husband and then, for the first time since she'd arrived, mentally jotted off a prayer.

Save me from myself.

At least from the men in my life.

And this was why, for all the terrifying and creepy elements they brought with them, Shea much preferred the company of ghosts.

Shea was exhausted. She could see the dark circles under her eyes too, and that did nothing to boost her self-confidence.

Holt had stopped by last night, shortly after Pete arrived, having heard of the events of the day and wanting to check in and make sure she was okay.

After an awkward exchange between the men, Holt had wisely taken his leave, yet Shea couldn't help but wish she could have followed him. She noticed Holt move a bottle of wine to the back seat of his truck before pulling away. Instead, she'd closed the door and shown Pete to one of the claustrophobic spare rooms in the attic just off the spiraling lighthouse stairs. Then she'd gone to bed, ignoring further research on Jonathan Marks, opting instead to toss and turn.

Giving up on sleep, she patted on some cooling aloe eye gel and tugged her uncooperative dark curls into a thick braid that had pieces springing out of it within seconds. She threw on jeans and was just buttoning a blouse when Pete entered the keeper's bedroom.

Shea yelped and clutched her shirt closed. "Warn a person, Pete!" She'd forgotten that getting to the main floor required traipsing through the lightkeeper's bedroom, where she was dressing.

He shot her a perplexed look. "Sure." Pete kept moving and left the room, unaffected by her annoyance and the brief glimpse he'd gotten of her in her bra.

Husbands were the worst. She could dress in nothing but plastic wrap and Pete would be completely oblivious.

Shea sank onto the edge of the bed and drew a deep breath. This trip wasn't going the way she'd imagined it. Now she had her husband to contend with. She'd exhausted prayers for her marriage months ago. She'd exhausted prayers for herself a few weeks ago. What was the use when they didn't change anything anyway? All she could see as the next best move was to center herself on her own needs, evaluate the toxicity in her life, and then make the necessary changes.

A pang of regret warred with a twinge of anger. She'd been raised to believe that marriage was forever, that vows were sacred, that faith was the fabric of one's life. Now she was realizing that her dreams were tired of being ignored, her vows had become a prison, and faith was nice but only when it worked.

It left Shea feeling lost at sea . . . or lost at lake might be more appropriate. A bit like her research.

She sucked in a determined breath. Enough was enough. If Pete was going to hang around like a lost puppy, then fine. She would manage. She had for the last decade. And in some ways, it was nice to have Pete around. He was reliable at least. Yet it was all so difficult for her to sort out in her head, let alone try to talk to Pete about it. And the image of Holt and the bottle of wine in his truck? Why was romance always just out of reach? Why was happiness and feeling cherished as elusive as Annabel's ghost?

13

ᴊONATHAN MARKS?" The historian nudged his glasses up his nose.

Shea watched the balding man from behind the counter. She'd left the lighthouse that morning in the guise of taking a walk, and she'd ended up three miles away in the small remnants of the once promising Silvertown. In the 1870s, the city had been expected to become the epicenter of a silver boom. In the end, silver had become a short-lived dream.

The historian unwrapped a piece of chewing gum, and the minty smell permeated the otherwise musty smell in the small house that doubled as the Silvertown Historical Museum. Two rooms really, with the main attractions being a wall filled with cheaply framed black-and-white photos and a taxidermic black bear in the far corner, along with a sign that boasted it was the largest bear taken in the twentieth century on the shores of Lake Superior.

"Jonathan Marks," the historian repeated. He clucked his tongue as he chewed the gum. "I knew him back in the day. It's been a while since I heard the name."

Shea glanced at the name tag on the man in front of her. "Chuck, I'd love to hear about Mr. Marks."

Chuck eased his short frame onto a stool and adjusted his position until he found a comfortable spot. It seemed every man she met of late was testing her patience. Shea looked around for her own chair or stool, but since there was none, she leaned forward on the counter.

"Yep." Chuck nodded, oblivious to Shea's search for a place to sit. "I went to high school with Jonathan. Then he left for the university and didn't come back to this area until about 2000 or so." Chuck's mustache stretched as he smiled. His cheeks were ruddy, and the mustache made the middle-aged man appear like a mash-up of youthful pubescence and a man whose age had snuck up on him and caught him unaware. He laughed. "Jonathan was *all* about Y2K. Remember that? The computer chips weren't set for the millennium change, and the world was going to experience a crash. He said he moved back here where he could live off the land. He bought the lighthouse, which at that time hadn't been made into a historical landmark."

"When was the lighthouse put out of commission?" Shea interrupted.

"The sixties," Chuck answered. "There wasn't any need for it. I'm surprised the government ran it that long since Silvertown never was a port. They kept it lit mostly for the potential of shipwrecks on some of the outcroppings and rocks. But now? There's no need with all the navigational equipment on ships these days."

"What do you know about Jonathan's death?" Shea didn't bother to tiptoe around her intentions.

Something flickered in Chuck's eyes. "Yeah. That. Super tragic. Put a gun to his head and just pulled the trigger. My brother was with the police department then and was one of the first people on the scene. It was pretty gory."

"Most gunshot wounds are."

"'Specially to the head." Chuck patted his hands on his knees for emphasis. "Brains and all, you know?"

"I know." Shea grimaced. "Someone was telling me that Jonathan was anti-guns?"

"Yep. Had been since high school," Chuck affirmed.

"So how did he come by a gun to end his life with?"

Chuck wagged a finger in Shea's direction. "Now you're asking the questions the cops asked. My brother, Tim, told me it was a 9mm handgun. The autopsy report said the gun was consistent with the angle of Jonathan holding it to his temple. But it was the right-side temple, and Jonathan was left-handed. So foul play was introduced as a theory based on that, as well as Jonathan being so anti-firearm."

"Did he have a reason to be anti-gun?"

"Anti-gun?" Chuck's voice went up a notch. He lifted his shoulders and dropped them in a shrug. "Not sure. I mean, it's not exactly a popular opinion around these parts. We've a lot of hunters and the like."

"But hunters don't hunt with a handgun, do they?" Shea inquired.

"Not likely, but there's still a use for them. Protection when you're out hiking—wolves are making a comeback now. There are the black bears too, though typically they're more scared of us than we are of them. Still, if you come up on a mama bear—"

"Where did Jonathan get this gun?" Shea asked, cutting him off.

Chuck lifted his hands in acquiescence. "No one knows."

None of it made sense to Shea, and she voiced her skepticism. "It seems there would be some record somewhere. I mean, guns have serial numbers."

Chuck's expression told her he agreed with her. "Yep. They do. But he might've purchased the gun out of state. Like next door in Wisconsin, where you can sell your gun to a friend, and no one is the wiser. Jonathan could've bought a handgun somewhere and been legal about it but not have its serial number registered under his name. The bigger question was motive—who would want him dead? Jonathan wasn't popular around Silvertown or Ontonagon. He riled folks up with his talk of how we were destroying the environment with the logging and mining, polluting the lake, and so on. He was also known for being a drunk. Spent every evening at the Dipstick Saloon. Man drank old-fashioneds like they were so old-fashioned they were going extinct. He'd always talk a lot when he did. Depression ran in his family, and a week or so before he died, he was at the Dipstick and going on about ways a man could off himself and leave behind the stress and darkness of the world. To be honest, he seemed a bit excited to die."

"That's awful." Shea couldn't fathom being that low in life as to wish death on oneself. But she knew it was a very real place all too many found themselves.

Chuck nodded emphatically. "But there's the even weirder part about it."

"What's that?" Shea leaned her elbows on the counter to take weight off of her feet.

"About a month before Jonathan died, he mentioned to others in the Dipstick some very odd things happening at the lighthouse. Slamming doors, footsteps in the hallway, the water turned on in the middle of the night when no one was there to do it. He was determined Annabel's ghost was really in the lighthouse, and she didn't want him there."

"Are you insinuating *Annabel's ghost* killed Jonathan?" Shea had to find a human explanation for his death. Gone crazy and run himself off the top of the lighthouse? Sure, she could believe that. But Shea couldn't wrap her belief around the idea Annabel's ghost herself somehow pulled the trigger that resulted in Jonathan's death.

Chuck slid off the stool and made a pretense of getting busy straightening a stack of brochures. "I think folks bring up that Annabel legend because it makes a good story. As if an old ghost could pull a trigger or would even *want* to."

"What do *you* believe happened?" Shea asked.

Chuck matched her intent gaze. "I believe blaming a popular legend is an excuse. It sensationalizes Jonathan's death and gives it a whole lot of attention and builds a mystery around it. Before you know, the authorities want to shut all the hoopla down, so they go with their gut and claim suicide." Chuck gave the neat stack of brochures a kindly pat. "The bigger question isn't whether Jonathan was killed by Annabel's ghost, but *if* Annabel was haunting him, why it drove things so far as to have Jonathan end up dead? Either the haunting drove him to suicide, or it drove someone to murder him. There's the rub if you ask me."

"What'd you find out?"

Holt's appearance just outside of the museum caught her off guard. Shea stopped on the porch and tried to temper her expression into the appropriate smile of a married woman, as she knew she should. Man, but it was hard.

"I'm sure it's nothing new to you." She widened her smile, unable to hold in the warmth.

"Chuck has always been in the murder camp when it comes to Jonathan Marks." Holt tipped his head toward his pickup. "Need a ride back to the lighthouse?"

"Actually," she answered, "I was going to head down to the Dipstick. Just to look around."

"I'll come with you." Holt fell into place beside Shea as she skipped down the steps toward the gravel parking area.

The woods grew up all around them, and from where the museum was located, she could peer up and down the highway and see the entirety of Silvertown: the museum, post office,

111

Dipstick Saloon, country store and gas station, and a couple of houses that looked to be half home and half boutique shop.

Their shoes crunched on the gravel as they hiked down the road toward the bar. No sidewalks were available, just the gravel on the edge of the asphalt highway.

"Soooo . . ." Holt dragged the word out long enough for Shea to have an idea of where he was going. "I didn't know you were married."

"We're . . . separated." Shea wasn't sure if that was the actual truth. If someone were to ask Pete, he'd probably have no clue that she was considering this trip a separation. A test.

"Ah." Holt nodded. "Marriage is tough."

"You've been married, right?" Shea cast him a sideways glance as the Dipstick Saloon came closer into view.

"Briefly. My high-school sweetheart and I got married, which is kinda what you do in a small town, eh?" They both laughed. "She left about a year later. The call of the city. I was too small-town for her by then. We were shortsighted teenagers, I guess."

Shea didn't elaborate about why she agreed with him, but her "Mm-hmm!" came out far more emphatic than she'd intended.

That was the thing that sucked about being in her mid-thirties. She was already well on the way to the midpoint of her life and yet her twenties were still visible in the rearview mirror, which meant she saw the foolhardiness of her younger self and yet—Shea stole a glance at Holt beside her—she still had enough impulsive youthfulness in her to want to be foolhardy all over again.

"Here we are." Holt opened the door of the Dipstick Saloon for Shea, and she entered, immediately taking in the Upper Peninsula vibe of taxidermy, neon beer signs and mirrors, the smells of grease and cigarette smoke, a pool table, and a few pictures on the walls of the Porcupine Mountains.

Even though it was late morning, Holt shimmied onto a stool

at the bar and gave the silver-haired woman behind it a grin that deepened his dimples.

"Holt boy, you son of a gun. Since when do you pop into the Dipstick for lunch?"

"Never. It's always for supper. But today is different." Holt slapped the bar in jest. "So serve me up a cheeseburger."

"You serious?" Penny raised her brows, the crow's feet beside her eyes deepening.

"Never more serious. What do you want, Shea? It's on me."

Shea approached and slipped onto a stool next to Holt. It was a bit early for lunch, she thought, but then—why not? "A cheeseburger is fine."

"No, no. Get her a pastie. She needs to try one." Holt negated Shea's order with both authority and a sense of humor.

Penny turned green eyes in Shea's direction. "You've never had a pastie, hon?"

"I don't even know what that is." Although Shea had to admit she'd heard of it since Wisconsin bordered the U.P.

"An Upper Peninsula delight, brought here by the Cornish miners, these handheld beef pies are perfection. With some rutabagas and potatoes chopped up in them? Mm-mmm!" Penny's description had made Shea's mouth water, until she heard the word *rutabaga*, which lent to some trepidation at the spicier root.

"But." Holt leveled a stern look on Shea. "Do you dip it in gravy or ketchup?"

"Ummm." Shea had no idea how to answer.

Penny burst out laughing and waved Holt away. "Don't mind him, hon. That's an age-old debate you'll never give the right answer to." Then she disappeared back into the kitchen.

Holt twisted on his seat. "Penny has been running the Dipstick since I was in my teens."

"She seems like a nice person," Shea said.

"She is. A local, and a good one to ask questions of."

And that was what Shea intended to do.

When Penny returned to the bar, she wiped the counter with a damp rag, then tossed it into a bucket of soapy water on the floor behind her. "Okay, what are you having to drink?"

"Coke," Shea answered.

"One Coke." Penny turned to Holt. "And you?"

"Spotted Heifer."

"One Spotted Heifer comin' up."

Shea was a bit surprised that Holt was going to have the Midwest ale at this time of day, but when she saw his callused fingers wrap around the bottle, it sort of completed the picture of the rugged Upper Peninsula man.

Penny interrupted her observation. "Holt told me yesterday you're staying in Annabel's Lighthouse."

Shea nodded. "I am."

"Seen her yet?" Penny's eyes sparked.

Shea chuckled. "Well, no, not exactly. I did hear the floor creak the other night. That's creepy enough." She didn't add that she could almost swear she'd heard Annabel respond when she told her to be quiet.

"And a lightbulb burned out on you, right?" Holt added.

"Oooooh." Penny's face contorted into a melodramatic look of caution. "Annabel is not a fan of modern conveniences. I'd light a lamp next time instead. Keeps her calmer."

Shea smiled as she sipped her Coke. She liked the laid-back nature of today. Much better than yesterday and having her windshield shattered for no apparent reason. Which reminded her . . .

"I was talking to Edna Caraway yesterday," Shea led.

"Oh boy." Penny exchanged knowing smiles with Holt.

"Oh boy?" Shea said.

"No, no." Penny shook her head, refusing to explain. Her little silver seashell earrings bobbed. "Tell me what story Edna told this time."

Holt leaned over to whisper loudly, "Penny thinks Edna makes up half of her history."

Penny swatted at Holt. "I just think she's an old lady with nothing else to do but try to remember stuff an old lady can't remember. She's riddled with dementia."

"She is?" Shea drew back. Edna hadn't struck her as someone struggling with memory issues.

"That's what Marnie told me. Her daughter. We went to school together back in the day." Penny's explanation made sense in a way, but then the fact Marnie hadn't told Shea about her mother's dementia seemed a bit strange. Maybe Penny wasn't meaning to come across critical, but her blunt, inconsiderate declaration about Edna's state of mind gave Shea a nudge of caution.

"Anyway"—Penny leaned her elbows on the bar—"what'd you learn?"

Shea didn't want to bring up the broken windshield, although she had a feeling that Penny somehow already knew, and it dawned on Shea that Holt had to have heard from somewhere too, seeing as he'd shown up at the lighthouse last night to make sure she was okay.

"Well." Shea hesitated, then decided to go for it. "Okay, so Edna mentioned that Annabel might be behind the vandalism to my windshield." Stupid didn't begin to describe how Shea felt after posing the idea.

"Ahh, yes. The 'Annabel is protective of her story' angle." Penny dropped a wink in Holt's direction. "That's not unique to Edna, though, I will admit. It's been said that after Annabel's lover died decades after her own death, it always seemed as though Annabel never liked people nosing around and asking questions. Anyone digging into her story found themselves with strange things happening to warn them off."

"Who was Annabel's lover?" Shea had to admit, the story of Annabel and the lighthouse got odder every time she learned a little bit more.

"Shhh." Penny's expression lost its humor in a way that made Shea believe she truly was being serious now. "We don't talk about it out loud. That's the worst thing you can do. Speak of Annabel's lover, and her ghost goes berserk."

Shea offered up a nervous laugh and glanced at Holt, who took a draw from his bottle and raised his brows as if to say, You're on your own on this one.

Penny's eyes shifted left to right as though concerned someone might overhear them. She leaned closer over the bar. "The more you dig into the story of who Annabel and her lover were, the spookier it gets. Take Jonathan Marks, for example."

Shea straightened.

Penny tapped the glossy bar with a long, red fingernail that was chipped on the end. "He went from being a smart conservationist, lobbying the government on behalf of the environment, to hiding out in the lighthouse and eventually shooting himself in the head."

"Was he researching the lighthouse?" Shea asked.

Penny tugged on her shirt with its beer-brand moniker. "He *wasn't* until he moved into it. His sole purpose for moving in was to get the place registered as a historical site and work on sprucing up the property. Of course, Annabel . . . well, she seeps in slowly, like the tide, until suddenly you're swept up in her story—good or bad."

"I didn't realize Jonathan Marks was into Annabel's legend," Holt admitted.

Penny glanced at him, her eyes wide. "Oh yeah. Jonathan used to come in here and tell me all the things he was trying to figure out. Then it went from research to an obsession. It was really strange. He came into the bar one night just before closing, around one in the morning. He was a mess, an absolute mess. He said he'd had a sense he was being watched as he tried to sleep. Someone hiding in his closet. He investigated further and said there was the shadow of a woman staring out at him as he lay on the lightkeeper's bed, and when Jonathan sat up, the vision dissipated."

"Every closet is haunted. We learn that when we're kids." Holt jabbed a hole into Penny's story.

She jabbed the air back at him with her finger. "You may not believe, but I do. I saw Jonathan that night, and let me tell you, that man was all scientific and statistics before he moved into the lighthouse. Then to go and kill himself? I don't believe it."

"Did Jonathan have issues with Annabel too? I don't mean haunting him; I mean like my windshield getting shattered?" Shea had to ask even though the stories were sounding more ludicrous by the minute.

"Mm-hmm." Penny gave a curt nod. "Little things mostly. There was the time he was picking up his laundry from the laundromat in Ontonagon. Yeah, and there was black soot all through his clean clothes."

"Soot?" Holt questioned.

"Yes. Like old coal soot from the stove back in the lighthouse. Only the clothes had been washed." Penny held her palms up toward the ceiling. "Figure that one out. Someone sabotaged his laundry."

"Doesn't sound too *ghostly* to me." Holt twisted his bottle on the bar. "Sounds like a kid's prank."

"So, essentially, the argument goes that Annabel's spirit can't rest in peace because people keep trying to find out what happened to her?" Shea summarized.

Penny's red lips drew into a thin line, emphasizing the fine wrinkles around her mouth. "Partly. I think the lighthouse has secrets, more than we realize. *That's* what makes it—and Annabel—an enigma. But she needs to be left alone."

Penny cleared her throat as she took a step back from the bar to retrieve the cheeseburger and pastie for Holt and Shea. She hesitated, then spun and leveled a look on Shea.

"I will say this, though. Things got really weird with Jonathan when he uncovered the story about the girl who showed up at the lighthouse about twenty years after Annabel died. Rebecca, they called her. Jonathan found some mention of the girl in the copies of the lighthouse log. There wasn't a lot of detail. A few pieces of historical documents said she was Annabel reincarnated, but the really strange thing? Silvertown went a little crazy about that time. It was right when the silver mining dream was ready to burst wide open, and the town was in the process of becoming a port. People started seeing Annabel more often. A miner even reported that Annabel's ghost sabotaged the stamp mill to halt the miners from harvesting the silver ore. Jonathan was dead two days after he told me that little tale. He thought there was some connection there—between the lost girl and the dead Annabel."

"What do *you* think?" Holt's tone was serious, and Shea felt her breath catch in her throat.

Penny turned away to refill Shea's soda. "Doesn't matter what I think. I just know that one day Jonathan Marks wore a business suit and championed climate-change awareness and gun control. The next day he looked like Shaggy from Scooby-Doo, drinking every night and telling others the lighthouse needed to be destroyed so that Annabel's spirit would move on. And then he took a bullet to the head. Whether by his own hand or Annabel's or someone else's, who knows?" Penny's eyes locked on Shea's. "Fact is, he was the last person I know to try to understand Annabel and the lighthouse and, well, the cursed story killed him."

14

REBECCA

A wind blew out of a cloud, chilling my beautiful Annabel Lee . . .

Annabel Lee

ABEL SLAMMED THE DOOR. Rebecca startled from where she sliced the last of Niina's bread as she attempted to help make lunch for the two lightkeepers. His eyes were wide, and urgency in them she'd not witnessed since her arrival. He motioned toward the inner sanctum of the house. "Go, Rebecca! Now. Go to the oil room."

"What?" Dazed by his sudden appearance as it cut through the otherwise quiet day, Rebecca stared at him in confusion.

"Go!" His eyes widened even further, and he leaped forward,

grabbing her arm. The knife slipped from her grasp and clattered onto the cutting board.

She shrank away from him, and Abel dropped his grip as if touching her had burned him. Apology spread across his face, but he didn't voice it. Instead, he shot a harried look over his shoulder toward the door, then back to Rebecca.

"Please, Rebecca. Trust me. There are men coming. You need to take refuge in the oil room, and don't come out until they are gone."

"Are they—?" She bit her tongue. How would Abel know if they were the men who had assaulted her? But his imperative pushing her into hiding made sense now. She nodded and hurried from the kitchen just as someone banged on the door. Scurrying around the corner, she ducked into the oil room, careful to avoid the window. She pulled the door shut, leaving it open only a crack so she could hear.

"—saw her last night." The man's voice was gruff and unfamiliar.

"Saw who?" Abel's attempt to sound nonchalant didn't fool Rebecca at all. She heard the brief quiver in his voice, and he must have noticed it also, for he coughed as if clearing his throat to cover it.

"Annabel's ghost." The man spat the words as though it were an accusation.

Rebecca shrank into the corner, her back against the wall, an oilcan on the shelf near her shoulder. She was careful not to kick a box of lantern wicks as she pulled her knees up to her chest.

"And you know what that means!" Another man's voice broke in.

"No. No, I don't." Abel's tone was controlled now.

"It's a bad omen, Abel, and ya know it. We already had the shipwreck—come to find out it sank with the supplies for Hilliard's mine. Set us back by weeks."

"Edgar and I have nothing to do with Annabel—or her—her

ghost." Abel's words made Rebecca hold her breath. *She* had been on the shore last night. Had the men seen her and believed *she* was Annabel? Or had they seen the same apparition Rebecca had, wilting into the waves and disappearing? Maybe it hadn't been just her own vision. Maybe Annabel really *had* made an appearance.

Abel was speaking again, this time more insistent. "I'm telling you, whoever you saw, we had nothing to do with it. Do you think we conjure Annabel's spirit? No!"

"Sure you do!" The original man's voice rose. "We all know she thinks this place is her own. This lighthouse and the land around it. She don't want Hilliard and his mines here."

"That's superstition, man, and you know it!" Abel snapped.

"Do I now? Not after what I seen last night. And so did others. On the shore just like they describe her. Pacing the sand like a wraith. She's real as real can be."

"She hasn't done anything." Abel defended the dead woman's spirit—or perhaps he defended Rebecca, for she was almost certain it was her the men had seen. "And what do you want us to do about it anyway? We can't catch a ghost and lock her up. If you saw Annabel, then she'll do what she wants, there's no doubt about that, and you can rot in your superstitions." There was a bitter edge to Abel's voice now.

"What's next? You say she's not done anything? She's caused a shipwreck. She lost our supplies. Next, she'll be going after *us*! The men are shook up."

"Don't be daft," Abel shot back. "Annabel's ghost doesn't control the weather. There's nothing Edgar and I can do about *your* superstitions."

"You listen here, and you listen close." There was a chill in the man's voice that made Rebecca hug her legs tighter. "If I see her again, I've no problem—"

"No problem what?" Abel interrupted. "Are you going to kill a dead woman?"

Silence was his answer, and then finally there was the stomping of feet, the men walking away. But then they turned and came back. One of them said, "You're still not welcome in town, you know that, Abel."

It was an unsettling declaration, and Rebecca strained to hear, wondering why these men held Abel so responsible for the supposed actions of a spirit.

"Do you see me in town?" Abel retorted. "You think I have any desire to be there?"

"Keep it that way," the man concluded. "And make sure your mother keeps her nose to herself too."

A yell split the tension. Rebecca recognized Edgar's growly vibrato, the one that emanated straight from his gut. "Get off my property!" His shout was followed by loud thwacks and thumps.

Rebecca dared to crane her neck to look out the window covered by white sheer curtains. Two men jogged away, Edgar chasing them as fast as he could hobble, waving an oar in the air and attempting to bring it down on the back of one of the men.

A tiny smile toyed at Rebecca's mouth even as she absorbed the gravity of the moment. The puzzling questions piled up inside of her. There was a hatred in the men that went deep and spoke to a history that was darker than their words stated. A hatred for Annabel's ghost, yes, but also for Abel. Which made little sense. He would have been a young child when Annabel was alive. He had nothing to do with her, and he was obviously not her son or anything sensational such as that because it was apparent Niina was his mother. Even *they* had said as such.

So why were Annabel and Abel linked so closely in the eyes of the mining community in Silvertown?

While the answers to those questions evaded her, Rebecca knew with certainty it was her on the shore the men had seen last night. Her own vision of Annabel had been brief, while the men had stated they saw Annabel pacing the shore. Rebecca held her hands over her abdomen as she considered the weight of that. The small mining community believed her to be a ghost, and there was no mention of a missing woman. If she had been from Silvertown and had somehow gone missing, wouldn't it stand to reason that they would assume it could have been her before they leaped to the conclusion of Annabel's ghost? Even Abel had been harried, wanting her to hide on the men's arrival. Abel must have assumed the men were looking for her, not to confront him about a ghost.

But no. There had been no mention of her. Just a superstition. A belief. The overwhelming awareness that the miners frantically searched for a dead woman's ghost, while flesh-and-blood Rebecca huddled in a corner, crashed over her with the ferocity of the lake's frigid waters.

It was a lonely, vicious realization that shattered Rebecca.

No one was looking for her.

She was not missed—by anyone.

She felt him crouch before her, but Rebecca kept her eyes closed and her face turned away. Something deep inside told her she had always questioned her place, but now it dawned on her that it was more than that. It was a *knowing* that she was truly alone. That the memories that teased just out of her reach did not hold promise of desperate reunion with family who was besides themselves to find her. Instead, they hold no promise of reunion whatsoever.

Abel moved, and the air between them shifted. A whiff of the lake came off him and awakened her senses. Rebecca had no doubt he was staring at her, his gaze boring holes into her skin, her soul. Yet she didn't dare open her eyes. She couldn't bear to see whatever lay in the depths of his look. Disdain? Pity? Compassion? She feared any of them would be her undoing.

"They're gone now, Rebecca."

She managed to pry her lids apart, and for a long moment

she drew strength from his sharp blue eyes that mimicked ice but somehow still mirrored a strength that promised protection.

"It's not your fault." Abel tipped his head toward the window. "Those men, they're from Hilliard's mine. They're sore about the ship going down. The silver mine has been underperforming, and this is a setback. Not to mention there's so much wild superstition in the area about Annabel."

"It was me they saw last night," Rebecca breathed.

"I know."

"You didn't tell them. Why?"

Abel frowned. "Why would I tell them? We don't know who hurt you and . . ." His eyes dropped to her abdomen and rose again. "And there's no reason to put you in more danger."

Did Abel know about the babe within her also? Rebecca's cheeks warmed even as she responded. "But we don't know *why* I am in danger—at least I don't." She leveled a look on Abel, and he averted his eyes. "If you know something . . . something about me, please tell me."

He glanced back at her, an uninterpretable look in his eyes. It was as if he warred with saying more yet believed he should say less. "It's too much." Abel squeezed the bridge of his nose with his fingers and drew in a steadying breath. "Just trust me, Rebecca. *Please*."

He hadn't given her a reason to, but he hadn't given her a reason *not* to either. Rebecca searched his face, and he didn't look away this time. Their eyes met in a silent plea, her for more knowledge and him for her not to ask more questions. "Edgar and I aren't turning you out to a mining community of men."

"Why do they hate you?" Rebecca didn't miss the shadow that crossed Abel's face.

He offered her a resigned smile. "Why do men hate other men? There's always a reason, and it's usually jealousy or greed or maybe one man thwarted another's success."

"And which one is your story?" Rebecca dared.

Abel's expression steeled, and he gave a short shake of his head. "Doesn't matter. The fact is this lighthouse is the best place for you and the best place for me. Edgar can go to town if we need supplies. You and I will stay away from the madness of silver and copper ore and all the chaos it creates."

"You never wanted to be a miner?"

Abel pushed himself up from his crouch before her and extended his hand. Rebecca tentatively reached up and took it. He helped her to her feet and then released her immediately. "No. There is nothing innately wrong with it. In fact, I suppose it is necessary. But . . ." He let his words hang as he turned to stare out the window. "I love the water. I love the lake. I love the roar of the waves, the unbridled power. It reminds me of God. So gentle one day, so far beyond our comprehension the next. I don't think He should be questioned flippantly."

"I question Him." Rebecca's admission surprised even her.

Abel looked to her, curiosity in his expression.

"I question why He allowed this to happen to me. W-why I am in this condition and don't even know who I am."

If being in her situation was teaching her anything, it was that each day was unpredictable, and each day was as dangerous as the one before.

———

Nighttime was becoming her nemesis.

Rebecca sat up in the bed and stared at the doorway, certain only moments before she'd heard it creak open. It was open too, but only a crack, which could be blamed on the shifting of the lighthouse.

An overwhelming sense of not being alone was what had awakened her. That eerie sensation that someone was there but just out of reach hung in her mind. She squinted into the corners of the small bedroom. Aside from Kjersti's trunk—which she dared not open on her own out of respect for her family—there was nothing else in the sparse room to imitate a figure. It didn't appear as though Annabel had come calling. For that, Rebecca was both grateful and curiously disappointed. She surveyed the room again. The dresser was too bulky to be mistaken for anything but what it was. Rebecca swung her legs from the bed and padded across the wood floor to the basin and pitcher that sat on the bureau's top. She poured water into the basin and splashed it on her face, urging the cold to startle any remaining sleep from her.

The floor creaked outside her room and Rebecca froze, her hands poised around her face as she bent over the basin, water dripping down her cheeks.

Silence.

Rebecca snatched the tea towel that hung over the bureau's mirror and dabbed at her face.

The bedroom door began to swing open.

Rebecca spun, staring as the door moved as if of its own volition. A few inches, pausing for a moment before continuing its slow swing, until soon Rebecca stared wide-eyed into an empty hall.

She took a tentative step forward, her bare toes connecting against the cool, wood floor.

Squinting into the darkness of the hallway, Rebecca strained to see. But no one was there.

The door ended its journey when it reached the wall behind it, the knob bouncing with a quiet *thud*.

All privacy gone, Rebecca held the tea towel to her chest as if it were a shield. "Hello?" Her whisper was shaky.

There was no response.

"H-hello?" She tried increasing her volume, hoping Abel would speak from the hallway. Hoping he had merely gone to check the lantern on Edgar's behalf and was returning to his room, that the weight of his footsteps had somehow instigated the swing of the door and—

The floor creaked again.

Rebecca stilled.

She couldn't tear her gaze from the open doorway, the wall beyond it, and the darkness that enveloped the hall. Only a crack of light from beneath the door to the spiral staircase of the lighthouse provided any illumination, and it revealed nothing that might explain the noise.

Rebecca had just taken a few more tentative steps to the doorway when a rush of cold air swiped through her. Bumps rose on her flesh. Her hip bumped the edge of the small table by the bed that held the pitcher and basin, and the pitcher tipped, crashing onto the floor. Shattering, water splashed on Rebecca's legs, the porcelain exploding into shards.

The cold air dissipated, but as it did, it stole her breath. A phantom, reaching inside of her and wrapping vengeful fingers around her lungs and squeezing. Black shields closed over her eyes. Rebecca screamed, grabbing for the bed even as her foot came down on a sharp piece of the broken pitcher, the stabbing pain of it only adding to the intense disorientation of the moment. She wrestled to stay conscious, to stay alert, and she cursed the weakness that enfolded her. Fumbling to find the bed, Rebecca blinked against the darkness rising before her vision. In that brief second, a ghoulish face of a woman pressed in close to hers, blackness for eye sockets, her mouth gaping, and her breath frigid but ripe with the stench of smoke. Like a fire made of ice.

"Go away, Annabel!" Rebecca moaned as she fell into the oblivion that sought to claim her, missing the bed and collapsing onto the porcelain that littered the floor.

15

I T'S NOT GOOD, ABEL."
Rebecca heard Niina's voice before she opened her eyes.
Her body hurt, her head hurt, and worst of all, the awful
image from the previous night remained trapped behind her
eyelids. That woman. It couldn't have been Annabel. The Annabel
that had visited before, had wandered the shore, even the Annabel that had disappeared beneath the waves—she had been
ethereal. Distant. A gentle but unsettling spirit. The one from
last night had been sheer terror.

Niina continued to whisper, and Rebecca strained to hear.

"Is it the baby?" Worry tainted Abel's voice.

"No, no. Not that."

The brush of material and a whiff of musty air pushed
through Rebecca's haze. Was Niina rifling through Kjiersti's
trunk, releasing mildew and memories, or did Annabel's ghostly
visit still haunt her senses?

"The men I met on the way here. They're looking for her."

"For Annabel?"

"*Annabel?*" The mockery in Niina's tone directed at the miners
was easy to decipher. "No. For *her*."

"Rebecca?"

"*Joo.*"

"I'd hoped they thought she was dead." Abel's words sliced through Rebecca as full consciousness returned. She remained still, unwilling to open her eyes and cut their conversation short. She knew the moment they knew she was aware, they would bite their tongues, give her those awful pitying looks, and pretend they knew less than they did.

"I had hoped so as well. But these men were *his* men. Not the superstitious ones from town who think Annabel holds some sort of power."

"This isn't good." Abel echoed his mother's words.

"And what happened here?" Niina must have toed a bucket filled with the remnants of the pitcher because glass clanked against tin.

"I don't know," Abel breath released in a heavy sigh that Rebecca felt reverberate through her body as though somehow he felt her pain, had inherited her fear, and was at an equal loss as to what to do next.

She stirred then, mostly because she felt she would be discovered eavesdropping and secondly because her body ached from holding still.

"There now." Niina's hand brushed Rebecca's hair back from her forehead.

Finally, Rebecca opened her eyes and met the concerned, motherly face of Niina. Behind her towered Abel, and hovering in the doorway behind Abel was the stoop-shouldered and very silent Edgar.

"She's good then?" Edgar's relief was evident by the tone of his voice.

"She'll be fine." Niina nodded. She met Rebecca's eyes. "You rest. You've not been going easy on yourself or the baby since you arrived here, and that's unwise." The reprimand was soft, as though Niina didn't hold her completely at fault. Niina turned to her son. "I'm going to go make tea for Rebecca. You stay with her."

Abel nodded as his mother pushed past him. They weren't demonstrative, mother and son, but there was an evident bond of familial loyalty between them that pricked at Rebecca. It stung her deep inside and revealed something she had never had. Never experienced. Or, at least she didn't think she had.

Rebecca frowned. That was a memory, wasn't it? The unbidden realization that she wasn't close to whoever had been or was her family?

The mattress sagged beneath Abel's weight as he lowered himself onto the edge. He searched her face. "What happened last night? I heard you scream, and then the crash. Edgar heard it up in the lighthouse. We both came running. You were all cut up from the pitcher breaking, but we couldn't get you to come to."

The memory was still as vivid as when it happened. The opening door, the creaking floor, the burst of frightful cold air, and then the black, sooty holes where the woman's—Annabel's?—eyes should have been. Her breath—the smoke-filled breath—all so real, and now it felt so like a dream. A conjured vision, real but not real. It wasn't like the other night when Kjersti's and Annabel's ghosts had come to visit. This was more like a mist. Rebecca wondered if she'd actually seen it, or if her mind was playing cruel tricks on her.

"I-I dropped the pitcher," Rebecca finally answered.

The doubt in Abel's eyes told her he didn't believe her, and the way he studied her told her he was able to see through her emotions. His eyes narrowed, scanning her features, telling her without words that he knew. He knew of her fear, her confusion, her loneliness. That she was lost inside of herself, was something he understood—and how Rebecca knew that Abel understood this was a mystery. He had not said a word and yet their exchange of looks communicated more than any vocabulary could have in that moment. Someone had once told her that when you met a kindred soul, it took no introduction, and you could sit by them for years with no names exchanged and you would be closer to them than one's own family.

Rebecca bit the inside of her lip.

Someone had once told her . . .

A sprig of hope flickered inside of her. If she was remembering little things, perhaps the big things would be soon to follow.

"All right." Abel nodded, even though he had been waiting for her to expound on her story of last night. "I'll leave it at that." Yes. He knew. He knew she was withholding, and while part of Rebecca was alarmed Abel could read her so well, another part of her was drawn to the safety of that. To have someone else wish to slip in alongside of her, to guide her—it was tempting to tell Abel all she knew. Which, admittedly, wasn't much.

But then he seemed to know something too. What had he told Niina? He'd hoped they had thought Rebecca was *dead*?

Abel cleared his throat, and Rebecca met his eyes. "They are looking for you. Men. My mother met them on her way here after Edgar went to retrieve her."

"Do you know them?" Rebecca pretended she hadn't already heard the conversation between Abel and his mother.

He shook his head and lied; she was sure of it. "No. But you must stay here, Rebecca, in the lighthouse. You mustn't go out— even to the shore. If the miners from earlier thought you were Annabel, then these men will know you are *you*."

"And they're dangerous?" Rebecca pressed, wondering why Abel wouldn't tell her what he'd meant when he identified them earlier as "*his* men"—*who* was this *he* Abel and Niina had referred to?

Abel's look told her the answer should be self-evident. "They attacked you already and left you in this state. Of course they are dangerous."

"I don't understand." She didn't mean to sound so pitiful, but her words came out before she could bite her tongue and suppress her confusion.

Abel leaned forward but didn't reach out for her, his expression urgent for her to hear him. "Do you have any idea, any idea at all what happened to you that night before Edgar found you?"

Rebecca strained to remember. Perhaps if she offered a little of her truth, Abel would reveal some of his. "The other night, I had a memory of a man shouting at me. We were on a rock outcropping, and the lake was splashing my dress. That's why I left the lighthouse, to see if I could find this rock. But—"

There was no need to reveal the vision of Annabel.

"Do you remember this man?" Abel's brow furrowed.

"He's faceless. I just recall his voice. He was so angry, so aggressive. The fear I felt was, well, it was strong . . ." Her voice trailed as she remembered, hearing the words again in her mind in all their vitriol.

Abel ducked his head, a strand of dark hair falling over his forehead. "There are men—we've already told you about them. Hilliard and his mine. The investors. Silvertown is growing, and Hilliard has big plans. If you crossed them in any way, they would want retribution." He waited as if that might engage a memory for her, or trigger something more she could provide him.

But Rebecca knew nothing. The name "Hilliard", the mine, even Silvertown felt as distant and imaginary as if it had been another life. Rebecca stilled. It *had* been another life. It had been the life before she had lost her memories.

She could only offer Abel a look of regret. She had nothing to give him for answers. "I-I don't remember. I don't know. What could I have possibly done to anger someone like him?"

Abel's mouth thinned, and he nodded in acceptance of her reply, though he gave her no answer to her inquiry. Instead, he drew in a deep breath and closed his eyes as if to center himself. When he opened them again, Rebecca was looking directly into

JAIME JO WRIGHT

those icy blue depths, only this time they had darkened. A storm was brewing inside Abel. She could see it. *Feel* it.

Yes. She could feel Abel the same way, it seemed, he could feel her. He was a tempest, he was brewing, his emotions were barely controlled and just as the lake, the calm was merely a façade for the rough waters that lay just beneath the surface. No.

She and Abel could sense other. Somehow, Rebecca knew they *understood* each other. They would not be able to keep their secrets much longer.

She stared out the window, her palm resting on her abdomen. It was firm beneath her hand, a small mound that could barely be seen, telling her she was not far along in her pregnancy.

But it meant that she had known a man, been *close* to a man, created a *child* with a man—and yet she could not recall him. Could not summon up the slightest remembrance, and it curled her insides with an anxiety Rebecca didn't know how to rein in. The questions she now considered were awful ones: Had she been happy to be with child? Did she love the child's father? Had something far more dreadful left her with the pregnancy and that was part of why she was in trouble—in danger even?

"You are a chilling reminder . . ." The man's words could be in reference to her and the babe. Perhaps they reminded this man of mistakes made, or perhaps it jeopardized his future in a way she and the babe were best gotten rid of. A scandal perhaps, or worse. She might be some man's secret, and the babe what threatened to expose him.

Rebecca strained to remember as she watched the lake rolling in with its steady waves. Edgar stood on the embankment, his hand over his eyes to shield them from the sun. It was a beautiful spring day, nature beckoned, and she was imprisoned in the lighthouse to avoid being seen.

"Do you fear the child?" The voice came in a whisper over

Rebecca's shoulder. She glanced behind her. No one was there, yet she could see the icy eyes surrounded by curling dark lashes. She could hear the tempered anticipation in her voice.

It was another memory.

It was of Kjersti.

Rebecca closed her eyes to allow the memory entrance. To remember Kjersti, if she couldn't remember Abel or Niina or Edgar.

"Do you fear the child?" Kjersti asked.

"I fear the future." That had been Rebecca's response. She had trusted Kjersti. Kjersti had been her closest friend . . . she thought.

"It will be all right." In the memory, Kjersti was folding linens, dry from the clothesline. *"You'll see. You're safe now. The babe will be safe too."*

"Will it?" Rebecca asked.

Kjersti paused, her hands gripping a pillowcase. *"Abel will make sure of it. As will Edgar. My mother will stay in town, and she'll listen . . . she'll hear if something is amiss."*

"I'm afraid." Rebecca's admission coiled within even now as she remembered.

Kjersti allowed the pillowcase to fall onto the pile of unfolded laundry.

Rebecca noticed that Kjersti had shadows under her eyes. Beads of sweat dotted her friend's forehead.

"Don't be afraid, Rebecca," Kjersti whispered.

"Are you all right, child?"

Niina's voice startled Rebecca. She jumped, spinning from her view out the window, lost in her memory of Kjersti.

"Don't be afraid."

The joy of retrieving a lost memory was shrouded in the turmoil of all the ones still swirling inside of Rebecca, unknown and yet to be seen.

Niina came alongside Rebecca, her shorter, rounder form bringing with it the smell of freshly baked cinnamon bread. She was unaware of the tumult within Rebecca. Unaware that Rebecca had remembered her daughter, Kjersti, which confirmed in Rebecca's mind what she'd assumed. She *had* known Niina and Abel and Edgar before being found on Annabel's grave. They did have a story, and whatever it was, Rebecca had been hiding here. At the lighthouse. With her babe, with Kjersti . . . She stilled, confusion swelling within her. But no. Kjersti had died here at the lighthouse. With fever. Had Kjersti's death been more recent? As in two or three months?

Rebecca's hand found the mound of her abdomen. She couldn't be more than three or four months along, could she? She was small, her pregnancy barely seen.

Niina's voice broke through her spinning thoughts, her question inane enough to bring Rebecca soaring into the present and leaving the questions deep in her subconscious.

"Do you know how the Porcupine Mountains got their name?"

Rebecca shook her head. She looked back out the window, a wistful feeling coming over her. Wistful and wishing . . . but wishing for what? That she could be free? That she could remember? That fear could be exchanged for joy? For hope?

"The Indians say that years ago, a giant porcupine took a drink from the Lake of the Clouds and was frozen for all of time." Niina's smile was indulgent of the story.

Rebecca held the lake in her focus. "It's a sad story in a way."

"It is." Niina nodded. "And you feel trapped here, like the giant porcupine, don't you?"

Rebecca gave a small laugh. "Yes." No use denying it.

Niina matched Rebecca's stare through the windowpanes. "If you were a man, I would advise you to disappear into the mountains and be rid of this life. Start a new one. Only you are not a man, and you bear a new life inside of you."

"I know." Rebecca stifled some irritation that Niina would

feel the need to remind her of what was such a weight inside of Rebecca.

"The babe is small inside you." Niina's words increased Rebecca's anxiety.

"Child," Niina continued, "I can see you're going places in your mind, entertaining fears, and that is understandable. You have experienced so much in such a short time."

"How do *you* know?" Rebecca snapped before she could bite her tongue. "I'm sorry, Niina, I—"

"No, no, it's all right." Niina shook her head. "I only wish to encourage you. To help you not drown in despair." She sighed. "However, I know . . ." Niina left her sentence unfinished.

Rebecca eyed her. "You know what?" Niina was Abel's mother. She likely knew the same things Abel was keeping from her. "What do you know, Niina?"

Niina flushed and made a pretense of wiping her already dry hands on her apron. "I know you are a good person. I can see it in you."

It was gracious, but it wasn't what Rebecca wished to hear. She decided to be more direct. "*Do* you know me, Niina?"

Niina frowned in genuine confusion. "Of course I know you."

"I mean, do you know me from before? Are you holding secret who I truly am?"

Without hesitation, Niina shook her head and refused to answer truthfully. "Rebecca, your memory will return to you. Give it time. You must give it time." She patted Rebecca's arm and then motioned toward the kitchen. "I must go check on the bread."

16

SHEA

So that her highborn kinsman came and
bore her away from me . . .
Annabel Lee

ANNABEL'S LIGHTHOUSE
PRESENT DAY

PETE WAS STILL THERE. Shea grimaced as the lighthouse came into view. Holt must have caught her look because he bid her goodbye rather quickly and veered off toward his place. Shea noticed two legs sticking out from underneath Pete's truck that he'd driven to the lighthouse the day before. She stopped and gathered her wits. A glance over shoulder told her Holt was out of sight and a guilty sensation washed over her. But it shouldn't, she argued within herself. She had come here to the lighthouse for *her* and her career, and once again, Pete was inserting himself.

"What are you doing?" She didn't mean her voice to sound as sharp as it did.

Pete's voice was muffled. "Checking the exhaust. I thought it sounded a bit loud on the way here." He maneuvered his way out from under the truck and pushed himself off the ground, brushing his hands together to wipe off any debris. "It's getting rusty, but I don't see anything serious."

"How long are you staying?" Shea didn't like herself in that moment. She heard the edge to her words. She sounded bitter. And she didn't want to turn into a bitter wife. But it was hard not to. It was hard to look at her husband after just spending lunch with Holt and comparing the two. Holt was *interested* in what she was doing. He gave her eye contact. He shared in the conversation and even bought her lunch. Pete was just—busy. Fixing things.

"I don't know." Pete was also oblivious to her tone and was horrible at reading her emotions. He looked over his shoulder at the lake. "This place is nice."

Nice? How about beautiful, or gorgeous, or entrancing? But no. Pete could barely make his way through the basic thesaurus of synonyms.

"Yes. That's one reason I came here." Shea bit her tongue before she added, "Because you never brought me."

Pete redirected his gaze back to hers, and she saw a flicker of something. Hurt? Or maybe irritation. Frankly, she couldn't read him anymore like she used to.

He proceeded to answer and disregard her not-so-veiled complaint. "I'd like to stay until your windshield is repaired. I'll check on the battery, probably replace it to be safe. I'd like to check the fluids too since I'm here. After your drive from home, it wouldn't hurt to check."

"I'm sure they're fine." Her car was newer than anything Pete drove.

"Probably." He offered a nonchalant smile and lifted his brows. "You want to get lunch?"

Well, there was Murphy's Law in action. Her cheeks warmed. "I'm not really hungry."

"Okay." Pete didn't seem to care. He patted the side of his truck like it was an old friend. "I saw there is a bar down the road a couple of miles. I was thinking of getting a burger."

Fabulous. Just what Shea needed. Penny to meet Shea's husband after she just had a mini lunch date with her bachelor landlord.

"Why don't I make you a grilled ham and cheese?" she offered quickly.

Pete's surprise was evident. He rubbed the back of his neck for a moment. Shea noticed his dark hair had gotten longer, and he needed a haircut. "Yeah, I guess."

"Okay." Shea took his acquiescence and ran with it. She started for the lighthouse. "I'll just get it started then."

"I'll follow," Pete stated.

Great. That wasn't her intention, but follow he did.

"If you were going to shoot yourself, would you shoot yourself in the head?"

Pete choked on a bite of his sandwich. "Do you *want* me to shoot myself?" he countered.

"No!" And Shea was stupidly relieved to realize she really, truly didn't. "No. I was thinking about a man named Jonathan Marks. He used to live in the lighthouse about fifteen years ago, and they found him dead with a gunshot wound to the head."

Pete considered for a moment. "It'd be a quick way to go." He took another bite of his sandwich.

"But is that how you would do it?" Shea pressed.

"I've never actually considered how I'd kill myself." He gave her a sideways glance and a raised eyebrow.

Shea knew she was being gruesome, but at least with Pete, she didn't have to pull any punches. One plus of being married to a man who had no emotional reaction to anything. Ever.

They sat outside at a picnic table in the yard that overlooked the lake while Pete ate his lunch. The sun was warm, the breeze remarkably light considering they were lakeside. At least it was a pleasant backdrop to the darkness of her train of thought. Shea couldn't let it drop. She peppered Pete with another question—he might as well earn his stay.

"And the gunshot wound was to his right temple. He was left-handed. Can you shoot yourself easily with your less dominant hand?"

"What have you been watching?"

"Just go with me here." Shea brushed him off. "If I were to shoot myself, I would hold the gun to my temple like this." She demonstrated with her finger pointing at her right temple, her hand in the shape of a gun. "The left side would feel super weird, and I don't think I'd want to risk messing up my shot by using my less dominant hand."

"I'm not sure it makes much difference," Pete replied. "Unless you're really bad at holding a gun to your head, left or right, dominant or not, the bullet goes into your brain."

"But why use your less dominant hand? Why not do what's easiest?"

"So people like you would still be talking about it fifteen years later," Pete teased.

"Funny." Shea twisted in her seat on the top of the picnic table next to Pete. Both of them rested their feet on the bench, where most people usually would have sat. "The police ruled Jonathan's death a suicide. Some of the locals say he had a severe personality change prior to his death."

"Consistent with suicide then," Pete observed, then took another bite of his grilled ham and cheese.

"I suppose." Pete had a point, and Shea didn't like it. She liked the theory of murder—if for no other reason than it added intensity to the retelling of the ghost of Annabel's Lighthouse. A man murdered after going crazy digging into a century-old legend? Her editor would eat it up. But a death by suicide? It totally killed that angle, and she was back to writing about a ghost legend like other ghost legends—more of a historical recounting with spooky elements but less of an exposé. Which, she supposed, is what she'd originally set out to do.

"What would be the motive to murder this guy?" Pete asked.

Shea glanced at him. "He was getting too close to the actual truth about Annabel's ghost?"

"Who's Annabel?"

Shea gave him a cursory rundown. It wasn't lost on her, all her internal whining about Pete never sharing her interests, and now here they were, perched in front of a scenic view and discussing the topic of her next book.

"A dead man and a ghost." Pete played devil's advocate better than Shea expected. "Well, a ghost story isn't a typical motive for murder, especially one over a hundred and fifty years old."

"Unless Jonathan uncovered something."

"Buried treasure?" Pete suggested.

"Sure!" Shea perked up, a little surprised Pete was still engaging in their conversation. "Or some elusive truth someone wanted kept buried. Apparently, he was researching another bit of history surrounding the lighthouse. A woman named Rebecca who showed up here in the late 1870s, and she didn't know who she was. It sounds like she had amnesia or something."

"I'd start there then." Pete sniffed, balling up the paper towel his sandwich had been wrapped in.

"And look for what?" Shea knew Pete wouldn't have a clue, but she asked rhetorically, more to herself than to him.

"I don't know." Pete surprised her with an answer as he pushed himself off the table. "But the bigger question, if you opt for the murder theory, is why Jonathan Marks digging into all of this would have any effect on someone wanting to kill him?" Pete shoved the wadded paper towel into the pocket of his jeans. "I'm going to go patch up that woodpecker hole in the trim over the back door."

The swift change of subject whiplashed Shea from her investigative thoughts, and she frowned. "Holt will do that. This is his property."

Pete shrugged. "I don't mind helping. Gives me something to do. I'll give him a call and make sure he's okay with it."

"Ope!" Shea's voice squeaked.

Pete shot her a quick look. "Is that all right?"

"Yeah. Yeah, that's fine." She answered too quickly, and she knew it. Pete's eyes narrowed, and then his expression normalized. "Great."

"Have fun." She was still too cheery.

Pete lifted his hand in a backward wave as he hiked back toward the lighthouse.

Shea spun around to face Lake Superior again, noting how it blended with the sky at the horizon. She had to pull herself together. She hadn't done anything wrong by sharing a pastie—which had been better than she'd expected—with Holt. It hardly equated to an affair.

She hated to admit it, but Pete was right. What had Jonathan Marks stumbled upon that would be worth someone killing him over? Or had he truly just lost himself in it all—Annabel's ghost notwithstanding—and was driven to end his life? Pete had made sense. If she found nothing, then it made the argument that there might be a hidden motive for murder a moot point—at least in relation to Annabel's Lighthouse. But in the process, she might find something intriguing to add to her book. And if digging into this bit of the lighthouse's history really had driven Jonathan Marks crazy, then—well, that added some spice to the story as well.

Shea shoved off the picnic table. Best get to it, she determined, before Annabel decided to break another window—or worse.

17

SHE PROBABLY HAD INSOMNIA. Shea stared at the ceiling, knowing even as she thought this, that there was an entirely different reason for her not sleeping. The fact that Pete's snoring could be heard an entire floor above in the attic was part of it. The other part was because to get to the bathroom, he had to come down the metal spiral stairs of the lighthouse, through her room—the lightkeeper's room—into the hallway beyond. Horribly distracting, considering Pete went to the bathroom twice a night, and because the last time she'd bothered to see him past eleven o'clock at night was at least a year ago. And during that time, he had for some reason decided to start sleeping without a shirt.

He might be the most boring man alive, but there was something to be said about naked broad shoulders in the moonlight.

With a growl, Shea rolled over in the bed, punching her pillow. The podcast on her phone had long since expired, and now she was conjuring up *feelings* for her husband. The heart was fickle, but at least she didn't have to feel guilty about these thoughts since Pete *was* her husband after all.

Nevertheless, she had no intention of a midnight jaunt to the bedroom upstairs. Seduction was the furthest thing from her mind. She had come here to *be alone.* She snatched up her phone and thumbed through a few bookmarked sites that were inspirational and meant to help encourage self-care. She needed to remember that despite her book research, her other reason for coming here was to get back in touch with herself. To heal. To rest. To bandage her tired, sore heart.

What was it her favorite women's retreat speaker from church had said when she'd attended last year? *"Until you take care of your inner self, your whole being, and find yourself grounded firmly where you need to stand, you can't take care of anyone else. Even Jesus went off to be alone. So should you."*

That was all Shea had needed to hear, even though she wasn't fond of the chic and cute speaker, who claimed to be forty-seven but looked to be twenty-three. Well, if becoming self-grounded was church-approved and helped her stay young, then sign her up!

Except life was creeping in already. Pete. The broken windshield. The convoluted murder-suicide or whatever it was that had happened. Wasn't self-care about reflection, coffee, quilts, a sepia-toned filter with neutral colors that inspired a hygge lifestyle beautiful enough for the socials? Not to mention, it seemed like the more she focused on her own self-care, the more she tended to push Pete away. To push others away. To disconnect from those around her.

Shea sat up. She needed something to drink. Water. Cranberry juice. Fruit punch. Anything. She hadn't explored her inner self much, let alone her faith, and being raised in a traditional Christian home had made her bored by the time she reached her late twenties. Enter marriage with Pete and . . . maybe that was the issue! Was she simply bored?

The low ceilings of the building attached to the lighthouse made the cramped rooms even darker as Shea made her way from the lightkeeper's room on the second floor down to the kitchen. She opened the small fridge—which Holt had called the "icebox"—and observed the few groceries she'd stocked it with. Cranberry juice it was.

After pouring a glass, Shea wandered the first floor aimlessly, stopping to look out the windows and catch different nighttime views of the property, the lake, the woods, the dark outline of the Porcupine Mountains in the distance. It was all so primal. So wild. So beautiful at night. The moon was a thumbnail, but the sky was clear, reflecting off the lake.

There was a small room off the kitchen and sitting area that Shea recalled had originally been the oil room. Having read up on the lighthouse before she'd come, Shea knew it was in this room where the keepers had stored the oil for the light, until lighthouses made the switch to kerosene instead of colza oil. Kerosene's fumes were far too toxic to store in the lighthouse. It would be unhealthy for those living in the lighthouse. Shea peered out the window in the now empty oil room, whose shelves bore vintage books and knickknacks as decor instead of for function. Across the yard, closer to the woods, was a small shed, built strong to weather the fierce Upper Peninsula winters. That had been the oil shed where the kerosene had been stored during the later lighthouse years.

Shea leaned toward the glass, brushing her forehead against the windowpane. She hadn't explored the shed yet, although it didn't appear all that interesting. But maybe there was something there she should log in her research. Old cans of kerosene or even a scent might still linger that she could include in her book to capture the essence—

Two hands slammed against the outside of the window in front of Shea's face. A dark, hooded figure blocked her view of the shed, and an even blacker liquid mashed between the skin of the hands and the windowpane. It ran down the wrists and the glass. The window trembled from the force of the hands, and Shea flung her glass of cranberry juice, a scream ripping from her throat as the hands smeared down the window. The figure seemed to sink to the ground, vanishing below the window.

Shea scrambled away, her shoulder colliding with a shelf that sent a bookend flying and a line of books toppling like dominoes. She spun wildly and charged from the oil room, her arms stretched out ahead of her to avoid running into anything. Her hands slapped against a bare chest, and Shea careened backward, managing a terrified fall onto her backside. She tried to scurry away as the figure drew near, bending over her.

She screamed again, slapping the hands that gripped her arms.

"Shea." Pete's voice broke through her panic.

Shea began to calm.

"—the heck?" Pete's frown was barely visible in the dark inner room of the house.

Without another thought, Shea flung herself against him. Pete wrapped his arms around her, just as he used to do when they were younger. Only now it wasn't for romance. It felt necessary for her survival.

Shea knew she looked a fright, but she didn't care. Her spiral hair was springing in directions altogether reminiscent of attempting to catch a radio wave. Her hands were jammed into the pocket of her blue hoodie, and her flannel pants touched the tops of her bare feet, which were shoved into flip-flops. She was bordered by two men, one her husband, one her landlord, and both were investigating the window. They all stood outside, Holt's large flashlight illuminating the area. Pete had insisted they call Holt after calling the police, who were half an hour away in Ontonagon. Holt would want to know, Pete had stated blandly. He was altogether unbothered by the event.

"Looks like blood." Holt held the light at an angle to see the smears left behind on the glass.

"It *is* blood," Shea insisted, warding off a shiver. "I saw it on the hands when they slapped the window!"

146

"Maybe," Pete said. "Corn syrup and food coloring can make good fake blood."

"Why don't you taste it?" Shea snapped sarcastically. Both men eyed her, and she dipped her head. She was scared. Freaked out. If either of these two guys had been standing in the oil room when the ghoulish invader had slapped their hands on the glass—well, they'd be more agitated too.

Holt crouched and shone the light on the ground below the window. "The grass isn't even trampled."

Pete squatted beside him, and Shea decided to join them, not wanting to be left out. Holt was right. The grass showed no signs of anyone ever having stood there.

"Where did you say this person went after hitting the window?" Holt asked Shea over his shoulder.

"The person sank," Shea answered.

The guys both twisted to look at her.

"Sank?" Holt frowned.

"Yes, sank down below the windowsill and just *disappeared*." She knew she sounded a tad bit off-center from normal.

"So whoever it was bent down to get out of sight?" Holt clarified.

Shea winced. "I mean, if I was to say what it *looked* like? It looked like a hooded phantom with human, bloody hands that simply dissipated as they sank into the earth."

"Oh," Holt said.

Pete sniffed and nodded. "The ground is dry, so I suppose someone could have stood here and not left any indentation."

Headlights swept across the yard as a vehicle came up the highway and turned onto the gravel drive.

"That's the police." Pete stood and went to greet them, still clad in his cotton sleep pants.

Holt stood also, but he lagged behind and looked down at Shea, his eyes searching her face. "Are you all right?"

She drew in a steadying breath and nodded. "Scared," she admitted, "but I'm fine."

"I'm sorry about all this," Holt stated.

"It's not your fault." Shea shook her head. "I don't know what's going on. I mean, if stuff like this happened when Jonathan Marks lived here, then I can see why the man went off his rocker."

Holt's hand gave the middle of her back a quick rub of reassurance, and Shea took strength from it, even as Pete and a police officer made their way toward them.

"Officer Ford." He gave a short nod.

"Can you fill me in on what happened?" The officer retrieved a notepad and pen.

Shea spent the next several minutes recounting the tale.

The officer took notes with the assistance of Holt's flashlight. He leaned in toward the window and studied the blood on the glass, shaking his head.

"Yeah, that's not blood. I don't know what it is, but it's not blood. Probably corn syrup."

Pete shot Shea a glance. She looked away.

Officer Ford tilted his head toward the door. "Mind if we go in where I can have more light?"

"Sure." Pete led the way, followed by the officer and then Holt and Shea.

"I thought for sure it was blood," Holt muttered. "He didn't even take a sample."

"I'm guessing Ontonagon doesn't have a CSI lab?" Shea whispered back.

Pete and Officer Ford glanced back at them as they entered the house. Once inside, they crammed around the kitchen table, where Officer Ford collected more details.

No, trespassers hadn't been a common occurrence of late, Holt informed him.

No, he didn't have any history of vandalism to the property.

Yes, they knew tourists were coming into the area to the Porkies to camp and hike.

Yes, it probably wasn't unrealistic to assume they knew about the ghost story and had creeped around the property for the adventure of it.

Officer Ford tapped the notepad with his pen. "That's probably what it was. Someone from the big city wanting to play ghost hunter."

"What about the blood? Why would someone smear blood on the window to scare the pants off me?" Shea asked.

Officer Ford looked her way. He shrugged. "Well, it's not blood. It's not paint either. I can take a sample if you want, and we can have it sent to a lab. It'll take a few weeks—"

"Don't bother." Holt's mouth thinned. "If you know for sure it's not blood—"

"It's not," Officer Ford assured him.

"Then what's the point?" Holt finished.

"Just trying to make you feel at ease, that's all." Officer Ford sucked in a breath and glanced around the room. "Been years since I've been in here."

Shea furrowed her brow.

"Years?" Holt inquired.

"Yeah." Officer Ford grimaced as though he probably shouldn't have given voice to his thoughts. Now he seemed to feel obligated to explain. "I was here when Mr. Marks was found."

"You were?" Shea's attention was sparked.

Pete's foot pressed down lightly on hers beneath the table. Why was he trying to squelch her curiosity? She pulled away and ignored him.

Officer Ford nodded. "Yeah. I was new to the force back then."

"Do you believe it was suicide?" Shea's question brought all three men's eyes to her face. Shea flustered for a second. "I was just curious. I . . ."

"It was ruled a suicide." Officer Ford's expression was sincere. "No question in my mind."

18

Rebecca

To shut her up in a sepulcher in this kingdom by the sea . . .
Annabel Lee

ANNABEL'S LIGHTHOUSE
SPRING, 1874

"C OME." EDGAR'S RASPY VOICE startled Rebecca, and she looked up from the book she was trying to read. It was dusk, with night settling in quickly. The wind had become stronger and more insistent, and she could hear the waves crashing against the shore from inside the house. Abel and his mother were in the kitchen, their voices a low murmur. "Come," Edgar repeated, motioning with his gnarled hand.

Rebecca laid the book of poetry aside and stood from the sofa to follow Edgar. The lightkeeper led her upstairs and through his room to the door that opened to the spiral staircase. She expected him to halt at the door to the attic rooms, but instead he continued the climb upward.

She had not been to the lighthouse—not to the lantern or the gallery outside of it. Now, as night descended, the wind grew in intensity and whistled through the tower, causing the metal steps to clang beneath their feet.

"This lantern wasn't here when Annabel was alive. Neither was this house." Edgar's words floated back toward Rebecca. His large feet lumbered up the steps, and when they reached the top, she was surprised at how narrow the circular walk around the lantern was.

Edgar busied himself with some maintenance to the lantern while he filled the air with his words. "Back in the day, this area was mostly Indians and trappers. I was friends with a man named John Bell at the time. He had a house he'd hewn from logs himself, along with a shop and a storehouse. Married a Chippewa woman and they had a little boy. John treated his wife well, and she kept a good home. But the Chippewa wanted the White man to pay his dues. They threatened to burn down John's buildings, but he convinced them to leave his place be, giving them pork, flour, and corn as a kind of payment. We went on to trap and live in relative peace, but now and again a group of White men would try to canoe up the Iron River just over yonder in Silvertown. But you can't get a canoe upriver more'n fifty rods because of the rocks and the falls. And it was visitors like them that made us aware this area wouldn't stay wild much longer. The Chippewa knew it too."

Rebecca listened as Edgar droned on. She'd never heard the old man speak so much, and she wasn't certain why he was telling her this now.

Edgar pushed back the canvas that hung over a portion of the glass, which was there to protect the lens from the sun's rays. "Only ten years later, the White settlers moved in and began mining for copper—that was when I first saw Annabel."

Rebecca looked at him in surprise. Edgar had not admitted to knowing Annabel personally. She waited. He rounded the lamp and opened the door to the gallery. Motioning for her to follow, Edgar stepped out into the night air. The wind was cool and brisk, nipping through Rebecca's cotton dress. The waves below rolled onto the shore with whitecaps forming. She saw a flicker of lightning off toward the horizon. The Porcupines to the east were dark blue mounds of wilderness.

Edgar gripped the rail and stared at the lake. Rebecca shirked the cold, unsure why Edgar had brought her here, and why was he speaking of Annabel? The expression on Edgar's face had changed, going from a sharp-eyed, grouchy lightkeeper into a softer, more sentimental version of himself.

"Annabel was the daughter of one of the miners. She was young, motherless, and she cooked for the men."

"Were you ever a miner?" Rebecca raised her voice to be heard over the growing insistence of the incoming storm.

Edgar shook his head, his white hair ruffling in the wind. "No. Never a miner. I trapped and fished. I knew these waters. I knew the woods."

"And you knew Annabel," Rebecca added.

Edgar gave a nod. "I did." He moved to go back to the lantern, and Rebecca followed once more, glad to come in from the cold wind. Edgar closed the door of glass and latched it tight. "Annabel was a beautiful soul, Rebecca. Don't let anyone tell you different."

She waited, still confused as to what had brought this on, why Edgar was telling her the story.

He stopped his busyness and met her gaze. "There comes a time here at the lighthouse when Annabel pays each soul a visit. Some see her as a beautiful phantom, while others see her dark side. The vengeful side. The side of Annabel who never wanted to die."

A chill made Rebecca shiver.

Edgar didn't seem to notice, yet his wrinkled face softened as he looked at Rebecca. She was surprised when she noticed tears glistening in his eyes.

"I loved Annabel."

His vulnerable admission ripped through Rebecca.

Edgar reached out as if he were going to touch her cheek with a callused, fatherly hand. Instead, he pulled it away, a lone tear trailing down his weathered cheek. "Now you know my secret."

Rebecca allowed a silent moment to pass. The water below them rolled ashore, crashed against rocks, and lulled them into a peace that was mysterious and foreboding all at the same time.

"Why are you telling me this?" she finally asked.

Edgar leaned forward, his elbows finding a familiar position on the rail that encircled the gallery. "Because we all have memories, Rebecca. Yours will come back to you, and when they do—" he hefted a deep breath, letting it out slowly as if weighing his words—"don't forget how you loved."

Concern edged its way into Rebecca's spirit, unsettling her more than she already was. "I don't understand."

Edgar nodded, staring out over the lake again. "Horror can erase love. It can make love drown beneath its weight." He was quiet for a moment, then added, "Sometimes love has to be rescued, and sometimes it's simply too late."

The wind whined outside the lighthouse, and what made things worse was her being enclosed in the attic bedroom. Enclosed and alone while the storm brewed. Thunder rumbled in the distance. Or perhaps it was closer and being cordoned off in Kjersti's room made it seem farther away.

There were no ghosts tonight, only the lingering haunting of Edgar's words. She paced the floor, debating whether to head down to the kitchen to witness the storm for herself. No doubt Edgar was still awake, tending to the lantern and keeping an eye on the storm. He reminded her of everything she couldn't remember. He'd spoken of horrors and of love, and Rebecca was certain now that she had recalled Kjersti first because Kjersti was safe. Kjersti had been a friend to her, a haven. But the rest? The unremembered parts? Abel and Niina? Were they horror or love? Rebecca wanted to know and yet she didn't. She wanted to demand they tell her what they knew of her, yet it was fear that kept her from doing so.

She crossed the room to the wall that separated her from Abel. Splaying her hand on the wall, she felt the coolness of the plaster. It was probable he slept while Edgar kept watch. One of them needed to rest so that if they needed to swap roles at some point, they could. For a moment, Rebecca thought she heard Abel. Heard his footsteps, the creaking of the floorboards beneath his feet.

Rebecca had shared moments with Niina, now with Edgar, but Abel? He kept his distance, though she felt his brooding gaze when she wasn't looking. She knew his protective nature was there, and yet she didn't trust it. She didn't trust *him*. Something about Abel felt dangerous, but in a way that was different from the fear she felt toward her attackers, more than two weeks ago now. This fear confused her. It created butterflies of the unknown in her stomach and made her want to sequester herself when Abel entered the room. But she didn't know why. She didn't—

The bedroom door opened.

Rebecca whirled and knew she had not been imagining it. Abel *had* been pacing his small sleeping quarters. He stood in her doorway, presumptuous in his entrance, wordless and brooding.

"What do you want?" she breathed, clutching at the neckline of her nightgown.

Abel's eyes were intense. The blue of them had faded until they appeared to be like ice. She believed she had seen hot iron once at a blacksmith's shop, and the smithy had told her it wasn't the blue flames that burned hottest; it was the white flames. White like the flame of Abel's eyes.

He closed the gap between them in a few long strides, and before Rebecca could react, Abel reached for her. His arms were strong and unfamiliar, muscled with the potential of force, and yet Rebecca knew she could break free at any moment and he would release her.

"I want you to remember," Abel said hoarsely. His hands held her at her waist, dangerously close to her abdomen.

Rebecca couldn't breathe. She couldn't think. She had not expected this—not at all. It was as if Abel was someone who'd been caged and had finally broken free, but now he restrained himself. Or did he?

"Do you remember?" He searched her face.

Rebecca winced, wishing she could give the lighthouse assistant whatever it was that he wanted.

Abel pulled her toward him. She didn't resist, while at the same time Rebecca knew she should. Needed to. She needed to push him away. Raising her hands, she laid them on his chest, intending to shove him back. But his chest moved up and down in barely controlled breaths. It was emotion, suppressed emotion.

"Do you remember Kjersti?" he asked.

Rebecca stilled. She'd not expected him to ask that.

"She saved you." Abel leaned forward, his breath warm on her cheek. She felt the stubble on his jaw as he spoke into her ear. His hands still held her waist. Rebecca maintained the spreading of her hands on his chest.

"How could you forget my sister?" Accusation and desperation merged together in his question.

Rebecca pulled back enough to meet his broken expression. This man, he had loved his sister. He had loved Kjersti. Rebecca could see it wounded him that she might have forgotten someone so precious and, based on his statement, someone who had rescued her.

"I remember Kjersti," Rebecca whispered.

Abel's eyes flickered.

"I remember Kjersti," she repeated.

Abel released her, staggering back. He stared at her, his eyes sparking with surprise, maybe hope, and something else she didn't understand. And then he spun and fled the room, the bedroom door closing with a bang behind him.

Rebecca stumbled to her bed, sinking onto the edge, her hands trembling.

Kjersti. This was about Kjersti.

For a moment, she had thought—or maybe she had hoped?—the emotional boiling within Abel was about her. But no. It was grief. Grief was what haunted Abel, the lightkeeper's assistant. Grief was what followed him. So desperate to keep his sister's memory close, he couldn't bear that Rebecca had forgotten Kjersti along with everything else.

Rebecca lay back on her pillow, shaking. The shock of it both confused her and frightened her. Grief. A hot tear trickled down her cheek. Kjersti. Yes. She had lost a dear friend. She knew that now. She knew that not long ago she had, more than likely, stood by Kjersti's grave, within distance of Abel, and buried her.

Kjersti was what bound Rebecca to Abel. Kjersti and nothing more.

~

The storm blew in strong and persistent during the night, and Rebecca was wide awake, along with Abel and Edgar, who were busy tending the light and keeping watch.

"I don't see any ships out tonight." Abel struggled through the door, ducking as the wind and rain blew in behind him. He pushed it shut and swiped his rain hat from his head. Drops of water fell onto the wood floor in the narrow entry. He avoided her eyes as he asked, "Is Edgar in the lighthouse?"

Rebecca turned from the stove, where she had just added

coal to the firebox. "Yes." She had the sudden urge to grab a dish towel and wipe away the rain that dripped down Abel's face. The impulse stunned her, but instead she remained frozen near the stove.

"Good. I'm going to go see if he needs anything." Abel strode through the kitchen on a mission to assist the lightkeeper. When he disappeared around the corner, Rebecca collapsed onto a chair.

Would that God had not stolen her memories in such a way! There were feelings, glimpses of the familiar, of repetition, as though she had experienced pieces of these moments at one time. And yet her memories were blurred, her mind shielded by a fog—no, a blustering storm—that whipped the recollections into wild waves that forced them deeper into the cold depths of her subconscious.

Right there. A breath away. It was as if she were drowning, but if she could just reach up, her fingers breaking the surface of the water, she could grab ahold of something firm with which she could pull herself back to safety.

The door blew open with such force, Rebecca screamed. Sheets of rain splattered the entryway, and a gust of freezing wind blew her hair across her face like a whip. She tried to collect her wits against the sudden shock of nature's intrusion. Rebecca hurried toward the door to latch it shut again. A tenuous smile touched her lips as she did so. Annabel had probably shoved the door open in her spiritous vengeance. Was it perhaps a desperate attempt to return to the man who had loved her—Edgar? The stories ricocheted in her mind as Rebecca held her forearm over her face to shield herself from the wind and the rain. She reached for the door that banged against the wall with each gale of wind.

A beefy hand appeared amid the darkness just outside the entry and yanked her into the storm. Rebecca's scream was drowned by the roaring of the waves off the lake as they lifted and fell in the distance.

A sharp pain shot through Rebecca's arm as she was hauled into the steely grip of a stranger whose face she could not see. Another man appeared then, and a rag was shoved into her mouth, pushing her tongue back against her throat and inducing a violent gag. Rebecca doubled over but was jerked upward. Her feet lifted from the ground as the man who had forced her from the lighthouse hoisted her over his shoulder. Rebecca squirmed and twisted, kicking and screaming deep in her throat.

The second man's hand cracked against her face, and he shouted a command that was washed away by the violence of the lake's fury.

Rain soaked through her dress, chilling her to the bone. Her breath was stolen as her body slammed against her captor's shoulder. She could see nothing but rain as it battered her face. She heard nothing but the grunts of her assailants as they ran into the night.

19

REBECCA LAY SPRAWLED on a wood floor covered in debris and dirt. As her eyes began to focus, so did the run-down shack around her come into focus. Its condition didn't appear to be much better than the way she felt. Wind whistled through the cracks in the shack's frame even as Rebecca's head pounded with sharp waves of pain. The rag was no longer in her mouth, thank God, but her tongue was dry, and the corners of her lips were cut and raw from the force of it being thrust into her mouth.

Rain pelted the sides of the shack, and water dripped from a hole in the roof, landing in a puddle next to her. The splash of a drop finally startled her into full awareness. She blinked rapidly against the darkness that was cut through with the faint light of a lantern sitting on the floor across the small, barren room.

Her feet were bound at her ankles, her wrists bound behind her back. Rebecca attempted to wiggle and push against the floor with her feet so she could manage a sitting position.

Heavy footsteps told her she was not alone, and sure enough a pinching grasp around her arm was confirmation of that as she was pulled up from the floor and half thrown against the wall.

She squinted up into the face of her captor, and a second shadow appeared behind him. Both men were unfamiliar. The one closest to her was built like a bear, with a beard that covered so much of his face she could see only his nose, his eyes, and a small portion of his cheeks. His hair was wet, as were his clothes.

Bending, he examined her face for an intimidating second before speaking. "You're a lot of trouble."

The accusation only confirmed in her mind that these two men had to be the assailants who had sent her fleeing into the woods before she landed on Annabel's grave.

"What do you want?" she whimpered, hearing the plea in her own voice and cursing the weakness she heard in it.

"What do we want?" The bear turned to his partner with a growling laugh. "As if she doesn't know!"

The partner was also strong, but leaner, with a face that Rebecca could see was closer to her own age, handsome in a way, but no less wicked. There was a gleam in his eyes, and she knew he had been the one to slap her across the face. This man was perhaps more dangerous than the bear.

He squatted in front of her while the bear stayed upright, his thick arms crossed over her chest as if to dare Rebecca to try anything.

As if she could.

The rope cut into her wrists and ankles. Her face burned from the abuse. She couldn't even begin to assess the baby— the *baby*.

A fresh wave of terror ripped through Rebecca. She was not staying alive for herself, there was her child. A child she had no association with, no motherly bond. A life forming inside of her she wished away for a split second, so she didn't have to be concerned for its welfare. What risks she took with her own life didn't just affect her now, they affected the babe. But this was also a life, a new life for whom she was responsible.

The man who had slapped her reached out to touch her cheek.

Rebecca winced and shrank back, but his callused fingers still grazed her skin where he had assaulted her.

"Sorry about that." His words meant nothing, and even in the dim light, Rebecca could see the sickening enjoyment in his eyes.

"Who are you?" she asked.

"Who are we, Bear?" He looked over his shoulder and called the man by the very word Rebecca had been imagining him to be.

Bear's laugh was mocking. "She doesn't know, Mercer."

"You don't, do you?" Mercer leaned in so close Rebecca could smell his breath. Cinnamon. Strange how a man could smell good and have such chiseled features and could also have eyes so devoid of empathy or mercy.

"Where is it?" he demanded.

"I don't know what you're talking about." And she didn't, though Rebecca had a feeling that she *should* know. That she *did* know. That if she could only swim through the torrents of confusion—

Mercer's hand cracked against her cheek again. Rebecca cried out, her head whipping to the side. Hot tears trailed down her face.

"Do you think we're not serious, Rebecca?"

He knew her name.

She shook her head, unable to speak. Her tongue was bleeding where she'd bit down on the force of Mercer's smack.

"Where is it?"

"I really don't know!" Rebecca cried. She pulled her knees up to her chest as best she could, but Mercer's hand shot out and pushed her knees back to the floor.

"Don't play with me."

"I'm not!" Rebecca sobbed.

"Do you want me to send Bear back to the lighthouse to pay a visit to old man Edgar, the lunatic? And to your *friend*?"

She knew he was referring to Abel. The threat was obvious,

and Rebecca looked to where Mercer crouched next to Bear. The man glowered down at her with beady eyes.

"Please . . ." Her words caught in her dry throat. Rebecca coughed wildly, and Mercer's patronizing pat on her chest did nothing to help. Rebecca squirmed so he'd move his hand, which had invaded her privacy.

"What do you think, Bear?" Mercer pushed off his knees and stood.

"Storm's not lettin' up." Bear's resistance to going back out into the weather might be the saving grace for Edgar and Abel.

Rebecca prayed she could remember whatever it was Mercer was after.

"Then we wait it out." Mercer kicked at the lone chair in the room, a straight-backed wooden one. It spun perfectly in line for him to flop onto it. His lazy sprawl indicated he intended on going nowhere. Bear turned his back to Rebecca and moved to the cold fireplace, kicking at ash and long burnt-out remnants as if wishing for a spark to ignite into a fire that would give off warmth.

They were all wet. The cabin was chilly.

Rebecca began to shiver. She couldn't control the trembling of her head or her shuddering breaths.

"She's cold." Bear's observation brought a snort from Mercer. "Good. Maybe that will force it out of her."

"Just t-tell me what it is you w-want." Rebecca's plea was reinforced by the stuttering caused by the cold.

Mercer's movement was swift, and in a second he was on the floor, straddling her legs, his hand squeezing her chin as he forced her to look at him. "The papers. *Where* are they?"

Knowing made it worse because it brought no clarity to her mind.

"You're a tough one." Mercer released her chin by whipping her head to the side. He sat back on her legs, his weight bearing down on her knees. "It's okay. I'll wait." Crossing his arms, Mercer seemed to make himself comfortable on top of her lap, even as his weight crushed her and stole any ability to calm herself.

He tilted his head, studying her. "Do you even have them?"

Them. The papers. Rebecca tried to make sense of what he was saying. If she had any papers, she didn't recall them, but they must be why she'd been attacked in the first place. What had she done? Had she stolen them?

Mercer reached out and tweaked her chin, lifting it with his thumb and forefinger, watching her close.

Rebecca stared down her nose at him, wary but unable to give him any answers even if she wanted to.

"Did you give them to your lighthouse friends? Or maybe you gave them to Aaron."

"Aaron?" Something in Rebecca sparked. She knew Aaron. Yet she didn't. Her breath quickened. But she did. Aaron. Aaron.

"Did she?" Bear asked.

Mercer's weight on Rebecca's legs was painful. She whimpered, trying to dislodge him.

"Aaron." He released her chin and tapped her chest with his forefinger. "Your little brother is mixed up in this, isn't he?"

Her brother.

Rebecca did everything she could to steel her reaction. There was no good reason to let on she couldn't remember this Aaron—this brother—of whom they referred. But now the foggiest image danced in her mind. A young man, more than a boy but not yet full grown, light hair like hers, hazel eyes like hers . . . and she remembered a smile, a laugh. Arms hugging her and then giving a playful shove.

Aaron. Her younger brother.

"Did you give them to him then?" Mercer interrupted her attempt to remember. "If you did," his added, his voice lowering menacingly, "then he's in a heap of trouble too."

"No!" Rebecca retorted. She must protect Aaron, even though she could not fully remember him.

Mercer leaned into her, his face inches away, the weight of his body hurting her legs. "Then where are the papers, Rebecca?" he spat. Saliva dotted her face.

Rebecca didn't answer. She couldn't. She still had no idea what Mercer was talking about.

20

SHEA

The angels, not half so happy as in heaven,
went envying her and me . . .
Annabel Lee

ANNABEL'S LIGHTHOUSE
PRESENT DAY

W ANT TO GO HOME?"
Pete stood in the doorway of the lightkeeper's
bedroom, coffee mug in hand, leaning against the
doorjamb.

Shea wrestled the blankets away from her shoulders as she
sat up in the bed, bleary-eyed and wishing she could take a
longer nap after not sleeping much last night. "What time is
it?" she asked.

Pete glanced at his watch. "Three p.m."

"No, I don't want to go home." Shea sprang from her afternoon

165

nest in bed and straightened her shirt over her leggings. She ruffled her curls and then gave up and reached for a baseball cap she'd hung on the bed rail. Smashing it onto her curls, she wiped the sleep from her eyes. "I want to find out what's going on."

Pete frowned, the blue of his flannel shirt making his eyes more vibrant. "I don't know if it's safe."

"I'm not afraid of corn-syrup blood," Shea retorted with a small grin. If Pete should know anything about her after a decade of marriage, it was that when challenged, she stiffened her upper lip and met it. She wasn't the type to run to the hills, cry foul, or give up.

"Then I'll stay longer."

Okay, that wasn't what she'd meant. "I don't need you to protect me, Pete." Shea patted his chest as she slipped past him and out the door of the bedroom. He followed. "I will be fine."

"I kinda like it here, though." He either ignored or didn't pick up her subtle hint that he wasn't particularly welcome. "I'm surprised."

"I told you that you would three years ago when I asked you to come to Silvertown for our anniversary." Rebecca jogged down the narrow stairs to the sitting room and into the kitchen. She looked around for her purse. Finding it, she rifled inside for her keys, then remembered she didn't have a car. "Can I take your truck?"

Pete's expression remained placid—like usual. "Sure."

"Great, where are your keys?"

"I'll drive." He set his mug on the table and edged past her toward the entryway, removing his keys from his pocket and exiting the house.

Shea released a puff of frustrated air and closed her eyes, seeking internal fortitude and patience. "Why?" She moaned to herself and then followed Pete out the door.

He was already in his truck and waiting when she reached for the passenger door. She didn't get in but waited until Pete looked at her.

"Pete, I want to do this by myself."

"I know" was all he said.

"Then can I take your truck?" Shea pressed.

Pete twisted in his seat to give her a direct look as she stood on the ground with the passenger door open. "No. I'm going with you." There was an edge to his voice that made her bristle.

"Seriously?"

"Yeah. Seriously." Pete's eyes took on a steely glint. "I don't care how much you don't like my company, Shea, I'm not messing around with your safety."

She snorted. "No one is trying to kill me, Pete."

"A busted windshield?" he countered.

"Vandalism."

"Fake blood on the window and a creeper outside?" he shot back.

"A tourist being stupid." Shea used the police's reasoning.

"A man suspiciously dying in the lighthouse." Pete made it into a statement.

"Fifteen years ago." Shea had the distinct feeling she was losing this battle.

"A ghost with a vendetta against anyone who lives in the lighthouse."

"Oh, for pity's sake!" Shea half laughed in exasperation and half glared at him. "Pete! You don't believe in ghosts."

"No, and I don't believe in coincidences, and I don't believe in leaving you hanging out to dry."

"You're not," Shea reassured her husband, at the same time realizing that one thing was certain about Pete. He could always be counted on. He was predictable. A creature of habit. But that included being there when she needed him—if not emotionally, at least physically. "I *want* to be left alone. It's why I came here in the first place."

"To get away from me," Pete added, yet there was no hurt in his voice or expression.

Shea hesitated. They'd never had a frank discussion about their dying relationship. She'd just been really good at expressing herself when it came to what she wasn't happy with, and Pete was really good at not expressing that he cared.

"Pete—"

"Get in, Shea." He patted the seat next to him in a friendly gesture. "You may not like me here, but I don't like you here alone. So we're at an impasse."

"You're acting like I can't take care of myself." Shea climbed into the cab of the truck.

"Why do women think when a man wants to protect them, they're assuming the man thinks the woman isn't tough?"

Shea had no answer to that, so she shut the door as Pete fired up the truck.

"Where are we going?" he asked as he shifted the vehicle into reverse.

Shea drew a steadying breath. She wanted to rant at him, but at the same time, a piece of her melted as she stared straight ahead, trying to figure out how Pete had pieced together a question longer than two words.

"I'm trying to find Captain Gene." Shea leaned against the counter at the diner, very aware of Pete hovering behind her and making a pretense of looking at postcards on a rack. It was obvious that even though he'd come with her with an intent to protect, he was trying to be considerate and stay out of her way.

Marnie gave Shea an apologetic smile. "Hon, I don't know what to tell you. The last time the captain was in the diner was just after Christmas."

"I have this gut feeling he could fill in some of the blanks surrounding the history of the lighthouse," Shea said, her shoulders dipping in disappointment. Out of all the locals she'd been advised to chat with, Captain Gene seemed too interesting not to try to find.

Marnie tucked a piece of graying hair behind her ear. "And Mom couldn't give you enough info?"

Shea smiled kindly. "We were interrupted by the windshield thing."

Marnie rolled her eyes. "That was awful. Mom is still talking about it. But seriously, she'd love to still chat with you! Fill in any blanks she can for your research."

Shea glanced over her shoulder at Pete, then back at Marnie. "Do you know anything about a woman named Rebecca? Apparently, she was tied to the lighthouse as well, and Jonathan Marks had been digging into her story when things got . . . weird."

Marnie's face fell, and a shadow crossed her eyes. "Oh. That story."

Shea waited.

Marnie tapped her fingernail on the counter and gave Shea a frank stare. "I don't understand what all the hoopla was about. Jonathan was so interested in it, though, and then . . . well, you know. Just everything about that lighthouse consumed him."

"You knew Jonathan too?" Shea asked.

"Too?" Marnie questioned.

"I was talking to Penny at the Dipstick Saloon and—"

"Oh." Marnie shook her head. "Penny." Then she glanced around to make sure no one was eavesdropping and lowered her voice. "Penny gets a little vicious. You need to be careful with her."

"What do you mean?" Shea asked. She felt Pete step closer behind her and knew something in Marnie's tone had piqued his curiosity.

Marnie sighed, "Oh, gosh, I hate talking ill about folks, but Penny sort of had a *thing* for Jonathan. Even back in high school. And when he moved back to the area, at first it was like he was too good for her, and then for some reason things changed.

While staying at the lighthouse, he started confiding in her or
. . . or something."

Shea waited.

Marnie sniffed, straightening a pile of diner receipts, stabbing them through with the metal prong of the receipt holder.
"Penny never really liked me. She thinks my mother tells stories.
She has all sorts of her own theories—especially when it comes
to Jonathan being killed."

"What do you think happened?" Shea was willing to set aside
her quest to find the elusive legend, Captain Gene, in light of
Marnie's willingness to confide.

"I don't know." Marnie's gaze was direct and honest. "I really
don't. Whether he was just done with life or something more
nefarious happened." Marnie sighed. "I just know that nothing
about Annabel's Lighthouse has ever been just nice, sweet history. There's something off there, like a curse. And this *Rebecca*
. . . I don't know about her. My mother might." Marnie reached
out and gave Shea's arm a pat. "Believe me, there are times I wish
that lighthouse didn't exist." Her eyes brightened then. "Oh! Did
you chat with August Fronell? Remember how I mentioned to
you a few days ago that he's the other whiz about the area? He
might know about this Rebecca character."

Shea had forgotten about him. She *had* heard his name the
first day scouting in Ontonagon, so it'd be worth following up on.

"Thanks, Marnie." She offered a grateful smile to the woman,
who returned it.

"Anytime, hon. And, really, don't be shy to knock on Mom's
door. I promise, we don't make it a habit to have bricks thrown
through the windshields of our guests' cars."

Shea laughed even as Marnie lifted her hand in a wave to
Pete. "Nice to meet you!"

He dipped his head in his silent way.

Marnie leaned forward. "Gosh, hon, you do have a looker
of a hubby, I tell you!" A conspiratorial wink and her declara-

tion floated over Shea's shoulders right to Pete, whose mouth twitched only slightly in the wake of the compliment.

Shea led the way out of the diner. She'd not told Marnie that Pete was her husband, but apparently word had gotten around town fast. And a looker? Shea gave Pete a sideways glance. Dark hair. Blue eyes. Average. *Average* was the word she'd always used to describe Pete. But for a moment, she saw him through Marnie's eyes. Square jaw, broad shoulders, unshaven whiskers . . . he was all right, she supposed.

But all right didn't make up for everything else. Everything she thought she wanted but didn't have. Everything she had but didn't think she wanted.

"Fronell?"

"Hmm?" Shea's head shot up, and she realized they were standing next to Pete's truck. He was waiting for her next move. "Oh. Sure. Yes."

"K." Pete rounded the truck to the driver's side and hopped in.

Shea climbed into the truck also, wishing for the first time in a long while that she could continue to see Pete through Marnie's eyes. Attractive. A "hubby." It was sexy and endearing simultaneously, though right now Shea could see only Pete. Just good ol' Pete.

They'd uncovered that August Fronell lived in the local nursing home after Shea had given Marnie a quick call back at the diner to ask. She should've just asked when they were there, but Marnie's comments about Pete had more than distracted her.

When Pete pulled into the parking lot of the one-story, sprawling center, Shea grimaced. "Eek. I hope I die before I get to this point."

"Why?" Pete hopped from the car.

"Because." Shea followed. "Think about it. No family to visit you. A bunch of strangers taking care of your day-to-day needs. I value my independence too much."

Pete shrugged as they walked side by side into the facility. "Might be nice."

Shea gave him a sideways look. "How so?"

"Three meals a day. Nice nurses."

"Nurses, huh?" Shea shot him a look. "I get it."

Pete didn't answer, he didn't even smile, he just held the door for Shea, and she entered ahead of him. At the registration desk, she got the directions to Mr. Fronell's room, and they started down the appropriate wing.

"I need to ask him what he knows about Annabel, about this Rebecca, and about Jonathan Marks," Shea said, even though Pete didn't seem to take much interest in anything but following her. "I'm curious if *Rebecca* even plays a part in the story, or if she's just a rabbit trail. I *do* need to stay focused on my book too. I don't know if my editor wants me to go too deep into the conspiracy theories surrounding the history of the lighthouse or focus strictly on Annabel's thread."

Again, no response from Pete, but it didn't matter because they'd reached the door of Mr. Fronell's apartment. Shea knocked. Waited. Then knocked again.

"Door's open!" a wobbly voice hollered.

Shea pushed it open and was instantly assaulted by the scent of peppermint, stale air, and the heat of a thousand fires. The elderly man must've had his thermostat set to eight-two. She noticed Pete push his sleeves up his arms after he closed the door.

August Fronell was a small man. His frame was bent at the shoulders, and his ears looked too large for his face. Wispy white hair was neatly combed, and he wore dress pants and a cardigan as though he were a little old accountant who'd forgotten he was retired. He sat in a wheelchair, his feet encased in black orthopedic shoes.

"Mr. Fronell, I'm—"

"Shea Radclyffe." The man was sharp as a whistle, as were his brown eyes. "Heard rumblings you were in town asking questions for your next book."

"You've read my books?" She smiled in pleased surprise.

"Nope. Not a one," Mr. Fronell retorted.

Pete gave a suspicious clearing of his throat.

Shea quickly swallowed her humble pie. "Well, you heard correctly. I have a lot of questions, if you'd be willing to chat with me?"

Mr. Fronell eyed her for a second. "You'd be better off chatting with Gene."

"Captain Gene?" Shea's interest perked at the same time she felt instant disappointment. August Fronell didn't seem to want company.

"Gene's the one who knows everything. 'Course, no one takes his stories seriously. Just stories, they all believe."

"And you don't?" Shea inquired.

Mr. Fronell gave her a sharp look. "Gene don't lie. What Gene says, is. That's the truth of it."

"When you say he knows 'everything' . . ."

"I mean everything." Mr. Fronell nodded. His hands massaged the arms of his wheelchair in a reflexive motion he probably didn't even realize he was doing. "He knows the truth about Annabel's Lighthouse and everything that ever went on there. Not to mention Pressie."

"The mysterious creature of Lake Superior?" Pete inserted to Shea's surprise.

Mr. Fronell smiled, his gaze bypassing Shea to take in Pete. "You betcha! You heard of Pressie?"

Pete nodded, and Mr. Fronell didn't seem to take offense at Pete's lack of words.

"There's a lot more hiding in the depths of Lake Superior than folks realize. Pressie, the shipwrecks, dead bodies, loot, treasure—it's all there."

"Treasure?" Shea interrupted skeptically, and Mr. Fronell shot her an almost irritated look.

"Sure. Shipwrecks carry more than just basic cargo."

To Shea's surprise, Pete said, "I was reading a book on the sinking of the *Edmund Fitzgerald*."

Mr. Fronell snapped his fingers. "I was around for that one. It was 1975, and that shipwreck was one for the books. I was friends with a fella from the other ship the *Fitzgerald* was on the waters with."

This had nothing to do with Annabel. Shea was growing antsy, but Pete followed Mr. Fronell's wave to take a seat, and he lowered himself onto the couch.

Shea stood in disbelief at the sudden camaraderie between the two men. The very unhelpful camaraderie.

"Did you know that in '94 they found a body of one of the crew members?" Fronell's grin wiped away any irritation from earlier.

"I didn't." Pete shook his head.

"Yep. And they've retrieved the ship's bell—all two hundred pounds of it. You can see that in the museum in Paradise."

"We should go." Pete glanced up at Shea.

He had to be kidding. But Shea let the men talk. Fronell was warming up to Pete, and in the meantime she was collecting her thoughts and how to segue from shipwrecks to Annabel's Lighthouse.

Pete looked back to Fronell. "So aside from the *Fitzgerald*, do you know of other shipwrecks?"

Fronell waved him off with a throaty chuckle. "All sorts of them. There's over ten thousand in the Great Lakes."

"Ten thousand?" Shea interjected.

Fronell seemed to have forgotten she was there, and he startled. "Only about three hundred and fifty or so in Lake Superior," he added with a scowl. "Don't know that they count the little ones in there."

"Little ones?" Pete prodded.

"Yeah. Like Annabel's," Fronell said.

Shea sent Pete a wide-eyed look. He'd totally gained the man's trust and then somehow expertly directed the conversation back to the point Shea had tried to start at. Only this time Fronell was relaxed—as long as she didn't interrupt.

"Annabel was in a shipwreck?" Pete pressed.

Fronell crinkled his nose. "Not really. Her skiff broke to pieces in the waves. She drowned. I don't think they tabulate those little ones into the calculation of ships lost in the lake."

"Why was Annabel in a skiff on the lake?" Shea inserted, taking the liberty to ease herself onto the arm of the couch by Pete and hoping her question didn't shut Fronell up.

He seemed to tolerate her inquiry. "A spat with her husband, they say. An' if we knew Annabel's last name, we could maybe figure out who her husband was. Anyway, Gene knows more, but she was married to a man in Silvertown back in the early days of the copper mines. She was married and died the same year, I think it was, and she was one of the few White women in the area at the time. Story goes, she and her husband got in a fiery spat, and Annabel pushed out in the skiff right as a storm was blowing up. Nothing her husband could do but watch as the skiff was tossed about and broke apart. Couldn't get to her. She died just off the shoreline where the lighthouse is today."

That was more than Shea had ever heard.

"Did they recover her body?" she had to ask.

Fronell gave a short nod. "They did. Buried her in the woods not far from the lighthouse."

Another new discovery. Shea bit back a smile of excitement.

Fronell continued. "Her grave was marked by an old stone. Probably tipped and grown over by now. I last saw it back in the 1980s, but there's been no reason to go back there."

"Have you heard of a woman named Rebecca?" Shea asked.

Fronell's head whipped around, and he skewered her with a look. "Why do you ask?"

"Um . . . the name just happened to come up in my research." Shea tiptoed around the truth. She was hesitant to bring up Jonathan Marks, especially as she still sat there speared by Fronell's dark eyes.

"Leave Rebecca out of it. It'll go better for you and everyone else."

Shea frowned. "But—"

Pete's hand on her knee stopped her, and she stared at him with annoyance. Pete ignored her. "Rebecca is more off-limits than Annabel." It was a statement acquiescing to Fronell's directive.

The elderly man shifted his attention to Pete and gave him a nod. "Annabel has turned legend. Folks round here love a story of a ghost set on vengeance or love—both are debated. But only a few of us old-timers know of Rebecca—and we don't talk about Rebecca. She did no good for this area. None at all."

"But . . ." Shea started, then bit her tongue. It hadn't once crossed her mind that Rebecca might be disliked according to the historical accounts. That she might be someone not worth remembering, maybe even a villainess in the story of Annabel.

"*Gene* is the only one who has the right to talk about Rebecca," Fronell finished. And it was final. Shea could read it in his expression and knew it by the way Pete stood and shook hands with the man.

The conversation was over, although now Shea wanted to find out more than anything who Rebecca was, why Captain Gene had the right to speak of her, and where in the Porkies the elusive captain might be?

Annabel

THERE'S A WISTFULNESS IN DYING.
　　The world becomes quiet around you.
　　But I can see your face. I can see in your eyes how you wish me dead.

So I will die.

For you.

I will die because of your hatred and your desperate love.

I will die for all you gave to me and all you refused me.

When death comes calling, I answer it.

When the tempest swells, I row into it.

My life is worth nothing, but you—you are worth everything.

There is a wistfulness in dying, for the loss of what was, what is, and what could be.

The loss of *what could be* is what haunts me most.

It's the *what* that will *never* be that will chase after you when I am gone, riding on the cold breath of my watery vengeance. I shall never release you, my heart and my soul. You are what gave me breath. You are what gave me death.

I made my vows, and I shall keep them.

Even in death we shall not part.

21

REBECCA

Yes!—that was the reason (as all men know,
in this kingdom by the sea) . . .

Annabel Lee

ANNABEL'S LIGHTHOUSE
SPRING, 1874

SHE WAS SHIVERING UNCONTROLLABLY as morning dawned and light enveloped the shack. Mercer had long since removed himself from his seat atop her, but Rebecca still writhed from the violation of his weight, even though he'd done nothing to take advantage of her otherwise.

Bear snored in the corner of the cabin, and somehow Mercer did as well. Both men were oblivious to the chill of the room, the dampness of their clothes, and the fact that Rebecca's wrists dripped blood on the floor as she worked to loosen her bindings.

She had been able to wriggle enough space between the ropes

around her wrists that she could finally pull her hands free of them. Still, the action was painful, her skin raw. Rebecca bit down on her lip to distract her from the pain of her hands as she tugged her right hand free. When it came loose, she shook off the rope with her left hand and then paused.

Both men still slept, so sure they were that she was subdued by their domination. And in a way, she was. She was terrified by every sniff and grunt they made in their sleep. Now, as she pulled her arms around to her front, she caught her breath as her muscles cramped from being held back for hours. Rebecca's breaths came in little gasps as she forced herself to relax and let her muscles cease screaming at their new position. She buried her wrists in the damp fabric of her dress, taking small comfort from the coolness found there against the abrasions on her skin.

The bindings around her ankles were looser, and after Rebecca watched Mercer and Bear for long seconds to be sure they still slept, she leaned forward and worked at the ropes until her feet were free.

Desperate to scramble to her feet and run toward freedom, Rebecca forced herself to remain still. If she moved too quickly, she risked startling them awake. Assuming she was lucky enough to get out of the shack, Rebecca had no idea which direction to run to for safety, and she believed she could not outrun either man.

Rebecca shuddered to think what Mercer would do were he to catch her. The hatred in his eyes was the kind that pleased a man to feel wicked, and no pleading or begging would sway him toward mercy. Mercer's intoxication with hating her would drive him to abuse her more thoroughly, more violently.

For the babe, she could not risk it.

No. To escape, she would need to move quietly in a methodical fashion so as not to awaken the men. And then, once out of the shack, she would need to quickly decide which direction to run.

Listen for the waves.

Keep the sun to your east.

Look for the mountains.

Rebecca silently recited her three points of reference in hopes they would make sense once she was free.

She eased onto her feet, every nerve in her body on fire from being bound. Glancing down, Rebecca made sure her toes were securely engaged with her slippers so that she wouldn't stumble. She stealthily tiptoed toward the door of the shack.

Bear snorted, and she froze, staring at him as he leaned against the wall, his chin tucked into his chest and his hairy face just shy of appearing fully beast with no sign of man. Assured he was still asleep, Rebecca focused on Mercer. His eyes were narrow slits, and he was watching her with a thin smile of pure enjoyment.

"Going somewhere?" His voice sliced through the stillness.

Rebecca lunged for the door.

Mercer leaped to his feet, but Rebecca managed to evade his first grab at her, slamming her hand against his face and connecting with his nose harder than she had even intended. Mercer growled as blood spurt from his nose.

Rebecca ran. She forgot about the east, about looking for the Porcupines' ridgeline. Instead, she sprinted toward the sound of the lake. The waves. She plunged through the woods, her feet trampling ferns and sticks, hopping over a downed tree, a branch catching her dress. It ripped at her waist, but Rebecca continued to flee, hearing the shouts of Mercer and Bear behind her.

A glimpse of the water through the trees beckoned her. She surged ahead, breaking free from the forest. Her feet connected with the sand of the shore, crunching over driftwood and stones. Boulders and a cliff outcropping were to her right, so Rebecca veered to the left, seeing only shoreline, more driftwood and rocks. She heard the endless cadence of wave after wave coming ashore.

The water. If she ran into the lake, she could let it take her away, for drowning would be preferable to Mercer and Bear.

Delirious, Rebecca cried out as she twisted to see Mercer breaking free from the woods mere yards behind her. She had no time. The sand sucked at her feet like shackles holding her back. The only sand that would be firm enough to run on was the wet sand.

Rebecca raced toward the water, her slippers peeling off as she ran, and now the tender skin of her feet met the freezing cold of the lake.

Mercer was gaining fast, but Rebecca pushed forward, splashing at the edge of the lake as she sprinted along the shoreline. An outcropping rose up ahead, and without thinking it through, Rebecca veered toward it, seconds later stumbling to a slippery halt on the black basalt.

This was it. She'd been here before.

The outcropping.

You are a chilling reminder . . .

"Ha!" Mercer's laugh filled the air. He stood on the shore, and Rebecca realized she had allowed herself to be cornered by him. The lake was at her back, her body balanced precariously on the slick rock.

Mercer stood on the shore and waved his fingers. "Come on now. You've nowhere to go."

Rebecca looked over her shoulder at the lake. It wasn't horribly deep here, but if she were to jump in, the water would still swallow her with its numbing temperatures and insistent waves.

Concern flickered on Mercer's face as he read her thoughts. He glanced past her to the lake and then back again. "Come here, Rebecca."

She considered.

You are a chilling reminder . . . The words repeated again in her mind. The man's voice wasn't Mercer's, and in her soul she knew it didn't belong to her brother, Aaron, either. What should she do now? If she obeyed Mercer, she would return to captivity and perhaps endanger Aaron even more, if she couldn't produce whatever it was Mercer demanded. But if she leapt into the lake . . . would she join Annabel permanently?

What about her baby?

Rebecca stared at the water.

"No!" Mercer's shout was muffled behind her.

Rebecca wasted no time. Flinging herself into a wave, she dove underwater. Her breath was stolen in an instant. The frigid cold locked her lungs, and she could not inhale either air or water. Tiny spears attacked her nerve endings, which protested the inhuman coldness of the lake.

She no longer worried about Mercer or Bear. When her feet hit the sandy bottom, she pushed off with all her strength, rising to the top of the waves and standing. The water was chest-high, and even as her face broke into the air, Rebecca's mouth was still open, still gasping to take in the blessed oxygen that would allow her mind to clear.

A wave careened into her, pulling her under with a force that sent her to the bottom of the lake. Rocks grazed her legs, and she couldn't find her footing, as the rocks were slippery and cut into her feet. She was deep enough that the force of the insistent waves continued to hold her under just as her nose and mouth broke the water's surface for air.

She was going to die.

She was going to drown.

She was—

Arms hooked under hers and hauled her upward. Rebecca clawed at the air and at the hands holding her. She was able to suck in small amounts of oxygen even as the cold syphoned the remaining energy from her body.

Her shoulders collided with wood, which scraped her back as she was yanked from the lake. The edge of a flat-bottomed skiff bruised her as she fell into the boat, a sodden and breathless pile.

Oars lifted over her head as someone lowered them into the

lake and began a steady but urgent rowing, keeping parallel to the shoreline.

Rebecca managed to look up at the silhouette of the man. It was neither Mercer nor Bear. She noticed the grim set to his face. When he glanced down at her, she saw the man was Abel. There was murder in his eyes, and Rebecca knew in that moment he would kill for her.

"Get blankets." Abel's command was a distant echo in Rebecca's ears. Her body was jostled as he carried her into the lighthouse after hefting her from the skiff. "Lock the doors. Set a watch."

Edgar's voice muttered something in return, and for a brief second, Rebecca felt the lightkeeper's gentle hand on her cheek.

"God help her." His words brushed over her as Abel carried her through the house. It was tricky getting up the narrow stairway. Rebecca tried to open her eyes, tried to lift her arms to wrap around Abel's neck, but her body refused to cooperate.

Abel was in Edgar's room and seemed to have no intention to go farther. Maneuvering up the spiral stairs of the lighthouse to the attic was out of the question. He didn't bother to ask permission as he laid her on Edgar's cot. His fingers found the buttons of her wet dress, and he hurried to remove it.

"I'm sorry," Rebecca heard him breathe as he finished stripping her of her wet garments, doing his best to cover her with a blanket as he did so.

Garments removed, Abel tucked another quilt around her body, leaving her feet exposed. He sat on the end of the cot and rubbed them vigorously with his hands, inspiring her blood to flow and bring warmth to her toes.

"S-so c-cold," Rebecca struggled to tell him.

"I know." Abel wrapped the quilt around her feet and climbed onto the cot next to her, pulling her blanket-clad body into his arms. He held her for several minutes, the warmth of his body enveloping her.

Once her teeth began to chatter less, he lifted his face to peer into her eyes. "I'm going to go heat some rocks for the bed warmer. Stay here."

All she could do was nod. She had no intention of going anywhere. For the first time in what seemed like days, warmth was beginning to spread through her extremities. Exhaustion pulled at her, but fear was awakening again, and Rebecca struggled to sit up. There was a window at the head of the lightkeeper's cot, and one to the left of her, with the cot pushed into the corner. When Edgar slept here, it would provide him with a perfect view of the lake and the light from the lantern, as well as ships in the distance. Now it gave Rebecca a clear view of the shore. If Mercer and Bear were coming . . .

No.

She saw no one. No one but Edgar, who was standing in the midmorning sun, a rifle propped in his elbow, his stooped shoulders as straight as he could make them. No longer did Edgar look like a weathered old lightkeeper. Instead, he appeared to have summoned the man of his youth, a fierce defender ready to go to battle.

To battle for her.

Footsteps alerted Rebecca to Abel's return. He entered, a steaming mug of tea in one hand and a long-handled copper bed warmer in the other. He slid the warmer beneath the blankets and then helped to prop pillows behind Rebecca so she could receive the mug of tea.

"Do you have much pain?" Abel's eyes were gentle, but as he took inventory of her raw wrists, they darkened.

Rebecca allowed the sip of hot tea to soothe its way down her throat and warm her insides. "My body is sore, bruised," she answered.

"But is there pain . . . ?" Abel stuttered to a halt. He met her eyes. "In your . . . where the babe is."

It was a tender subject, but Rebecca was startled to realize she'd forgotten her pregnancy for the moment. Escape had been foremost on her mind, followed by the acceptance of death. The baby fled her thoughts in the traumatic moments of earlier.

"I-I think I'm all right. I think the baby's all right too." She didn't know, of course, not really. And she didn't know what she should feel on a normal day of being an expectant mother when the child inside her kicked or squirmed.

"Who did this?" Abel's voice was grave. He hadn't released her hand, and his thumb brushed over her knuckles in a possessive sort of way she didn't understand or expect.

"Two men." Rebecca was thankful that at least this time her mind had not erased the abuse. "A man named Mercer, and another who goes by the name Bear."

Abel's jaw tightened. "All right."

She knew then there was no law in the area, no real authority Abel could seek out on her behalf. She also knew that on hearing their names, it had confirmed whatever information Abel possessed and had not shared with her.

"Who are they?" She drew her hand away from Abel's.

· Abel swallowed, clearing his throat. "Did they tell you what they wanted—why they took you?"

"They asked me to tell them where I'd put the papers."

Abel frowned. "The papers?"

Rebecca shook her head, thankful that the bed warmer had ceased the involuntary shivers. "I don't know. I can't remember. They thought I was lying."

"But you weren't?" Abel looked sheepish the minute he asked.

"I wasn't lying." Rebecca gritted through her teeth, hurt and suddenly irritated that Abel would even raise the question she might be pretending her memory was lost. "But I—do I have a brother?"

Abel froze.

Rebecca held the tea between her palms, and a protectiveness washed over her. She did. She could see on Abel's face that he knew him too. "Aaron," Rebecca supplied.

Abel stared at her.

"If they hurt Aaron, it will be all my fault." Rebecca set the mug on a side table and struggled to free herself from the blankets.

"Rebecca." Abel pressed gently on her shoulders to push her back against the pillows. "You're in no condition to help him."

"But you knew I had a brother," she accused, unable to quench the ferocity that filled her. A ferocity she would have expected to feel for her unborn child but was so raw and visceral when it came to Aaron, the young man she could barely see in her mind.

Abel raked his hand through his hair, agitated, his breath expelling shakily. "We're trying to keep you safe, Rebecca. And I don't know what happened. The attack you suffered was horrific and—"

"What are the papers they're asking for?" Rebecca demanded.

Abel looked bewildered. "I don't know."

"And my brother, where is he?"

He shook his head. "I don't know that either."

"What *do* you know? Tell me!" Rebecca slammed her fists against the mattress, glaring at the man who eyed her with caution and not a little wariness. Something had awakened in her, and while it wasn't all clear, she knew. She knew what she had to say. Leaning toward Abel, she clenched her teeth. "You loved your sister. We both loved Kjersti. So why should I have any less devotion to my own brother? Why would you keep him from me?"

Abel's face darkened. He blinked repeatedly, and Rebecca thought she saw tears for a moment, and then they dissolved. "I'm not keeping Aaron from you. I'm keeping *you* from Aaron. To keep you safe." He took a step back and said, "Stay here. Edgar will watch over you. I've no doubt that if Mercer or Bear show their faces around here again, they're dead men."

Rebecca was stunned that Abel would refuse to tell her more, and stunned that he would leave her here, separated from her family. "Where are you going?" she demanded.

Abel hesitated before giving a reply. "I'm going to fetch my mother. You need her."

It was a half-truth, Rebecca knew. Abel was going to fetch Niina, yes, but he was on a mission to do something else as well.

"Abel?" Rebecca stopped him, and he turned in the doorway to look at her. "Who am I?"

She knew that he knew.

"Get some rest, Rebecca," Abel said, then disappeared into the hall.

22

SHEA

That the wind came out of the cloud by night,
chilling and killing my Annabel Lee . . .
Annabel Lee

ANNABEL'S LIGHTHOUSE
PRESENT DAY

SHEA HAD DODGED PETE the morning following their interlude with August Fronell while he was out combing the shore for fossils. He'd been reading a book about fossils in Lake Superior last night before she'd gone to bed, and he'd barely looked up when she said good-night. The day together had been a mixture of uninterpretable emotions. One moment she was irritated he was there, and the next moment Shea had little glimpses back into the early days of their marriage when they'd done things together, when they'd worked well together.

August Fronell was an example of that. Shea couldn't help

but be impressed at the way Pete had directed the conversation and won the elderly man's friendship. That Fronell's mind was sharp, was clear, and he hadn't been manipulated by Pete, but genuinely won over. The only piece of the conversation that had bothered her was when they'd bidden Fronell a thank-you and goodbye, and Pete had promised to pay him a visit in the future for a game of chess.

Chess? The future?

Pete should be getting ready to go home now, despite his husbandly ambitions to protect her from ghosts and snooping tourists.

Shea bounced on the seat of Holt's truck as it hit a pothole. Yes, Pete should go home. Although she noticed Holt was more standoffish today. Friendly, but not nearly in the warm way he had been when she'd first arrived at the lighthouse. Yet he'd been willing to pick her up this morning and take her to Ontonagon to get her car. The windshield was repaired, the message on her voicemail had stated this morning. It was a stroke of luck Holt was on the lighthouse grounds working on maintenance issues, and so Shea had left a note for Pete—so he knew where she was and wouldn't interrupt her by trying to track her down—and garnered Holt's assistance.

"I can drop you off at the glass repair shop first." Holt kept his attention on the road ahead, bordered by wilderness. The trees whizzed by on either side, with Lake Superior being an occasional blue glimpse between thick trunks and forest growth.

"Thanks." Shea smiled but suddenly felt awkward. Silence drifted between them, and then she ventured, "Do you know where I could even begin to look for Captain Gene?" He seemed to be the universal answer for who the best person was to talk to about the history of Annabel and the lighthouse.

Holt gave her a sideways glance. "Not a clue. Well, that's not entirely true. They say he has a cabin somewhere in the Porcupine Mountains State Park."

"You can live on state park land?" she asked.

Holt's chuckle eased some of the tension. "Nope. You can't. Which is why they *say* Captain Gene has a cabin there, but no one has ever found it."

"Where else might he live?" Shea's question followed the swift deduction that, aside from Ontonagon and Silvertown—with Silvertown being a pit stop on the way through to the Porkies—there wasn't much else for options in the northern wilderness area.

"I personally believe he's a drifter." Holt checked his speed-ometer and let off the gas a bit. "I think he just roams and lives off the land, and no one really questions it. Even if he strays into state land, Captain Gene is just, well, a fixture of the area. Kind of like Pressie, you know? Rarely seen, debated existence, legendary intrigue and local fame."

"So local enigma spots local lake monster and . . . huh." Shea cut off her line of reasoning.

"What?" Holt pressed.

"Well." Shea thumbed the screen on her phone. No signal. "I'm just thinking, even if Captain Gene had a lot to tell me, how could any of it be substantiated?"

Holt's chuckle helped Shea relax despite her skepticism about Captain Gene. "Shea, if you're writing a historical record, then Captain Gene won't be in the bibliography of reliable resources. But then neither would Edna, or August Fronell, or really any veteran of the area. This place is steeped in lore and legend. It was that way long before the Europeans set foot here. So if you're wanting verifiable historical facts?" Holt clucked his tongue. "Good luck with that."

"I've been deducing that very thing." Shea opened the notes app on her phone and typed in a few key words: *conspiracy, legend, theory*. She'd need to contact Pat, her editor, and reassure herself that he'd be okay with the book taking a more legends-and-lore feel rather than a historical recounting like her others. "Why is

Captain Gene considered the authority on all things Annabel's Lighthouse anyway? No one's been able to clear that up for me."

Holt slowed as a white-tailed doe pranced across the highway. He watched carefully for any more, but none followed. Speeding up, he answered, "Captain Gene worked on the lake as far back as the mid-fifties. He has roots here that run deep. He's fifth generation to the region."

"How old is he?"

"Probably in his nineties."

"And he lives off the land?" Shea's disbelief carried through the cab of the truck.

"He's a tough old geezer who prefers his own company. Heck, he could be dead for all we know. No one's seen him since last Christmas."

"That's what Marnie said." Shea sagged back against the seat and blew out a sigh. "I feel like I'm fighting a losing battle trying to find him."

"You probably are," Holt agreed. "To be honest, it's better if you don't worry about the other angles to the lighthouse's past. Like Jonathan and this Rebecca person. Just focus on Annabel. There's enough there to write about, isn't there?"

"Is there?" Shea asked doubtfully, glancing at her phone again. Still no signal, and the only reason she was curious was that she expected Pete to text her. That was what a guilty conscience did to a person—it made them look over their shoulder. But all she'd done was ask to Holt for a ride. Nothing more. She gathered her wits and continued, "I have a very basic ghost story. I don't know that anything I've learned about Annabel will be enough for an entire book."

Shea felt defeated. Annabel's ghost was an interesting story. The fact she'd been married was a good start, but hardly an entire chapter's worth of material. And since she'd died in 1852, the records were sketchy and slim. "I probably should've gone to the Pacific Northwest like my editor suggested."

It also would have been far enough away for Pete not to follow. And honestly, far enough away that Holt would never have entered the picture.

Shea felt grimy. Inside. Nothing here was working in her favor, and now? Now she was beginning to not like even herself. Her self-confidence was waning, and that familiar roiling in her stomach that she'd been trying to get away from by coming here to write and engage in self-care was returning.

She wanted to blame Annabel and the lack of historical documentation. She wanted to blame Holt for being so kind and considerate and stupidly good-looking.

She really wanted to blame Pete for disrupting everything.

But mostly she blamed herself for ever letting things get so bad. No, not bad. More like *stagnant*. Like pond water covered with green slime because there was no freshwater flowing in. And stagnancy stunk. Literally. She'd smelled dying ponds before.

As the woods finally cleared, Lake Superior broke into view. It stole Shea's attention and her breath for a moment.

Like the lake, freshwater came with its own unpredictable currents. It was untamed. It was dangerous. It was cold and unforgiving, yet it was gentle and beautiful at the same time. Avoiding the stagnancy wouldn't result in a vibrant life; that required flooding it with freshwater.

Which could only mean one thing really.

A storm was coming, and Shea was going to need a lighthouse to show her the way out of it.

Shea's throat hurt from asking so many questions. She sat in the driver's seat of her newly repaired car and ran a mental inventory of the places she'd visited to inquire as to the whereabouts of Captain Gene. Part of her wondered if he even existed or if he was just a convenient way for the locals to send wannabe mystery-solvers like her on a wild goose chase.

She'd been to the diner and had coffee with Marnie. The dear soul had given her a few more options to check into. The supermarket manager's mother's cousin had worked with Captain Gene back in '84. Maybe they'd have an idea where the old man was. Then there was the privately owned and run pawnshop with the retired shipman who apparently had been pals with Captain Gene. But for the most part, the town seemed to be tight-lipped, as if Captain Gene were a secret and they were protecting him. Or maybe he was protecting them somehow. The library kept archives she could peruse on microfiche if she wanted. She could probably dig up records on Gene while researching the history of Ontonagon and Silvertown.

Shea preferred to interview people yet living if possible before desperation drove her to a library and the migraine-inducing time spent with old newspapers. So she'd followed Marnie's lead and visited the supermarket manager whose distant cousin now lived in Nevada somewhere; they'd since lost touch with each other. The pawnshop shipman wasn't much help either. He'd been more interested in selling her something than answering questions. One lead he'd given had led her back to the retirement community to chat with another resident, who pretty much repeated word for word August Fronell's advice: "Leave Captain Gene alone."

Now, hungry and discouraged, Shea noticed Pete's text had finally come through once her phone connected to the Wi-Fi at the retirement home. She sat in the parking lot and checked the message.

You alive?

Hesitating, Shea considered not answering, but then a pang of guilt shot through her. It was Pete. He was there for her. She owed him an answer at least.

I'm fine. Just got my car and am doing some research.

There. That was an acceptable response, right?

She shrugged it off and started the car, veering back onto the road from the retirement home. What if the ninety-something old man really was dead? What if Captain Gene had wandered into the woods and had frozen to death during the brutal Upper Peninsula winter? No, it didn't make sense that anyone in the twenty-first century would be living off the land in an environment that wasn't conducive to survival. The U.P. could average sixteen feet of snow during the winter months. How was a ninety-year-old man going to hole up and live in those conditions? If he had a cabin, it would've been found by someone by now, and there was no way he'd be in any condition to disappear so deep into the sixty thousand or so acres of the Porkies that no one would see him.

No. Shea concluded that Captain Gene had to be a well-kept secret. Someone in Ontonagon knew where he was. Someone in Silvertown knew. Someone somewhere was making sure the old man had food and water and a place to stay warm. There was no way anyone could convince her that Captain Gene was anything less than a legend that would carry on in these parts *ad infinitum.* But there was also no way he was anything more than an old man staring down death somewhere safe while his body continued its journey toward the grave.

She didn't mean to be harsh, but realistically it was ludicrous to fall for the tales that claimed Captain Gene was still out there, a wanderer. The man was simply too old.

Her phone rang via her car's Bluetooth and startled Shea as she drove out of Ontonagon. She tapped the answer button on the steering wheel. "Hello?"

"Shea?" It was Holt.

"Yep, what's up?"

"You need to get back to the lighthouse. Now." The urgency in Holt's voice stiffened her spine and brought Shea into full alert.

"What's wrong?"

"It's Pete. He fell."

"Is he okay?" Shea knew he probably wasn't if Holt was calling her. A broken ankle? Leg?

"Shea, he fell from the lighthouse."

Her foot pressed harder on the gas pedal. She gripped the steering wheel tighter. "What? Where?" She didn't understand.

"He fell from the gallery—from the lighthouse balcony."

"Oh no . . ." Shea breathed, her throat closing in instant panic.

"Drive careful, Shea, but get here ASAP. I called the EMTs, but . . . I think it's bad."

23

THE FACT THE AMBULANCE PASSED HER on the highway going toward Ontonagon from where she'd just been did nothing to make Shea feel any better. She had spun on the gravel shoulder, turning her car back toward Ontonagon and the hospital and thought *she* was driving fast. She floored the gas pedal, remembering her childhood when her mom, for fun, would yell "pedal to the metal!" and take off at top speed from a stop sign. Probably not the best of parental choices, but it was a happy memory. Until now. Now when Shea had to apply it in an emergency. How had Pete fallen from the lighthouse of all places? A person didn't just lean and flip over the side!

Shea pounded the wheel as trees whipped by on either side. Pete. Predictable Pete. A tear escaped her eyes, and then another. When had they grown so platonic? When they were younger, Pete had been the hometown boy, the one she wanted to plant her roots with. What had changed? Was it her? Was it her overblown romantic notions? Too many streaming-service romances that had gotten under her skin?

Thankful there were no four-way stops or intersections to

make her slow down, Shea glanced at her speed. Seventy-five? She could raise that by at least ten. Cops out here were few and far between, and the greater risk was in hitting wildlife. She increased her speed while considering literally flooring it.

A memory of Pete when they were newly married flooded her senses. He'd been at the kitchen table eating cereal. Shirtless. Wearing boxers. It was a Saturday morning, and twenty-something Shea had thought he was the sexiest thing since Mr. Darcy himself. She'd come up behind him and wrapped her arms around his neck, running her hands down his chest. The man had jumped—literally startled—sending his cereal bowl flying, milk spilling everywhere. His look had been incredulous. Stunned. Confused.

"What the heck are you doing?" He wasn't angry; he was one hundred percent taken by surprise.

Shea recalled her laughter as milk dripped down his chest, but Pete had just stared at her. The shock of the moment had stilled him into wordlessness. Her smile had waned. He'd reached for a washcloth and begun cleaning up. He didn't reprimand her, but he certainly didn't respond the way she'd expected him to. The standard belief was wink at a man and he'd come running. But Pete? He liked predictability. She liked to act on impulse.

Even then the gap had widened between them. She'd even taken to reading books to see if her new husband was maybe on the spectrum somewhere. She'd asked herself how she'd not noticed his inability to do things on the spur of the moment. But there was no magic diagnosis. It was just Pete. She was just Shea. Back then she'd accepted it. Now?

Shea swiped at the tears that trailed down her cheeks. Guilt rolled in her stomach. Guilt about her attraction to Holt. Guilt that she was tired of Pete. Guilt that she still prayed he would somehow change and become, what, different? Fun? Affectionate?

Another memory slammed into her. That night a few years

ago when she'd been sick with stomach flu. He'd stood in the bathroom with her. He retrieved a cold washcloth for her forehead. He cleaned up the mess. He'd sat in the chair next to her until she fell asleep. When she'd awakened the next morning, he was still there. Bright-eyed and bushy-tailed with a mechanic's manual on his lap. *"You good?"* he'd asked blandly.

She'd nodded. Then he had gone about his day.

Shea threw her head back against the headrest as she pushed the gas pedal even more toward the floor. He was boring. But he was there. He was *there*! How many women would *kill* to have a husband who was there. Always. Reliable. Never wavering. Maybe there were no clandestine kisses. Maybe he was immune to feminine wiles, but that was sort of nice too in a way. She knew he was faithful. When they were together, it was only her. He didn't whisper dramatic words and memorable one-liners that could be the script for a romantic movie, but he was . . .

"Please, God," Shea prayed aloud, "don't let Pete die."

"Is Pete okay? What's going on?" Shea demanded, wrestling against Holt's grip.

"Shea."

"Let me go, Holt!" She wrenched away, took two steps, and then was caught again by Holt, this time with an arm around her waist, pulling her toward him. She knew everyone in the hospital was staring at her, but she didn't care. Shea searched his face with desperation. What she saw sent cold waves through her body. "No. No, no, no." She shook her head. The pulsating realization of grief knocked her knees out from under her.

Holt caught her against him. "He's alive."

Her breath caught, and she snapped her head back to stare at Holt. "He's alive?"

"He is. It's not as bad as I first thought."

The relief she felt didn't assuage the worry. "Tell me what happened." There was steel in her words. She was losing patience. "No. First, I need to see him."

Holt released her when she shoved away from him. He raked his hand through his hair. "They won't let anyone see him yet. He's getting a CT scan and an MRI."

"What happened?" Shea's resolve was crumbling.

"I stopped by to work on some repairs to the oil shed," answered Holt. "I saw Pete on the lawn, directly under the lighthouse. When I got to him . . . he was pretty messed up."

"What do you mean 'messed up'? Did he say anything?" Shea curled her fingers into the front of Holt's shirt.

Holt winced. "He was in a lot of pain, Shea. His arm or shoulder—it has to be broken. He tried, but—"

"But what?"

"All he got out was—"

"*What?*" Shea slammed her palm against Holt's chest.

He stumbled back, frowning. "'Annabel.' He said 'Annabel.' But he didn't elaborate. He was writhing in pain."

She snorted in disbelief and stepped away from Holt, scanning the hospital for a nurse, a doctor, anyone who could give her a better explanation. She took off toward the nurses' station.

"Where are you going?" Holt hurried after her. "Shea!"

"No." Shea waved him off, blinking back tears that burned.

"But—"

She leveled a fierce look on Holt. "You want me to believe that Pete thinks a *poltergeist* pushed him off the lighthouse?"

Holt grabbed at Shea's arm, but she wrenched it away.

"I'm only repeating what Pete said, Shea. But they won't let you see Pete, not yet. And you need to calm down. You're too panicked."

"I'm going to see my husband." Shea glared at Holt, trying to piece together a fall from a lighthouse. None of it made one iota of sense. "While I go see Pete, I suggest you come up with a heckuva better story than that a ghost shoved Pete off the gallery!"

She didn't blame Holt. Not really. He was trying to help, to protect her even, but the idea that Pete's only response was "Annabel"? It was stupid. It was asinine. It was horrific. And while Shea didn't believe that a ghost was behind Pete's fall, she couldn't shake the reminder of Penny's declaration from the other day about Jonathan Marks:

"Fact is, he was the last person I know to try to understand Annabel and the lighthouse, and . . . well, the cursed story killed him."

Penny had been speaking of Jonathan, but now Shea was terrified it applied to Pete as well.

⁓

She had never felt so alone in all her life. Maybe it would've been a good idea to allow Holt to accompany her to Pete's room. They had told her she could wait there—at least it wasn't ICU. That was a good sign, wasn't it? They had taken Pete back for who knows what litany of tests, and now she sat in the room staring at an empty hospital bed, thinking over every possible good and bad scenario she could.

Holt had to have heard Pete wrong. Annabel? It just didn't make any sense. But if Pete fell from the lighthouse, how was he even alive? The ground below the structure was essentially a geological rock plate hidden beneath the grass. There was no give in it, no bushes to soften a fall. Either a miracle had taken place, or Holt had misread the situation, or—

"Mrs. Radclyffe?"

Yesterday Shea would've grimaced hearing that. Now she didn't care. She shot to her feet as a doctor entered the room. She had kind green eyes and a smattering of freckles across her nose. Her scrubs were clean but wrinkled, and she wore a white jacket. All in all, her expression was one hundred percent unreadable.

"How's Pete?" Shea was breathless.

No death. Please, no death.

The doctor extended her hand. "Emily Sturgeon," she stated by way of introduction. "Pete is going to be all right."

Shea's relief was palpable, and she collapsed onto the chair she had been sitting in.

Dr. Sturgeon continued, a smile of understanding on her face. "Your husband sustained a proximal humeral fracture."

Shea blinked. "A what?"

"A bad break to the upper left arm. He also has soft tissue injuries. But there are no internal injuries, and no head injury."

"That's good," Shea said.

"*Very* good. Getting hit by a car is no small thing."

"A car?" Shea stood again, confusion warring with relief. "I thought he fell off the lighthouse."

Dr. Sturgeon's eyebrows winged upward. "Well, that would've resulted in far more severe injuries, if not been fatal. No, your husband said he was hit by a car. I'm not sure where you heard the idea of the lighthouse."

"The man who found Pete—he said he was lying at the base of the lighthouse," Shea informed the doctor.

Dr. Sturgeon gave a small laugh, revealing straight white teeth. "I'm guessing he assumed as much, given where he found your husband near the lighthouse. Anyway, Pete is on an IV of pain medications to alleviate the stress to his body. From what I can tell, there are no bone fragments that have shifted out of place, so surgery doesn't appear to be necessary. We're getting him into a sling and such. He'll need to keep that shoulder immobile for at least two weeks. I'll want to do an X-ray next week to make sure the fracture is healing properly."

"If it's not?" Shea swallowed the panic that was still unnecessarily rising in her.

"If it's not, then we'll reassess. Sometimes surgery ends up being required. But let's not borrow trouble."

"Okay." Shea nodded vehemently. Funny how she hadn't prayed in weeks, but suddenly today it seemed as if praying was all she was doing.

"One other thing," said Dr. Sturgeon. "When he first came in, he was understandably in a lot of pain and a bit delirious. He said the name Annabel. Seeing as it was a hit-and-run, the police were wondering if you knew who Annabel might be?"

Shea wrapped her arms around herself to steady her nerves. "No. No, that's just some research he and I were doing together. I-I'm not sure why he'd mention her. Annabel died in 1852."

"Oh! Well, Pete hasn't mentioned her name again. In fact, he doesn't even remember saying the name Annabel. Which is understandable. The shock of the impact, the pain, all of it can lead to some wacky things being said. The good news is there's no evidence of a concussion—although he's sure to be groggy from the meds when we bring him back to his room."

Shea gave a nervous laugh and nodded. Then a question popped into her head, and she voiced it without thinking it through first. "If Pete was hit by a car . . . the lighthouse isn't even by the road. How did he end up by the lighthouse?"

Dr. Sturgeon's eyes widened, more in consideration of the question than in surprise. "I'm not sure what to tell you. I know the police will want to follow up. There's already been a report filed."

Shea winced.

"But Pete is going to be okay, and that's what matters most," the doctor concluded.

"So someone hit him with their car and then sped off?" Shea still couldn't wrap her head around what had happened.

Dr. Sturgeon grew serious. "From what he has claimed, yes. And his injuries are consistent with that."

"Thank you." Shea had no intention of enlightening the doctor any further with where her mind was beginning to go. If it wasn't Annabel—which was ludicrous—then the only person who would even be *around* the lighthouse with a vehicle in the driveway would be . . . Holt.

Dr. Sturgeon, oblivious to Shea's swirling thoughts, reached out and touched her elbow. "Pete will be fine. After a scare like that, I want to keep him here overnight to monitor his condition and help with pain management."

"Thank you," Shea repeated.

Shea hated harboring suspicions regarding Holt, but she also couldn't fathom who else might have driven to the lighthouse, struck Pete with their car, then left him there to writhe in pain. Pete would have been welcoming to whoever had pulled into the drive, likely standing close by where he was vulnerable to someone wishing to do him harm. No doubt he believed they would stop their vehicle. And if she took the scientific position that ghosts do not exist, nor do they have the power to exact vengeance on the living, then the only logical conclusion was that someone alive—*very* alive—wanted Pete dead.

24

Rebecca

But our love was stronger by far than the love
of those who were older than we . . .
Annabel Lee

ANNABEL'S LIGHTHOUSE
SPRING, 1874

THEY WERE BOLD ENOUGH to come and take her from the lighthouse. Right under our noses!"

Edgar's growl traveled into the room, where Rebecca lay propped against pillows, feeling useless and shaken still, even though she'd slept safely through the night and under Niina's ministrations.

"Shush." Niina spoke louder than the woman probably realized. "Abel says they were looking for papers. Do you know anything about that?"

Edgar's grunt was his answer.

"If we can help her remember, then maybe he will leave her alone," Niina continued in a hoarse whisper. "Let her live her life."

Edgar snorted. "Not with the baby. If he finds out about that, then everything could change." Hatred laced Edgar's voice. "We need to tell her. Enough with this addlebrained idea that we're keeping her safe. We obviously aren't!"

Guilt over eavesdropping gnawed at Rebecca's insides. Yet the secrets they withheld from her chipped away at her trust in Niina, in Abel, and possibly even in Edgar—although his confession about Annabel left her feeling a bit of ownership in his own heartbreaking secrets.

"You already know what happened when Rebecca learned the truth the first time! It's why she's here, and why she can't remember." Niina's tone grew bitter. "Besides, he doesn't believe she's his to begin with, does he? Why would he want the child when it isn't his either? She's got enough to worry about with Aaron, so why add to it?"

Silence drifted into the room, and Rebecca strained to hear in case Edgar was responding far quieter than he had been. Instead, she heard his booted steps as they charged from the lighthouse.

The interplay plagued Rebecca. Who was this *he* they had referred to? Their insinuations startled her into a vague recollection. A man. The argument on the outcropping. His anger. This time the memory came with words.

"You are not faithful! Not to our name! Not to anyone but yourself!"
Not faithful.

A stifling weight settled on Rebecca's chest. The kind that sprang from guilt, from shame. She had stepped out on her husband? Was that it? Was that how she'd become with child? From another man?

She could remember now, the betrayal in the man's voice. While she couldn't make out his image, or remember who he was, she could hear the oppressive truth.

"You are not faithful."

Who had she been before this all began? The very idea that she had willingly entered another man's arms than that of her husband—it appalled her. It tightened her stomach, and the hardening of her womb mimicked what had to have been the hardening of her heart. She was a worthless woman, if that were the case, and her child the result of sin that would forever tarnish her and the child. It would be known as a bastard. She would be identified as a loose woman. That was why she had run, wasn't it? Why she'd been chased through the woods. She'd found no mercy from her husband, no forgiveness for the sake of her babe, no covering by his name to protect the innocent unborn in light of her deeds. And she must protect whatever remained of the reputation for the sake of her brother. He couldn't be associated with her if the babe had been illegitimately conceived!

But her flight was somehow compounded by the mysterious papers. What papers? And why would she have taken them to begin with? Why abscond with something this man—to whom she'd been unfaithful—would want? Was it retribution? A form of vengeance in lieu of his rejection?

Rebecca could not fathom that she was so vindictive, and yet here she was, recovering in a bed that was not her own, with child by a man who had no face, being hunted for something she had more than likely stolen, and barely able to remember her own brother, whom she would die to protect.

"Ah, you're awake!" Niina's voice was perky as she entered the room, jolting Rebecca from her internal war. She held a tray that held cookies and tea, and her short, rotund figure brought with it the scent of freshly baked bread. It was a smell that Rebecca associated with Niina now. The woman's own perfume of sorts that lent a motherly nurturing to her persona, one that Rebecca ached to trust.

But trusting Niina brought risks that Rebecca was afraid to

face. The risk of knowing the truth about herself. The risk of knowing for certain that Niina and Abel and now, more than likely, Edgar had kept the truth from her as to who she was.

"Do you feel any movement?" Niina rested her hand atop the blankets that covered Rebecca's abdomen.

Rebecca shook her head. "Aside from a tickling sensation, no. I don't." Maybe the baby had died. Maybe she carried within her a lifeless form, having taken the brunt of the consequences of recent events—the brunt of the consequences of her sins. Rebecca's breath caught.

"A tickling?" Niina's face split into a smile. "You're feeling the fluttering of the babe! He's telling you he's going to be just fine."

"He?" Rebecca could hardly believe those little featherlight tickles were the child. Surely she would have known. Surely a mother who had conceived a child out of love would have the sense to know when the babe began to give evidence of its life. Tears of oppressive guilt wadded in her throat.

Niina was ignorant of Rebecca's feelings. Instead, she busied herself pouring Rebecca a cup of tea from the kettle on the tray. "He or she. We won't know until the child pokes its little face into the world, and we hear that first cry." Niina handed Rebecca the teacup. "But I picture him as a boy."

"Why?" Rebecca asked.

"I . . . I just do. My eldest was a boy. Abel. And a daughter"— tears shone in Niina's eyes—"well, it's hard to imagine a girl when Kjersti left us not so long ago. It's selfish of me, I know. I'm sorry." She lifted the corner of her apron and dabbed at her eyes. "A boy seems hardier. Less susceptible to illness, I suppose. I wouldn't survive another loss of a child—a babe most assuredly not."

It was a very personal answer to a child Niina had no claims to. Rebecca could take it no longer. "Niina?"

"Hmm?"

"Who am I?"

Niina's startled expression told Rebecca she was right to con-front the truth.

She knew Niina was not going to be forthcoming. "Tell me. I know you know. I know Abel knows. Even Edgar knows more about me than I do."

"And you remember nothing?" Niina lowered herself to the edge of the bed, her expression growing strained.

What should she tell Niina? That she remembered Kjersti most of all? That the daughter and sister so grieved over came to her in her sleep—or in spirit—and that Rebecca knew her? Or did she tell her that she knew she had a brother, that his name was Aaron? That she could barely remember more about him except for this wild assertiveness inside of her that would do anything to protect him? Or did she tell Niina of the cold words that plagued her, from the man she knew now was somehow at the root of it all? Perhaps she was to blame for it all. Maybe she was the villain, and the others were merely . . .

Rebecca shoved aside her swirling thoughts and gave a simple response: "I remember small things. Words said to me. Awful words that, if true, mean I'm not a good person."

"No!" Niina's declaration surprised Rebecca. Her eyes were stern as she raised her index finger. "Don't let anyone tell you that you've made bad choices. Ever. You've made your choices, and you live with them because they were *your* choices. Not his."

"Whose?" Rebecca asked. "Tell me who you're talking about? Who wants me harmed for the sake of some papers? Who hates me enough to care nothing of my bearing a child?"

Niina's chest rose and fell with a sigh. She looked at her hands and then reached out and took the teacup from Rebecca. Once she'd set it on the tray, she repositioned herself on the mattress to face Rebecca, taking Rebecca's hands in hers and looking her in the eyes. "Your father," she said.

It was unexpected. She had thought to hear Niina admit to Rebecca's husband's name. But her *father*?

Niina pressed forward. "I don't know what your few memories tell you, but the one after you is your father."

"My father?" Rebecca asked, breathless with disbelief.

Niina searched her face for a moment before nodding. "Yes. And he will not cease coming after you until you turn over to him the papers you apparently stole."

"What *papers*?"

"We don't know," Niina admitted. Her grasp of Rebecca's hands tightened, and a shadow passed over her face. "All we know is that you are the daughter of Walter Hilliard, the sister of Aaron."

"Hilliard." Rebecca repeated the name, recognizing it not as her own, but from the stories Edgar and Niina and Abel had told her shortly after her arrival at the lighthouse. "The man who—"

"Yes." Her reply was curt and filled with distaste. "Hilliard, the mining baron. The man who is convinced Silvertown will become a great source of wealth."

"And somehow . . ." Realization began to dawn on Rebecca. She swallowed, the truth bitter in her mouth. "Somehow I am threatening that success."

"Yes." Niina nodded slowly, concern etched in every crevice of her face. "Your father has never . . . thought highly of you. And now, if you took something that belongs to him, something to do with his mining investments, then—"

"Then I am my father's worst enemy," Rebecca finished. Tears burned in her eyes.

"You're a chilling reminder to me."

Those words, the words that had driven her to the lakeshore, had come from her father. It was he who had stood on the rock outcropping with her, anger infused in every pore of his body. It was not her husband to whom Rebecca had been unfaithful; it was her father. She had soiled his name. She was with child by someone, and he hated her for it.

"Yes, I'm my father's worst enemy," Rebecca repeated in a whisper.

Niina said nothing to correct her.

Rebecca finished buttoning her dress. It was time to leave the sanctuary of the lighthouse—if she could even call it that. If she removed herself from the lighthouse, she would remove Abel, Niina, and Edgar from Hilliard's—her father's?—reach. She didn't wish them to suffer only because they tried to protect her from the man she had blocked from her memory.

"You're not to leave the lighthouse!" Niina hurried after Rebecca as Rebecca made her way through the kitchen.

Every muscle in her body screamed. She agonized at the thought of leaving and risking finding herself back in the clutches of men like Mercer. If he worked for her father, then her father had set few boundaries for his cronies, and Rebecca was walking right back into harm's way.

"Wait for Abel," Niina begged as Rebecca opened the door.

She shook her head, fighting against the tears, but more so against the fear, the hurt, and the darkness of the unknown. "I can't stay. I can't put you all in danger."

"But we *want* to help you!" Niina's words bounced off Rebecca's back. She dared not look at Niina, dared not face the woman who had withheld the truth from her to keep her safe.

Rebecca understood the stark reality that being protected was not customary for her. It was a feeling, a state of being, she had long ago given up hoping for. Rebecca now knew that she had been standing alone since she was a child—except for Aaron. *He* had not been her protector, only *she* had protected him. Her younger brother who, even now, was as alone as she had been.

Faint memories were returning even in the last hour as Niina danced around Rebecca, urging her to wait for Abel, threatening to retrieve Edgar to have him lock Rebecca away for her own safety.

Rebecca recalled the faint image of herself as a child, a man glowering at her, the back of his hand connecting with her cheek. She couldn't recall what she was guilty of, just that she was guilty. If this were the case, if she bore the weight of transgressions, if she carried the rancor of the man who was her own father—her own flesh and blood—then she herself brought only trial on others.

Rebecca's feet sank into the grass. Niina had stopped following, but called to her from the lighthouse, "Rebecca, *please!*"

Her breath hitched as Rebecca fought back a sob. She cared enough about these three who had fed her, bathed her, shown kindness to her not to put them in further danger for her sake. She had to return—for Aaron. She could see his face more clearly now. He was fifteen, she thought. He was hardly a man and yet no longer a boy. She needed to be there for him. This was all her fault . . .

"Rebecca!"

This time it was a male voice, and it was sharp.

She stopped in her tracks, teetering on the edge of the embankment that led to the shoreline. Spinning, she saw Abel approaching, his long strides determined. Niina's voice carried over the wind and the sound of the waves. "Bring her back to us, Abel!"

Even as the sun broke through the clouds and warmed Rebecca's skin, she shivered at the determination she saw on Abel's face as he drew nearer.

"Have you lost your senses?" Abel asked.

Rebecca bit the inside of her lip to keep it from quivering. Yes, she was certain she *had* lost her senses. She had lost them the moment Edgar found her at Annabel's grave. She had further lost her way when she couldn't recollect the past. She had lost her way when Annabel visited her, when she brushed Rebecca's hair from her face and cooled her skin with her fingers. She had taken comfort from ghosts: Annabel, Kjersti. Worse, she had lost her way when she became controlled by men who abused her for reasons she didn't understand. Why then would she bring anyone with her if she were so lost? To have them join her in the darkness of the world she lived in. The questions, the lack of answers, the fear, the need to flee?

Abel stepped closer to her, caution tensing his body, as if he half expected her to throw herself over the embankment. "Don't do this. Don't leave," he pleaded.

"I have to," Rebecca said with a raised voice, so he could hear her above the waves. The rolling waters that hypnotized with their glistening color and lulling pattern. They were gentle today—unlike the rising tide in Rebecca's heart.

"You don't." Abel reached for her, but Rebecca moved back, maintaining some distance between them.

Abel's bottom lip was split and puffy. Dried blood had coagulated on a cut in his cheek, and his left eye was swollen, bruised with the evidence of a battle.

"This!" Rebecca gestured to his injuries. "This is why I must go. I'm only hurting you all by staying. I'm putting you in danger, and I don't even understand why. How can I fix what I don't understand?"

Abel shrugged off her concern. "It is nothing. It will heal."

"Mercer did that to you?" Rebecca demanded to know.

Abel winced, obviously not wanting to tell her the truth.

"He did," Rebecca stated.

Abel shouted over the ruckus of the waves. "He deserved it, and he fared worse!"

"You'll only *make* things worse, Abel!" Rebecca felt a pull toward him that she didn't understand. "For me and for Aaron! For my baby!" She could drown in his eyes, as much as she almost had in the lake. Yet she knew in that drowning it would end up killing him. She just *knew* that the man Niina said was her father—Hilliard—would see Abel as an inconvenient obstacle, one that should be disposed of.

Abel took the final few steps toward her, grabbing hold of her shoulders with the desperation of someone who knew he was losing a battle he could not win. "Rebecca—"

She pulled away from him instantly. "I can't stay. I know you have only tried to protect me, but I will not—"

"Don't be foolish." His words were insistent but not critical. They held an element of begging that made tears spring to Rebecca's eyes. "Please, Rebecca. Let me take care of you."

"I don't need to be taken care of." And she meant it, though she knew it was a ridiculous thing to say considering how she had relied on him. "Let me go. I'm not your responsibility. I-I am apparently *his*. My father's."

Abel's face darkened. "Your father doesn't claim you! Hilliard cares only for himself and his financial legacy."

"But he's my *father!*" Rebecca shouted back.

"You don't understand!" Abel's jaw was set in a stubborn line, icy fire spitting from his eyes.

Rebecca spun to leave, to flee from Abel, from the lighthouse, from the inevitable draw that would be her undoing. It was the open wound of need that made her ache to find refuge here in Annabel's lighthouse, regardless of its ghost, of its curses. If evil could be traded for evil, Rebecca would bear the haunting of Annabel for eternity if she could only return to what moments before had felt like a prison.

No.

No!

She was in prison even here, standing on the shore of Lake Superior, her hair whipping wildly about her. She was caged by the knowledge of a man whose will superseded her well-being. She was never to be free. Never to be her own person. Even her mind had locked her away behind bars made of foggy, dark memories.

Abel's hands once again grasped her shoulders, turning her gently yet firmly to meet his frigid yet somehow warm and inviting gaze. "What about your babe?" he asked. "Think of the child. You must protect it from those who seek to harm you!"

"What about my brother?" she snapped. "There's no one to protect *him* from my father." Rebecca's eyes burned, and she did little to hold back the tears that rolled down her cheeks. "I don't know this child or its father, but I know my brother. I can *feel* him. And I will not desert him." She spat the words, which were like a confession being dragged from her unwillingly.

"Rebecca, you—"

"Stop!" She slammed her palms into Abel's chest, shoving him away from her. "Leave me." The agony of her blocked memories, the trauma of her latest assault, and the dread of what she was yet to face all overwhelmed her. It hindered any ability to conceptualize her next steps. And the baby's presence inside of her had stolen the last fragments of a life that had once been pure and hopeful.

Abel stiffened, his chest heaving. "I won't let you go."

"You *must!*" Rebecca yelled. The waves had grown fiercer, crashing now onto the rocks below, spray shooting upward.

"No!" Abel set his mouth in a grim line. "You will not return to your father!"

"I will!" She took another step backward.

"Please, Rebecca, don't do this."

"Let me go, Abel."

"I can't!" he insisted.

"Why not?" she screamed.

"Because your baby is *mine!*" Abel's declaration rose louder than the waves, louder than the wind, and louder than the pounding of her own heart.

Air escaped her as though she'd been gutted. She stared at Abel with her mouth agape, his bold claim having ripped the words from her throat.

Abel's eyes were pleading. He didn't touch her, but he might as well have. He might as well have bound her to him in that moment and in a way she could not make sense of. "Your baby is mine, Rebecca. *I'm* the father."

She closed and then opened her mouth again to ask questions, to try to comprehend the meaning of what she'd just heard.

Abel's voice dropped in volume as he bent close so that she could hear him above the lake's insistent roar. Rebecca felt his breath on her face. She could imagine she felt the pounding of his heart resonating so loudly between them that the vibrations collided with her own.

"I belong to you, Rebecca. You are my *wife*."

25

SHEA

Of many far wiser than we . . .
Annabel Lee

ANNABEL'S LIGHTHOUSE
PRESENT DAY

AFTER A PHONE CALL with her editor Pat, Shea had a bit of leniency regarding not only the direction of her manuscript but its deadline as well. Considering she'd spent the night in the hospital, running on restless sleep in a semi-comfortable recliner, and already sick of cafeteria food, Shea had officially called off the mission of writing and self-care for this trip.

The trip was now one of mere survival, and a huge part of her was ready to end her stay at the lighthouse and take Pete home the minute he was released from the hospital.

A groan from the bed alerted Shea to Pete's wakening. He'd

been awake much of yesterday, though Dr. Sturgeon had strongly advised Shea against drilling Pete for details about his fall while he was still heavily medicated.

"The details will come out eventually. We don't want to stress him out right now. If things look good, he can go home tomorrow." Dr. Sturgeon's smile was laced with directive, and Shea had complied.

Until now.

Pete was very aware of her as she met his eyes. There was a clarity in them that hadn't been there even earlier this morning.

"My arm is pounding," he muttered.

"That's understandable." Shea moved from her place at the hospital room window and slid onto a padded chair with wooden arms that faced the bed. "You're lucky to be alive." Shea was taken aback by a sudden onslaught of emotion, knowing how close he'd come to losing his life.

"You did ask me how I'd kill myself if I tried." Pete's awful attempt at humor earned him a glare.

"No, I asked you how you'd shoot yourself, and that was for research purposes only. Please don't make jokes about this." Shea's sense of humor was nonexistent at the moment.

Pete glanced at his injured arm, then up at his IV and the monitors that measured his vitals. "When can I get out of here?"

"This afternoon hopefully," Shea informed him. "But it's important you keep that arm and shoulder immobilized." She hesitated, then went for it. "What do you remember, Pete?" Her phone was burning a hole in her pocket, and she'd have no qualms about extracting it to call the police if Pete gave her the name of whoever had struck him with their vehicle.

Pete closed his eyes for a long moment, and when he opened them, he squinted as though the daylight bothered him. "A car?"

"Did you recognize it?" She was careful not to plant the idea that she suspected Holt in any way.

Pete considered her suggestion. "No. I don't think so. It was a car, though, and Holt drives a truck—if that's what you're think-ing. I do remember Holt being there after I was hit and calling 911."

"Were you hit somewhere near the lighthouse?" Shea pressed. "Holt thought you fell from the gallery."

"No. I mean, I remember being hit hard and sort of rolling there. The car came down the drive and then right into the yard at me. Whoever it was knew what they were doing."

"Did you see Holt before you were hit?" Shea asked.

Pete gave a little snort, then grimaced from the pain of it. "It wasn't Holt, Shea."

"So some random person pulled into the drive, onto the yard toward you, and struck you? Then they just took off . . ."

"Yep." Pete wasn't elaborating, but then it didn't seem as though he had much more to add.

Shea shook her head. "I don't get it. Why would someone do such a thing?"

"I dunno. That's for the police to figure out."

"Holt said you mentioned Annabel's name. In fact, that was *all* you said before you passed out." Shea provided Pete with everything she knew and then waited while he digested the information.

"I don't know why I said that." Pete's answer was unhelpful.

"Did you see the driver?" Shea asked. "Maybe what happened has something to do with the lighthouse. I mean, Jonathan Marks was killed there after people started nosing around."

"The car's windows were tinted," Pete said, recalling a few more details now. "I didn't see a face. Just a form. It could've been a man or a woman." Pete ran a hand lightly across his jaw, his palm making a scraping sound against the stubble on his face. "Do I get to go back to the lighthouse with you?"

"Get to go back? It's not Disney World, Pete." Shea blew out a sigh. "I'm not sure I want to go back myself. The book isn't worth all this. Someone tried to kill you!"

"Sure, but . . ." Pete attempted to push himself up on his pillows and then groaned again, immediately stopping when it was apparent his arm and shoulder protested. "Shea, I'm all in now."

"All in?"

"Yeah." He didn't expound on that as Shea moved to help him adjust the pillow he was struggling with.

"That place is dangerous," she stated as she eased the pillow beneath his hurting shoulder. "Or more to the point, *someone* is dangerous. And you saying the name Annabel after getting hit irks me. That's a weird thing to bring up at such a moment with your life hanging in the balance—the name of a dead woman?"

"Is it?"

"Pete." Shea leveled a look on him.

"What?" Annoyance flashed across his face.

"Isn't it obvious? For whatever reason, someone out there is *not* happy about our digging into the lighthouse's history and its secrets. I don't know what's going on, but it's not worth the advance on the book. I'm going to take you home."

"You know what?" Pete stated suddenly. "I'm kind of done with this."

"With what?" Shea reared back, perplexed.

"You."

"*Me?*"

With his good arm, Pete shoved aside the blanket that Shea had just tucked up for him. "Yes, you. You're bossy. You're entitled. You tell me what to do and where to go and how to do it. You're not easy to get along with, Shea."

"I am too!" He was taking this way too far. Here she was at his bedside, worried about his welfare, and he was taking it out on her.

"And you argue with me all the time."

"I do not," Shea retorted. She crossed her arms and glared down at him.

"Listen." Pete paused and shook his head. "I can't do this."

"Do what?"

"This!" He waved his hand in a circle. "I can't do anything right for you, so I leave you alone, and then that's not even right. What do you want me to be? Casanova? Mr. Darcy?"

So he *had* been listening at some point.

"I wouldn't mind a little Mr. Darcy! You don't buy me roses for Valentine's Day, you don't give me a kiss when you walk through the door, and you get more excited about your truck than you do about me."

"Because if I pay attention to you, I don't do it in the right way." Pete's glower matched her own.

They stared at each other for several seconds, neither one of them blinking. It was uncomfortable, but Shea would be darned if she was the one to break the standoff.

She didn't. Pete did. "I'm not saying I've got it together, Shea. But at least I try."

Shea's eyes burned. "I try too, you know."

"Do you?" Pete pressed.

"Of course I do. I'm here, aren't I?" Shea sank onto the chair, drained of energy and warring between the stress she'd been holding in the last day and a half and the frustration of a dying marriage.

"But you left me," Pete went on, sharing more with her than he had in months.

"I left you for a research trip. That's nothing new." Shea's retort sounded weak even to her ears. She tried to strengthen it. "And you don't like to travel. You never want to come along anyway."

Pete sniffed. A light sniff that was derisive while also being careful not to jar his ribs. "I overheard you talking to your friend about how you needed 'self-care.'"

"What's wrong with self-care?" Shea snapped.

Pete locked eyes with her. "Self-care? Nothing. Self-indulgence? That's a problem."

"I'm not indulging in anything but trying to be alone and figure out who I am! That's even biblical."

"Really?" Both doubt and sarcasm laced his tone.

"Sure. Jesus went off by himself."

"To pray!"

"And to rest!" Shea argued.

"Because He needed to prepare to give more of himself, not become one with himself and His own self-importance."

Agitated, Shea sucked in a breath and pushed up from the chair. Pete was as dense as they came, and this was the evidence of that. Arguing theology while recovering from being hit by a car? That summarized Pete in a nutshell. He never just focused on the root issue—what *she* needed. It was always something else. Always . . .

At that moment, the essence of Pete's argument slapped against Shea's consciousness. Her needs. What about his? What *about* his? Shea marched to the window and turned her back to Pete in the bed. She hugged herself as she stared out the window. The sunny spring day was happy. It was pleasant. And here she was arguing the philosophy of self-care with the man she'd tried to get away from to begin with.

"And Holt?" Pete's question bounced off her back.

"What about him?" Shea's question echoed off the windowpane.

"You two have a thing?"

Shea looked over her shoulder at Pete with exasperation. "Of course not."

"But you like him."

Well, she had before she thought he might have hit Pete with his car. But since Pete had eliminated that possibility . . . "He's a nice and helpful man."

"Everything I'm not?" Pete challenged.

Shea faced him. "He's *attentive*, Pete. He cares about what I do. The other night? When that person scared the pants off of me in the lighthouse and smeared fake blood on the window? You were all business. The police pulled up, and off you went to talk to them, whereas Holt stayed behind to make sure I was okay. He made sure I was *okay*, Pete," she repeated, hoping he'd get the point.

Pete's eyes widened. "Really? You wanted me to stay and coddle you instead of taking care of the situation? I'm trying to take care of you, Shea. I've fixed your cars, and I drove up here to make sure your windshield got repaired. Then I drove you around and helped you with your research. I spoke to the cops, I mean . . . what? You'd rather I stop all that, snuggle with you, and watch a movie? Sure, I can do that. Let's snuggle when we get back to the lighthouse, and then you can take care of everything else. I'll just dote on you like the princess you are, and I'll stop doing everything I do to take care of you—to take care of *us*!"

Shea swallowed. The fact Pete had strung that many words together stunned her. The fact he was throwing a list of deeds at her as if they were his Get Out of Jail Free card was ridiculous.

"I just want to be cherished, Pete." She choked back a sob that made its way up completely against her will.

"Yeah? And taking care of you isn't that?"

"I don't need to be taken care of—I need to be loved."

"Maybe I do too," Pete stated. "Maybe I need to know you respect what I do. That you respect *me*. That you don't see me only as your butler or your handyman. I may not be the romantic lead of a movie or the model on the cover of some novel, but if making sure you can live your dream to travel and write while I try to get through my anxiety that something might happen to you—well, if that doesn't tell you I love you, then I don't know what will."

"Maybe say the words," Shea retorted while simultaneously beginning to feel like a spoiled, mean girl.

"Fine. I love you." Pete spit them out, and yet Shea knew he meant them. "I always have. I thought you could see that. Everything I do is so you can be content, so you can live the life you love. But if you want some hunky, doting hero like Holt, then go for it. I don't know what else I can do. Because we could snuggle and be all sappy with each other, but when stuff like this happens? When one of us almost gets killed? You realize then what you came close to losing, and I guarantee you, Shea. You find out it's not the romance you'll miss. It's that your car started this morning, that there's money in the bank to pay the mortgage. The fact that we do life together, and sometimes it's just redundant and dull and stupid. But you know what? There are people in this world—couples—who would *kill* for a routine life. We're comfortable. With each other. I'm *comfortable* with you, Shea. Why is that a bad thing?"

Shea's chest heaved as her breaths came in rapid succession. She stared at her husband. What Pete said made sense. It was also disappointing. Comfortable was boring, wasn't it? Comfortable meant there was no more spark, no more interest, didn't it?

Pete's eyes glistened, and he shut them as though trying to hide the rare emotion.

"I just want you to want me," Shea managed to squeeze out around the lump in her throat.

Pete didn't open his eyes, but his response stunned her. "Yeah. Same here."

26

PETE HAD WANTED TO RETURN to the lighthouse, and the entire argument had shifted his stubbornness into high gear. Maybe it was that a half-hour car ride was better than the six-to-eight-hour drive to get all the way to their home. Maybe he was making a point. Regardless, it was still the longest thirty-minute car ride Shea had ever been on, and since Pete was in pain-management mode, she had the entire time to self-reflect.

She didn't like a minute of it.

In truth, Shea still believed she wasn't completely at fault. Yet little snippets of Pete's outburst at the hospital made too much sense to be ignored, and it was that left-brained logic that warred with her right-brained need for emotional attachment.

Where was the balance? *Was* there a balance?

To make matters worse, now that Pete had called her out on her attraction to Holt, she didn't want to see that man again. Not to mention, her own suspicions of Holt made her wary, even if she couldn't put a finger on a direct motive.

They'd arrived at the lighthouse by early evening, and after getting Pete situated, Shea made a late supper, served it to him without a word, then settled into her bed with a book. But she was far too distracted to get involved in a story. Instead, she lay there staring at the ceiling until well past two in the morning. When sleep finally claimed her, it was fitful and filled with dreams of Pete getting hit by a car, with Annabel's ghost hovering just beyond the crime scene as if responsible for it.

She woke up on a mission, and Pete noticed from his position on the sofa where he'd chosen to sleep that night.

"I'm going to find out who this Rebecca is and where Captain Gene is and all this nonsense about Annabel's ghost once and for all," Shea explained in response to Pete's wordless question.

He'd been watching her go to-and-fro, busying herself collecting her notebook, purse, filling her water bottle, and more. The wordless treatment was worse than if he'd just been nosy.

She halted. She'd not bothered to check on him in the night. He preferred not to be babied, instructing her to leave his pain meds on the coffee table and he'd "figure it out." Now she felt like she should at least try to be the bigger person.

"Did you sleep all right?" she asked.

Pete raised an eyebrow. "Sure."

They were still at an impasse. Shea decided there was nothing she could say or do at the present time that might solve their dilemma. "Well, bye then. If you need anything . . ." Whatever. He would *figure it out*.

"Have fun" was all Pete had to say.

Shea didn't stick around to see if he'd add anything more. She slipped her feet into a pair of leather mules and swung open the door.

"Oh!"

Penny stood just outside the door, her hand poised to knock, a large cake pan in her other hand. Her bright red lips stretched into a smile.

"Good morning, hon!"

Shea quickly gathered her wits about her. "I was just heading over to the Dipstick to see you!"

"You were?" Penny held out the cake. "And here I am making sure you get that handsome husband of yours fed. He needs sugar to heal, that's my prescription!"

Shea stepped to the side and invited Penny in. The tiny bar owner walked straight to the table to set the cake pan on it. "Chocolate cake with chocolate icing." She reached into her pocket and pulled out a can of cherry pie filling. "It's not particularly gourmet, but my mama swore by adding cherries on top. Our own version of German chocolate cake, I guess."

"Sounds great!" Pete hollered from the sitting area.

Penny made herself at home and went in to see him.

Apparently, Pete had eaten more meals at the Dipstick than Shea realized. He and Penny—who was almost old enough to be his mother—seemed like the best of friends.

Interesting.

Shea watched the two interact for a moment. She was suspicious of everyone now. Rightfully so, she believed.

"I'm just so glad you're still with us!" Penny perched on the footstool near Pete's spot on the sofa. "And that you came back here!"

Shea leaned against the doorjamb. "A few days ago, Pete was suggesting it was too dangerous for *me* to be alone."

Penny's laughter pealed. She waved toward Shea. "My late husband was always like that too. Making sure I was taken care of and never doing anything to take care of himself. I had to watch him like a hawk or that man would've died way sooner than he did by cause of sheer stupidity." She laughed again, Pete joined her, and Shea managed a smile.

Penny grew serious and looked between the two of them. "I did want to let you both know something, though."

"What is it?" Shea pushed off the doorjamb and took a few more steps into the room.

"Well," Penny started, "right after Pete was hit, Holt took off on a fishing trip to Canada. I think he needed some time away and it'll do him good."

"He what?" Shea was dumbfounded. Holt hadn't said a word about a planned fishing trip.

"Mm-hmm." Penny nodded. "And he's put me in charge of this lighthouse, so if you need any landlord-type stuff, just give me a ring. But since it was rather sudden, and I . . . well, I wanted to ask if he'd said anything to either of you about the fishing trip? Seeing as you're his guests and all."

"Not a word," Pete replied.

"No, he never said anything to me," said Shea. Which could be proof that Holt was behind at least some of what had happened to Pete. Shea's prior attraction to Holt turned into a deep distrust of the man.

"Okay then." Penny hefted a sigh. "Maybe I'm too much of a worry-wort. And not to be out of line, but I think Holt has a little bit of a thing for you, Shea, and, well—he knew there are boundaries in place."

"Good," Pete gruffed.

Penny patted Pete on the knee. "Now don't get all riled. Holt is a good man. He'd never steal another man's wife."

This conversation was entirely too uncomfortable. Shea opened her mouth to interrupt, but Penny continued, not seeming to notice Shea as she directed her attention to Pete.

"I'd advise you to be careful, though. I'm not sure who was behind this hit-and-run, but it was obviously very intentional. Still, you know how this place affected Jonathan Marks. Something about the lighthouse gets into your psyche and messes with your mind."

"The police are actively investigating." Pete's statement made Penny's brows raise.

"Well, good! But that could take forever and a day!"

"My thoughts exactly," Shea muttered.

227

Penny's earrings bobbed as she turned her head as if look-ing for something. Spotting it, she sprang from the footstool. It was the painting on the wall. The one Jonathan Marks—according to the documentary—had died under. "See this?" Penny's fingernail tapped the vague form of Annabel's ghost near the lighthouse. "Don't underestimate her. Annabel has a lot of influence on this place. She always has, and she always will."

"Why do you think that is?" Pete asked the question in Shea's mind, though it was one she'd already asked and had received no satisfactory answer to.

Penny eyed him. "I'm not sure, but I do know this." She re-turned to her seat on the footstool. "Folks discount the impact prior generations have on us today. I know some don't know their family trees beyond their grandparents, and that's unfor-tunate. Do you know what happens when you throw a rock into the lake?"

"It sinks," Pete replied.

"Well, yes," Penny chuckled, "but on a day when the lake is calm, you can see the ripples the rock creates on the water, and you can watch it as it sinks to the bottom. The water is cold and clear. The effects of that rock being thrown into the lake change an otherwise consistent pattern. Even if it's just for a moment, those ripples reach farther than that rock ever would on its own. And as the rock sinks, it touches other rocks and debris that it never would have otherwise." She looked up at Shea, who stood frozen, listening to Penny's words with a layered reaction she didn't know how to process.

Penny continued, "You see, how Annabel lived left its effect on others around her. Enough so that today, over a hundred years later, we're still being touched by the fact she once lived here. We can blame it all on Annabel's ghost, or we can realize it's the ripples she caused that affect us today."

"In what ways?" Pete had a way of drawing people out that

was fast becoming a surprise to Shea even after a decade of marriage. Why hadn't she noticed that about him?

Penny cleared her throat. "Well, if it weren't for Annabel, then Jonathan Marks would still be alive, I'd bet my bar on it. If it weren't for Annabel, he never would've gone out of his mind. I'm sure of it. And if it weren't for Annabel . . . my dad wouldn't be such a hermit."

"Your dad?" Shea inserted.

Penny looked up at her. "Yes. My dad. Captain Gene. Didn't Holt tell you he is my dad?"

No one had told her that Captain Gene was Penny's dad. Not Marnie—who had said to watch out for Penny—not August Fronell, and definitely not Holt. Penny swore on her mother's grave that she didn't know where her father was, in keeping with his reputation of disappearing. But Shea had immediately attempted to interrogate Penny further.

"Oh no." Penny lifted a hand. "I'm not going to talk about this stuff any more than I already have! Not that I have much to add."

"How could you not?" Shea winced when she realized her question was a bit rude.

Penny's chuckle reassured Shea it wasn't taken that way. "Because I know what happens to people who dig into Annabel's story." She took her index finger and swirled it in a circle beside her temple. "And Dad never wanted to talk about it anyway. Said too much trouble came from digging up the past. Sometimes you have to let the ripples in the water settle and allow everything to go back to normal."

"Shea isn't capable of doing that." Pete managed to twist enough to give her a faint grin. Then he winced and returned to his prior position, tending his arm.

"You're a curious one, Shea, I'll grant you that." Penny pushed to her feet. "I should go now. Leave the two of you to kiss and make up."

"Pardon?" Shea said.

Penny pursed her lips. "You really think I can't tell when two people have built the Great Wall of China between them? I was married once too." She reached down and patted Pete's shoulder. "You be a man and give your wifey some hugs and kisses. And you . . ." Penny approached Shea and gripped her hand in a squeeze. "Don't take that man for granted. I can see he's a good one, and you've got him right where every woman would want theirs. He's going to be in the palm of your hand with that busted arm of his, so now's your chance to get some time with him when he's not playing grease monkey on the cars."

27

REBECCA

And neither the angels in heaven above nor
the demons down under the sea . . .

Annabel Lee

ANNABEL'S LIGHTHOUSE
SPRING, 1874

REBECCA STARED UNSEEING into the expanse that was Lake Superior. The window of the oil room had become her escape, and once she was safely back inside, Abel had left her there, alone. She'd had nothing to say after his pronouncement that he was the father of the child that was swelling her abdomen. He knew her better than she knew herself merely because he could recall and she could not.

She was numb. There had been no rejoicing, no sudden resurgence of memory or understanding. There had only been a

231

long stretch where she had no words and Abel beseeched her merely by his expression to come back to him.

That there was an innate pull toward Abel had been evident from the first day Edgar had brought her to the lighthouse.

"*Anishinaabewi-gichigami.*" Now, Edgar came along beside her in the oil room. His presence was unexpected, and yet Rebecca didn't mind it. Of anyone here at the lighthouse, Edgar was now the least intimidating. He didn't come with expectations. He was just Edgar, the lighthouse keeper. The one overseeing the lake who ensured each ship and crew made its way in the darkness.

Maybe he could help her as well.

"That is what the Ojibwe call this lake." Edgar leaned on a long stick of smoothed driftwood that he brought into the lighthouse, stabilizing his bowed legs. His floppy fisherman's cap squashed his white hair, but from her peripheral vision, Rebecca could see he was following her stare across the waters rather than demanding she give him her full attention. "Annabel loved the lake."

Rebecca inhaled a steadying breath scented with lake water, drawing it deep into her lungs.

"I hear Abel told you he's the father," he stated.

"Yes," Rebecca answered flatly. She didn't care to speak of Abel, not yet. But then a part of her did, and perhaps Edgar would be the safest person to talk to about it.

"The story of love consumes a soul. Remember what I said? Don't forget the love? There's often no other thought but that." Edgar's words hung in the room between them.

"Do I love him?" It was the question that plagued her the most. Rebecca hated herself for the pained expression in Abel's eyes. She agonized trying to summon recollections. There was no question she was drawn to him, had even trusted him, and something in her desired to be close to him. But there was no tangible memory to cling to. No recollection of their love, let alone the conception of the babe she now bore.

"Only you can answer that. It'll take time," Edgar acknowledged.

"And I've lived here at the lighthouse? With both of you?"

"Since Kjersti concocted her plan to get you away from your father in the first place." His explanation confused her.

"Kjersti?" Rebecca struggled to remember.

"Yes, Kjersti. You two had been friends for a while. Kjersti and Niina lived in Silvertown not far from the Hilliard house. And Kjersti knew about your father."

"You mean that he was greedy?" Rebecca offered.

Edgar's expression turned dark when he looked at her. "No. That he flat-out disowned you, that he abused you your whole life. You'd visit Kjersti with a black eye and with no good explanation."

Rebecca was beginning to understand. Kjersti's concern. A black eye. Yes, she could remember—vaguely, but still, it was there now that she'd been reminded of it.

Edgar sucked in a resigned breath. "Kjersti convinced her brother, Abel, to marry ya. Get you out of that house before Hilliard did something worse to ya. I doubt that man has one ounce of affection for you."

Rebecca recognized the dull cold in the pit of her stomach. It was coming back. Like a rainstorm where the rain came down harder and harder, pelting her with its fierceness. Yes. Her father.

"You are a chilling reminder . . . unfaithful . . ."

"My father was furious with Abel and me," Rebecca said, remembering more pieces of her story now.

Edgar studied her. *"Furious* is the right word for it. Abel and you stayed here at the lighthouse. We had no idea Hilliard would just about lose his mind over it. But then after Kjersti got sick—" Edgar stopped and swallowed hard—"nigh on about six weeks ago—"

"Six weeks!" Tears sprang to Rebecca's eyes. No wonder Kjersti

was fresh in her memory. No wonder Abel could hardly speak of her. Aside from her attack, Kjersti's death would've been the most traumatic thing to have happened. Abel was still reeling from his sister's passing. Niina was hiding behind Finnish fortitude.

"Six weeks." Edgar nodded. "You blamed your father."

"For Kjersti's death." Rebecca knew then. The memory of her fury. "We couldn't get her treatment. That's why she was in the lighthouse instead of with Niina as Niina was ailing. My father stood in the way of Kjersti because she convinced Abel and I to marry—out of convenience—so I could leave the Hilliard house."

"Yep," said Edgar.

Rebecca clenched her teeth. It was coming back like the nightmare it was. "My father hated my besting him and leaving, as much as he despised me when I was at home."

Edgar turned, his eyes scanning the vast breadth of Lake Superior. "You left the lighthouse after Kjersti died. You were not only angry, but you were petrified for your brother's safety. You said if—"

"If my father could allow all of this horror, then Aaron would be the next one to suffer," she finished.

Then there was Abel. Her cheeks warmed. Abel had tried to rescue her months ago. He had taken her as his wife—on Kjersti's plea and due to his innate protective nature. Convenience. And yet . . . there had been more.

"The babe." Rebecca put her hands to her hot cheeks. She was beginning to remember that too. She remembered feeling the awkward bride, and later, the palpable relief she experienced when she'd moved to the lighthouse. She remembered sleeping in Abel's room. That first night he'd slept on the floor. That arrangement went on for days, weeks. And then with his steady presence, his eyes, his quiet spirit . . . one night everything changed between them.

Edgar leaned on the driftwood stick as he pointed out the window. "That's the earth this lighthouse stands on. Seems fittin' it was built where Annabel died. But love here in these wilds? It's not an easy place for love to survive. It's beaten and abused. Life ain't simple, not as it should be. Love should be straightforward, but then people threaten the ways of it. They have their own plans, their own schemes. Dirty deeds lend a man to do more wickedness, and all in the name of love."

Rebecca waited, sensing there was more, though Edgar seemed to talk in riddles.

"You're a Hilliard." Edgar summarized what Abel and Niina had only danced around. "And then you became a Koski. Abel's wife. Rebecca Hilliard Koski." He shifted to look at her. "When I found you days ago, we knew your father would stop at nothing to exact his anger. But these papers? We don't know about that. We don't know what you did when you left the lighthouse to go back to Aaron."

Panic surged through Rebecca. She drew back from the window and stared at Edgar. "Is Aaron all right?" How had she not thought of that yet? Where was he? Was their father punishing him for her deeds?

Edgar held up his palms to calm her. "Niina has seen him. He's fine. Not a speck of a bruise to be seen, and he smiled at her. That's all they can do; they don't dare speak to each other. But every indication is your brother's all right."

"How did it come to this?" Rebecca cried. "What did I do when I left here? I hurt Abel, and now I'm carrying his . . ." She couldn't think of that now. With all that she could remember, her feelings for Abel were the most confused, a torrent of whirling emotions. And then there were the papers. Those blasted, mysterious papers! "I don't remember what I took from my father. I don't remember why they were chasing me—why they almost killed me!"

Edgar shook his head and sniffed. "Awful things happen, an'

when they do, sometimes your mind can't look at them. That's what yours is doin'. You can't look at the awful and you can't hear the painful, so your mind has told everyone 'no more.' All we know is your father hates you for leavin' to be with Abel. But your father hated you just as much for stayin' with him. An' now he believes you've crossed him by taking those papers, an' if it's what I'm guessing, you took something of immense value regarding his silver mines, the stamp mill, and who knows what else? The men he sent after you the first time tried to get it out of you. That's when your mind said enough was enough. You blocked the images, the memories, the people. Your mind wants to start fresh, but you can't."

"And I can't stay here, Edgar," Rebecca added. "Regardless of my carrying Abel's child. I put him and Niina and you in danger each moment I don't face my father and supposedly hide whatever it is he thinks I have."

"You can't go back to your father." Edgar's black eyes bored into hers. "He'll kill ya. You're not runnin' from us again. We're family, an' that baby is family. Whether or not you an' Abel can figure things out between ya."

"Why does my father hate me so?" Rebecca breathed.

Edgar's expression grew disdainful. "Because the man is a fool. He doesn't believe you're his child."

Rebecca's mind spun, trying to piece together the puzzle that was her life.

Edgar struck the floor with his walking stick and mumbled something under his breath.

"What did you say?" Rebecca pressed.

"I said he's an envying demon who doesn't know the good of what he had." With that, the lightkeeper hobbled from the room, looking especially stoop-shouldered, especially tired, and especially old.

Rebecca knew then that despite the gaping holes in her story and the unknown tales of Edgar and Annabel's story, they shared one thing in common: *Anishinaabewi-gichigami* was a coffin for the hope of ever being loved. It allowed its wild waves to grow into what was good and then pulled it apart until only broken pieces were left behind. Pieces better sunk to the depths and forgotten about.

She had tried to forget, but the waters did not seem to allow her to.

Beating on the lighthouse door brought Abel's footsteps pounding across the floor. He cast a wordless glance at Rebecca, who sat alone at the kitchen table. It was the wee hours of the morning. She had spoken to no one after her conversation with Edgar, but neither had she left the lighthouse as she'd planned. Niina had left to go back to her cabin in Silvertown, Edgar had retired to the lighthouse, and Abel . . . he had given Rebecca a wide berth. The air between them sizzled with sparks that needed merely the right question or statement to erupt into emotional flames. They were flames Rebecca didn't know how to put out or how to contain or even how to properly tend. She must avoid the flames. Only now, it seemed, the flames had come to their front door.

"The stamp mill's ablaze!" It was a boy's voice at the door.

"The mill?" Abel verified.

Rebecca pushed up from her place at the table.

"*Joo!*" the lad responded in Finnish. "Flames higher than the trees! All available men must come before it spreads to the woods."

Abel sprang into action, grabbing his hat, sliding his feet into his boots.

Rebecca hurried to the entryway "What can I do?" The boy at the door eyed her with suspicion, and she drew back.

"Nothing," Abel said. "Stay here." He shoved his arms into his slicker. It wasn't raining. Perhaps he wore it to protect against sparks and flames. Abel hesitated, seeming to debate within himself, before turning and pushing his face close to hers. His icy eyes reflected a hardness in them. "Do *not* leave the lighthouse," he told her.

Rebecca simply nodded. She wanted to say *be careful*, but the words stuck in her throat.

"Tell Edgar what's going on." And with that, the door slammed behind Abel.

Rebecca opened it and rushed outside. Black smoke billowed over the treetops, suffocated the sky and the fresh air. Abel and the boy raced to a sturdy wagon and climbed aboard. Even as Abel took his seat, the boy had already whipped the two horses into action. They were stocky breeds, not meant for speed, but they would reserve Abel and the boy's energy to fight the stamp mill fire.

Movement behind Rebecca drew her attention. Edgar approached the doorway, a question etched on his face.

"The stamp mill is on fire." Rebecca's explanation brought a darkness to Edgar's expression.

"They'll blame you for this." His statement made Rebecca go cold.

Her incredulous stare was returned with frankness. "Hilliard will say you started the fire. He will say you're out to destroy him."

"Whatever reason would I have to do that!" Rebecca cried in utter disbelief. It made no sense! Did her father think she was the devil himself, bent on wickedness?

"Because of *her*," Edgar spat. He looked beyond Rebecca. "He'll think it's because of her. She bewitched him just like she did everyone else. He'll say she's bewitched you too."

"Who? Who has bewitched me?" Rebecca didn't feel bewitched, but then maybe that was why her memories had been stolen from her. Maybe that was why, in the depths of her heart, she knew she would die if something happened to Abel tonight, and yet she could not grasp whether she loved him at all.

Edgar gave the side of the lighthouse an angry slap. He reared back and brought his hand down a second time, ignoring how a corner of one of the bricks sliced into his callused hand, drawing blood.

"Annabel!" he said between gritted teeth. "We will never be free of her."

28

SHEA

Can ever dissever my soul from the soul
of the beautiful Annabel Lee . . .

Annabel Lee

ANNABEL'S LIGHTHOUSE
PRESENT DAY

FINGERTIPS AS LIGHT AS THE TOUCH of a wispy feather traced along Shea's neck. They were warm as they trailed down to her shoulder, and then in an instant they shifted. A frightening cold, so cold that it burned her skin. Nails speared her skin like icicles, and Shea lay there frozen. An oppressive weight held her down. She tried to suck in air, but it was as though something had closed off her airway, blocking the passage to her lungs. She was drowning. She was drowning, and she couldn't break free . . .

Shea shot bolt upright in bed. Her T-shirt clung to her, soaked through with sweat. Rivulets of sweat trailed down her face. She flipped off the covers and leapt from where she'd been sleeping—no, where she'd been having a night terror.

The dream had been so real! So terrifying! One moment she had been enveloped in the sensation of love and warmth, and the next it was as if someone had thrown her into the depths of Lake Superior and then stood by to watch as Shea fought for her last breath.

Annabel.

Shea shook the webs from her fuzzy mind. No. A ghost couldn't induce a vision. She couldn't influence Shea's mind like that or twist her thoughts. But then the mind could conjure many strange things while in a dream. The vision was still vivid in Shea's mind, only this time, as she replayed it, she saw herself in Annabel's place, with Pete standing on the shore.

No. No.

Pete would never have stood on the shore like that. Pete would have plunged into the waves to rescue her. He would have battled the freezing temperatures. He would have drank the entire lake if need be. That was Pete; he took care of what was necessary. For her.

Was that not romantic enough?

Shea whimpered as her conflicted emotions sent a wave of guilt through her. She spun from the bed and yanked her curls back from her face, tying them into a knot where they would hold for a bit until she could find a hair tie.

She sought refuge in the kitchen, snatching a cold Coke from Holt's "icebox." The vintage word for refrigerator now soured on her tongue. Holt. Holt had disappeared to Canada like a guilty man on the run.

But guilty of what? He had tried to *save* Pete, hadn't he? He'd been the one to call the EMTs and to summon her.

And what about the tales of Annabel and the mysterious Rebecca that had consumed Jonathan Marks—until his bloody death in the very sitting room beyond where she stood? It was all horrendous, but Holt could not have any ties to it. Fifteen years ago, Holt would have more than likely been away at college.

He'd have no incentive to murder Jonathan! Not to mention, Holt didn't come into possession of the lighthouse until years later. There was no motive. None. It made no sense.

Shea popped open her Coke, strode through the entryway, and opened the door to the chilly spring night. Lake Superior was insistent with its waves, but not angry. Shea wandered across the yard, barefoot, toward the embankment. She stared over the dark expanse of the lake, glowing in places where the moon reflected off its surface. The Porcupine Mountains and the forest were mounds of blue, dark against the clear night.

What was she missing? In this entire morbid story surrounding the lighthouse, what was she missing?

Annabel. A woman drowned, left to die by a husband who allegedly stood by and watched as she sank beneath the waves. An unknown lover—maybe the lighthouse keeper? But what part had he played in the thwarted love and the horrible death?

Rebecca. An unknown piece to a story that seemed unimportant, yet Shea was told not to ask about her? Yet, Rebecca was potentially intertwined with Jonathan.

Jonathan. A pacificist, a naturalist, a scientist, supposedly as unmoved by emotion as a rock, losing his mind and committing suicide rather than face Rebecca's story.

Captain Gene. A mysterious man who had fathered Penny, but whose whereabouts were unknown, along with the supposed missing pieces that would put definition to the story of Annabel, the life of Rebecca, and the reason for Jonathan's death.

It all hinged on Captain Gene.

But someone—a force, a person, a spirit?—didn't want the truth exposed. They were stifling the truth and convoluting the channels until all that was left was muddied water, a story of broken hearts, and death.

So much death.

Shea blinked as her eyes focused on movement down the shoreline. Her breath caught at the sight of the wispy, white vision of a woman, a lantern swinging by her side, her night-gown blowing against her legs. Long, white-blond hair blanketed her shoulders. Her pale skin was illuminated by the moonlight.

"Annabel," Shea whispered.

She stepped forward as the woman moved toward the water, entering it, the waves lapping at her legs. Shea was helpless to do anything, to say anything. She stared in shock as Annabel walked deeper and deeper into the lake, until finally she turned and looked directly at Shea. ·

A moment passed, their gazes meeting across the expanse as though connecting across time.

Go to him. Shea heard the voice in her head.

Annabel slipped beneath the waves.

"I know you won't believe me, but it was Annabel. I saw her."

Shea plopped onto a chair next to Pete. He was sitting propped up on the couch, a mound of pillows supporting him. His hair was ruffled, his cheeks covered with a day's growth of whiskers.

"Say that again?"

"I said I saw Annabel, Pete. Last night on the shore. She was carrying a lantern, then just walked into the lake and disappeared beneath the waves."

Shea didn't add the part when she'd heard Annabel whisper *Go to him.* Which made no earthly sense. She could hardly hear a whisper beside her with the crashing of the waves, let alone hear a whisper from several yards away.

Go to him. What did that mean? Go to Pete?

Pete held up a hand. "Okay. Let me . . . let me focus."

"Is it time for your pain med?" Shea offered, popping up from the chair to go retrieve it.

"Shea." Her name on his lips brought her attention back to him. "You need to calm down."

Shea shook her head. "I feel like I'm on the cusp of figuring it out *and* losing my mind. If I could just find Captain Gene, then I think we can solve everything! And sidenote, I don't believe in ghosts, but I'm seeing them! Do you not see the problem here?"

"Hey." Pete spoke with firmness this time. "Calm. Down." He emphasized each word, and it caught Shea by surprise. He never told her what to do. That was her job. She told *him* what to do and—

Shea snapped into awareness and heard her own fickle thoughts, the wildness in her words. She stared at Pete. "Am I losing it? Like Jonathan Marks did?"

"Hardly." A slight smile quirked Pete's mouth upward. "Sit down, would you? Take a deep breath."

Shea did as her aloof and boring husband requested. Only he didn't seem aloof this morning—or boring. No, he seemed different somehow. What had changed since their last massive blowup? Him? Or maybe her?

"I don't know what to do, Pete." She was surprised by the watery sound of her voice.

Pete reached out to her with his good arm, and she took his hand. "You're not losing your mind, Shea. You've undergone a lot of stress the last few days, and I know you're not sleeping."

"I am," Shea admitted, "but fitfully."

"Right. And then there's us." Pete let his words hang for a moment before continuing. "It's a lot. I get it."

Shea bit the inside of her lip. She felt like she might *cry*, for pity's sake! "This was all for a book. A stupid book. And now— look at you. I don't know who I am anymore. I don't *like* who I am, but I don't know what I'm supposed to be."

There.

She'd said it.

Out loud.

She'd admitted to her weakness. Shea didn't know who she was anymore, or maybe who she had ever been. She just knew what she *wanted*. A dream. A carefully calculated dream of a bestselling book, a life of traveling and exploring, a husband who doted on her and shared her interests, and . . .

"I wanted you to think I hung the moon." Shea whispered her final thought aloud.

Pete's eyes turned glassy. His grip on her hand tightened.

"Why would I think that?" he asked.

Shea's gaze shot up to meet his in surprise. There was honest confusion.

He continued, "Why would I make you larger than you are, larger than you're capable of being? That's not fair to you. To have expectations of you that you can't *fulfill*? Why would I do that?"

That took her aback. Shea tried to catch up to what Pete was saying. "But—"

Pete scowled. "Stupid love songs and stories—they put ideas in people's heads that are unrealistic. Hang the moon, swim the ocean, go to the ends of the earth. Am I supposed to make you my god? Am I supposed to worship you? How would that be *kind* to you, Shea? Those expectations would crash and burn really fast."

Shea blinked. It was all she could do. His words made sense but were so counter, so different from how she had wished him to be. She *had* wished Pete would hang the moon for her, fly to the stars, spin the world on its axis.

Pete's thumb moved back and forth, caressing her hand. "I chose you, Shea. The good, the bad, the ugly, the day-to-day mundane of you. I chose you because that's the gift I was given. I just had to say yes to it. And I did. I mean . . . God gave me you. No bells. No whistles. Just you."

Shea couldn't breathe.

Pete finished, "And I've always been content with that."

29

S HEA AND PETE PULLED TO A STOP in front of Edna's
house.

"This is it," Shea stated.

Marnie had invited her there, and Shea was going to take
her up on it.

"I'll just sit here," Pete said, his arm held secure in the sling.
He was sore—that much was obvious—but he'd also been quietly insistent that he accompany her.

"Okay. But if someone throws a brick at the windshield, be
sure to duck." Shea did a double take. "What?"

There was a look on Pete's face, but it wasn't appreciation
of her dry humor, and she didn't understand it. He gave her a
quick smile. "Nothing."

She searched his face for a second and then, "Okay. I'll be
back as soon as I can."

Within moments Shea had knocked on the door, and Edna
greeted her with a warm welcome.

"Oh, I thought you'd never come back to see me after that
ridiculous windshield incident." Edna looked over her shoulder.
"I see you brought someone with you to watch the car. Good

girl." She lifted a frail, age-dotted hand in a wave to Pete, who returned the gesture.

"What can I do for you?" Edna led the way into her living room and motioned for Shea to sit down.

Shea decided to waste no time sharing her latest theory. "Well, I've been researching Annabel's story—"

"Yes, I know." Edna's smile stretched across her powdery soft face.

"Yes, and I came across the name Rebecca."

Edna's smile waned.

Shea didn't let that deter her. "I know that Jonathan Marks had been digging into her story, but I haven't a clue where to start. Do you know who this Rebecca was?"

Edna slowly shook her head, her permed curls holding in place. "Nooooo . . ." She dragged out the word as if trying to remember, but Shea could tell the woman was lying.

"How about Annabel's husband?" Shea tried the whiplash technique of changing directions quickly.

"She was married, yes," Edna responded as if by instinct. Then a slight frown creased her forehead.

"And her husband's name?" Shea pressed.

"That's up for debate." Edna's tone grew cheerier again, as if she were returning to more comfortable ground. "Annabel was married, but it's all a big question as to who her husband was. You see, the story goes that when she died, her husband—"

"Watched from the shore," Shea finished. "Yes. Yes, I'm aware of that. I'm trying to piece together whatever it was that Jonathan Marks pieced together. Wouldn't Annabel's marriage be public record?"

"In 1852? Back then this place was wilder than the Wild West, my dear. There *were* no public records. And as for Jonathan . . ." A slight hardness entered Edna's eyes. "Shea, you need to be careful you follow in his footsteps. Annabel remained quiet over the years. Stories and legends were what we lived on, until Jonathan decided to dig into the past. It's not a good thing to awaken a spirit."

"Why?" Shea leaned forward in earnest. "What is it about a woman's long-ago drowning in Lake Superior that would still affect so many people here, today, in the twenty-first century?"

Edna tightened her lips.

Shea saw the elderly woman warring with herself. She latched onto the woman's moment of weakness. "Please, Edna, tell me."

"Greed." Edna's one word seemed to suck the air from the living room. She had grown serious, and her voice had a tremor now. Shea couldn't tell if that was because of Edna's advanced age or because she was nervous. "Greed," she repeated. "That's the root of it. It's the root of most of mankind's problems."

Shea waited, praying Edna would continue.

She did. Only this time she fixed her eyes on the lamp on the end table near Shea and allowed herself to go deep into her thoughts.

"Back in the days of Annabel, the European settlers were mostly trappers, with some being miners. As time went on, silver was discovered in the area we know today as Silvertown. A man named Hilliard was the one responsible for most of Silvertown's growth. The town began to boom and showed great potential. The proof of that was the building of the stamp mill. Hilliard used the promise of wealth to garner the financial capital to keep Silvertown growing. He had investors lined up from here to Philadelphia, but he desperately needed more to realize his grand plan. Two things then happened that set in motion what is still in motion today. That's where your Rebecca comes in—and more than likely why Jonathan drove himself mad and committed suicide."

Shea noted Edna's belief in Jonathan Marks's suicide over murder. She would circle back to asking about that later. She gave Edna her full attention. "And the two things are . . . ?"

Edna lifted a finger. "One. The stamp mill burned down. Hilliard claimed it was arson. History records it was accidental, that a witness came forward saying there was a fire started in a coal stove that got out of control. Either way, it was a significant loss. It would mean an even bigger loss for Hilliard if his investors started pulling out as a result. How do you maintain the financial backing for a major project in the mining industry if those of means get cold feet? Even so, Hilliard might have recovered had it not been for his daughter."

"Rebecca." Shea filled in one piece of the puzzle.

Edna nodded as she lifted a second finger. Her reluctance to continue seemed to be behind her now. "Two. Rebecca. Hilliard claimed his daughter was behind the stamp mill's destruction. He also claimed that Rebecca had stolen some important documents from him—documents that would guarantee him the investors he needed. Among these stolen papers was a map that showed a very rich, very abundant deposit of silver ore deep in the wilderness somewhere. A deposit that wouldn't be exhausted for decades and would promise great wealth and economic opportunity. But without the map, well, you know how many thousands of acres of wilderness there are around here?"

Shea repositioned herself on the edge of her seat. "And how does all that affect things here today? Why don't people like to talk about Rebecca?"

Edna, not at all in a hurry, reached for a glass of water sitting on the small table near her and took a few sips.

Shea told herself to keep calm. She suddenly wished Pete were here to lay a hand on her knee, so she'd stop bouncing it due to nervousness.

Edna coughed, wiped the sides of her mouth with a handkerchief she pulled from her shirtsleeve, and continued. "The map was never found."

Shea's knee stilled.

Edna paused as if to add a bit of dramatic impact. "That's what drove Jonathan Marks crazy. Trying to find out where Rebecca Hilliard stashed the map that showed the location of the silver ore deposit."

Shea frowned. "Couldn't Hilliard have had another map drawn up? He had to know where this supposed vein of silver was."

Edna nodded. "Perhaps. But while the map might've been the reason Jonathan Marks went haywire because he was on a treasure hunt, back in Hilliard's time I think it was less about the map and more about the other papers that had Hilliard in such a tizzy. Silvertown went bust shortly after the stamp mill burned. Hilliard lost all his investors. He lost . . . everything."

"What happened to his daughter, Rebecca?"

Edna shook her head. "She disappeared into the annals of history. But she was blamed for the economic downfall of Silvertown. She essentially made off with its future and it turned into a ghost town. Jonathan thought he'd figured out some tie between Rebecca and Annabel's ghost and the map. Some *big reveal*, but then he just gave up. He killed himself."

Shea considered Edna's words. "Jonathan found out something he'd been passionately pursuing, but instead of revealing it, he decided to end his life?"

Edna nodded. She rubbed the end of her nose with her handkerchief. "Poor Jonathan. He was . . . such a damaged soul."

Jonathan's death made less sense now than ever to Shea. Who killed themselves when they were supposedly on the cusp of their greatest find? She bid Edna goodbye and made her way back to Pete and the truck. Once she slipped into the driver's side, Pete waited for her to speak.

Shea twisted in her seat to face him. "If I were to tell you I had super big news, would you expect me to kill myself?"

"You ask the weirdest questions," Pete retorted.

"Well?" she persisted.

"No. I'd expect you to come out with it and tell me."

Shea could tell Pete was waiting for the repeat of her conversation with Edna. Instead, she leveled a direct look on him and said, "Jonathan Marks was murdered. I'd bet my book on it."

30

REBECCA

For the moon never beams without bringing me dreams . . .
Annabel Lee

THEY KNEW WHERE TO FIND HER, and with the opportunity provided by the distraction of the stamp mill in flames, Edgar was one man against ten. This time Hilliard had sent more than Mercer to the lighthouse, and he was no longer acting covertly.

A rifle butt slammed into Edgar's midsection, and the old man went down to his knees on the lawn, his rifle falling to the ground. The group of mercenaries encircled him—bearded faces, grungy clothes, the physique of miners, the sooty remains of the stamp mill fire marring their skin.

Mercer bent over Edgar. "Hand her over!"

Rebecca burst from her hiding place in the lighthouse, where Edgar had demanded she stay put after spotting the incoming small army of miners. Where Abel was, they didn't know, but it was just Edgar now against much younger, much brawnier men. Men with few scruples.

"Stop!" Rebecca screamed at Mercer. Anger filled her at the sight of Edgar. He was still doubled over on the ground, yet he was waving her back into the lighthouse as if it could somehow save her. It wouldn't, Rebecca knew. Mercer and his men would bust into the place and take her anyway, but only after beating Edgar.

She could not let that happen.

"Leave him alone!" Rebecca staggered toward them, her hand on her abdomen as though she could protect the child Abel claimed was his.

Mercer straightened, and his eyes narrowed. "Ah, so you're finally going to come on your own free will."

Rebecca fought the urge to look at Edgar. She couldn't lose her resolve, and she knew he was beseeching her with his every movement and expression. *Go! Hide!* She could practically hear his unspoken demands.

But she was done with hiding. Finished with running from memories that were like ghosts lurking in the back of her traumatized mind. Finished with denying that her father was a greed-driven man with no conscience when it came to her.

Mercer tipped his head toward one of the men, and they stalked toward her, grabbing her arm and jerking her forward.

"Leave her alone!" Edgar grunted, attempting to push himself off the ground.

Mercer brought a boot down on Edgar's shoulder and sent him floundering onto his back. He bent over Edgar. "You knew this was coming, old man."

The next moments were chaotic. Rebecca was taken to a wagon, where the men hoisted her into the back with little care. Her leg hit the wagon frame, and she bit her lip to avoid crying out.

Mercer's laugh followed her as the wagon jerked forward. Rebecca curled up on the wagon bed, trying to drown out Edgar's shouts. Shouts from a man who decades earlier would have had the fortitude to fight a good fight but now was prohibited by the limitations of an old man's body.

The wagon jolted over the rutted road, each pothole slamming Rebecca against the rough wooden planks. It felt as if hours had passed before she saw glimpses of Silvertown, its rugged shanties and flat-fronted buildings boasting a mercantile, a blacksmith shop, and a saloon. A thick, suffocating blanket of smoke filled the air. It settled over the small but burgeoning town like a fog.

Moments later, the wagon pulled to a stop in front of a square, plain-looking building. Rebecca noted the plaque on its door: HILLIARD MINING. A sickening anxiety assaulted her. It was one thing to face a father whose selfishness and greed seemed to have no bounds. It was an entirely different thing to face him knowing they had a lifetime of history together—history she could recall only snippets of, and those snippets were not pleasant ones.

It was startling how quickly she remembered him. The memories she'd buried deep in her mind suddenly rose to the surface with a terrible force.

Walter Hilliard.

Her father.

He sat behind a desk, his blue eyes unyielding and cold. There was no hint of familial concern or care for Rebecca's well-being. Instead, he watched as Mercer pushed Rebecca into a chair opposite Hilliard. He watched as Mercer ducked from the room and shut the door. Then he leveled his attention on Rebecca.

"You're a lot of trouble for me, Rebecca."

Her father. He was a fierce man, driven, savvy, and demanding in his expectations. Rebecca met his gaze briefly, then averted her eyes out of habit.

Don't look him in the eyes.

Don't show signs of defiance.

Comply.

Obey.

Respect.

That had been her motto since Rebecca was a child. She remembered it now. She remembered the way the back of his hand would bruise her as a little girl when she dared to question what he'd ordered. She recalled the glimpses of him at night when he was dressed in casual attire, reclining by the fireplace, reading a book and looking like the ideal father figure. It was a poignant memory, especially the one time when she had attempted to include herself by merely starting a conversation and he had sworn at her for disrupting his peace. Then he'd struck her, for no other reason than that she had been born.

"Did you think that burning down my mill would ruin me?" Hilliard wasn't going to dance around the purpose of his hauling her back into his possession.

"I didn't—"

"Stop." Hilliard held up a hand and leaned over his desk, his broad chest a wall of power. "I will not allow you to avenge any wrongs you believe I have done against you. You will return those papers to me at once, and then I'll wash my hands of you and your pathetic excuse of a husband."

Rebecca longed for a moment of peace to summon the broken pieces of her memory, including the depth of who Abel was to her. She could feel it in her soul now, and a part of her quaked for Abel to barge in and salvage what was left of her. But he couldn't—she wouldn't let him. Her father would ruin Abel. Ruin the lighthouse.

Let him ruin only her . . . and Abel's child.

Rebecca was careful not to touch her abdomen and bring attention to the existence of the babe.

"Where is my brother?" she attempted. "Where is Aaron?"

Her father chuckled. "Home, where he should be. He's fine. If you think I'd harm my son—I would never. He *is* my son. His mother gave me an heir, and I will treasure that."

His mother. Rebecca didn't miss the inference. Another piece slipped back into place. Aaron was her half brother. Her father had remarried when she was five. Aaron's mother was with them until shortly after Aaron's birth, and then she had died.

"It doesn't have to be this difficult, and yet you have bucked me every step of the way." Hilliard moved around his desk and leaned against it, glaring down at her with judgment in his eyes. "Where are the papers? The map?"

"I don't know what you're talking about," she said with a nervous tremble in her voice.

Hilliard's face darkened. "Stop lying."

"I'm not!" A desperate sob caught in her throat.

"You are, though," he insisted. "You're trying to ruin me, Rebecca, and I won't allow it."

"Why are you doing this?" Rebecca honestly didn't know what had inspired her to supposedly steal the elusive papers to begin with. And she didn't understand why her father had no qualms about abusing her to retrieve them.

Hilliard let out a burst of derisive laughter. "Why? Why!" He threw his hands in the air in exasperation, and Rebecca flinched back in her chair, afraid he would swing them at her next. "Because you *despise* me, that's why. You're like your mother. Wicked and subversive, and you feign meekness while you practice your wiles and trickery behind my back."

A flash of recollection fluttered across Rebecca's mind. That night. The night she had run through the woods before Edgar had found her at Annabel's grave. She had stolen something. She remembered now. She recalled sneaking into this very room, taking a roll of papers from her father's desk and slipping away into the night. A shout. Mercer chasing after her. Her escape to the woods, which became a nightlong attempt to evade him. Then Mercer caught up with her, and his assault was bruising. She had broken free using her teeth and her knees, had grabbed the papers and hidden in the underbrush until finally Mercer moved on. Still hunting for her. Rebecca remembered falling to the ground that was Annabel's grave. She remembered nothing more until Edgar's face came into view.

"Give them to me, Rebecca. The papers and the map." Hilliard held out his hand as though she would pull the sheaf of papers from under her dress.

"I don't know where they are." Though she spoke the truth, her father didn't believe her. A cry escaped her as the back of his hand connected with her cheek. A few choice names erupted from his mouth.

Rebecca doubled over, shielding her face from another back-handed slap.

Hilliard grabbed her by the collar of her dress, yanking her to her feet. "You are pathetic—just like your mother!" Spittle dotted Rebecca's face as he held his mere inches away. "You have inherited her spirit. Pretend humility while cloaking a rebellious nature, one that's determined to bleed me dry." Hilliard shook her, and Rebecca whimpered. "You'll be the death of me if I'm not the death of you first."

"Please!" Rebecca begged, hating the weakness in her voice.

Hilliard released her with a shove, and she fell back onto the chair.

In that moment, as she shrank within herself under the weight of Hilliard's threats, the room seemed as if it had faded away. Rebecca now floated somewhere in the past, the long-ago wish she had whispered as a child on her lips. *"Who is my mother?"* she'd asked him.

Hilliard had refused to give her a name. He refused to give Rebecca's mother the honor of a remembered legacy. Instead, he had spoken only of his second wife. Aaron's mother. A good woman, but not one Rebecca remembered well.

The room swirled and came back into focus. Rebecca gripped the arms of the chair, and suddenly she knew that her mother was more central, more key, to all of this. The survey and papers, the burned-down stamp mill, the silver ore, the lighthouse . . .

"Who is my mother?" Rebecca's question had an edge to it that matched the steel in her father's demeanor.

He stared at her for a long, horrible moment.

"Who is my mother?" Rebecca repeated, anger rising within her.

"Your mother?" Hilliard's laugh was both rude and hateful. He entrapped Rebecca in his cold, hard gaze. "Your mother drowned in the lake."

Rebecca didn't breathe. She couldn't breathe. She knew. Before Hilliard ever said her name, Rebecca knew. And it terrified her.

"Your mother is Annabel." Hilliard spat the words as though the name itself were filthy. "Annabel who haunts the lighthouse. Annabel who haunts the shores. Annabel who haunts the miners. Annabel who will *not* remove this curse from me!"

"What curse?" Rebecca asked. "Please, I don't understand."

"*You!*" Hillard's admission stole the last shred of hope from Rebecca's soul. "You! She saddled me with a daughter who isn't even mine. You pathetic bastard of a girl!"

31

SHEA

Of the beautiful Annabel Lee . . .
Annabel Lee

ANNABEL'S LIGHTHOUSE
PRESENT DAY

SHEA SLIPPED ONTO A BARSTOOL, and Penny set the requested Coke in front of her, bubbling over ice with a plastic straw. "So you think that Jonathan was murdered?" Penny confirmed, leaning her elbows on the bar.

Shea took a sip of Coke. "I have a strong suspicion. There's potential motive for someone to take him out, and zero motive for Jonathan to have done it to himself."

Penny nodded.

The strains of country music filtered through the bar as they shared a companionable silence, both lost in their thoughts.

Shea had left Pete at the lighthouse. Now Shea was trying to collect the fragments of her research.

"I found out the Rebecca that Jonathan Marks was researching was actually Hilliard's daughter," Shea said, watching Penny's reaction closely because she wasn't sure at this point whether she trusted anyone in Silvertown or Ontonagon.

Penny's lips thinned. "Edna told you that?"

"Yes," Shea replied. "It was Edna who told me, although there are no online records or anything to corroborate it."

Penny nodded. "I suppose that makes sense. They wouldn't have kept detailed records—not back then when these parts were just being inhabited by settlers. So that means Jonathan's theory was probably correct."

"You know about his theory?" Shea frowned, wondering why Penny hadn't offered it up prior to this.

Penny adjusted the earring in her ear that was on its way to freedom. Pushing its hook back through the hole, she smoothed the side of her peppery-gray hair. "Pieces of it. Not much."

Shea searched for the right questions and came up short. "I don't know where to go from here. Did Jonathan have a journal, or notes, or keep his research in the cloud? Was he close to anyone around here, someone he might have confided in?"

Penny started folding a square cocktail napkin into an origami crane.

"Penny?" Shea raised a brow, sensing Penny was way too interested in the napkin.

Penny bent a wing into place, then pressed the crane flat against the bar. "Fine." She lifted her eyes, and there was an admission in them that surprised Shea. She hefted a deep breath. "Jonathan and I were . . . well, we were in a relationship."

"I know." Shea clapped a hand over her mouth. "I'm sorry. I didn't mean—"

Penny winced. "Marnie tell you? Well, Jonathan and I never really told anyone, but she's as nosy as they come."

Penny ran a fingernail along the seam in the back of the paper crane. "I've not spoken about my relationship with Jonathan because I feel if someone was willing to kill him over a ridiculously old history lesson, then they might be willing to do it again." Sheepishness spread across Penny's face. "I don't want to be involved, Shea. I don't have any *need* to be near this story." There was a bitterness in her tone that Shea wanted to respect, and yet she couldn't help but feel distrustful of Penny. Was she being completely forthright with Shea . . . in anything she said?

"Penny, when I spoke to Mr. Fronell, he said the only person who had the right to talk about Rebecca was your father, Captain Gene. Edna was reticent to talk about her too, even though she finally did. Is it really because she's still being blamed a century later for the downfall of Silvertown's mining opportunities?" Shea gave a doubtful look to Penny. "What is it about this Rebecca that is so sacred that it's your father's 'right' to talk about her and no one else?"

Penny looked away and then turned and disappeared between the hanging doors that separated the bar from the kitchen.

Well, that went well. Shea reached for the paper crane and fiddled with it as she considered her next move. A few moments later, Penny returned, a cardboard box in her hands.

She plopped the box onto the bar in front of Shea. "Open it."

Shea met Penny's frank gaze, then slowly she unfolded the cardboard flaps. Inside were a pile of notes, newspaper clippings, a beat-up old book about Annabel's Lighthouse, and a sheaf of dot matrix printed paper.

Penny pointed at the dot matrix papers. "Have a look at those."

Shea pulled the first page from the box. It was a family tree of sorts, listing Penny's name, her father's, and those of relatives that branched off until showing the current generation and time.

"Now take a look at the next page," Penny directed.

Shea flipped the page, reading aloud, "Your dad's father was Timothy, who was born in 1932."

"Keep going."

"His father was Ralph."

"And?" Penny led.

Shea leaned forward, unsure if she was reading it correctly. Her eyes shot up to Penny, and Penny's face confirmed the truth. "Ralph was the son of Aaron Hilliard? Who is Aaron Hilliard?"

"Keep looking," Penny urged. "Those are Jonathan's notes. I don't know where he found out all this stuff or if it's even true." She didn't look pleased. In fact, she looked quite nervous.

Shea followed the hand-scribbled family tree. "Aaron is a half brother to Rebecca, and Rebecca is . . . the *daughter* of Annabel?" Shea couldn't help the higher octave in her voice. "Why didn't you just come out and tell me this at the very beginning? You're Annabel's great-great-great niece!"

Penny pursed her lips. "When Jonathan discovered that, that's when things went wrong for him. I didn't want the same to happen to anyone else. But you're too deep into this now. After Pete's accident, well, now it all just needs to end. I just want it to go away."

Shea grappled with the logic of it. "Is this because of that missing silver map?"

Penny's face was ashen with withheld secrets. "If the map still exists—if the *silver vein* still exists—it could impact this area in so many ways. Conservation and land rights are likely to be contested—it would be opening a huge can of worms. Not to mention if someone finds the map to the silver vein, if it's on private property, they could offer to buy the land without mentioning what they knew, and then all that silver would be theirs. There are so many ifs and buts, Shea."

"You mean . . . ?"

Penny nodded emphatically.

Shea completed her thought aloud. "If there *is* a silver vein in these woods, then the bust of the 1870s needn't have happened. Whoever finds the map can potentially revive it and that creates—"

"Land war potential. Conservation issues. A whole mess, not to mention a lot of locals will want to dig into it and revive the wealth," Penny inserted.

"And lay claim to it. Which means the value of what Rebecca stole from her father is very significant."

"Also," Penny went on, "if you're a local, you probably believe that Annabel's ghost will do anything to avenge any wrongs committed against her—and against her daughter."

Shea sat straighter on her barstool. "You're not saying . . ."

Penny's lips flattened in resignation before she answered, "They say if a person gets too close to Rebecca's secret, they also get too close to Annabel. And Annabel isn't a friendly ghost where her daughter is concerned."

"Or her legacy," Shea added.

～～～

"But no one knows if Jonathan Marks ever found the map," Shea concluded, recounting her conversation with Penny.

Pete rested in a lounge chair in the yard not far from the lighthouse and almost directly in the spot where he'd been hit by the car. The chair was padded with pillows, and he wore sunglasses to block the setting sun that reflected off the lake. It was quiet tonight, restful, almost as though the lake were relieved to have some of its secrets revealed.

"I can't get over Annabel being a part of Penny's family tree." Shea shook her head, bending forward in her lawn chair to rest her elbows on her knees. "There's so much I could put in my book now, but then I'm not sure about the infringement on privacy. Penny wants nothing to do with the map. In fact, she doesn't really want to talk about this with anyone."

"I guess finding Captain Gene isn't important now," Pete said.

"Isn't it? If anyone would know if the map was ever found, I would think it would be him!" Shea declared.

"Why?"

She twisted to eye Pete as though he'd not even been listening. But then maybe his mind didn't work like hers in connecting invisible dots. "Jonathan would have known the connection between Penny and her ancestry all the way back to Annabel. As conscientious about things as he supposedly was, if he'd found the map, he would've known the map at least—maybe not the land where the silver vein might be—should technically belong to Captain Gene, the next of kin."

Pete lowered his sunglasses a bit. "Captain Gene."

"Yes. He's Rebecca's nephew many times removed. Technically, Captain Gene is a descendant of Hilliard, who originally owned the bulk of Silvertown." The breeze picked up and lifted some of Shea's curls and blew them across her face. She pulled them away, paying no mind to Pete's silence because it was customary. "Anyway, someone must've killed Jonathan because he had either found the map, and they wanted it, or he knew where it was." Shea hesitated. Her conclusion still seemed questionable. "But why kill him if only he *knew* where the map was? Did he tell his killer before he died? Or did he *have* the map, and they killed him to *get* the map?"

"You're making my head hurt," Pete grumbled.

Shea ignored him. "The other thing is, I can't get past the whole story of Annabel's ghost."

Pete seemed to agree. "Yeah, that's weird. It's a stretch for anyone to believe Annabel's ghost smashed your windshield or drove that car into me."

"Right?" Shea said.

She was enjoying the fact that Pete wasn't off in a garage working on his cars and trucks. She had his attention, and she really liked that. She also wondered at his sudden willingness to engage with her. Maybe it was because his convalescing was forcing Pete to have to slow down. Or maybe he had really listened to her—listened to what her needs and desires were—even though, she had to admit, she'd shown herself to be acting selfishly as well.

"Edna said that Annabel's ghost was quiet throughout the decades until Jonathan came along. I find that suspicious," Shea mused.

Pete shot back a quick answer. "Maybe Annabel's ghost is only a cover. You know, for someone who's dead set on getting their hands on that map."

Shea's eyes widened. She looked at Pete. "Wait . . ."

"What is it?" Pete asked.

"Edna Carraway is the one who first told me about Annabel being protective. Penny said Edna sometimes shares 'dementia-inspired' tales. And I was at Edna's house when my windshield was vandalized."

"So?" Pete scowled. "What's the connection?"

Shea frowned. "I know Edna didn't do it, but if she concocted the idea of Annabel being protective of her legacy, then someone else had to have adopted the same idea."

"You have someone in mind?"

"Marnie." Shea leveled a look on Pete. "It has to be Marnie."

"Edna's daughter? The waitress at the diner?"

"It makes sense—at least that Marnie would *know* about the concept of Annabel's ghost and her protective nature."

Pete summarized, "So you think Marnie is after the silver map, and she's the one who killed Jonathan Marks for it? Now *you're* stretching, Shea."

He was right. Shea collapsed back into her lawn chair, staring over the lake and wishing Annabel's ghost would just walk up to them and tell them what had happened. "I'm never going to figure this out, am I?" Shea mumbled.

Pete's low chuckle was her answer, followed by a contented

sigh. "Probably not. But, if nothing else, Annabel has done one thing."

"What's that?" Shea asked.

Pete smiled. "She got you and me talking again. I'd say that's a big accomplishment—for a ghost."

It dawned on Shea in the middle of the night—like most things did when she was lying in bed wide awake with insomnia.

Annabel's grave.

Penny had mentioned it wasn't far away from the lighthouse. And if so, maybe there was a clue there that would help Shea put all the pieces together.

She knew she should wait until morning to go check it out. But as alert as she was, dawn seemed ages away. So Shea slipped from bed and dressed quietly in a pair of jeans and a sweatshirt. She left a note on the kitchen table just in case Pete woke up looking for her in the next fifteen minutes. She didn't intend to be gone long, but the moon was almost full, the lake was calm, and the evening had been beautiful. All she needed was a flashlight and she'd be good to go.

Finding one in a kitchen cabinet, Shea flicked it on and exited the lighthouse. In the moonlight, the lighthouse itself towered like a sentinel, dark and unyielding, but also dormant. Its lantern no longer glowed as it had back in the day when it was essential for ships traversing Lake Superior.

Unsure where exactly Annabel's grave was located, Shea started off toward the woods. This was also in the direction of Silvertown. Because the woods were sparser here, the area seemed more conducive to a graveyard. She swept the flashlight's beam into the woods as she hiked between the trees. Exploring the woods at night was sort of fun—except a nagging sensation told her it was probably foolhardy if her theories proved to be true. Her theories were based on the argument that none of the recent happenings that involved damage or injury were accidental.

If someone was lurking in these woods, which were in the shadow of the lighthouse, and now Shea was announcing her nosy presence with a flashlight, scanning the area with its beam . . .

Smart, Shea. Real smart.

She flicked it off and plunged herself into darkness illuminated only by the moon. Yeah. She hadn't thought this through. Shea was turning to traipse back through the woods toward the lighthouse when the toe of her shoe collided with something hard and sharp sticking up out of the earth.

"You're kidding me," she muttered under her breath, then squatted close to the ground, daring to flick the flashlight back on. Sure enough, the corner of a gravestone stuck out from the fern and the undergrowth.

Shea set the flashlight on the ground and made quick work of pulling wet leaves and other debris from atop the stone, and then she sat back on her heels.

There in carved letters was Annabel's name.

Date of death said 1852, but there was nothing else. No other clues. Nothing to confirm Shea's theories and recategorize them as facts.

"Hello, Annabel," Shea whispered almost reverently. She ran a finger along the etching of the name. "What have you been hiding all these years? Why is the lighthouse so important to people?"

As if Annabel heard her, the breeze picked up, sending leaves swirling around Shea. Surprised by the sudden gust of wind, Shea fell onto her hip. Her left hand shot out to brace herself, and her palm scraped against another stone, buried beneath more debris.

Another stone?

Shea clawed at the moss and leaves that covered it. Like Annabel's grave marker, this one also lay flat on the ground. Forgotten, untended, a story untold.

She grabbed the flashlight and held it over the name etched in this stone—this unknown stone.

Edgar.

Just a name.

No date.

Nothing to memorialize this man who had once lived.

Nothing to tell her why he had been laid to rest beside the tomb of Annabel and her lighthouse.

32

REBECCA

And the stars never rise, though I feel the bright eyes . . .
Annabel Lee

ANNABEL'S LIGHTHOUSE
SPRING, 1874

WHAT DO YOU MEAN, you don't remember?" Hilliard asked.

His hard stare brought back the memories Rebecca didn't want to recall. More and more flooded her consciousness. The moments she'd hidden under her bed as a child when her father had stormed around the house in a drunken rage. The times she had planted a pretty smile on her face at dinner functions, where he paraded her around to potential investors. They had traveled to places like Philadelphia and Washington, D.C., St. Louis and Detroit. Hilliard was always mingling with investors, politicians, men driven by the pursuit of power.

Rebecca had lived in her father's shadow, managed each day under his thumb, and had known from a young age that she was no more to him than a tool.

"I asked you a question!" Hilliard's sharp demand brought Rebecca back to the present.

Her heartbeat was erratic, her breaths coming in short gasps. Panic wrapped itself around her.

"I don't remember," she whimpered, desperately wishing she *could* remember where she had stashed the papers. Wishing she could remember as well *why* she had taken them in the first place.

Hilliard marched to the door of his office and jerked it open. "Mercer!" he shouted.

"Yes, sir?" Mercer's voice sent shivers through Rebecca's body.

"Take my daughter to the shack and keep her there until she complies and tells you where the papers are."

"Yes, sir," Mercer said.

Rebecca's breaths came faster now. Mercer strode in and hauled Rebecca by her arm from the chair.

"No!" She cried out against the pain of his brutal grip. "Father, please!" Rebecca pleaded, tears staining her face. He had to have some mercy in him, some element of concern or of conscience. But she saw none of that on his face or in his eyes. Instead, selfish ambition and greed shadowed her father's countenance despite the well-trimmed beard and dark sideburns, his overall debonair appearance. He was a man who was used to having his way.

Hilliard put out a hand to stop Mercer as he tugged Rebecca toward the door, her feet stumbling over themselves.

"This is your last chance, Rebecca," Hilliard warned. "Once you are out of my sight, your welfare is out of my control."

Rebecca sucked in a gulp of air. "You're a monster," she whispered.

Hilliard's face hardened, and he pointed to the door. "Take her. Get those papers and map from her. Do whatever you need to. I will not lose this town because of the impulse of that woman's illegitimate offspring!"

Mercer shoved her out a back door, away from the small town's main street. The air was still thick with smoke. Miners and a few women scurried on missions likely related to the stamp mill—their livelihood—which now, according to Hilliard, lay in ashes. Mining would be slow and worthless without the mill. To move the quantity of ore necessary to maintain strong economic growth, the mill had to be in working order.

Mercer half threw Rebecca into the back of a waiting wagon. Bear was there, and he hauled her up and in, her legs scraping on the wood floor. He held her down with a boot to her midsection, and Rebecca froze. Any struggle from her would only result in pressure from his foot, and that in turn might harm Abel's baby.

Abel's baby.

It was how she thought of the child now. Her loyalty to the babe was due to her loyalty to the man who had shown her kindness. He had withheld the knowledge of their marriage—of his fatherhood—she could only assume because he didn't wish her to flee again. The world around them had begun to spiral out of control, not the least of which being Kjersti's death. Grief and fear had a way of making souls make hard choices—and not always the best ones. She should know.

The wagon hit a rut that jolted Bear's balance. His foot came off Rebecca, and she rolled to the far side of the wagon, away from him. As fast as she could, she gripped the side and pulled herself into a sitting position.

"Please, someone! Help—!" Her screams were cut off as Bear's arm came across her mouth, dragging her back against him.

But in that moment, Rebecca's eyes latched onto another's that emerged from the hazy, smoke-filled street. Niina's horrified expression summarized every ounce of Rebecca's terror.

She was alone in the shack that Mercer had brought her to before. The place she had escaped from, an act he'd obviously recalled because her hands and feet were bound tighter now, and Bear stood sentinel outside the rickety door made of wood planks. She could see daylight through the top and bottom of the door. She could also see the heels of Bear's boots. She was not going anywhere, even if she could wriggle free from her bindings.

Rebecca allowed the tears to come, though they had been falling longer than she'd realized. She wasn't strong; she wasn't a fighter. No, she had always been compliant, easily manipulated, well aware that things would go better for her if she didn't go against Walter Hilliard. The man who claimed he was not her father. The man who had raised her because of her dead mother, Annabel. Was it true? Was he truly not her father? Or perhaps that was the thin thread of reason that had made Hilliard keep her close to him. To raise her anyway. Maybe he questioned it too. Maybe Annabel had never told him whether Rebecca was or wasn't his, and Hilliard had drawn his own conclusions.

Annabel. Rebecca closed her eyes, and Edgar's story returned to her. Had he loved her? He claimed to have. The unrequited love in his words, in the old man's tone, haunted Rebecca now.

Annabel had been a miner's daughter, Edgar had said. Hilliard had told Rebecca that she was not his child. Edgar had loved Annabel. Hilliard had married her.

Rebecca's heart began to race. Two men, one woman, a child—Rebecca—and Annabel's death. This was a legacy. A legacy of one woman torn between two men.

She strained to remember the date of death on Annabel's gravestone—1852, it had a said. She would have just been born. Was she . . . was she Edgar's daughter? Rebecca's watery gasp echoed in the shack, and Bear's boot slammed against the door.

"Shut up!" he demanded.

Rebecca bit down on her tongue, willing away the sob that stuck in her throat.

Edgar was an old man, at least twenty years Hilliard's senior. He would have been in his fifties when Rebecca was born, and yet Rebecca knew in a wild land like the Porcupine Mountains, age meant little when love blossomed.

She squeezed her eyes shut against the burning tears. If God had mercy, then He would come down from His heaven and clear everything up until all of it made sense. He would fill in the blanks and give answers to the questions of this tragic story.

Love wasn't supposed to be this way. It was supposed to be giving, a wellspring of joy, with a willingness to serve and sacrifice for those one held dear. Instead, in Rebecca's story—no, in her mother Annabel's story—what passed for love had taken on the grotesque shape of selfishness, of a motivation not for the well-being of the other, but for oneself.

At least for Hilliard it was that way.

Rebecca didn't know Edgar's story. She didn't know her mother's story either. She just knew Annabel's, the woman who had given her life, then drowned while she had been married to Hilliard. Not to Edgar. Which meant that if Hilliard was right, an affair of the heart, if not more, had occurred *while* she was wed to him. Edgar would have been an interloper in a marriage perhaps based on greed or selfish desire on Hilliard's part, or desperate need on Annabel's. Or perhaps they had both at one time imagined love.

Whatever its beginning, it soured, became divisive, and then Edgar entered . . . and then Rebecca was conceived and later born.

And Annabel had drowned.

A horrible supposition entered Rebecca's mind then.

Annabel had drowned—a woman alone in a skiff? On Lake Superior, with waves that could easily topple such a boat, unless of course the one at the helm had the benefit of expertise?

Why had Annabel left the shore to row onto the lake anyway? What had driven her to face the violence of the lake's mouth?

Rebecca stilled at the imagery entering her mind. Blue eyes as cold as the lake but filled with a protective warmth that countered the chill. Abel.

Not long ago *she* herself had entered the mouth of the lake—to escape a worse evil, yes. Yet the wildness of the lake was preferable to the violence that had loomed behind Rebecca. But Abel . . .

He had been there.

He had risked his life to envelop her in his embrace.

He had claimed her and their babe.

And suddenly, in the force of what love was *supposed* to be, Rebecca remembered everything.

33

SHEA

H E CAME OUT OF NOWHERE, his hand clapping over Shea's mouth, pulling her hard against him and behind a grove of trees.

Shea squirmed to free herself, her cries muffled against his palm.

"Shhh!" Holt's breath against her ear silenced her. "You need to be quiet!" His hoarse whisper was frantic, not threatening. Shea remained stiff beneath his clutches, but she nodded until finally he removed his hand from her mouth.

The graves lay just ahead of them, their newly exposed faces staring up through the treetops to the moon that glowed above.

"What are you doing here?" Shea hissed.

Holt tugged on her, drawing her deeper into the woods. "Come with me."

"No!" Shea pulled against him, extricating herself from his grip. "Tell me what's going on!"

Holt looked in all directions. "Seriously, Shea, you need to trust me. We have to get out of here."

"What about Pete?" she asked, her mouth set in a hard line. She knew it! She *knew* it! Holt had been behind Pete's injuries.

Yet her suspicions were instantly challenged at the wave of concern that swept across Holt's face in the moonlight. "Pete's *here*? At the lighthouse?"

"Yes, where else would he be?" Shea snapped, crossing her arms.

"The hospital, I was hoping, or home." Holt looked warily over his shoulder. "He'd be safer there. Like you would be."

"What's going on?" Shea demanded.

"Why did you come to the graves?" Holt growled, his accusation riddled with urgency. "Why couldn't you leave it alone!"

"How could I?" Shea raised her voice, and Holt instantly shushed her. "After everything that has happened?" she whispered. "Even Pete wanted to see this through."

"No one *sees this through*!" Holt snapped. "They never have!" He motioned for her to follow as he changed course to wind back around to the rear of the lighthouse.

Shea followed but with caution. "Where are we going?"

"To get Pete!" Holt ducked under a branch, then held it up for Shea to step under. "You two need to go home. I had no idea when you rented my lighthouse that you were going to be this persistent."

Shea stopped in the middle of the woods, forcing Holt to face her in the night. The moon cast a blue glow across his handsome face that was now contorted with what Shea could only identify at fear. Outright fear.

"Did you hit Pete with the car?" She had to ask, even though the odds of Holt giving an honest answer were slim to none.

Holt reared back in shock. "What are you talking about? Of course not!"

"Then who did?" Shea demanded.

"How would I know?" Holt motioned to her. "Come on!"

"What are we sneaking around for?" Shea began following him again, though reluctantly. "Please tell me what's happening."

Holt twisted, his sigh squelched by not wanting to make noise. He took a few steps back toward her and lowered his face to hers. She could feel his breath on her skin.

"I should have just asked you to leave. I should have said the lighthouse was closed and terminated your stay."

Shea rolled her eyes at him in the dark. "Well, if you wanted me gone, yes, that would make sense."

"But . . ." Holt raked his hand through his hair. "At first I wanted you to write the book."

"Because you wanted the publicity?" Shea asked.

Holt nodded sheepishly. "If the lighthouse was haunted, and you wrote about it, I'd never be shy of bookings ever again. So I crept around the lighthouse at night to make noises. I rigged your light to pop like a ghost killed it. I made corn syrup to look like blood and smeared it on the window."

"That was *you*?" Shea couldn't help but give him a look of sheer exasperation.

"Yes." She could see the whites of Holt's eyes in the night. "I'm not proud of it! But that's what people tend to do after reading about a haunted lighthouse. They want to visit it."

Shea shook her head. "I'm a writer, and you knew I eat that kind of stuff for breakfast!"

"I realize now it was totally wrong! But—I needed to get some publicity for the place and—" Holt's chest heaved, and he released a sigh. "Listen, when you booked the place, you said you were a writer. I wasn't surprised you were interested in Annabel—anyone who comes here is. But I thought you were going to keep it simple, not dig into it like an archaeologist! Shea, it's this sort of research that might've gotten Jonathan Marks shot. And look what happened to Pete? We can't play around with this anymore. This is something longtime local legend the old-timers around here take very seriously!"

"Point made," Shea said. She was discovering that all on her own.

"I'm not here to hurt you or Pete. I'm here to get you away from the lighthouse. Let Annabel and Rebecca and Edgar . . . everyone else— just let them all be."

"Why?" Shea challenged. "What if their story needs to be told. For Penny's sake. For Captain Gene's sake, her father. If all this stuff really happened, then there could be a silver map somewhere around here that belongs to Penny and her father. They deserve it. They shouldn't have to lose out on their legacy just because someone out there thinks they're owed it!" Shea threw her hands in the air, her words ending with a hiss.

Holt grimaced as the sound of tires crunching on gravel alerted them. He yanked her down behind some trees as the car parked yards away from the lighthouse, the headlights off. The engine purred and then was silenced. A car door opened, and a form emerged from the driver's side. The driver was male, stoop-shouldered, and he hesitated as if trying to find his footing before starting toward the lighthouse.

Holt leaned into Shea and whispered in her ear, "What room is Pete sleeping in?"

"One of the attic rooms," Shea answered.

"Okay." Holt sucked in a steadying breath.

Shea reached out and gripped Holt's arm. "Why? Who is that? And what's he here for?"

Holt's look was grim. "You should have that figured out. You're the one who wanted to meet Captain Gene."

Thoroughly confused, but knowing this wasn't the time to interrogate Holt, Shea followed behind him as they moved ahead slowly, staying out of view in the tree line. When a stick snapped beneath her shoe, she froze, but Holt waved her on. It was apparent that Captain Gene hadn't heard it, as evidenced by his hunched form continuing to lumber his way toward the lighthouse as if he owned it—or maybe as if *it* owned *him*.

Shea was perplexed. Why was Holt slinking around the edge of the woods to avoid being seen by Captain Gene? A ninety-something man couldn't pose much of a threat, could he?

She tugged the hem of Holt's shirt. When he glanced over his shoulder at her, she whispered, "Why are we sneaking around like this? Let's just go talk to him."

"You don't *talk* to Captain Gene."

Holt's answer was unsatisfactory, and Shea told him as much. "I'm going to talk to him." She pushed out ahead of Holt, and he clamored for her, gripping her wrist in a viselike hold that pinched her skin.

"No!"

More annoyed than cautious at this point, Shea spun and rammed her finger into Holt's chest. "I'm not afraid of an elderly man. I'm not afraid of Annabel's ghost. I *am* afraid of what's going on that threatens anyone who dares to investigate. So how about we just end this once and for all so that no one else gets hurt?"

"Or *killed*?" Holt growled back. "You mean killed, right? Because that's what happens when anyone messes with Annabel's story."

"Again with the cryptic nonsense. Doesn't anyone around here tell the truth about anything?"

Holt gave a quick shake of his head. "We don't have time for this. We need to reach Captain Gene before he can enter the lighthouse."

"And then what? What's he going to do if he gets in the lighthouse?"

Holt's response sliced through Shea like a razor-sharp knife. "He's going to protect his family. He's guarding family. A family that started more than a century ago. You don't understand what you're digging up here, Shea, and if I'd not been so stupid and greedy, I'd have sent you packing the day after you arrived."

"Why? What do you mean he's 'guarding family'?"

Holt hesitated, then said, "Just *trust* me, okay?"

"Why should I?" Shea snapped. She didn't trust Holt as far as she could throw him. The fact was, at this point, she was confused enough to wish she'd insisted she and Pete just return to their mundane and boring lives back home. But she was also invested enough that she knew she'd never be content with that—not now, not after all that had happened.

Moments later, they had reached the back door of the lighthouse, which stood ajar, inviting them in like unsuspecting victims. Only they did suspect . . . something. Shea just didn't know what it was. Yet concern for Pete urged her to follow Holt in silence, at least until she was better able to assess the situation.

She noticed wet footprints across the wood floor of the kitchen. Large feet, the soles probably those of rubber boots. They were staggered, and Shea noted that a set of the prints were only partially applied, and one of the kitchen table chairs was cockeyed from its normal position. It appeared Captain Gene was unbalanced of body. He hardly posed a threat!

Willing to play along with Holt's melodrama, Shea continued following him through the spotty darkness. Narrow strips of light filtered through from the moon shining through the windows, just enough to negate the need for a flashlight and for Shea to make out Holt's face. He stopped at the doorway to the lightkeeper's bedroom—her room—and held up a hand.

Captain Gene stood across the room, his hands braced on the doorway that led to the spiral stairs and Pete's room. The elderly man's shoulders lifted and fell in heavy breaths as he struggled with the effects of advanced age. Again, hardly a threat.

Shea put a hand on Holt's arm.

He waved her off, slipping into the shadows of the room, just out of view of Captain Gene.

Shea narrowed her eyes. Was Holt going to pounce on the man? A surge of empathy for her intruder, and irritation toward her would-be protector, flooded her then.

"That's it!" Shea's words cracked through the silence.

Holt jumped, and his shoulder struck the wall, sending a small oil painting of a black bear careening from its hook and sliding across the floor. Captain Gene fell against the doorway, clutching the jamb for balance, his eyes growing big in his wizened face.

Shea flicked on the light switch, thoroughly finished with the subterfuge.

She got her first good look at Captain Gene, and for a moment her world tilted like a ship on the crest of a tidal wave. Dark eyes set in his wrinkled face, shaggy white hair sticking out over his ears. His nose was rounded on the tip like a cuddly Santa Claus, but it wasn't red and chapped from the cold. Instead, it was weathered from the buffeting wind, the years spent in the Porcupine Mountains. His flannel shirt was half untucked in his faded, navy-blue trousers. His jacket was a khaki-colored slicker with a patch over the right side of his chest, boasting a pine tree in green embroidery and the words *Protect the Trees*. But it was his eyes. His expression. His startled stare that burrowed into hers that was so eerily familiar, Shea could only swing to the younger version of Captain Gene, who now stiffened in the corner of the room.

"You!" She shifted back to the captain, calculating the visual evidence of what was still remarkably unclear to her. "You're . . ." She couldn't finish.

It was very apparent that Holt and Captain Gene shared a large amount of DNA. If someone put Captain Gene's life into rewind, the years would strip away the influence of age from his face and body. His form would straighten into a broad-shouldered stature. His eyes would become less lined, less sunken in his face. His hair would grow blonder, and he would essentially become like Holt, and Holt would become Captain Gene. It was only the decades that separated them. The decades and, apparently, the truth.

Captain Gene seemed to recover from Shea's impatient outburst. He held his arm out toward Holt, his palm extended, whether to shush him or keep Holt at bay, Shea wasn't certain. He was stern when he faced Shea, and Holt was, strangely enough, obedient and silent.

"It is time for you to go." Captain Gene's declaration was controlled and authoritative. It was as though his age alone demanded compliance.

But Shea was not the compliant type, and Pete lay upstairs with a busted arm. There was no way she was going to leave him behind. "Give me one good reason why I should go."

34

REBECCA

Of the beautiful Annabel Lee . . .
Annabel Lee

**ANNABEL'S LIGHTHOUSE
SPRING, 1874**

S HE'D WANTED THIS MOMENT TO COME—had ached for it, in fact—but with the onslaught of recollection came the assault of pain such recollection caused. They came in waves, forceful and strong. They held Rebecca under the waters of memory and dared her to try to swim to the surface and break free. But breaking free from such reminders of pain was as impossible as saving a doomed ship after it had foundered and slipped below the waves.

Rebecca no longer struggled against her restraints. Instead, she sagged against the wall of the shack, desperate to regain some sort of hope, some semblance of reason to keep fighting—

and she couldn't find any. That was how it had all begun in the first place. When one lost the will to fight, one was left with only defeat. If defeat became the bed in which she was going to lie for the rest of her life, then any risk to escape it was no risk at all. She would merely dodge death for as long as she could until it came and saved her from this agony she'd lived in since childhood.

She would not bring her own babe into such a world. Rebecca knew she would be judged harshly for that were someone savvy enough to read her mind. But a babe had never been a part of the life Rebecca struggled to escape to. She would never submit an innocent into this world of darkness, of selfish entitlement. And it wasn't Abel's decision—he didn't know, *couldn't* know—what it meant to grow up in such darkness. To cower in the corners beneath the doom-filled sound of heavy feet thudding against the floor on a mission to find you. Ghosts? What were ghosts in the wake of human hatred?

Maybe she should throw herself at Annabel's mercy and allow the spirit of her mother to take her once and for all, to rescue her from this evil as any mother should do—as *she* would do—for her own child.

Maybe death was better than life. This was a riddle too many misunderstood. Kjersti had already gone before. Eternity was supposed to be filled with hope and grace, and wouldn't that be a better place to dwell?

But the babe! If she ceased to live, the babe would too, and then she would be a killer—like her father was threatening to do with her. But how could she bring a child into this dark and awful place?

Rebecca closed her eyes against the battery of her internal conflict. The shack was growing chilled. She could hear Bear outside the door, grumbling and growling to himself. The smoke from his pipe—a sickeningly sweet scent of tobacco—wafted toward her through the cracks in the wooden door.

It all came down to this.

This shack.

This place Hilliard, her father, believed would be where Rebecca finally confessed, revealing where she'd hidden the papers—papers she now remembered were the numbers— columns of them—and notes—pages of them—that would prove he'd been partaking in fraudulent business practices. Proof that his investors would be horrified to learn. It would ruin Hilliard. It would ruin his investors if they didn't find out the truth.

And then there was the map. The map of a silver vein? If true, she could see why Hilliard was gambling, fixing numbers and moving funds. He would start to mine a new vein—one that wasn't going belly-up—and then the investors would never know of the money he'd stolen.

The miners and their families coming to Silvertown, com- ing to the Porcupine Mountains, deserved better than Hilliard's schemes of wealth. She had seen the papers. She had seen what they exposed. She had also seen other fraudulent papers, ones she hadn't bothered to steal. The modified ones that Hilliard exposed to his investors, promising a controlled wealth of silver in an area where silver would go dry in months.

The truth was that there was no wealth to be had unless her father was able to strike it big with a new vein. Otherwise, there were only investments to be lost—or siphoned into other accounts her father had. Filtered away in small amounts, but enough to fund the new mine, the new vein. Unless Rebecca exposed him, revealing the fraud and hiding the map which led to the silver vein.

Now, Rebecca stared at her feet, her toes growing numb from the bindings around her ankles. She blinked away tears as Abel threatened to invade her fortitude and what small determina- tion she had left.

Abel.

Dear Abel.

He had been an unexpected promise amid the brutality of the world in which Rebecca lived. It wasn't until last year that she had seen him during the trip she'd made to Silvertown with Hilliard. Abel and his mother, Niina, and his sister, sweet Kjersti.

Rebecca couldn't stop the tears that trailed down her cheeks at the memories of Kjersti. It was she who had befriended Rebecca. It was Kjersti who had been the first glimmer of hope. It was Kjersti who had convinced Abel to rescue Rebecca with their flimsy marriage.

"It will break your bonds to your father when you become Abel's wife!" Kjersti had promised.

An elopement with a virtual stranger whose propensity for empathy and protection was juxtaposed with her father's intoxication with coldness and abuse, which had proven only to compound the problem.

Hilliard had been furious. His pride had taken a major blow. Rebecca was no longer a Hilliard; she was Rebecca Koski now. And that loss of control incensed Hillard.

The lighthouse became their refuge.

The hospitality of Edgar had become their burgeoning hope.

The days of respite away from her father had opened Rebecca's heart to trust again.

Abel's tenderness . . . his gentleness . . .

She remembered that night. The first time had been needful, surprising, a consummation of their marriage that was both meaningful and filled with unknowns. Expectations. Feelings. Unspoken words. But the second time?

It was after she had nursed the feverish Kjersti for several days, agonizing that her dearest friend was slipping away from her.

"*Never be afraid of him,*" Kjersti had urged Rebecca that night. "*He will take care of you. For me. Abel will take care of you.*"

And he had. Rebecca had slipped from Kjersti's room as her

friend slept. She had sagged against the wall, fighting back tears of desperation. Hope was always stolen by the anger of this life. Her father, Kjersti's inevitable death, and her comforting but mostly platonic marriage to a man who—

Abel had exited his room at that moment.

He had seen her pain.

He had held her.

His fingers had traced her cheek.

The tenderness—it was the tenderness that had engaged Rebecca that night. Perhaps it was her presence of comfort that had engaged Abel. The strangeness of their situation, the understanding of necessity that had settled between them, the undeniable need for intimacy in crushing circumstances—perhaps it was those that had brought Abel and Rebecca together.

Rebecca's eyes flew open as Bear punched open the shack's door, busting into the reminder of what love might have been had she not crossed her father in such a detrimental and final act.

Abel.

In his way, Rebecca knew he had grown to love her. In her way, if she could only come to know what love was, then maybe . . . no . . .

Rebecca lifted her chin in preparation for Bear and his inevitable bruising fists.

No.

She did love Abel. In her way. It was the kind of love that ached at what could have been. The kind of love that knew their babe should not be made to suffer as she had suffered all these years. It was the kind of love that knew her sacrifice would set them all free.

And maybe she didn't understand it properly.

Maybe she was misguided.

But it was all Rebecca knew.

Love meant giving oneself for another. Though no one had ever done that for her, she would do it for them.

35

SHEA

And so, all the nighttide, I lay down by the side . . .
Annabel Lee

ANNABEL'S LIGHTHOUSE
PRESENT DAY

IT WAS A LITERAL STARE-DOWN. Shea and Captain
Gene refused to look away from each other, and it was only
when the sound of feet on the metal stairs of the lighthouse
alerted them that they shifted to see Pete poke his head into the
room.

"What'd I miss?" Pete appeared to have no sense of danger,
but the quick assessment he gave Shea announced to her he
was far more aware than he portrayed. He shifted his attention
to Holt. "You're back."

Holt had been silent to this point, and now he seemed to collect himself. He took a step toward Captain Gene, whose arm

was still stretched in Holt's direction as if to keep him at bay, stiffening his arm even more.

"Don't say nothing." It was a command that Captain Gene shot at Holt, and it was made with a familiar, patriarchal dominance that was easily recognizable.

"Well, somebody had better," Shea stated.

Pete's form blocked the way to the lighthouse.

Captain Gene lowered his arm a few inches.

Holt hefted a breath that could only be compared to a tightly wound sigh of anticipation.

Shea wouldn't have been surprised if at this moment the ghost of Annabel had swept through the room and cut through the thick tension that was collecting like a pile of washed-up driftwood.

"Grandfather, I presume?" Shea offered the only explanation she could think of to qualify the familial similarity between Holt and Captain Gene.

"You could say that." Holt grimaced but kept his attention focused on his grandfather.

"Penny's your *mom*?" Shea attempted to connect the dots in this messed-up version of a haunted lighthouse. The mother and son had never once let on or even acted that familiar with each other!

"Yes," Holt snapped.

Captain Gene's balance seemed to give out for a moment, and Pete shot out an arm, wincing against the pain from his injured ribs as he half caught the old man.

"Sit down," Pete stated.

Captain Gene took the opportunity to sink onto the bed that Shea had slept on since she'd arrived at the lighthouse.

The convoluted state of the night, the facts, the story, and even the history of this place were a jumbled mess. The sense of danger had dissipated. Shea attempted to gain full control of the moment, though Pete's quick look told her she should probably still proceed with caution.

"I'm so confused." Shea directed her statement to Captain Gene, whose dark look was his only answer. "Holt?" She turned to her host with expectation.

Holt shook his head, sealing his mouth in a tight line of silence.

"What does it matter if we find out?" Shea laughed in disbelief. "Is this part of the rental fee?" she ventured, not fighting the sarcasm in her voice. "Rent a lighthouse, live out a ghost story, and enter a world of local lore and mystery?" She waited for a moment. "Because I'm sort of tired of it. And it's costing us quite a bit of sleep and physical safety."

A look at Pete summarized what she meant. Pete met her eyes, and there was a strange glint in his. What was that about now? Warning? Caution? He rarely tried to put her in her place, so the look was unfamiliar, yet it bit at Shea's inner concern. She frowned.

"Let me take him home." Holt's request stilled the room. "I'll get the old man out of your hair. I'll refund your money. You can leave in the morning, and we'll all agree to just call it over with."

Shea opened her mouth to reply but was held back by Pete's expression of caution.

"Good idea." Pete's insertion was unwelcome, and Shea sucked in a breath to protest. Pete lifted his hand, and the motion silenced her more from surprise than obedience. "Get him out of here."

Holt stepped toward his grandfather, but Captain Gene scowled. "No, no, young man—stay away."

"It's me. Holt." Holt stated.

Captain Gene's face furrowed in confusion.

Pete reached out and touched Shea's arm. "I think he has—"

"Wait," Shea interrupted, before Pete's words fully registered. "Do you know where the silver map is? The one that's been supposedly hidden for over a century?"

Captain Gene's eyes darted to hers.

Shea drew in a breath. "You *do!*"

Holt growled under his breath and stalked to Captain Gene's side, reaching down and hoisting him from the bed. Captain Gene wrangled his arm from Holt's grip. "Let me go!"

"Yeah. Let me help." Pete stepped farther into the room to assist Holt with Captain Gene's removal from the lighthouse.

"No!" Shea held up a hand toward Pete. "I want to know where this map is. If Captain Gene knows . . . is that why you've stayed under the radar all these years? To keep it hidden? Is it really that big of a treasure map?"

"Shea." Pete's voice held warning.

She glanced at him, then at Holt. There was a tension in the air that warned Shea. Warned her that she was consumed—by the story, the missing map, by everything but the people in front of her.

"Let's get the captain home," Pete said to Holt.

"Yeah." Holt led Captain Gene from the room.

Pete moved past her, following the two men from the lighthouse. She followed on his heels.

"Pete!" she called, trying to get his attention.

But he waved her off, intent on making sure Holt and Captain Gene were taken care of.

"Pete, I still have questions. And what if you can't trust them?"

Pete's response was swift. "Then trust me, Shea."

Trust you?

The words penetrated her with a swiftness Shea was not prepared for. Yet his statement was more of a request than a command. It was a need for Shea not only to back down but to show Pete the respect due him as a fellow human being who might just know more than she did in this situation.

Trust Pete?

That required less of her and more of him.

That required a level of respect she'd stolen from Pete long ago when she all but wrote him off, as she grew weary of hoping and wishing and waiting to be cherished. And was that so bad? To want to be cherished? To want to be the center of someone's affection?

No. No, it wasn't.

Shea stared after the retreating backs of the three men. One hunched with age, the other with his back so ramrod straight it boasted of hurt and stubborn willfulness, and the third managing through physical pain but steady and straightforward. You got what you saw when you met Pete Radclyffe. There was no charm, no pretense, no romance, no butterflies. It was just Pete.

Her Pete.

The steady, mundane, always-there Pete who got things done and let her be her without argument.

So now he had asked her to trust him. Just trust him.

Like someone pulling scabs from her wounded heart, Shea stilled, not following the men any farther.

She *could* trust Pete, she just never *wanted* to. Because that meant she also accepted Pete as he was, and she'd always wanted more. And yet, in this moment, Shea realized she was catching a small glimpse of a long-existent side of Pete.

Sometimes steady was comforting.

Sometimes mundane was reliable.

Sometimes always-there was the most romantic thing anyone could ever be for someone.

The men disappeared outside and into the night, Pete following to make sure Captain Gene was situated in his car and Holt with him. It felt so anticlimactic to Shea. The long-awaited encounter with the captain had resulted in no real answers, just more questions. And Holt wanted them to leave? She couldn't just *leave*. But logic told her she could, and she should. There was enough done in the name of research for her book that her editor would work with her, and they'd end up with an acceptable manuscript. In fact, not having all the answers to the mystique around Annabel's Lighthouse would probably make the book more appealing to readers in the long run.

But to leave meant to close the book on everything else. On Edna's tales of Annabel's guardian, of Captain Gene's vanishing acts and his now sudden appearance for no apparent purpose, and of Holt's revealing relation to the old man?

Then there was Annabel. The story of Annabel. Of Rebecca. Of the silver ore map that, if one broke it down to bare bones, had to be the impetus for it all somehow. Find the map Rebecca stole a century ago, and it would all make sense. A veritable treasure map of the U.P. It would still have to go through the courts to determine ownership, wouldn't it? But the lure of it, the potential of a massive silver vein, in the present economy . . .

Shea stilled as the quietness in the lighthouse pervaded her thoughts. It was very still now with the absence of the men. And Pete. Pete hadn't returned yet. She moved to the window that looked out to where Captain Gene had parked his vehicle. It was gone. She searched the darkness looking for Pete.

Frowning, Shea hurried to the door and opened it. The lake greeted her, its waters rolling onto shore with an even cadence. The moon had dipped behind clouds, and aside from the light emanating from behind Shea, the world outside the lighthouse was pitch-black.

"Pete?" she called, taking a step outside the door. "Pete?"

Only the waves responded. Shea made her way around the corner of the lighthouse. "Pete?" she called again, this time louder. She reassured herself that Captain Gene and Holt had taken their leave. There had been no sounds of a struggle, so Shea couldn't imagine that Holt had suddenly turned against Pete and abducted him.

Annoyed at her imagination getting completely out of hand, Shea pivoted to return to the lighthouse. Maybe Pete had somehow slipped back in and past her as she'd been ruminating about life at the wrong time. Maybe he'd gone back to bed? The idiocy of that idea wasn't lost on Shea, but the sensation of being very much alone was creeping up and becoming more and more real.

She quickly entered the house and pushed the door shut, debating on locking it because it felt better to be locked inside. But if Pete was still outside . . . Shea decided to leave the door unlocked and returned to the kitchen.

A shuffling sound halted her in her tracks.

Shea looked up at the ceiling.

The lightbulb in its fixture flickered.

The hair on her arms stood at attention. Deliberate footsteps crossed the floor above her. Slow footsteps.

"Pete?" Her voice was shakier than she'd expected.

Shea tiptoed into the sitting area. The room was illuminated by a soft, yellow glow from a lamp directly beneath the painting of Annabel's ghost on the wall. It was where Jonathan Marks had died too, and suddenly Shea caught a vision of red on the walls and the floor. A vision of what it must have looked like to whoever had discovered his body. Blood spatter. Fragments of who Jonathan Marks had once been.

The serious turn of her thoughts brought with it the gravity of all she had been delving into. The adrenaline of the night, her almost intoxicated insistence to know what had happened—to push the old captain to tell her things—no. She had pushed too hard. Her obstinacy had been insensitive, driven by the lust for the hunt, if not the treasure. She had been wrong. This wasn't child's play—it never had been—it was dark, and it was riddled with a story that made no sense, and its threads were tangled with every aspect of this place. Annabel. Rebecca. Silvertown. Holt. Captain Gene. Penny. Even Edna and Marnie and the man at the historical museum. The Porcupine Mountains and the lake boasted tales of hardship, of vicious winters and blistering summers. It captured the spirit of its original people while it inhabited the dreams of newcomers. It was a place of rock and earth, of greed and ambition, of nature and wanderlust.

The lake was a place of ghosts.

A chilling breath blew across the back of Shea's neck. She could almost hear Annabel's sigh behind her, and Shea whirled to face her. To see with her own eyes once again the woman who haunted this place and these shores. The woman that the stories all seemed to return to. The woman whose spirit held the secrets to her mystical breast and teased with her gentle memory and her vengeful recollections.

But Annabel wasn't there.

No one was.

Very aware of her aloneness, Shea was drawn to the light-keeper's room. The light was still on, the room still empty. The door to the lighthouse was propped open, and Shea moved toward it, stopping to stare up into the abyss that spiraled upward.

A shadow person swept out of view as Shea's eyes focused on the lantern room above her. A vaporous form that boasted of having lived once but now only haunted.

"Annabel?" Shea finally called out the name of the woman long since dead. Dead for more than a hundred and fifty years. She stepped onto the metal stairs, tentative and questioning her own sanity.

A clanging sound responded, staggering down toward her, pinging against the stairs like a stone having been tossed toward Shea. Only there was no stone.

She hesitated at the door that led to the attic bedrooms. It was open, the hallway dark, the rooms dark as well. "Pete?" she whispered.

No answer.

This was ridiculous. She was chasing a ghost. Literally.

Another clang from above jerked Shea's attention back to the dark, unlit lantern. She took a few more hesitant steps before freezing, her hand gripping the railing, white-knuckled and tense.

Humming.

The melodic sound of a woman's soft hum drifted from the lighthouse, wrapping itself around the stairwell and embracing Shea in a hypnotic hold.

". . . soul my soul . . ." it sang, taunting and chilling Shea.

The wind outside picked up, the lighthouse moaning against the unexpected stress of the lake's breath on its frame.

Shea knew then. She knew it was not over.

There was one more person she must face to find the answers that haunted her. The answers that had woven themselves into Shea's soul and bound her to this place. The answers that mocked her belief of what love was and her loyalty to herself and to Pete. The answers that convinced Shea that the past would always be very much alive because the past echoed through the lives of its offspring and continued on. Curses that didn't die when a grave was backfilled. Wrongs that weren't concluded when the water drowned the body and sank it to its depths.

Shea had to face Annabel's ghost.

She took another step upward into the lighthouse.

This ghost would be faced in the dark.

36

REBECCA

Of my darling . . .
Annabel Lee

ANNABEL'S LIGHTHOUSE
SPRING, 1874

WHERE IS IT?" Mercer's hand connected with Rebecca's cheek, and she tasted blood as her lip was cut by her teeth.

She knew. She remembered now. She could tell him exactly where she'd hidden the damning papers and the map. But to tell would be to ensure the success of Hilliard, and he would only continue to take advantage of those less fortunate.

Rebecca had witnessed it her entire life. She had seen Hilliard trample others for selfish reasons. She'd carried the weight of his fabricated love for her as his daughter in the public eye, and

296

then his hateful disdain for her as the girl he believed was not his own when they were home alone and in private.

She tilted her chin, summoning courage from God and from the images of Abel and Edgar and Niina in her mind. Summoning courage from the fluttering of the babe in her womb.

Bear hauled Rebecca up from the chair, spouting a vile name for her. Her arms were yanked back so hard that she cried out in pain. She could not balance on her own with her feet bound, so Bear held her while Mercer went nose to nose with her. She could sense the seething power that emanated from his eyes. The man was consumed by the desire for it, and it had been bestowed on him by Hilliard. Mercer would take full advantage.

His hand shot up to grab her chin, his fingers biting into her skin. "I will make you tell me where you hid the papers, and your suffering will mean nothing to me."

Spit dotted her face as Mercer dug his fingers into her cheeks. Rebecca whimpered.

He chuckled low in his throat. "You are nothing to your father. He will say you were lost in the wilderness, that the wolves must have eaten you. You will disappear, and that pretend husband of yours can weep for a day and then move on with his life. You save no one by staying silent—so save yourself!" Mercer whipped Rebecca's head to the side as he shoved her face away.

If she were brave, she would have raised her throbbing face to him and glared into his eyes. As it was, Rebecca was terrified.

Remember Abel.

Mercer slapped her across the face.

Remember Niina.

Another brutal punch took her breath away.

Edgar.

She gasped for air, her throat clawing for the bliss of oxygen as Mercer stole it with his hand around her throat.

"Who are you protecting?" he sneered.

Bear held her against him as Mercer pressed in.

"Did you give the papers to that lightkeeper? Is that who has them? Edgar?"

Rebecca couldn't hide her wince. No! No, she hadn't! But it hadn't occurred to her that in trying to rid the region of her father and his greed, that Mercer would conclude she'd taken Edgar—or anyone—into her confidence to help.

"You did, didn't you?" Mercer's eyes sparked with awareness.

"No," Rebecca whimpered. She truly had not, and now she must make Mercer believe her. "They don't know anything. Please! Leave them alone."

"Ohhh." Mercer's laugh was matched by Bear's. "She loves them," Mercer ridiculed. "She loves the old man." Mercer palmed Rebecca's face, shoving her head back against Bear's chest. "Did you know how much your father despises that old lightkeeper? And that you *live* there with his apprentice? It disgusts me. It disgusts your father."

Rebecca tried to comprehend Mercer's words. He must have read the question in her eyes.

"Your mother—dear Annabel—oh, the stories I've heard. Her beauty. She may have been Hilliard's wife and your mother, but she was Edgar's lover and the bane of Hilliard's existence."

When she didn't react, Mercer jerked her away from Bear, throwing her to the floor. The roughhewn floor dug into Rebecca's skin, and her shoulder was bruised when it took the weight of her body upon impact.

Mercer stood over her, a cruelty emanating from him that bewildered Rebecca. He reached for a knife holstered on his belt and slid it from its sheath. A quick glance at Bear revealed his face draining of color beneath his beard.

Rebecca caught the glint of the knife as Mercer straddled her.

"Why don't we have another discussion about where you hid those papers?"

Rebecca felt the edge of the blade lightly trail down her arm. "Shall we?" Mercer's question demanded an answer.

SHEA

Every step up the spiraling stairs was laborious. Her feet felt heavy as she lifted them. The humming had not ceased. The ethereal voice drifting down through the lighthouse was worse than if the ghost of Annabel had just moaned like most ghosts were supposed to do.

She hadn't forgotten Pete—hadn't forgotten that he had all but vanished. But the draw toward Annabel pulled Shea up. A century ago, this lighthouse would have smelled like oil—kerosene maybe?—and light would have brightened the interior. Heat would have radiated throughout the space. The wind and growing storm outside would have been met by the barrier of hope given off by the refuge of the lighthouse. But now? Now the wind was in charge, the lighthouse almost seeming to sway from the force of it. It had only been minutes before—hadn't it?—that Shea had looked out across the lake and seen the calming rhythm of the waves. Now she could hear them increasing in volume, pummeling the shore as a storm rose up from its slumber.

". . . soul my soul . . ." the voice hummed again, and Shea pushed herself forward. The bumps on her skin coincided with the chill in the air—air that almost suffocated her with its oppressive anticipation.

What did a person say to a ghost? To a haunted spirit back from the dead. Or if it were haunted, had it truly died? They said spirits didn't pass over until they were at peace. Was this the result? A tempestuous spirit of Annabel humming and teasing and toying with the senses?

And yet the very idea warred not only with Shea's reason but with her faith. Her fledgling, worn-out, oft-ignored faith.

"Annabel?" Shea made herself call out.

The humming ceased.

The air went still.

Shea gripped the rail, only steps away from reaching the top and the narrow walkway that ran around the lantern. She swallowed hard, willing away her fear in exchange for the need to face her—face *it*. That overwhelming sense that Annabel wasn't real, that instead *she* was an *it*. A disembodied fragment of error passed on through the decades. Unrequited, mismanaged, abusive, selfish love that didn't understand what it meant to love. To truly, wholly love with sacrifice. Love that didn't taunt and torment, but that held steady when the wind blew, that shielded the other from the storm as best as one could, that did everything opposite of what Shea had done for Pete.

Annabel was a whisper.

This was real.

At last Shea reached the walkway, and the form on the other side of the lantern became very real.

It was a woman, her long dress reminiscent of the olden days. Her hair hung in long strands of silvery feather-like wisps. Shea could not see the details of her face, but for a moment Annabel did not seem young at all. She looked . . . old. Shea strained to catch a better glimpse of the woman's face. Her eyes were dark orbs in the shadows. Her figure was unfamiliar.

Shea took a step toward Annabel, the lantern's prisms between them dark and unlit. The wind and the waves were growing in strength; Shea could see the waves from the top of the lighthouse. The glass in the windows rattled, and the gallery outside seemed to shudder.

"Annabel . . ." Shea began, then bit her tongue.

This was not Annabel. This was not a ghost. The woman before her in the darkness was real, solid, and the humming had begun again.

". . . soul my soul . . ." She hummed in a high-pitched vibrato that sent eerie shivers through Shea.

One step closer. Just one step closer and she might be able to identify who—

Shea's scream was cut off as the woman flew toward her, arms outstretched, fingers wrapping around Shea's throat.

37

Rebecca

. . . my darling . . .
Annabel Lee

SILVERTOWN
UPPER PENINSULA OF MICHIGAN
SPRING, 1874

SHE WANTED TO LIVE! The realization coursed through her as Rebecca prepared to die, though, knowing that life had led her here to this moment.

"I'm sorry," she whispered under her breath to Abel.

I'm sorry, she spoke from her heart to her unborn babe's. *I'm sorry you didn't get to live. I'm sorry I couldn't protect you enough to bring you into this broken world. I'm sorry you will not know your father.*

But I'm not sorry that I love you.

A grunt shocked Rebecca back to the present. Mercer's knife flung from his hands, and his body careened off hers as another

302

man barreled through the shack's door and into him. A booted foot caught Rebecca in her hip, and she cried out, rolling away even as her bindings prohibited quick movement.

Bear shouted.

A resounding gunshot filled the room, deafening Rebecca's ears to only a high-pitched whistle. She winced, her vision blurred from the abuse her face had already taken by the hand of Mercer. Seeing his knife a few feet away, Rebecca tried to wriggle toward it.

A man shouted, and then the sound of a fist cracking against skin and bone urged Rebecca to try harder to reach the knife. From her peripheral vision she saw the still form of Bear lying on the shack's floor. A pool of blood was spreading from beneath him.

Chaos by her feet ensued as two men rolled on the floor, grunting and shoving, along with the brutal noises of fists and feet waging battle. Rebecca reached the knife and worked her bound wrists around it, holding the handle as stable as she could with her forearm while working her bindings against the blade. It was awkward, and the knife nicked her wrists and hands, but the bindings gave way, freeing Rebecca to scoot into a sitting position and sweep the knife along the ropes at her ankles.

"You son of—" The words were muffled as the new man rolled atop Mercer and leveled a fist into the man's face.

Rebecca's mouth fell open, and she screamed, "Edgar!" Never had she expected the man coming to her aid with such ferocity to be the old and arthritic lightkeeper. Mercer struggled beneath him, his face bloodied but fixed in a grin that said he was gaining the upper hand. He shoved Edgar off of him, and the old man careened into the wall. A rifle lay off to the side where it had fallen, obviously the weapon Edgar had used to silence Bear, though it was of no use to him now.

Rebecca scrambled toward the rifle, but Mercer dove in front of her and grabbed it. She heard the resounding click of the rifle's lever action, and both she and Edgar stilled. Mercer struggled to his feet, his nose dripping blood, his eye swelling.

"You should have stayed away, old man!" he growled at Edgar, who matched him for injuries but seemed far worse for the fight. Edgar hunched against the wall, gripping his midsection and gasping for breath. But his eyes were narrowed, his expression hard.

"Leave her alone!" Edgar shouted.

Rebecca's fingers closed around the knife that she had freed her bonds with.

Mercer adjusted the rifle against his shoulder. "Where are the papers?" he demanded.

A genuine look of honesty crossed Edgar's face. He looked at Rebecca and then back at Mercer. "I don't know where they are."

Mercer stalked forward, jamming the barrel of the rifle into Edgar's chest. "Tell me or I'll put a bullet in you."

"Then you'll never find out where they are!" Rebecca mustered the courage to challenge him. "If you hurt him, I'll never tell you!"

Mercer spun, bringing the rifle with him to aim in her direction. "Where are they at then, you little chit?"

Rebecca hid the knife behind her back. She glanced at Edgar, who shook his head in warning.

Edgar. Sweet, darling, crotchety old Edgar. She didn't understand how he'd loved her mother if Annabel was married to Hilliard, but he had. If he was her father . . . Rebecca almost wished it were true. She shifted her attention back to Mercer. It would be wise to reveal where she'd buried the papers. It wouldn't thwart Hilliard's grandiose plans of power and wealth, but it would potentially spare Edgar now. Would Hilliard leave them to the lighthouse once and for all if she capitulated to the demands?

Rebecca opened her mouth to reveal the location just as Edgar pushed himself from the floor. There was viciousness in his eyes that stunned Rebecca into stillness and momentarily shocked Mercer. With a guttural growl, Edgar stumbled and launched himself at Mercer, shouting at Rebecca simultaneously, "Run!"

The rifle in Mercer's hands fired, and Edgar lurched backward with the blast.

Rebecca screamed and without thinking flew at Mercer, wielding the knife. She sunk it deep into the man's shoulder, and he dropped the gun, falling away in agony. As Mercer writhed on the floor, Rebecca fell to her knees, grabbing the rifle and pulling it with her even as she hurried to Edgar's side.

The elderly man lay on his back, his chest heaving. A poisonous red spread along his shirt.

"No, no, no!" Rebecca wept over him as she pawed as gently as she could at his shirt, trying without success to stop the bleeding. She grabbed at her dress, ripping the bodice until her chemise was exposed. She wadded the strip of material into a ball and pressed it firmly against the gunshot wound.

Mercer rolled on the floor behind her, spitting vitriol as he clawed at the knife that was embedded in his muscle.

"Edgar!" Rebecca leaned over the lightkeeper while holding the wad of material against his chest.

Edgar's hand curled around her wrist in a weak hold. His eyes were glazed but soft, with moisture in them that could only be attributed to unshed tears. "Get out of here, child," he rasped out, demanding she flee for her freedom.

"I won't leave you!" Rebecca cried, her own tears falling on Edgar's weathered face.

He lifted his hand to her cheek. "I'm old. I've lived my life. You . . . live yours now."

"Edgar, I—"

His eyes closed and then snapped open. "So many regrets."

Rebecca pressed a bloodied hand against Edgar's face. "Are you—?"

"No." He shook his head. "I'm not . . . your father. That's Hilliard. Though he don't believe it. Two can love . . . and not do all wrong. Annabel wouldn't."

Disappointment coursed through her. "But you loved her—my mother." Rebecca's statement filled the air between them even as she heard Mercer in the background, gritting out words she would never repeat.

Edgar grimaced, then gasped out, "More than I should have."

Rebecca frowned. "What do you mean?" She was desperate to know the truth—the truth about her mother Annabel and about Edgar. If he wasn't her father . . . then what? Had he tried to save her as she fled the hands of Hilliard? To rescue her from the icy waters of the lake?

Edgar's eyes widened, and for what seemed an eternity he stared deep into Rebecca's. "I saved us from him," he said. "Run. Go live." His eyes slid shut, and he expelled a long breath.

"No!" Rebecca screamed. She spun when she heard Mercer behind her, stumbling to his feet, the bloody knife in his hand which he'd pulled from his shoulder. She snatched up the rifle, pumped the lever, aimed and pulled the trigger.

SHEA

Marnie's fingers squeezed oxygen from Shea's throat, blocking her airway. Shea reached up and grabbed at the woman's wrists and threw her weight against the waitress, Edna's daughter. She'd not expected to recognize the woman in the lighthouse. Now she wrestled not with a ghost or an idea, but with a woman whose anger she felt in every clawing scrape left on Shea's throat.

"Get. Off. Me!" Shea shoved Marnie away from her, and Marnie fell against the lighthouse window. Her body crumpled to the metal floor, but Marnie reached for part of the lantern's mechanism, pulling herself to her feet.

"Where is it?" Marnie's breaths came swiftly, and the women stood in a sort of standoff, the lantern between them, the waves and the storm held at bay only by the grace of the lighthouse's frame and glass. Marnie's nightgown—eerie and all too familiar as the ghost of Annabel—fell to her ankles.

"Where's the map?" Marnie swiped blood from her lip where Shea had nicked her.

"I don't *have* it!" Shea shouted.

Marnie shoved her long hair back, hair that when waitressing had been pinned into a tidy roll. Now she looked like a crazed version of a human *trying* to be a ghost. "I won't let it go," Marnie spat. "You don't know what it means to have it!"

"How do you know you'll even have rights to the silver vein if you find the map?" Shea shot back. "Most of this area is state park land! Even if the map tells you where it is—"

"It's not about that!"

"Everyone thinks that Rebecca's secret should be kept." Marnie shook her finger at Shea. "The stupid map should stay hidden. But Gene knows where it is. He always has! But Jonathan found out where it was!"

Jonathan.

The name startled Shea.

"Jonathan Marks?"

Marnie's face shifted into a sneer. "Penny's *man*. I know he found out where it's hidden. It is *family legacy*. Family legacy, I tell you, and I will not be cut out!"

"Cut out?" Shea said, clueless as to what Marnie meant.

Marnie took a menacing step toward Shea. Shea backed away, glancing behind her to gauge the space between her and the stairs. If she could get to them, she could run. Run away from Marnie and the lighthouse. How had Marnie even gotten *into* the lighthouse to begin with? With Captain Gene and Holt and Pete, she would have had to pass them all to get in. Unless . . . she had snuck in *before* Shea had been stopped by Holt at Annabel's grave. Marnie had to have waited for an opportune moment to sneak into the lighthouse, and when Shea left the lighthouse tonight, she must have made good of the moment. Which meant . . .

"You've been watching us? Here at the lighthouse?" Shea accused.

"At least you figured that out," Marnie scoffed.

"Did *you* hit Pete with your car?" Shea glared at the woman, who didn't even flinch.

"He was in the way." Marnie's admission was unemotional. "He never even saw me."

"In the way of what?" Shea shot back, inching toward the stairs.

Marnie laughed. "*You!* I've spent my entire life trying to get out of Penny and out of Captain Gene where the map is hidden. Holt has been worthless. Messing with the lighthouse, inviting guests. At least when Jonathan lived here, I was able to toy with his brain and get him all mixed up about Annabel's ghost. The man thought he was losing his mind!"

"*You're* the ghost," Shea stated. Marnie was the footsteps. The woman on the shore. She was dressed to fool the occupants and play with their superstitions. She must have a key—some way to enter. "But why? How does haunting a lighthouse have any effect on its occupants?"

"It was supposed to make Jonathan leave," Marnie said with satisfaction. "It was supposed to make *you* leave." She grinned with clenched teeth. "I can't search this place with people here. I had time for a while, after Jonathan and before Holt turned the lighthouse into a rental. I have a key—I could search everywhere, but then . . . people. People everywhere. They never stopped coming!"

"I don't know where the map is hidden!" Shea's foot found the first stair, and she stepped down onto it.

Marnie was rounding the lantern. "That's what Jonathan said, but he was lying."

"But you shot him anyway?" Shea had already drawn that conclusion, yet now she voiced it.

Marnie clucked her tongue. "Well, it was a pity the gun misfired. I hadn't intended . . ." She paused, seeming to check herself. "He wasn't supposed to die. Then my pathetic nephew buys the lighthouse—Holt has always been in the way."

Confusion spread through Shea. She paused on the lighthouse step. "You and Penny are sisters?"

"Stepsisters," Marnie corrected. "Captain Gene married my mother, Edna, after Penny's mother died. My mother already had me, but I should have been his daughter too. I was just a child! Yet it was always Penny first. *Always.* And Captain Gene told me as much when I was a teenager. The family legacy— the *Hilliard* family legacy—would always be hers through his bloodline. She was *his.*"

Marnie's expression seemed to soften. Vulnerability entered her voice. "Haven't you ever just wanted to be loved for something? Without the Hilliard legacy, I'm just Marnie the waitress. The spinster. The daughter of the second wife, Edna. My mother doesn't care. She always loved the history, and when she and Captain Gene divorced over thirty years ago, she didn't care about losing the legacy. But I *do.*" Marnie's words stunned her. They were so poignant, so brutally true that they knocked the breath from Shea's intent to flee. "And I won't let Gene keep me away from that legacy—the silver, the money. It should also include me!"

Shea remembered the gravestone. *Edgar.* "And how does Edgar fit into the story? The lighthouse keeper?" she asked.

Marnie's expression went blank. "I have no idea who that is. An old lightkeeper, I suppose. Nobody important."

Shea nodded, accepting Marnie's response, and took another step down. "Marnie, even if you found the map, it wouldn't be yours. Not legally. It would belong to Captain Gene, and I—"

"Shut. Up." Marnie took three determined steps toward Shea, and Shea took another quick step down and away from her. Marnie's face grew taut, causing her face to contort. "It's all I have," she hissed, her words choked. "It's all I have."

38

REBECCA

. . . my life and my bride . . .
Annabel Lee

ANNABEL'S LIGHTHOUSE
SPRING, 1874

LEAVING THE SHACK, Rebecca left the dead men—including Edgar—behind. Once again she stumbled through the woods, this time fully aware of who she was and who she fled from.

Before long she found the shore, the lake, with the expanse of the Porcupine Mountains rising as blue-green mounds in the far distance. The smell of smoke, light but putrid, muddied the air. Smoke from the stamp mill that had burned for whatever reason and ruined the immediate growth of Hilliard's plans. She would face him, her father. Edgar had denied parentage, so it remained that Hilliard was truly her father—though he assumed an illicit affair between Annabel with Edgar.

Instead, they *had* indeed loved each other, but Annabel had apparently kept her body true to her vows, even if her heart did not. That meant that Rebecca was Hilliard's. As she should have been. That meant that Annabel had gone back to Hilliard—or never truly left him. Edgar's words haunted her. If Annabel had remained with Hilliard, how had Edgar saved her from him?

With no answers, Rebecca fought through the sand as she veered back toward the lighthouse. She looked into the woods in the direction of Annabel's grave. Her mother's grave.

A dry sob racked her chest. Edgar was gone. She had killed Mercer. Her father was a greed-filled man who would find his own ruin, especially once this was all exposed. She would never—*never*—tell where she'd hidden the papers. They caused too much pain and symbolized a world she wanted no part of. And she had Aaron to think of. Aaron to care for. He would carry on a Hilliard legacy too. His children and his children's children would carry the Hilliard blood.

"Rebecca!" A shout in the distance jerked her attention up.

A group of men came toward her, Abel leading the charge.

Rebecca succumbed to exhaustion and grief. She sank to the shore, the wet sand soaking through her skirt, her chemise bodice pressing against her abdomen in the wind and revealing evidence of their babe.

Abel sprinted up the shore and, moments later, fell to his knees in front of her, his hands light on her shoulders, searching her face with his eyes. "What happened? Are you all right?"

"Edgar—" Rebecca gasped.

"What about Edgar?" A miner came up behind them and demanded to know, concern on his face.

Rebecca looked over her shoulder. "Mercer and Bear are

dead." She would never breathe a word that she'd shot Mercer. Let them all believe Edgar to be her hero. "Edgar saved me."

The miner shouted and waved his arm toward the others behind him. "Is Edgar hurt?" he asked Rebecca, even as Abel's hands roved her hair and gently turned her face to assess the wounds left behind by Mercer's hand.

"He's . . ." Rebecca met Abel's eyes. "Edgar is gone." Her breath caught as shock ratcheted across Abel's face.

"He's what?"

"I'm so sorry." Rebecca's cry was muffled as Abel drew her close against his shoulder, careful not to hurt her with his action. She heard him bark at the men.

"Go find Edgar."

"You got it," a man responded.

Footsteps thudded in the sand.

A hand briefly touched the top of Rebecca's head in recognition. She lifted her eyes to the miner who had taken the lead now in the wake of Abel's preoccupation with her. "We're just glad you're all right, Mrs. Koski."

Mrs. Koski. Abel's wife.

Rebecca fell against the man she had once thought might love her. The man she had once allowed herself to be swept up in loving if only for shared need. The man she hoped would stay true to his promise to her and their child—if for no other reason than her child was going to live. Because of Edgar, her child would live in a world where selfish and greedy people served themselves more than others. Her child would need a father like Abel to keep it safe. It would need a man like Abel to prove that sometimes loving required giving oneself up for another. It was clear to Rebecca now that it was what Abel had done for her. Kjersti had requested her brother help save Rebecca from the abusiveness of her father. And now Rebecca would ask Abel to save her and their child one last time—for a lifetime.

SHEA

Shea scrambled down the stairs, Marnie pounding down them behind her. They spiraled toward the main floor and burst into the lightkeeper's room, and once through it, Marnie launched toward Shea.

"Let go!" Shea's hand shot forward, connecting with the older woman's shoulder. Marnie fell backward on the lightkeeper's bed. Shea stood over her, seeing the woman for the sad heap that she was. Driven by a lifetime of jealousy, a lifetime of wishing someone would be more to her than they were. She had conjured up a dream that didn't fit reality, and Marnie had derived a conclusion that could never be even if Rebecca's papers were found after decades of being lost.

"Marnie . . ." Shea started, then bit her tongue. What did she say to a woman who was so broken and so wrong when she herself had, in her own way, conjured up her own reality, her own expectations for her marriage? Instead of finding value in what she had, she found value in what she *wanted*. As extreme as Marnie? Certainly not. But the roots were all the same.

"Marnie," Shea started again, gentling her voice in hopes to break through the psyche of the woman who had killed Jonathan Marks for papers that likely no longer existed. The woman who had snuck around the lighthouse and its grounds, pretending to be the ghost of the legendary Annabel. "It's over, Marnie." Shea's words were not the ones she'd intended to come out.

Marnie shoved herself up on the bed. "No." She wagged her head. "It's not over. It will never be over." A tear trailed down her face.

Shea softened toward the waitress. The pitiable state of the woman was truly that she had distorted life into expectations that would never be fulfilled. "I know you. You want to validate who you are, but Annabel is a ghost—literally. She's been dead for a century. And Rebecca, the map? That's not something you can unbury and claim. You all have wrapped your lives around a century-old *treasure map*, and in the end you've lost each other!" Shea stumbled to a halt. Dreams. A person's dreams were nothing when shared only with themselves. A person's dreams could turn into obsession and ostracize them from love. While dreams could be beautiful and hopes very real, to live in them and to demand them to come true like one wished upon a star could alienate a person from others who could love them, because they were centered on their own personal achievement.

Her personal achievements. Shea had never wanted to see Pete so badly in all her life. He had stood by in the shadows as she'd pursued her own life, her own dreams, and as she'd held him with disdain for not being the romantic picture she had in her head. She had been infatuated with *Holt* of all people, whose part in this was involuntary and circumstantial at best, but who didn't hold a candle to Pete's loyal faithfulness.

What was love if it wasn't devotion? What was love if it wasn't steady and consistent?

Shea knew this now, as much as she knew that above all, Annabel lived. She lived in the lighthouse. She lived on the lake's shore. She lived in the forest and in the town. She lived in the people born here. She lived in Shea's own mind and in Shea's very soul.

Annabel was, after all, Shea herself.

Annabel's ghost was the epitome of what they all ran away from. She was the memories. The heartache. The abuses. The tragedies. The could-have-beens and should-have-beens. Annabel was the story that had never concluded because no one was willing to read its first pages in order to write its last.

Annabel's ghost was the love a person put to death so the idea of it could never be lost, but instead could be hoarded.

"Marnie." Shea reached for the woman's hand. "Let's put an end to Annabel's story tonight."

Marnie eyed Shea's hand with teary-eyed suspicion. She shook her head. "I can't."

"You can," Shea encouraged. She wanted Marnie's dangerous state of mind to be put in a place where she could receive care and no longer hurt those around her. But to do that, she had to show the woman that she was worthy of being cared about. That history could keep its old silver map—wherever it was stashed. But that was a feat Shea didn't know if she was capable of. She tried anyway. "Your mother—Edna—she loves you, doesn't she?"

Marnie's expression softened. "Mom always has."

"Then that's what you focus on." Shea pushed her hand closer to Marnie. "Focus on what you *do* have, not on what you don't have. Focus on what you can give, Marnie. Focus on what you can give."

39

SHEA

In the sepulcher there by the sea . . .
Annabel Lee

ANNABEL'S LIGHTHOUSE
PRESENT DAY

SHE WAS NEVER MORE GLAD to see lights from a police car than the moment the red-and-blue flashed through the lighthouse kitchen. Marnie stumbled alongside Shea, holding her hand with a heartbreaking sense of need. Shea couldn't wait to be free of the woman who only moments before had been strangling her and now trailed Shea like a hurting child.

The door slammed open, and the next few moments were a blur. Officers took custody of Marnie. Holt barreled into the room, eyes wild, until they landed on Marnie. "Marnie!" He rushed toward her, but the officer who had Marnie in custody held out his hand. Holt pulled up short as Marnie lifted her head and looked over her shoulder at him, a desperate apology on her face.

"I'm so sorry, Holt. So very sorry."

Holt stared at his aunt as she was led away.

Another figure pushed through the fray in a calm manner, and Shea's knees nearly buckled. Instead, she collected herself and pushed past Holt, stopping just short of flinging herself at Pete. His arm was still secure in its sling, yet he was wincing even as a smile touched his lips. Rain was beginning to dot their skin, the wind whipping her hair in all directions.

"Hey."

"Where on earth *were* you?" Tears pricked Shea's eyes. She wasn't angry now. She wasn't anything other than relieved and desperate to make it up to Pete. Make everything up to Pete. Everything she had stolen from him, she now wanted to give back.

"I drove Captain Gene's car back to the Dipstick. Holt and his mom—Penny—had been harboring his grandfather in the basement of the Dipstick. The old man has dementia, but he's always been a local hero of sorts. They've taken care of him while letting everyone believe he's off on his adventures—like a legend. But he's just an old man who has been battling age and the loss of his memories," Pete explained. "Penny said her father asked them to do that. He didn't want people to remember him as anything but Captain Gene, man of the Porkies."

It made sense, Captain Gene's actions earlier. His erratic behavior, the fact that no one knew where he was, that he couldn't tell anyone what he knew. Captain Gene was no longer with them, and all that was left was the shell of an elderly man lost in a maze of dementia-riddled confusion.

Shea felt her heart break a little—for the man's pride, for Penny's silent burden, and for her own impetuous insistence to solve the mystery once and for all.

"Why didn't Penny tell me Holt was her son? Why didn't Holt call her 'mom' for goodness' sake?" Shea stared past Pete toward the flashing lights, toward Holt's silhouette as he stood looking lost, his hands behind his head and elbows sticking out.

Pete shook his head. "All I can say is that it's a pretty dysfunctional family, and Captain Gene's current condition hasn't lent toward making it functional."

Shea tempered her words so that they didn't sound accusatory. "Why didn't you tell me you were going back to the Dipstick tonight with Holt?"

Pete gave her a quizzical look. "I did. I asked you to trust me. Of course, I had no idea Marnie was in the lighthouse, not until Holt mentioned that's why he was here in the first place. He was starting to put things together after I got hit by the car. He'd always wondered if Marnie was . . . well, if she was okay. Her sending you to talk to Edna about all the history, it never added up to Holt because Marnie didn't like anyone being in the lighthouse. Once he told me his concerns, that's when we called—I called—the cops."

Shea wrapped her arms around his left arm and gave it a hug since she couldn't exactly assault him with affection due to his other arm. "Marnie has been lurking around here since I first came. Since she hasn't been able to access the lighthouse the way she wanted, when I came, she thought my finding the map Rebecca supposedly stole way back in the 1800s might be her answer. Then Marnie was going to take it. She tried with Jonathan Marks—swore he knew where they were, but then she accidentally shot him."

"Accidentally?" Pete's eyebrow raised.

"That's what she claims."

They pushed into the lighthouse just as the sky opened up in full torrents. Within a few minutes, Holt burst in and then froze at the sight of them. He hesitated. "Can I . . . come in?"

"It's your lighthouse," Pete said.

Holt collapsed onto a chair at the table, head in his hands. "I knew it," he muttered. "I knew it."

Shea glanced at Pete before easing into a chair across from him. "Holt?"

Holt looked up, eyes red, hair tousled and damp from the rain and the horrific night. "I'm sorry, Shea. I didn't . . . well, I *hoped* my aunt Marnie wasn't responsible for all of this. And my mom, Penny—I was trying to protect her—and my grandfather— and—I didn't know—" Holt was legitimately at a loss, and Shea couldn't help him.

Holt lifted his eyes to hers. "I messed everything up—from the beginning until now. I wasn't even honest that Penny was my mother. But it's just how we function. Our family keeps each other at arm's length. We care, but we don't trust—not even each other, really."

Shea grimaced. She couldn't really say anything. In a lesser and more familiar way as far as society was concerned, she'd done the same with Pete. Cared, but kept him at arm's length.

Shea noted Pete at the stove, pushing more firewood into it to generate enough heat to boil water for tea. His back was to her and Holt. He managed as though nothing major had happened. She looked back to Holt. "Your aunt Marnie admitted to the hit-and-run with Pete."

Holt dipped his head. "I'd hoped that there was a different explanation." He let out a growl of frustration and guilt.

Shea reached across the table as if to take Holt's hand, but then she pulled back. "I won't say it's okay, Holt, but it's not your fault. What Marnie did."

Holt leaned back in his chair and crossed his arms over his chest, tipping his head back to stare at the ceiling. "She and my mom have always been on the outs. But I got along with Marnie in our own way. It's my grandfather, Captain Gene, that's a tough nut to crack. And now he's just gone, even though he's still here."

"He sounds like he made life rough on Marnie and your mom," Shea said.

Holt snorted. "Rough? Yeah, I guess that's true. I'm so deeply entrenched in it, between Marnie and Captain Gene and Penny—my mom—I can't even see the water for the land at this point."

Pete gave a short laugh of understanding. "It's not about any of that, Holt. It's about wanting to be a part of something. It's about family. It's about the ties that bind—or don't bind." Pete's gaze fell on Shea. "The fact is, when you let yourself get in the way, you cheat not only yourself but those around you of the chance to love you."

Shea's cheeks warmed, both out of guilt and in realization that Pete was staring deep into her eyes in a way she'd long wished for but had rarely seen, if ever.

He finished, "We get our priorities messed up. We forget that the ones we love are what's most important, no matter the cost."

Holt had left to head back to his place. The lighthouse was a quiet refuge from the wind and rain as dawn split the sky. The gray clouds kept the sun at bay, yet the light still stretched over the lake, over the woods, and across the lighthouse.

The tea had finally been made.

Pete slid a tin mug across the table to Shea, who took it and palmed it with her hands. He slipped onto the chair Holt had occupied not long before, and they sat in companionable silence. Shea was sure if she reached out, she could physically feel the unspoken words between them, and knowing Pete, he wouldn't know how to start. That was the deal with being married to a man of few words, who'd pretty much used up his entire vocabulary in the last few hours.

"Do you think we'll ever know where Rebecca hid the map?" Shea ventured. It was as good a place to start as any.

"I doubt it." Pete shook his head.

"Now that we know what happened here with Jonathan Marks and the recent hauntings, it's kind of—"

"Anticlimactic?" Pete raised his eyes.

Shea gave a nervous laugh. "Yeah. I mean, I shouldn't say that considering you're recovering from being hit by a car, but I just . . . I felt there might be more to the story."

"I'm sure there is," Pete was quick to respond.

Shea shot him a questioning look.

"Well," Pete went on, "if you were able to go back in history, what do you know?"

Shea contemplated the story she'd been able to unravel. "Annabel drowned in the lake. Hilliard, her husband, watched it happen from the shore. Their daughter, Rebecca, stole the map—out of spite toward her father perhaps? She never revealed where she hid it. Silvertown went belly-up. Captain Gene was in her family tree through a brother she had named Aaron."

"So why is there a grave?" Pete asked.

Shea stared at him.

"If Annabel died by drowning, did her husband pull her body to shore? Was it really her husband on the shore?"

Shea frowned. "What are you saying, Pete?"

"I'm saying it's a story. That's all it is. Records state Annabel drowned in the lake after the craft she was in overturned. That's all. There are no records of her body being retrieved. There are no grave records either."

"How do you know this?" Shea was taken aback by Pete's extra knowledge.

He gave her a pacifying smile. "You're not the only one who got into figuring out the mystery."

"So if there are no grave records," Shea ventured, "then someone had to have created a grave for memorial's sake. To keep her close to the lighthouse."

"The lightkeeper," Pete finished.

Shea stared at him. "That's right!" She snapped her fingers.

"I forgot that part of the legend. Annabel and her lover. Her lover wasn't her husband. It was the lightkeeper, wasn't it? The man who spent his life watching over the lake where she died."

Pete shrugged. "Who knows? It's a good guess, though. We'll probably never know."

Shea considered this, and then the name slipped past her lips. "Edgar."

"Who?" Pete asked.

Shea didn't answer. She remembered the extra gravestone. The name etched into its face. Edgar the lightkeeper lost to the annals of time. She dared a glimpse at Pete, who drank his tea quietly, oblivious to any further expansion of the conversation or else deep in thought about it. Maybe she'd made a bad habit of misinterpreting Pete's silence.

Regardless, the genealogy of Annabel didn't include a man named Edgar, but the ghostly story claimed the lightkeeper's undying love for her long after she'd drowned. Shea tapped her finger on her mug, not taking her eyes away from her study of Pete. She wondered what it would be like to love someone so much that you never stopped, long after they were dead and buried. Or . . . a darker thought overtook her, so dark that Shea stuffed it away and determined not to revisit it. What would it be like to love someone so completely and obsessively that you never wanted to share them with anyone else?

They had a lot of work to do, this Shea recognized as she packed her belongings in preparation to leave Annabel's lighthouse. Holt had waived the rental fees as penance for all the drama. Shea had what she needed for a book—more than what she needed—and much of it she would never use.

It seemed when a person dug into a story from the past, so many details revealed themselves. Ones that made the past so much less romantic and haunting and instead darker and more broken. She still had questions, but Shea had concluded she would never know the answers. She couldn't time-travel back and read Rebecca Hilliard's mind when she'd secreted away with her father's papers and map. Shea also couldn't reconcile exactly how Edgar fit into the equation—aside from the infamous story of being Annabel's lover.

Putting the pieces together, it was apparent that Annabel had been married to Hilliard, Silvertown's founder who'd gone bankrupt and had been imprisoned for fraud and conspiracy to commit manslaughter. Which meant Annabel had not been married to a very nice man—not at all. In Shea's romantic mind, it all made sense then, that Annabel would fall in love with an older, caring sort. But seeing as Hilliard had raised Annabel's daughter, Rebecca, it also was apparent Annabel had not left Hilliard except by death—the tragedy of being lost at sea. An escape? Perhaps. But a strange one.

Shea had mulled over the concept of Annabel's supposed craft sinking and her drowning. But why would a woman take a skiff out on the lake unless the waters had been calm? And if the waters were calm, there was no reason for a skiff to overturn or a woman to drown. Unlike the story of a tempestuous storm or a husband stuck on shore unable to reach her due to the high waves, logic offered a different theory. One that made Shea question if Annabel had, after all, died of drowning by accident . . .

The thought hung in the air as an arm slid around her waist. Shocked, Shea stiffened and spun within the circle of the arm to stare wide-eyed at Pete.

"What are you doing?" She drew back, questioning.

He tightened his hold. "Hi."

"Oh, hi . . ." The butterflies that rose in her were unusual and rare. It'd been years since Pete had been the cause of them.

His ice-blue eyes were like melting bergs, and Shea had the sudden thought that she was okay with drowning in those eyes.

"I'm sorry." Pete's words both stunned and confused her.

"For what?" Shea asked.

"For not listening to you. For working on my cars all the time. For being so busy taking care of things *for* you, that I forgot to take care *of* you."

"Oh." Shea's voice was small even to her own ears.

Pete's fingers grazed the side of her face. "I don't want to love you for me, Shea. I want to love you for you."

His words stung and healed simultaneously. Shea sucked in a steadying breath, bracing her balance by taking hold of his waist. "I haven't been exactly fair to you, Pete."

He waited.

She tried to gather her thoughts. "I came here to find myself, and I've realized that . . . well, with everything that's happened, with Annabel's story and her family's legacy, I see now that pursuing taking care of myself first isn't necessarily balanced. I need to take care of you too. Of us." Shea pressed forward. "Not that I don't need to take care of myself. I mean, my health, my emotions, yeah sure, but what I mean is . . . it's not just me. I didn't fall in love with you for me either, but that's sort of what it's become."

Pete nodded. He leaned forward, and Shea's breath caught. His lips touched her jaw. "It's become that for both of us, I think. In our own ways." He pulled back. "Should we have a do-over?"

Shea gave a little laugh. Gosh, if he kept acting like this, she'd fall in love with him all over again. But, she reminded herself, this time she'd do it with the intent of making him her teammate, her love, and someone she would serve. Love—true love—required humility and sacrifice. That was the long and short of it. Romance ebbed and flowed like the waves outside the lighthouse, and yet love for another carried through the storm. It shone like a light across the tempest, and it beckoned the loved one home to safety.

Love wasn't about her. It was about them.

As Shea leaned into Pete and tasted the first real kiss in a long time, she wondered briefly if there had ever been true love in this lighthouse. Or if it had always been thwarted by heartache and haunted by the ghost of a woman who had never really known what it meant to be truly, wholly, and completely cherished.

Either way, Shea decided as she laid her head on Pete's shoulder, breathing in the essence of him, she would start again. She would examine her intentions. She would rethink her motivations. She would consider Pete in all her decisions. Most of all, she would love as if their lives depended on it . . . because they did. And that was good and pure and everything that was right.

40

REBECCA

In her tomb by the sounding sea.
Annabel Lee

ANNABEL'S LIGHTHOUSE
SPRING, 1874

THEY STOOD SIDE BY SIDE, Edgar's stone propped upright, his name etched as best as Abel could manage into its face.

Rebecca stood, careful to leave some space between her and Abel. Niina bent and laid a bouquet of fern and wildflowers at the base of the stone.

"To think," she mused, "your mother lies here, and now Edgar." Niina met Rebecca's eyes. "He thought he kept it secret, but I know he loved her."

Rebecca couldn't shake the niggling feeling in her heart. The

327

kind that still hurt and made her question everything. Her father, Hilliard, had been arrested for fraud, and supposedly they would be pressing charges against him for conspiracy to commit murder against her. Aaron would be coming to live at the lighthouse too. He would be safe, though they would have much work to do to mend what Hilliard had broken. Rebecca knew in her soul that if Hilliard had been okay in allowing Mercer to kill her on Hilliard's behalf, it was no stretch of the imagination to picture him standing along the shore as her mother, Annabel, fought against the lake's waves and the force that pulled her under. Had he been indifferent to her death? Had there been a storm that kept him from saving her?

But what was worse were Edgar's words that would not leave her alone. *"I saved us from him,"* Edgar had said. Us. But Annabel had died. So how had they both been saved?

Niina's hand trailed along Rebecca's arm, and Rebecca snapped free of her thoughts to meet the woman's eyes. "Take your time. We're here for you, my dear."

It was a gift, the words Niina extended to her. Niina had shown her nothing but a mother's true love and concern, and that didn't slip past Rebecca as she considered how she would learn to love her own child.

Niina's footsteps sounded as she walked across sticks and leaves leading back to the lighthouse.

Abel cleared his throat and turned to Rebecca. "I'll . . . be at the lighthouse." He was the new lightkeeper now, she the lightkeeper's wife. Their bond of Kjersti had long since passed away with her, and now the bond of their child was a tenuous tie that kept them together.

"Abel?" Rebecca said.

He stopped in his retreat and turned back to her. "Yes?"

"You've been more than gracious to me." Rebecca made sure he saw the gratefulness in her eyes. "Thank you."

He shifted his weight, looking down at his feet before raising his gaze back to hers. "You're my wife, Rebecca."

"I know that." She swallowed hard against the tears that clogged her throat. "But . . ."

Abel frowned and took a step back toward her. "But what?"

She shifted away from him, unable to read the tenderness and concern in his eyes as anything other than obligation. "You married me to help me escape my father, and now . . . now I have. And with Edgar and my mother, I—" she paused and cast a glance back at their graves—"I don't know . . ." Her words trailed; they hurt her throat. They hurt her *heart*.

Fingers lifted her chin as Abel gently raised her bruised face to his. There was kindness in the ice blue of his eyes. And something else. Always there was something else that she couldn't define. It had been there that night outside of Kjersti's room when desperation had pulled them together. When he had taken her into his arms and closed the door with his foot behind them. When he had taught her what it felt like to be a wife, to be held, to be enveloped in the concepts of security and faithfulness. Even if it was a facade, and only for a moment, she had felt it. Craved it. Wanted it. Wanted *him*.

Rebecca wanted to love him. She ached to love him wholly. To show him gratefulness for the gift of caring for her. To bring a smile to his eyes when she gave him his firstborn. She wanted to gift him her love, but not with the risk of her taking it back. But how did she tell him? How did she tell a man who had loved her merely by action and sacrifice? Could there be more than that? Could they love with passion and heart and soul while building a life of day-to-day care and sustainability?

Was it too much to dream that a home could really be a place where she could rest in the *knowing* that she was there for Abel, and Abel was there for her?

"You ask too many questions." Abel's breath on her skin

awakened her to the realization he had drawn close. His lips brushed her cheek, and Rebecca frowned in confusion.

"I've not asked a question," she argued tentatively.

"Rebecca," Abel breathed. It was a whisper that caressed her skin, bandaged her heart, and reassured her that she was safe. "I will not leave you stranded." He kissed the corner of her mouth, a featherlight kiss that weakened her limbs at the same time it strengthened her spirit. "I will not watch you drown." Another kiss to the opposite corner of her mouth. "I will not treat you as anything other than my most precious treasure."

"But I . . ."

"But you what?" His lips moved against hers, and his breath mingled, intoxicating and comforting all at the same time.

"I don't know how," she admitted. It was her worst fear.

Abel drew her closer until she fit against him where she belonged.

"Let me show you," he whispered against her hair.

Rebecca gazed over his shoulder, the sunlight breaking through the treetops and falling on Edgar's and Annabel's stones. No. She didn't know *how* Edgar had saved them from her father. She had an intuition that all was not as it should have been, though—how could it? A love that left broken vows in its wake? A forbidden devotion shrouded in the unrealistic hope that somehow true love could be found.

No.

Her father, Edgar, Annabel? Their love had been broken. No matter how it all unraveled. It had been woven by ambitions and passions and everything but what Abel now offered to her.

Himself.

Just himself.

Nothing less and nothing more.

Love was patient, and it was kind. It wasn't proud. It didn't dishonor another. It didn't envy.

Rebecca closed her eyes against the grave markers, against

her father's map that she had buried beneath Edgar's marker in a tin box. Instead, she breathed in the promise that emanated from Abel's body against hers. Love protected, it trusted, it hoped.

And always, no matter the personal cost, it persevered.

ANNABEL

AND THAT IS THE WAY OF IT, I believe. All that we dreamed shall remain only that, a dream.

I feel my body settle to the rocky bottom, the sand sifting through my toes and fingers. The lake is binding itself to me, a flood of ice in my nostrils, my throat, my lungs.

Maybe one day I will be remembered. Maybe one day I will make you remember me.

My love.

Because in my death I have discovered that consuming love is nothing more than obsessive love for one's own contentedness. This is the reason you submitted me to the lake, pushed my body into its choking embrace, held me under and refused to allow me to breathe deep of the hope of life.

No.

You wished no man to have me but you.

Your love that once encircled me now imprisons me, and you will make me conform to the visions of what you hoped we would be. With my death, our love will be frozen in place. My love will be dead, and you will take with you only what you want. A mutilated version of who we once were.

Nay!

Oh, my love!

I had dreamed of loving you with my whole being. But I was wrong. My love was in error, and my heart misled me away from him and away from my child. My selfishness cost me her happiness, and it will cost her peace and hope.

So as my shoulders collide with the rocky earth, as my body becomes one with the waters, so too do I come to realize my own regrets.

I have loved with a love that was less than love. I have loved with a love filled with myself.

As have you, dear one.

As have you, the taker of my breath.

Edgar.

Author's Note

It's always been a wish of mine to write a story set in a lighthouse on the shores of Lake Superior, my childhood stomping grounds. The Porcupine Mountains is a place rich in lore and legend, steeped in the history surrounding its Native peoples, the early trappers and traders, the miners, and eventually even my own family's roots. It's a place of mystique, of wild beauty, a land that swirls with the ghosts of the past no matter which direction you look.

The Porkies will always be my most favorite place on earth. It's a secret place, one of new beginnings. I share it now with you.

ACKNOWLEDGMENTS

I must give an immediate shout-out to Schuil Coffee in Michigan for supplying the foundation to any good novel: coffee. Without your Hawaiian Hazelnut, this book would have been far darker than it already is—depressingly so.

Thanks to my agent, Janet Grant, who consistently checks in and makes sure I'm still moving forward. Her encouragement and support are what every writer dreams of in an agent. All the heart emojis here.

Massive thanks to Elizabeth Olmedo for literally reading and editing as fast as I could write, so that I could make my deadline and not send my editors more of a mess than the story already was. (Check out ElizabethOlmedo.com if you need editing services. She's amazing.)

A huge shout-out too to the team at Bethany House. You always take a story and make it shine. Rochelle Gloege, my editor, you really did serious work on this one. Your ideas and insights made it come together.

Finally, to the original people of the Upper Peninsula of Michigan. This land was yours, and yet onward the settlers came. Such seems to be the story of humankind—the turning over of land either peaceably or by force, through mutual agreement or by trickery. But you have mastered the mountains for centuries, your legends and history remain priceless to this day, and your influence is still great, which is something I will not overlook. Thank you to the Ojibwe nation for being such good caretakers of creation. Though we're in a new era now, may we all remember to treasure what God has gifted us with and breathe deep of the history this earth carries in its soil.

READING GROUP
DISCUSSION GUIDE

1. Have you ever visited the Upper Peninsula of Michigan, and if so, what are some of the highlights of your trip? If not, which sites do you wish to see the most?

2. Lighthouses are known as symbols of rescue because of their purpose in guiding ships toward safety, yet they're also woven through history with countless stories and legends. What are some of your favorite lighthouse stories, and why do you think so many of us love lighthouses?

3. Rebecca's struggle with amnesia allows her to block out childhood trauma and other conflicting memories, but those who are most protective of her help to inspire the renewal process for Rebecca to find new beginnings. In your life, who has played a key role in mentoring you in a positive and healing direction, and how have they done so?

4. Pete is a quiet representation of the hero who saves without demanding anything in return. What other fictional and real-life heroes can you think of who fit this description?

5. Shea might have been on a research trip, but her ulterior motive was self-care and reflection regarding her life and her marriage. In what ways do you think the idea of self-care is helpful, and in what ways do you believe it can be risky?

6. For decades, Annabel's ghost is said to have haunted the shores of Lake Superior and the lighthouse. Most of the sightings in this story came to be explained, while a few were left without resolution. What are your thoughts on ghosts, the paranormal, and phenomena that defy a clear explanation?

7. Captain Gene is a larger-than-life character whose mystique is overblown due to local legend and lore. Why do you think we like to embellish and exaggerate our image of people from the distant past, of historic places and events? Or do you believe our recounting of history is mostly accurate? Why or why not?

8. Have you ever seen or read about Pressie, the elusive "Loch Ness Monster" of Lake Superior? Do you believe these sightings to be real or made-up? What about the sightings of other cryptids?

Read on
for a *sneak peek* at
the next book from Jaime Jo Wright

THE BELL TOLLS
AT TRAEGER HALL

AVAILABLE IN THE FALL OF 2025

Keep up to date with all of Jaime's releases
at JAIMEWRIGHTBOOKS.COM
and on Facebook, Instagram, and X.

WAVERLY

S UCH ARE MY MEMORIES of the two weeks prior to Uncle Leopold's murder:

Darkness encases Traeger Hall like a shroud. It's a sort of black cape, like that which settled over the shoulders of a questionable man lurking in the bushes. The darkness never lifts—it hasn't lifted since I arrived one year ago at this oppressive manor.

Even if the sun is shining, somehow Traeger Hall remains in the shadows, perched on the top of a high hill, overlooking the small town of Newton Creek.

My uncle, Leopold Traeger, settled in Newton Creek decades ago when he was a much younger man. He built his impressive sawmill, came to realize considerable success, and the town rose around the creek that powered the mill. And Uncle Leopold made sure everyone knew who had begun it all when he built Traeger Hall on the highest point in the area, flanked as it was by massive oak trees on both its eastern and western ends.

The house was rectangular and crafted entirely of brick, with a broad veranda whose angles had all been set at ninety degrees, and on the east side stood the bell tower. Its huge bell has never been rung, and it will never be rung except in the event of the onset of deadly foes—which Leopold Traeger predicted *would* happen sooner or later.

"Always remember your composure, Waverly." Uncle Leopold's grouchy voice raised goose pimples along my skin. I was not a meek-mannered niece by any stretch of the imagination, and yet, when it came to my uncle, he could silence me with a mere look from his steely-gray eyes. "I have given you respite here at Traeger Hall and therefore you are representative of our entire enterprise."

My uncle's gray sideburns twitched along with his jaw. His mustache hung down either side of his mouth like inverted antlers. Under my silent perusal, his face hardened. "Have I made myself clear?"

"Yes, Uncle." Again, meekness was not feigned. I quailed under that expression of his. There was a reason Uncle Leopold had been awarded such great influence over Newton Creek. There was nothing measurable to a man with a heightened sense of confidence and knowledge. Especially, when battled against, he was time and again proven right.

That was both the gift and the problem of Uncle Leopold. He only argued when he knew for a fact he was correct, and he was *always* correct. He was beyond mathematical equations of the rational—common sense being the primary demand of all those around him—and he had little patience for unreasonable emotion.

And I had shown as much.

For which there was no grace.

I had dared to mourn my dead sparrow. A little feathered creature I had nursed all summer long after it had careened into one of the windows of the front parlor.

In life, my sparrow had been a tiny ray of sunshine in the otherwise dark world of Traeger Hall. And now it was dead. No gratitude given to Mrs. Carp's cat, which roamed Newton Creek as if it were equal to Uncle Leopold in both stature and authority.

"It was only a bird," said Uncle Leopold. "They come, and they go. Weeping and grieving are a ridiculous waste of time when we have other, more important things to attend to." A raised eyebrow was the exclamation point at the end of his declaration.

In that moment—and not for the first time—I wished my uncle dead.

Jaime Jo Wright is the author of thirteen novels, including the Christy Award– and Daphne du Maurier Award–winner *The House on Foster Hill*, and the Carol Award–winner *The Reckoning at Gossamer Pond*. She's also a two-time Christy Award finalist, as well as the ECPA bestselling author of *The Vanishing at Castle Moreau* and two *Publishers Weekly* bestselling novellas. Jaime lives in Wisconsin with her family and felines.

Learn more at JaimeWrightBooks.com.

Sign Up for Jaime's Newsletter

Keep up to date with Jaime's latest news on book releases and events by signing up for her email list at the website below.

JaimeWrightBooks.com

More from Jaime Jo Wright

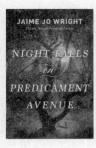

BETHANYHOUSE